W9-CBL-236

HUSH

Eishes Chayil

(also known as Judy Brown)

Walker & Company New York

For those who said I shouldn't,
For those who said I couldn't,
For those who said I wouldn't—
Dare.

And for the children who suffer.

Copyright © 2010 by Eishes Chayil
All rights reserved. No part of this book may be reproduced or transmitted in any form
or by any means, electronic or mechanical, including photocopying, recording, or by any
information storage and retrieval system, without permission in writing from the publisher.

First published in the United States of America in September 2010
by Walker Publishing Company, Inc., a division of Bloomsbury Publishing, Inc.
Paperback edition first published in March 2012
www.bloomsburyteens.com

For information about permission to reproduce selections from this book, write to
Permissions, Walker BFYR, 175 Fifth Avenue, New York, New York 10010

The Library of Congress has cataloged the hardcover edition as follows:
Chayil, Eishes.
Hush / Eishes Chayil. — 1st ed.
p.   cm.
Summary: After remembering the cause of her best friend Devory's suicide at age nine,
Gittel is determined to raise awareness of sexual abuse in her Borough Park, New York,
community, despite the rules of Chassidim that require her to be silent.
ISBN 978-0-8027-2088-7 (hardcover)
[1. Sexual abuse—Fiction. 2. Conduct of life—Fiction. 3. Jews—New York (State)—New York—
Fiction. 4. Orthodox Judaism—Fiction. 5. Judaism—Customs and practices—Fiction. 6. Suicide—
Fiction. 7. Borough Park (New York, N.Y.)—Fiction.] I. Title.
PZ7.C39725Hus 2010   [Fic]—dc22   2010010329

ISBN 978-0-8027-2332-1 (paperback)

Book design by Danielle Delaney
Typeset by Westchester Book Composition
Printed in the U.S.A. by Quad/Graphics, Fairfield, Pennsylvania
2 4 6 8 10 9 7 5 3

All papers used by Bloomsbury Publishing, Inc., are natural, recyclable products
made from wood grown in well-managed forests. The manufacturing processes
conform to the environmental regulations of the country of origin.

PART ONE
1999–2000/2008

CHAPTER ONE

2008

Devory?

Devory?

Devory, can you hear me?

It is hard to write a letter to the dead. It is easier to talk with you directly, as if we are having a real conversation. Sometimes, though, writing is strangely reassuring. When I finish the letter to you, I fold the paper into an envelope, tape it shut, and drop it into the mailbox. There is no address on it, no stamp or anything. It's just a small, white letter, and I can pretend it gets to you.

I am already seventeen. Do you know that? Soon I will be getting married. We all will. Sarah Leah, Chani, all the girls in our class. Do you remember us? Can you see us in heaven, or is memory a curse for only the living?

I know. I am already seventeen and I should not be talking to the dead. But still, it is the only way I can reach you.

My father is afraid no one will want to marry me. I heard him tell my mother that the *shadchan*, the community matchmaker, told him people would be scared to marry their son off to a girl like me after all that had happened. My mother said it was nonsense. She told him to stop annoying her and that no one thinks of you anymore. Everyone has long forgotten what happened.

It is true. Nobody thinks of you anymore. Even I forgot. They said it was better that way, not to remember. I don't know why I am speaking with you now, why I suddenly began thinking of you. But when I do, can you hear me?

I am not afraid like my father is. I am not afraid, because I believe in Hashem—G-d. They say there are three things that only Hashem controls: birth, death, and *shidduchim*—matchmaking. So I will get married soon, when I am eighteen. There is a *shidduch* up there, a perfect match, which was made in heaven just for me. I know it.

Do you believe in Hashem still? That is a ridiculous question. You are in heaven with Hashem. Right?

I am almost eighteen. You . . . you are still nine.

Please don't be mad at me.

Devory?

Devory, can you hear me?

CHAPTER TWO

1999

In my house there was a hat. The hat was made of black fur, and it was tall like my father, round as a pancake, and holy as Hashem. The hat was called a *shtreimel*, and it was worn by all righteous Jews in the world. All *shtreimel*-wearing Jews were *Chassidish*, and all *Chassidish* Jews belonged to a sect called *Yushive*. There were a few Jews that were righteous even if they didn't wear *shtreimels*— Moses, for example, who took the Jews out of slavery thousands of years ago, and King David, and Abraham. That's because there was no *Yushive* yet in their days, so it really wasn't their fault they weren't one of us.

I never knew that such a wise, divine, and stubborn hat could kill; that it could build such a pure vision and then destroy it so brutally. All the Jewish men I knew wore a hat, and though not all of them wore the *shtreimel*, their sacred hats kept the world secure and warm.

There were many kinds of hats roaming the streets of Borough

Park, where I lived. There was the taller, black fur hat called a *shtreimel*, worn by the *Yushive Chassidim*; there was the short, wide, brown fur hat, also called a *shtreimel*, worn by all the other *Chassidim*; and the bent-down—a regular, non-Jewish fedora of the 1950s that the non-*Chassidish litvish* wore.

But the *shtreimel* was the holiest. Its style was over one hundred years old and had begun in Poland with the founder of our *Chassidish* sect, the first *Yushive Rebbe*. He was a saintly man who had a direct relationship with Hashem. But then he died, and they found they couldn't pass down his holy relationship with Hashem, so they passed down his hat and had a direct relationship with that instead.

The fur *shtreimel* was originally worn by all *Chassidim* during the harsh European winter. But then the *Yushive Rebbe* commanded that for the Jews to survive, they must set themselves apart from the world in every way. This was a fundamental belief of the entire *Chassidish* movement, and the clothing of that day became the *Chassid's* safeguard against all evil. When the Holocaust scattered them, they carried their style of dress overseas to the new lands of Israel and America in the form of the *shtreimel* and the long, black belted overcoat called a *bekeshe*. The *litvish*, who were Orthodox but not *Chassidish*, came from Lithuania and also settled in large numbers in Brooklyn. Their dress was frozen in time too, but they wore the more modern bent-down hats and even ties.

Everyone knew that the *shtreimel*, being over a century older than the bent-down, was much holier, but my father always said that nobody could match the *litvish's* intense devotion to Torah learning. It was they, he explained to me, who had turned every Yid into a potential *Talmud Chacham*. We were the spirit and heart of the Jewish nation, Totty—my father—told me; the *litvish* were the mind. Together we form the soul.

My brother disagreed. He told me it was the *Yushive* that were the holiest—in heart *and* mind. And he was already *Bar Mitzvah*, so he knew what he was talking about.

The fur *shtreimel* was so holy it was worn only on *Shabbos*. Every Friday evening, my father would carefully take down the tall hatbox from its sacred place in the walk-in closet in my parents' bedroom. He would hold the *shtreimel* in the middle, then gently turn it around and around as he pulled it out so that all the fur would lie in one direction. Then he placed the hat on his head on top of the big black-velvet *kippa*—skullcap—and I knew that if King David had only worn the *shtreimel* he would have looked almost as tall and majestic as my father. He would kiss me *Gut Shabbos* and leave to walk to *shul*—temple. I would watch him out the window, his *shtreimel* bobbing regally down the street, until I could see it no longer.

The *shtreimel* was worn every single *Shabbos*, winter and summer. Even in the August heat of Brooklyn, the fur hat was placed faithfully on his head, and I knew that my father was not hot, because Hashem was somewhere inside the satin lining cooling him off.

The hat was completely holy because if a man was wearing it he carried Hashem on his head. It made the world a clear and safe place. And it taught me all I needed to know about right and wrong. If a man was wearing that hat he was right; if he wasn't, he was wrong.

The goyim always made trouble. That's why all the *Yiden* lived together in Borough Park, where goyim were scarce. Borough Park, like all of New York, used to be filled with goyim, but then about forty years ago the *Yiden* started moving in from the Bronx and Williamsburg and wherever else. Slowly at first, and then more quickly, the community grew. Every block had its own *shul*, every group its own school. The original ten blocks the community had crowded into was stuffed and squeezed until it burst. So families began moving farther out, closer and closer to Flatbush. Eventually Borough Park was so big it took up the whole world. Well, maybe not, but it certainly filled up most of it.

Borough Park was not a beautiful place. My aunt from Queens called it The Ghetto. She said she didn't know why *Chassidish* communities seemed to think there was an eleventh commandment that said, "Thou shall overcrowd and stack on top of one another, and there shall not be a blade of grass in sight." But she was impressed by the way we all took care of one another.

"Why, Gittel," she said to me, chuckling, "there must be two charity organizations on each block."

I proudly agreed. I had never been outside of Brooklyn, but all Jews knew that Borough Park was the most holy Jewish place after Jerusalem. Hashem was right there, hovering in our midst, because that's where all the *Chassidish* (and okay, even *litvish*) *Yiden* were. There were other Jews who lived outside of Borough Park, and even outside New York, but there was no place like Borough Park. This was the center of the world. There were some other countries on the map, like China and Russia and Australia, but they were merely decorations.

The strange thing is I didn't even live in Borough Park. I lived right near it, barely two blocks away, in Flatbush. Living two entire blocks away from Borough Park was a complicated matter, and I was the only girl in my class to do so. On the other hand,

I was also the only girl in my grade who got to live in such a large white house, with a spire that reached the heavens, a chimney, and a garden all around.

There were three families living in our white corner house: the Proukses, the Kreigers, and my family, the Kleins. The Kreigers were just another boring Orthodox Jewish family. But Kathy and Leo Prouks, who lived on the third floor of the house, were Christian, and everyone said Kathy was strange—even for a gentile. She had had a nervous breakdown ten years ago—or maybe twenty—and she had been different ever since.

Kathy had been living in the small attic apartment with her tall, silent husband, Leo, since just about when Hashem created the world. When my father bought the white house on the corner of East Tenth Street twenty years earlier, they'd already been living there, and they planned to live there forever.

Kathy was taller than my mother and had bright red hair that swung all over her pudgy face. She had small, deep hazel eyes, whose color, she said, smiling mysteriously, matched the dark grass that grew only on the moon.

My mother told us that she would never forget when the ambulance arrived to take Kathy away. She was screaming like a madwoman and the paramedics had to tie her, kicking and crying, to a chair. When she returned a week later, she was smiling and calm as if nothing had ever happened. My mother had wanted her to move out of the apartment, but her husband had cried and begged my parents and convinced them that she was harmless.

But I liked Kathy just the way she was. She was the only adult I knew who was still a child, and she never lied, which all adults did.

CHAPTER THREE

1999

Kathy Prouks was my first real secret. Nobody in my class knew that there was an actual gentile living in my very own house, and I dared not tell them. Only Devory Goldblatt, my best friend since forever, knew about her, and she claimed that Kathy wasn't a real gentile because she was so kind. She always had special kosher candies for us, and she said that being Jewish was beautiful.

Devory was my almost-neighbor. She lived just three and a half blocks away from me, on the Jewish side of the bridge, and we had always imagined that we were twins. We were born on the same day in the same hospital, and my mother said that we were both so ugly they couldn't tell us apart. Then she would laugh and say, "Oh, but you two were best friends from the day you were born."

Devory and I looked nothing alike. My mother said she was a blue-eyed skinny shrimp with stick-straight blond hair scattered in every direction on her head. Mommy called me a second version of Aunt-Leah-who-*nebech*-died-in-the-Holocaust. I disagreed. I had studied the ancient picture of Aunt Leah, and she was fat and plain and had ugly brown hair. I was chubby, average/cute, and had long, smooth hair I wore in a high pony. I also had chocolate eyes, which certainly were not the ordinary brown my mother remembered of she-who-had-*nebech*-died-in-the-Holocaust. I showed Devory the grainy picture when I went over to her house, and she agreed that definitely I was the prettier one.

Devory's house was small, but it housed eight children in three bedrooms and had three blades of grass in the front. The inside of the house was old and worn but clean, the smell of Windex and fresh chicken soup filling every room.

Devory's family was poor. Her father was a *maggid shiur*—a Torah scholar—who taught boys in *yeshiva*, and her mother was a high school *chumash* teacher in the *Yushive* school. They did not have money, my mother said, but they were a holy family because Devory's father was a great man who studied Torah many hours every day.

Devory thought my family was rich. We had a cleaning lady once a week, three entire bathrooms, marble floors, and fresh roses in flowerpots in every room. I did not know if we were truly rich, but Devory was jealous of my house and its five large bedrooms and nice furniture. I told her not to worry. She could live in my house anytime she wanted, so it was really half hers.

Our mothers had been close friends since high school, and they had almost all their babies at the same time. My seventeen-year-old sister, Surela, and Devory's sister Miriam were in the same class. So were my fifteen-year-old brother, Yossi, and Devory's brother Shmuli, who were both away in *yeshiva*. Then came my thirteen-year-old brother, Leiby, and Devory's sister Leah'la, who were a year apart; Avrum and Tzvi, who were both eleven; and Devory and me, who were eight. Six-year-old Sruli was the youngest in my family, but Devory had twin sisters who were five and then Chana'la, the baby, who was a year old. I told my mother it was unfair we didn't have twins, but she just laughed, then sighed in relief and said it was all up to Hashem.

Family Goldblatt was a prestigious family because they were related to all sorts of important *Rebbes*. The family connections were rather confusing, but the crucial matter is that the Gold-blatts were related somehow or other to the *Yushive Rebbe*'s family, and whoever is related—even distantly—to the *Yushive Rebbe*'s family is very important no matter how much money they have. When Mr. Goldblatt went to the *Rebbe* for a blessing, he—along with every descendant of the past seven generations—got the front place in the line.

Besides all this, Devory was a genius. Everybody said so. She read too much for her own good, and she had the brains of the *Yushive Rebbe*. It was too bad she was a girl so she couldn't be a *Rebbe*, but she could certainly be a big teacher.

Devory and I walked home from school together almost every day. Often she came over to my house and we'd play in my big back-yard and climb our cherry tree whenever my mother wasn't around. My mother had forbidden us to go near that thing after she had seen Devory dangling from a thick branch by one thin arm and said that one day that girl would kill herself acting like that, and what did she think she was anyways, a rag doll?

We were also fascinated by the witch's house on the corner; it was pointy and brown and hundreds of years old. Tovah, my neighbor who lived right across the street from that house, had told me that Mrs. Yutzplats, the last living witch of the world, lived there, and Tovah knew all about witches. Almost every Sunday Devory and I would go to Tovah's and sit on her steps to spy on Mrs. Yutzplats.

Tovah was my sometimes-sort-of-good-friend. It wasn't my fault. She was very sensitive and was always getting insulted about something or other. Maybe it was because she was more modern and wore knee socks that covered only half her leg, instead of tights or stockings that covered the entire leg, like we did.

Tovah didn't go to a *Chassidish* school like we did. Her father didn't wear any hat during the week, and on *Shabbos* he wore a fancy black hat from the 1970s. Her mother covered her hair at home with a snood, leaving one whole inch of her hair showing in the front. My mother, who tucked every last strand of hair into her turban when she took off her wig, strongly disapproved of such behavior. She said that a true married Jewish woman does not show as much as one piece of hair, and that in the Talmud it said Kimchas—a great big *Eishes Chayil*, a Woman of Valor—mothered seven sons who all grew up to be high holy priests because even within the four walls of her home they never saw her hair. Now that was modesty.

Jewish women cover their hair because that's what the Torah commands. Moses or Hashem or someone had proclaimed that a woman's hair is *ervah*—forbidden—and must be covered at all times, in all places.

But Tovah was proud of her family, and she would pull at her knee socks, with little pink hearts all over them, and smugly say that we were *nebbe*—nerds—because we had to wear ugly thick tights and outdated clothing. Devory and I stuck out our tongues at her and said that she was modern and would go to *gehenim*—hell—but deep inside I was dying to wear a denim skirt like hers and those cool hooded T-shirts that her mother always bought her.

My mother never bought us hooded T-shirts—they were too fashionable. And we certainly were not allowed to wear any denim. Nobody who was really *Chassidish* did; it was a *goyishe* material that came from the cowboys, and it was against school rules. When I complained to my mother that my clothing was *nebbe* she bought me a new *Shabbos* outfit in Wonderland, but Tovah gave one look and wrinkled her nose.

Devory's oldest sister, Miriam, had become modern too, even though she was from such an important *Chassidish* family. My sister, Surela, once her good friend, told my mother that Miriam's style of dress was ruining her name for *shidduchim*. How would her parents find her a match?

I asked Surela what was so terrible about the way Miriam dressed, and she explained to me that a *Yiddishe* girl was supposed to look different and to dress in a way that didn't attract any attention to her body. Someone who dressed in an immodest fashion was trying to be like the goyim, who cared only for their bodies and neglected their souls.

My mother nodded proudly from the other side of the kitchen. "That doesn't mean you have to dress in an ugly way," she explained, sipping coffee, "but with dignity. Fashion is created to bring attention to your body and to disguise what is really important about you."

My sister sighed. "You know," she said, pulling her short hair back into a tight pony, "I think it's that girl who Miriam became friends with—Raisy Berger—she really had a terrible influence on poor Miriam."

"Yes," my mother agreed. "The Bergers even get the *New York Times* at home."

"Raisy was always modern," Surela said. "And since they became friends"—she waved her hand dismissively in the air— "Miriam totally changed."

When I tried to explain our style of dress to Tovah the next Sunday, she said that I didn't know what I was saying, and that Hashem liked her and her socks every bit as much as He liked *Chassidim* and what they wore. She reminded me that her father was a big *Talmud Chacham* who learned much more than mine and that her mother did so many good deeds she would be going straight to heaven much faster than mine, and that we were just a bunch of *Chassidish nebs*, NEBS.

At that moment the Syrian Who Was a Jew at Heart and his dog passed by, and we were silenced. He lived in the middle of the block with his family and their dogs and though they were *Yiden*, they weren't religious at all. He once casually told my mother that he was a Jew at heart and that was all that really mattered. My brother told me that the Syrian's family was really pitiful because they didn't know how to be real *Yiden*. First, they had a dog; second, they wore pants and drove on *Shabbos*; and third, they had a modern, funny Hebrew accent and said things like "*Shabbat Shalom*," instead of "*Gut Shabbos*," and called their children names like Ya-el and Tehil-lah, while our names were Tzipoiry, Pessie, and Ruchel.

Tovah pointed at the dog and the Syrian Who Was a Jew at Heart and said, "See, *he's* not going to heaven. They don't even keep *Shabbos*!" and we stared at him as he walked away.

CHAPTER FOUR

2008

Dear Devory,

Yesterday was our last day of twelfth grade. Next week is our graduation. So much time has passed since it happened; does it pass in heaven also? Is there day and night and long years or is it just one long forever?

Rebbitzen Ehrlich, the Rebbe's wife, spoke to us yesterday in the auditorium after lunch. She told us about life after high school and how soon, soon we would be the future mothers and teachers of the next generation of Jewish children. We were already adults and within the next two years, with Hashem's help, we would all marry husbands who would learn the Torah and dedicate their lives to Hashem. She spoke about our obligation to Jewish continuity and how Hashem would bless us with many children for us to raise in His way. She also discussed shidduchim, the marriage market, and the matchmakers who would all start calling. How we must never,

ever forget the most important role of women—modesty. She said that it was a problem that ached her heart, how girls leaving high school suddenly start wearing skirts that are only two inches below the knee instead of four. "Why do you think Hashem suddenly doesn't see?" It was embarrassing how much makeup girls seemed to think they could put on, when a woman's natural inner beauty was what glowed most of all. And so on. I don't remember what she said after that. She spoke for too long and I began to think about you.

I don't know why. I had forgotten you for so many years. I liked it that way. I know you are angry at me, so angry. I know, because lately you started to come at night and I can't seem to make you go away. I found a picture of you last week. It was by accident; they had forgotten to throw it out. The picture was buried underneath a pile of old books in my mother's closet. Maybe she kept that one on purpose. Maybe she looks at it every now and then. It was so strange to see us together again. We were only seven or eight then, dressed like brides for Purim. Every year we dressed like brides. Remember?

Please stop coming to my dreams. Please stop. I can't sleep anymore. This morning, I went up to Kathy first thing. I haven't been up there in years, since right after it happened. I spoke to her. I spoke to her for a long time. She is just like she was. Nothing changed about her at all. I told her everything. Kathy said it was good to write letters to you. Kathy said that the dead could know and understand everything.

I have to go for now. My mother is here.

Your best friend,
Gittel

CHAPTER FIVE

1999

Devory and I strongly disagreed about adults. She thought it was fun being a grown-up; I said it was exhausting. Adults had to smile all the time. From the moment they walked out of the kitchen, no self-respecting adult dared not to smile. I knew that because I saw adults smiling at each other day and night. When they wanted to cry, they smiled. When they wanted to be alone, they smiled. When they were angry, they smiled. They all smiled and shook hands and asked each other how they were doing, and then walked away and cried, and frowned, and were angry.

Adults who only smiled when they wanted to were considered strange by others, and then everyone would smile at them more than ever. I always knew how lucky I was that Hashem made me a child, and I pitied the smiling adults. Devory said that I'd be an adult one day too. We would both grow and grow until, poof, we would wake up one morning as adults. I was horrified at the thought. I said that I couldn't be an adult because I smiled only when I was happy. Anyway, either you were an adult or you were not. There were simply no two ways about it.

Kathy was a child. I knew that because she wasn't just another smiling adult. I also knew that because she never told me how big I was, and she never told me my pictures were pretty when they weren't. When she told me that I was beautiful, I knew she really meant it. When I told her that I wanted to climb the tower on the roof from her attic apartment because then I could touch the heavens, she told me that I could touch the heavens from the ground too. She said that if I closed my eyes and spoke to Hashem and reached inside of me really high, I would touch the heavens—even if I was in the basement or in bed.

When Devory and I went up to visit Kathy, she was always happy to see us. She showed us pictures of her family, and we spoke strictly nonsense. Kathy told me that I was special and that when I prayed Hashem listened and smiled. I wondered how Hashem looked when He smiled, and she said that you felt it inside.

Kathy's attic apartment was small and cozy and crooked, with a sweet smell that always reminded me of the three bears' cottage in the woods.

Her kitchen was tiny and yellow, the chairs were wooden and creaked, and the refrigerator whined like an old man whenever she opened the door.

But my favorite room was the small living room with the mysterious *goyishe* pictures. Once I asked Kathy about a picture on her wall that had a man attached to a cross, bleeding all over and looking half dead. She said that it was J—, whose name we weren't allowed to mention—and that he was a saintly man, like Hashem, who did all sorts of miracles. I knew not to believe her. The goyim believed all kinds of nonsense and they made up miracle stories that could only have happened to *Chassidish* Jews. But I didn't want to insult her, so I kept quiet but laughed inside where she couldn't see.

I also loved the little Mary and baby statues, which I never told my mother about, and the big black TV, which I never told my father about, and the not-so-kosher candies, which I never told anyone about.

I stopped telling because once, when I was only six, Kathy gave me a square coffee candy and told me that it was kosher. But then my mother saw the candy, and when I told her that it was from Kathy she told me I shouldn't eat it, just in case it wasn't kosher enough. But the candy looked so good, and I was sure Hashem wouldn't mind if I ate just one candy that was just-in-case-not-kosher-enough. So I locked myself in the bathroom and hid behind the shower curtain. I knew Hashem couldn't see me behind the shower curtain. My teacher told us that Hashem's presence didn't rest in such places. I unwrapped the candy quietly, so that Hashem wouldn't hear from the other side of the door. I then made a loud blessing on it, just in case it wasn't kosher enough, and put it in my mouth.

It wasn't even good.

I was devastated. I had taken the pains to hide from Hashem but He had seen me and made the candy taste horrible. I was never going to eat a just-in-case-not-kosher-enough candy again. And I didn't—at least, not until the next one.

CHAPTER SIX

2008

It was Kathy who had told me I must come forward; it was her fault I was here now. She had said, "Go, Gittel, you must go. You are only seventeen and already you are dying inside. Nobody who saw what you did can live this way. God wants you to tell what happened."

But Hashem did not want me to go. He had stated clearly in the Torah that it was a violation of the divine, a transgression of the commandments, to speak evil of other Jews. I was only here because of that, to spite Him.

My parents did not know I was here, only two days after finishing high school, sitting in the police station of Precinct 66. I did not want to hurt them, to break them down, because it wasn't their fault, only Hashem's, how He allowed children to suffer.

A woman came into the room. She sat down behind the small desk. She held a pen and notebook and a file labled "Gittel." I told myself not to cry; I wasn't going to cry. I would only answer her questions exactly, precisely, and then I would go back home. She looked at me kindly. Then she looked at the form that I had filled out earlier saying that I was seventeen and a half, lived in Borough Park, and wanted to give evidence about what had happened. On her desk lay another form. It said "Devory Goldblatt, age nine." There were some lines scribbled underneath. No more. The woman raised her pen. She held it over the notebook. It hovered, poised, ready to write.

"Gittel," she said. "I'm Miranda. I am a social worker for the Department of Special Investigation in Brooklyn. So what is it you want to tell me?"

I began to cry.

CHAPTER SEVEN

1999

Right at the start of fourth grade, Devory and I realized that our friendship with a gentile, however nice she was, would hurt our social status, so we made a pact of secrecy. One Sunday we crawled under my bed and chewed furiously on the pack of gum we borrowed from my sister's drawer. My sister never let us have the gum but her drawer did. Pulling the stringy gum around and around each other's hands so that they resembled a mummy's, we swore that Kathy the goy would remain a secret known only to our souls and dreams till death do us part. Death, though, Devory said, yanking the gum off our hands, didn't apply to children, so it didn't really matter. I did not understand what she had said but agreed wholeheartedly.

We tried scrubbing off the gum with soap, but then my sister arrived home while we were still guiltily doing so and we fled the scene. We walked down my block, sticky hand in sticky hand, looking for adventure, and Devory said she wished she lived on a block like mine.

"Look," she said, pointing. "You have so much grass around your house. Only rich people have grass."

"I know," I said. "I like being rich. My father even told me that he has more than one thousand dollars deep inside his bank account."

Devory's eyes widened. She said, "Wow, I have only fifty cents."

Devory also said that all gentiles were rich because they all had grass on their front lawns.

Where I lived on the corner of the avenue, there were mostly gentiles. When my parents had moved into the house, my father had been the only Orthodox Jewish *Chassid* roaming the streets of the neighborhood. All of my parents' friends, huddled closely in the safety of Borough Park where all decent Orthodox Jews lived, could not understand him. But the house was huge, white, and cheap, and my father liked it—so he bought it right then for fifty-three thousand dollars.

There was only a narrow bridge separating Borough Park from Flatbush, but the two neighborhoods were worlds apart. My classmates were in awe of the *goyishe* world across the bridge, and I never disappointed them with my tales of goyim dancing around fires in their backyards burning Jewish books, and of Christian youth with long bloody knives searching the streets for Jewish kids. Devory once told them how she saw a priest walking down my street as I vigorously nodded my head. Everyone wanted to know what a priest looked like, but Devory, looking momentarily confused, said that a priest looks like a priest and that's all there is to priests.

Of course, none of it was true. Life in Flatbush was dreadfully boring. The streets of my neighborhood were wider, greener, and quieter than the crowded streets of Borough Park, and the goyim living around us confused me. My teachers always said that all goyim were evil inside, and I could hardly wait for the fiery explosion of blood and hatred so I could report back to my friends. But nothing ever happened in the goy-filled neighborhood, where my neighbors were quiet and clean and would smile at me when they helped me cross the street. Devory said that that niceness was all a lie. The goyim were secretly planning and plotting all the time and that one day, when the priest incited them, they would finally do something terrible.

But some of my friends were jealous. One day, after much huddled discussion in the corner of the classroom, Sarah Leah approached me with a large group. She indignantly informed me that none of my prayers mattered at all because I lived in a *goyishe* neighborhood and Hashem could never hear me from there. Hashem was settled firmly in Borough Park and only when you *davened*—prayed—there could the prayers reach the heavens. I told her that it wasn't true.

"My house," I informed her, "is three floors high and the peak of the tower on the right-hand side facing the avenue reaches the heavens. If I sat on the metal spire on the top of the tower I could touch the heavens myself, so my prayers definitely get up there."

"Nuh-uh," she countered. "It isn't true."

"Uh-huh," I retorted. "It is so." (Except that my parents never let me sit on the metal spire on top of the tower on the roof of the third floor, so I never reached heaven.)

"It can't be," she said, rolling her eyes. "My father even said so, and you could ask the teacher."

So I asked my teacher if it was true, and she said that it was nonsense. Hashem can hear you wherever you are as long as you are a Jew, but even she looked suspicious about where I dared live.

I stuck out my tongue at my ex-friend, but deep inside I was terrified. I hadn't told my teacher that there were goyim living on the third floor of my house. They were a secret hidden safely in the attic. Kathy Prouks was classified information. Only Devory knew, but that didn't count. And my twin neighbors who lived down the block were sworn to secrecy over a bar of white chocolate. We went to the same school, and they came to play with me all the time, so I couldn't keep them from seeing Kathy. They were a grade younger than I was, and I knew that none of my classmates would dare speak to girls a full grade younger than they were and certainly wouldn't believe so horrifying a secret from such an unworthy source.

For now, though, I hoped my secret was safe. My conscience, however, was not. For I knew without even asking my teacher that there was no way my prayers ever got up to the heavens with two goyim blocking the way up. And it broke my heart thinking of all these endless prayers I had prayed throughout my life rotting up there in the floorboards between the second and third floor.

Yet, if the sorrows of my troubled youth weren't enough, my friend Chani came over to me during recess one day and proudly whispered into my ear that she knew I had a *goyishe* neighbor living in my house and she was going to tell the teacher. I said it wasn't true, but she said she knew all about it from the twins down the block and even had a bar of white chocolate to prove it.

I shrugged my shoulders and walked away, trembling inside, but Chani ran after me and whispered that she promised she wouldn't tell the teacher or our classmates if I let her see the goyim when she came to play with me the next day after school.

Chani's mother and mine were good friends, unfortunately, so sometimes she would come over to play, and I knew I didn't have a choice. I told her all right, but only if she would give me half the bar of white chocolate. She did, and I happily munched on it. I would have forgotten all the world's problems if not for the mysterious glances Chani kept beaming in my direction until everyone wanted to know what was happening. She said she couldn't say because it was a secret, so I knew she would.

I asked Devory what to do now that our Kathy-the-Gentile secret pact was broken and all that borrowed gum had been for nothing. She said that there was no choice but to make another one after the furor had ceased because death had not yet done us apart.

The next day after school, I trudged home with Chani chattering excitedly behind me. She had never been in a *goyishe* apartment before and she knew that it was a sin, but it didn't really matter because afterward she would repent. And, anyway, maybe the goy wasn't really a goy, but only a secret Jew from a thousand years ago. Finally we got to the house that didn't quite seem to reach the heavens anymore. Chani asked me in a whisper where they lived, and I pointed up to the tower. She stopped dead in her tracks and stared at the place with her mouth slightly open until I yelled at her to come on already!

After supper I wanted to do homework, but Chani said no way—she wanted to see the goy now. We climbed up the forty-one steps to Kathy's attic apartment and I knocked loudly because Kathy couldn't hear well. Chani stood behind me trembling in awe and fear, ogling the brown door and the gentile that stood somewhere behind it.

Kathy finally opened the door and she was delighted to see me. Her curly red hair bobbed happily all over her face, and she was wearing a huge red shirt over long white denim pants. Kathy had always been fat, but I never noticed just how heavy she was until that moment. I walked into the tiny living room cluttered with furniture and plants and almost stepped over Kootchie Mootchie, Kathy's large, white furry cat that I had stupidly forgotten all about.

Chassidish Jewish families do not have cats or dogs because they are dirty and scary and not kosher. Chani, who had never seen a cat up so close, shrank back in fear, and I quickly asked Kathy to please, please lock up Kootchie Mootchie in her bedroom until we left. So out went Kootchie Mootchie, meowing angrily, as Kathy led us into the living room and sat us down on the sofa squarely in front of the big black TV.

Big black TVs were even worse than cats and dogs and were strictly forbidden in our little world. Kathy sometimes watched TV in the late afternoon, so I would always try to come up then because my mother told me not to. This time, though, I secretly kissed Hashem for seeing to it that the TV was off. There was also a large picture on the wall right on top of the TV with a pretty lady in a shawl looking down at a tiny baby in a cradle surrounded by a sheep and a goat. It was Mary and her baby of course, but I didn't dare say that I knew. Chani wanted to know if the nice-looking lady in the shawl was Kathy's grandmother, but Kathy laughed and said, "Oh, no, that's Virgin Mary."

Chani was about to ask further on just who that might be when Mr. Leo Prouks walked into the apartment and Kathy left the room. I thought desperately of a good explanation, and I told Chani that Virgin Mary was Kathy's husband's grandmother and the baby was Leo's father. Why else would the lady and the baby be hanging all over the place in the apartment? There was one picture near the entrance, another one in the kitchen, and another one I had seen once in the bedroom.

But Chani wanted to know why Kathy had a small statue of the lady and baby over there on the table, and what were the goat and the sheep doing there? I told her that that was the way the goyim did it in the olden times. All the mothers would stand looking down at the baby, who lay in a cradle near a goat and a sheep, because that was the way it was and that was that, okay!

Leo walked into the room then, and Chani turned pale at the sight of the big non-Jewish man, but he only nodded at us and set up a small standing tray near the armchair right where we were sitting. Leo was a silent man and I had always been a little afraid of him. He looked just like a *goyishe* man was supposed to, at least in all the books I had read. He was very large with curly, thick black hair atop a gruff, dark, silent face—and he even had a hoarse voice. Once, when I was little, he helped me fix my bike, and since then I wasn't afraid of him.

But Chani was, and she gave me a look that I ignored until Leo left the room and Kathy came back with a tray of all-the-way kosher candies. They were ultrakosher, she convinced us, setting the tantalizing tray of my favorite toffees in front of our faces. The grocer who sold them to her had a long white beard and looked like a rabbi. We recognized the familiar kosher company slogan scribbled across the candies and we each grabbed a handful.

Kathy giggled like an eager child and began blabbering to Chani about how she was my good, good friend since I was this teeny and just came out of my mother's stomach, and what a pretty baby I had been, and how my eyes turned from dark green to brown when I was two months and three days old, and she still had the card I made for her when I was in pre-1-A, and I had always come up to her to sing songs that I learned in school, and some other things.

I chewed fiercely on the sticky toffees and hoped Chani wouldn't believe what Kathy said or she would go tell everyone that I was friends with a goy. I was desperately trying to interrupt when Leo walked into the room holding a plastic plate heaped with food in one hand and a small cup of milk in the other. He set it all gently down on the tray in front of Kathy and told her she should eat. But Kathy pointed to the cup of milk, whined like my little brother did at supper, and said that she doesn't like milk in that cup—he should bring her the big cup.

Kathy acted like a baby sometimes, and I knew it was from the breakdown, but Leo didn't seem to care. He just picked up the cup, walked out, and soon returned with a large glass of milk. Kathy then pointed to the fork and whined that she couldn't eat with such a small fork, would he please bring her the bigger one. He brought her a bigger fork, cut up the chicken on the plate, and with a huge teasing grin told Kathy that there was an ice cream fudge in the freezer that he had brought home from the restaurant. She should eat it when she finished supper. Kathy laughed and said, "Oh, no, why did you do that? You know I shouldn't eat that." But Leo just laughed back, and when he finished cutting up the chicken he left the room.

Kathy told us that she was always trying to diet, but Leo didn't care how big she was and always brought her ice cream and goodies. Leo worked as a chef in a small restaurant somewhere far away. He would leave the house every morning at four a.m. and sometimes I would hear the steps creaking painfully as he strode down the stairs on his way to work. That was why he didn't eat with her, Kathy explained. He went to sleep at eight when he came home from work because he had to wake up so early. Kathy gobbled her food and told us that she would give us some but it wasn't kosher, and Hashem wouldn't be happy if we ate it.

I was about to tell Chani that it was time to leave when a barefooted Leo walked in wearing a blue-and-white-striped bathrobe. His hairy toes stuck out from beneath the long robe, and we were shocked that somehow they strongly resembled our fathers' toes. Leo bent over Kathy, and she looked up at him and quickly wiped her mouth. He stroked her cheek softly with one hand, and they gently rubbed their faces together.

Then they kissed.

It was a short kiss on the lips, but it confused me completely. I knew that goyim kissed, but I thought that was only in the TV box, where there was always a bunch of pretty people who slobbered over one another. Fat people never kissed like that, and definitely not ugly ones, and I could not understand why they had done that. I had never seen any couple kissing each other before and it made me feel funny inside. Then I thought that maybe it was because they didn't have children. The mothers and fathers I knew never acted that way. They just lived together and were mothers and fathers.

Kathy never noticed our stunned faces. She chattered on after Leo left, and I decided it was absolutely time to leave. Kathy walked us to the door and told us to please come again. We were such beautiful girls, and next time she would buy us kosher chocolate. I said maybe and quickly ran downstairs with Chani giggling all the way behind me.

My parents attended a wedding late that night. It was way past my bedtime, and my sister yelled at me to go to sleep, so I didn't. I wanted to see how late I could stay up. After all, if I ever mistakenly turned into an adult, my bedtime would be in the middle of the night. But really there were more pressing issues keeping me awake. My goyim-in-the-attic secret was out and I knew that I was in trouble.

There was no way Chani was going to keep Kathy a secret; she had such a big mouth, and by tomorrow morning I must find a solution or everyone would know everything and I would be lost forever. They would all know of the big, white furry cat; of the big black TV; of the statue of Leo's grandmother and her baby near the sheep and the dreadful goat; and most of all, that they had kissed on the lips together.

When I finally fled into bed after my parents arrived home, I knew I had no choice. Kathy had to die.

CHAPTER EIGHT

2008

I didn't really want to die. Sometimes, though, I wanted to fall asleep and never wake up again. Dying wasn't the same as sleeping forever. If you just slept forever, you never had to see the dead. You never had to look at them, at their agonizing sorrow, and answer questions they did not know to ask when they were alive.

- - -

I told Kathy that I couldn't do it any longer. The first time I came up to see her after all those years she smiled happily and said, "Gittel, you are a young lady, and even prettier than when you were a baby."

"Do you remember me from when I was a baby?"

"Of course I do." She laughed, remembering. "You had those green, green eyes, so pretty, and then one day when you were 'bout two months, they jus' turned a different color. Now you got dark eyes, nice brown dark eyes."

"Do you have pictures of when you were a baby?"

"Me? Oh, my pictures were still black and white."

"I've never see them. Let's look at them."

"I gotta drag 'em out from that closet." She pulled a folding chair to the corner closet. "Let me see, here it is, I can't reach this thing—take it."

She stepped clumsily off the chair. A picture fell out of the album. Kathy picked it up, panting lightly. "Oh, look at this—just look at this picture. It got only half of each of us here. See, here's me and here's Leo right when we got engaged. Look how nice and thin we were."

"Who made your marriage?" I asked.

"Made it? Nobody made it. We met at a dance on New Year's Eve in Greece, where he lived, and we fell right in love."

"What kind of love?"

"Love kind of love. The kind you fall into when you fall in love."

"What's that?"

"What?"

"Love."

"Oh, Gittel, one day you're gonna fall in love and know."

"We don't fall in love."

"Everyone does."

"We don't do such things."

Kathy sat down heavily on the couch. "Oooo—you just look— here's my niece. She's just a baby here. Now she's nineteen and all in love with Rob. He's her neighbor and they've been friends since eighth grade."

I was bewildered. "Do gentiles have a deadline for falling in love? Like we have to get married. Is not falling in love a terrible thing? Like for us not getting married?"

"Well, it's complicated," she said. "Let's look at the pictures now."

I sat down next to her on the couch in front of the TV. She showed me her two brothers and sister dancing in the garden. She showed me her father holding her when she was two, pigtails sticking out from the sides of her head. She showed me more pictures, but I don't remember because she looked up at me then and said, "Gittel, why are you crying?"

"I'm not crying."

"I see the tears in your eyes."

I could see the black-and-white pictures blurred and fading in front of me.

"I . . . don't know."

"Gittel, don't cry. Tell me what happened."

"I did."

"Tell me again."

"Why?"

"It will make you feel better."

"No."

And I cried and I cried and couldn't stop. I could hardly bear this when it happened because the tears always came without warning, sometimes in the kitchen or in school with my friends, and I would have to run to the bathroom or my room and tell them that it was nothing, just stomach cramps, because no one was allowed to know that I haven't forgotten. No one was allowed to remember what I knew. Sometimes I hit myself to stop it. I would hit myself hard on the head and in my face until it hurt, until I would get angry instead of sad, and then I would stop crying. But that day, I didn't. I cried and I told Kathy about Devory, how she was always knocking on my window.

"Devory?"

"Devory . . ."

"What does she tell you?"

"She doesn't speak. She only comes to my window every night, knocking. I can see her outside in the wind. Her hair is always wild, flying in the cold, and she wears the same light blue nightgown, the torn one that she got from her sister."

"Do you open the window?"

"I have to. If I don't she keeps knocking, and I can't go back to sleep."

"So why don't you open it right away?"

"I do, but then she just disappears. Last night I ran, I ran really fast, but as soon as the window is open she disappears. There is only wind."

Kathy stroked my hair. I wept.

"Tell her to leave me alone."

"Don't cry like that, Gittel. Come here. . . ."

"I'm so scared."

"I know."

My mother called my name. I could hear the door opening downstairs and her voice screaming for me, trying to find where I was. I sobbed quietly. I did not move from Kathy's arms. My mother called for me again.

"Gittel? Gittel, where are you?" Finally, the door shut. I would come up with an excuse afterward. She could not know that I was up here.

CHAPTER NINE

1999

I cried all the way to school the morning after I decided Kathy must die. I sat in the last seat of the van, where no one liked to sit, and bumped unhappily until we arrived. I didn't want to kill Kathy. I liked her. And what would her husband say? He really loved her and if she died he wouldn't be able to kiss her anymore. I was devastated, but I had made my decision. The advantages of Kathy's death were just too overwhelming, and I was sure she would understand.

I was first to arrive at school that morning and I stood outside the door waiting for Chani. As soon as I saw her traipsing through the swinging doors in the hallway, I ran over and soberly informed her that I had a big secret to tell her and she must follow me to the bathroom now. It was an emergency.

Chani followed eagerly, all the while promising that she had not told anyone of the great secret except only a little to our friend Goldy and someone else and her neighbor, but it didn't really count because she had sworn them to secrecy so they wouldn't tell anyone.

I took Chani to the last stall in the students' bathroom, solemnly closed the door, and then began to cry. I told her that Kathy had died in the middle of the night, and that it turns out, she was a secret Jew after all. She had suddenly become ill at about three in the morning, and an ambulance had come and taken her away. But it was too late. My mother had told me then that Kathy was really a hidden Jew from a thousand years before, and that she had even said the *Shema* before she had died, so all the stuff she did in her life didn't count anymore. Now that she was a Jew after all, we were not allowed to say any evil things about her.

I was so convincing about Kathy's tragic demise that I cried as deeply as I had when I lost my bicycle. Chani said that she felt horrible because she had told some terrible things about Kathy to Goldy and she started to cry too. She promised me that she would be my sworn best friend from then on, and she would always give me her snack. She would never, ever tell anyone anything about our deep and dark secret so that I should stop crying already. It was making her too sad.

We both sniffled and snuffled and dabbed at our tears with some crumpled toilet paper. Then, after we had solemnly sworn ourselves to friendship and secrecy forever, we walked out of the bathroom arm in arm, appropriately mournful, so that everyone would ask what had happened.

By the first morning break our deepest and darkest secret was out, and I was the new tragic hero of the fourth grade. Everyone struggled to give me a share of their snacks to secure a position in my new circle of friends. Devory, handing me some tissues, nostalgically reminisced about the warm past in Kathy-the-Secret-Jew's attic apartment. She said that she had always sensed Kathy was too good to be a goy and now that she was gone, life would never again be the same. Chani did all she could to console me in the face of the terrible tragedy and reassured me from the bottomest of her heart that she had not told anyone, except for a little to Goldy, and Devory, and Leah'la, who had promised not to tell anyone at all, except for Rivky, and Itty, and Roisy, so that I was well assured that nobody knew everything, and that everybody knew a lot of nothing, and it was all enough to maintain a position as queen of the class for at least a week.

After school they all gathered protectively around me as I told them just a little bit about Kathy and how she was really a Spanish descendant of a secret Jewish family from a thousand years before, but she never told anyone because she was afraid of her husband, Leo. But then it suddenly hit me that if she was a secret Jew, I didn't have to kill her. She could live and be a secret Jew too. But it was too late. She was already quite dead, and now I really couldn't stop crying. Then I sighed and said that I really could not talk much more now—I must go home quickly and see what was happening with the funeral.

I arrived at home a wiser and richer person. I now held in my immediate possession three bars of chocolate, two fancy lead pencils, and a new pack of Hello Kitty shiny stickers. As soon as I stepped off the van, I tore open the first chocolate bar and munched on it. "Oh well," I thought stoically to myself, "life must go on, after all." But then I opened the door to my house and there stood Kathy filled with life in a billowing orange dress, checking through her mail.

She asked me how school was, and for a minute I couldn't believe that it was actually Kathy. But of course she was alive. In school she was dead, but here she was alive, and I smiled, delighted at the simplicity of it all. I dropped my briefcase right there on the floor and generously offered Kathy a piece of my absolutely kosher chocolate. I then helped her up all forty-one steps, pushing her from behind, and she slowly made her way up the creaking, whining stairs, laughing merrily at my silliness.

CHAPTER TEN

2008

Dear Devory,

    I could not fall asleep last night. I was scared of you, that you would come again. I sat at my table all night trying to write you a letter. I wanted to tell you how sorry I am about what happened, how so much of it was my fault. But I could not find the words. I could not find the language one needs to apologize to the dead.

    I fell asleep at the table while thinking. When I woke up it was dawn. I still would not go to bed. Instead, to pass the time I said the tehillim, *the entire Book of Psalms. At seven my father walked into the dining room. I did not hear his footsteps I was so engrossed in the prayers. He wanted to know if I was ill, saying prayers so early in the morning. I told him, no, I was only doing the omen needed for an early, good marriage; reciting the entire Psalms for forty days*

*straight. He told me not to worry. Nobody remembered
anymore, and I, with my good name and family, would get
married in no time at all.*

*Devory, can the dead hear our prayers? When the words
come floating up, do they go straight to Hashem's sacred
domain, or does all of heaven know our desperation?*

Your best friend,
Gittel

CHAPTER ELEVEN

2008

Kathy and I watched some TV today. We watched a funny show, but in the middle I asked her to stop. I felt guilty, knowing it was wrong to do, especially now before marriage. *Rebbitzen* Ehrlich had warned us on the day of our graduation that we are responsible for all that entered into our minds. And if we allowed impurities in, it would taint our spirituality, impairing our ability to raise children the right way.

We sat quietly on the couch and spoke about Devory. Kathy wanted to know if I ever told anyone what had happened. I told her no.

"What about your friends?" she asked. "You got nice friends. I seen them sometimes, that one with the sweet smile, and that girl with the long pony."

I told her that we don't talk about such things.

She wanted to know why. I tried to explain to her. I said, "Because it didn't happen."

"They're scared?"

"They just act like nothing ever happened."

"But you just tell them it did. Things like that happen every-where. That's why there are laws to punish such evil deeds."

"I promised my parents I wouldn't."

"Why'd you promise them?"

"They said I will never get married if anyone knows the truth. Nobody will marry someone who is damaged by seeing such things."

"Why?"

I told her to stop asking why. There was no why. There was just what was.

Kathy's eyes crinkled up in that sad way. Then she showed me something. She shuffled to the corner of the tiny living room, moving slowly in her worn pink bunny slippers. On the floor lay a pile of magazines. On top was a small bag. Kathy pulled a notebook out from the bag. "Come sit near me," she said, holding out the notebook like it was a rare ruby ring. "Ain't it pretty? I got it in the gift shop by the train station. You could write your own prayers in it. It got flowers and angels on the cover, and pages and pages for when you feel sad or happy or just confused. See—it got an angel on every page. Different kinds."

But I told her that the angels aren't Jewish so I couldn't take the notebook back home or I would have to hide it.

"Angels ain't Jewish or Christian," she told me. "They ain't nothing. They're just angels." She still talks like that, with that funny "ain't."

But I told her she should look closer. These were gentile angels. "Look, they're barely dressed. And they don't have any beards."

Kathy just laughed. "Oh, angels ain't gotta be dressed. They ain't got beards. They live in heaven."

But I didn't argue with Kathy. She said it didn't matter, and the only thing that did was that I go to the police and tell them what had happened because it was a terrible thing to ignore something like that. I told her I couldn't, that it would be a *Chillul Hashem*.

"What's that?"

"A transgression of Hashem's name," I explained. "We Jews carry Hashem's name on Earth, and if I brought negative attention to us, Hashem Himself would be ashamed." I tried to tell her that the goyim would only use the story as a weapon against us. Maybe if I prayed more and repented more it would all go away; that's what everyone told me after it happened.

"Soon you'll be eighteen," Kathy said, sighing. "And doin' your own stuff." But I told her that soon when I turned eighteen, I would be married.

"You want to get married?"

"I don't know," I said, because it was a funny question to ask.

"It's nice to get married," Kathy said to me. "Marriage is for love."

"No it ain't—isn't," I said. "It's for children."

"Children come from love."

"They come from Hashem's commandment. He said to produce and multiply."

She said, "Oh, Gittel . . . God don't mean it that way." She then picked up the remote control and asked me mischievously if I wanted to watch some more TV with her. I told her I must go downstairs.

"Your mother knows you are here?"

I smiled. "Of course not."

She giggled.

"Don't tell her," I said.

"I won't."

I liked going up to Kathy. It reminded me of Devory, but in a warm sort of way—like she never really went away but was still cuddled up on the couch right next to me, listening to us talking.

CHAPTER TWELVE

1999

It was December in New York and Chanukah had arrived—a time for miracles and presents. Two thousand years ago Hashem made a miracle, and two thousand years later we still got presents for it. But most of all Chanukah was a time of beauty. It was a time of joyous remembrance of the Jews' triumphant defeat against the strong, evil Greeks who had tried to destroy Judaism.

In school our class made a big Chanukah sign. My teacher, Miss Goldberg, walked into the classroom one morning holding a stack of shiny gold and black papers, glitter, and glue. She placed the stack of papers on her desk and told everyone to take out their scissors and markers.

"We're going to make a beautiful poster for Chanukah for the whole school to enjoy," she announced. "The sign will show all the *Yiddishe* holy things on one side and all the *goyishe* Greek materialistic things on the other side. The gold is for *Yiden*, the black is for goyim. When we are finished we will hang it up in the hallway by the staircase so the whole school can see our artwork."

There was a titter of excitement. We loved making signs; it got us out of an entire morning of learning. Every year a different class made the same kind of Chanukah sign showing the difference between *Yiden* and goyim. Last year the sixth grade had done the *goyishe-Yiddishe* sign using white and black and it still hung glossy and beautiful in the auditorium.

"Who can tell me some of the items we should put on the *Yiddishe* side?" Miss Goldberg asked. We all raised our hands eagerly.

"A menorah," Shany screeched excitedly. Miss Goldberg nodded her head.

"A Torah!" Sarah Leah said.

"*Tzeddakah! Tzeddakah!*" Chani offered breathlessly.

"Excellent," Miss Goldberg said. "Now what about the *goyishe* side? Who can tell me what goes there?"

We all screamed at once. "Guns!" "Baseballs!" "Almost-kosher candy!"

There was hushed silence. Everyone looked at me.

"There is no such thing as almost-kosher candy," Miss Goldberg said, laughing.

"Um," I said, embarrassed. "I meant TV."

She stared at me a bit strangely. She then called on another girl and we all set about making the poster. Every girl received one gold or black paper with a picture to work on. Devory made the baseball, I made the gun, Chani was making the menorah in back of us. Devory cut out a crooked circle, drew some lines, then stared at it skeptically and announced that there was no such thing as a black baseball. I told her that it didn't matter. It was *goyishe* so it was black and that was all there was to it.

Then I wondered if Leo had guns in his house. Devory said no way, but Chani said that Miss Goldberg said all goyim did and she was the teacher, so she knew better. Anyway, Leo probably hid the guns and black baseballs inside the black TV.

Miss Goldberg explained to us that the evil Greeks tried to impose on the *Yiden* all such materialistic *goyishe* things, like guns and sports, that took the soul away from holy things. *Yiden* were supposed to sit and learn Torah all day and give *tzeddakah*— charity—and not waste their whole lives on silly things like baseball and hunting.

Miss Goldberg held up a Torah that she had cut out and pointed to it. "It says in the Torah that you could find beauty by the goyim— plenty. The Greeks were obsessed with beautiful things, but Torah, spirituality, a goy doesn't know what that is! And *that* is what really counts."

School was out for the first two days of Chanukah and my grandmother Savtah, who lived in Queens with my aunt, came over to celebrate with us. I didn't like Savtah. She was old and sick and cranky. She would order us all around, and nothing we did pleased her. But she was my mother's mother, and I knew that if I uttered one word of complaint I would be promptly and severely punished. "*Kibud Av Va'Em*, honoring one's parents, is the most important commandment," my father explained to me when I complained that Savtah was taking over my bed. "It comes before everything."

My mother didn't like Savtah either. They were always arguing over something or other, and it always ended with my mother stomping out of the room and angrily slamming the door. When I asked my mother why she didn't like Savtah, she looked horrified and said, "What? I love Savtah. Where did you get that strange idea into your head?"

"But you and Savtah are always fighting," I said.

"We are?" My mother looked surprised, then ashamed.

"*Oy*, Hashem." She sighed. "It's becoming more and more difficult."

My mother confused me. Three months before, my grandmother had had a stroke and my mother—convinced that Savtah would die—cried like I had never seen her do before. I couldn't understand her tears. I could barely wait till Savtah died. She was so old and ill and seemed mighty eager to get off the face of the Earth, and though I pitied the angels up in heaven (how would they ever sleep with her snoring so loudly?) I would have been relieved with the new arrangement—Savtah moving up to Hashem, us staying down here. My mother, though, seemed devastated.

My grandmother, typically, refused to die. She said that if she could survive the Holocaust, she would survive this too. I was afraid she was right. Three months later she was back on her shuffling feet, unhappy with everything.

My mother explained to me that Savtah had suffered so much in her life; she had been my age when her entire family was killed. "That is what makes her so difficult," she said. "She can't help it. She takes out her fears and insecurities on us."

Then my mother hugged me hard and said that I must learn to have more patience.

We had a fine time the first night of Chanukah. My mother made cheese latkes and doughnuts, and I got a purple jump rope sprinkled with shiny glitter that shimmered when I turned it. After opening the presents, we all put on a Chanukah play with my father as the head of the *Maccabim*—the heroic warriors of Hashem who defeated the Greek empire's army when they turned Jerusalem's

Holy Temple into a pagan place. Surela played Yehudis—the heroine—and I played the evil king.

Savtah laughed, watching me bellow about the Jews as my father charged toward me on his broom-horse. After the play was over and the Jews had once again triumphed over the Greeks, my grandmother asked me to make her tea. I brought her the simmering cup, placed it carefully on the table near her, and looked out the window across the street.

"Look," I told her, "the neighbors are putting up such pretty lights for *Cratzmich*."

Cratzmich was the word we used for Chr—as, which was forbidden to write or say, as it had something to do with J—. Savtah looked at me and laughed. "Pretty lights? Not so pretty lights."

"Why not?" I asked. "They *are* pretty."

She motioned to me to come closer.

"Come here, *maideleh*. I want to tell you a story."

I sat down near her on the couch, and Sruli and Avrum quickly joined us. We liked her stories. She pulled her sweater tightly over her thin body.

"My neighbors in Poland also had pretty lights." She smiled sadly. "I was so small, like you, Gittel, so small, and already my mommy and totty were dead. The Germans shot them in the head." She pointed her finger to her forehead. "Like that they shot them—after the neighbor took the Nazis to where they were hiding. And I was a little girl, hiding at the home of my father's old gentile friend who taught him music when he was a boy. My father gave him money, lots of money, to hide me well, to feed me, but the war was so long, and the money wasn't enough, and the old man was scared."

I fidgeted. I wasn't so sure I would like this story.

"It was his wife who was the real *rashanta*—that evil woman. I could hear them arguing from upstairs.

" 'You're crazy!' she would scream. 'You will be caught and then everyone will die! Tell the girl to go! You crazy man! She'll kill all of us!' Again and again I would hear her shouting at him to throw me out. The Germans were searching the area for Jews and a seven-year-old girl was too dangerous a visitor.

"One morning he gave me a piece of bread in a bag and told me that I must go. 'Little girl,' he said, 'I cannot help you anymore. Someone will tell the Germans and they will come. Go, little Jew. You must leave my house.'

"And that's how I left the basement, in the freezing cold winter, with snow up to my knees, wearing a thin summer jacket. It was late at night, and I was so cold I could not even think of fear. I ran back to the block that my family had lived on. I thought maybe one of our old neighbors would help me, because we lived on the block with a lot of goyim."

She pulled my hand into her cold ones. "I remember those pretty lights, so many pretty lights decorating the houses. And when I stumbled onto the block I could see all the decorated green trees through the windows. I went to two neighbors, two of them. I knocked on one door and rang the bell. I was so cold, I was shaking so hard, and when she opened the door, I couldn't even talk. I just looked at her.

"And you know what she told me, Gittel? You know what she told me?"

I shook my head.

"She looked up and down the block and told me, 'I can't believe you're still here! Get out of here, girl, get out! If anyone sees you they will kill you and me! Leave my house now!' And she closed the door in my face. I remember that door slamming in my face, Gittel, because they had a metal cross and that man nailed onto it, hanging on the door. And I looked at it right there in front of my face and I cried. I couldn't move, I was so cold.

"The other neighbor didn't even open the door. He just yelled through it, 'Go away from here! We have enough trouble without you!'

"So I hid in a garbage can. There was a big garbage can across the street near a boarded-up house, and I climbed into it and folded myself up into a ball so I would feel my body's heat. There was a small hole in the garbage can, probably the cats scratched it through, and I sat there folded up like that, staring through the hole at the pretty lights across the street, so many pretty lights strung all over the houses.

"Better to trust a dog than a goy," my grandmother warned me. "After I left the garbage can, I ran to the cemetery to hide. The guard dog from my father's factory followed me and didn't want to leave. I was scared it would give me away with its barking and forced it to leave. Such a fool I was. The dog was the only one that was loyal."

She let go of my hand and stood up.

"But, Savtah," I said, "the goyim here are different. They would never do that."

"Different?" She snorted. "It's in style to be nice today. Everybody likes each other; everybody respects each other. It's in style." She shook a finger at me. "Don't ever, ever trust them, *maideleh*. Nobody is different. They are the same people all over. Tomorrow the Pope will tell them not to be nice, and they will turn into Nazis in one week."

Savtah, though I didn't like her, was a great saint. My mother always said so. Even after going through hell at such a young age, she still prayed three times a day and said Psalms too. She always told us that a miracle had saved her, nothing else. Her brother, who was blond, handsome, and looked like an Aryan, was killed. And she, a seven-year-old obviously Jewish girl, with dark hair and eyes, survived.

"Don't ask me how," she would say. "I ask myself that every day."

In school we learned a lot about the Holocaust. All my class-mates' grandparents were Holocaust survivors. Once, the entire *Chassidish* world lived in Europe. The Ba'al Shem Tov, the founder of the *Chassidish* movement, lived in Ukraine. But then the Holocaust came and destroyed everything. Whoever sur-vived moved to Israel or America and built up the community again.

"The Holocaust taught us the greatest lesson we'll ever need to know," my teacher told us whenever she spoke about it. "Never, ever trust the goyim. Stay as far away as possible. In the end, they will only hurt you."

At ten p.m. the Chanukah flames were a tiny spark drowning in oil, and my mother ordered everyone into bed. I was pulling the nightgown over my head in my room when I heard my mother's surprised voice.

"Devory, what are you doing here? Why are you here so late?"

I raced downstairs.

"Go upstairs to Gittel's room," my mother was telling Devory. "I'm calling your mother."

"What are you doing here?" I asked happily. "It's so late!"

Devory didn't answer. She ran up the stairs to my room, sat on my bed, and pulled off her shoes. Her hands moved hurriedly.

"I'm sleeping here tonight and tomorrow. Shmuli came home from *yeshiva* and there's no room."

"Doesn't he sleep on the couch?"

"Sometimes, but he told my mother that the couch is too uncomfortable. Leah'lah should sleep on it, and he'll sleep in my room instead."

Devory pulled off her socks and rubbed her toes. She looked up at me and smiled brightly, suddenly, her eyes blank, as if she wasn't sure how she had appeared in my room.

"There's no room," she repeated.

I heard my mother's hurried footsteps coming up the stairs. She opened the door. Her snood had slipped back, showing tufts of black hair, and the skin near her eyes creased worriedly.

"Do you know that your mother is really worried?" Her voice rose, half-angry, half-confused. "You just walked out of the house without asking permission and walked under the bridge at ten o'clock at night! Your mother is furious! Get up now, put on your shoes, and Gittel's totty will take you home in his car."

Devory pulled at her toenails intently.

"There's no room at home."

My mother tensed, frustrated.

"Devory, enough of this nonsense. You can only come here if your mother gives you permission, and you know that."

"There's no room."

My mother snatched up Devory's socks and shoes and placed Devory's foot firmly on her knee to pull on each sock and shoe. Devory stared straight ahead. Her hands lay limply on her lap and she did not resist. My mother ordered Devory to stand up, then held her firmly by the arm and led her downstairs to where my father was waiting. Devory trudged slowly after him. Once, she looked back, and I thought, by the flash in her eyes, that she would run back upstairs, but my mother had closed the door behind them. She then turned to my sister, who was staring curiously from the top of the staircase.

"What is wrong with that child?"

CHAPTER THIRTEEN

2008

Miranda annoyed me. I had been sitting in the little room forever, it seemed, and every time I said something, haltingly, she would scribble it quickly in her notebook.

"I don't know why I am here," I muttered to myself.

I had been so certain last night. Devory had come to me again. She had pounded on the window desperately, and I could see her blue eyes boring in, looking at me. But I could not get to the window. I ran and ran, reaching out frantically for the sill only a few feet away, but it kept moving away from me as if I were on a conveyer belt running frantically in the same place.

As Devory pounded on the glass, I could see the question in her eyes, the terror and rage. Then I heard footsteps in the hallway. I bolted to the door. My heart stopped. I knew it was my mother or father and that they did not know Devory was really alive.

I woke up then, weeping from fear. I could not breathe. And I knew that I would go and tell that day, or I would never go back to sleep again. Maybe it would make her go away. Maybe she would finally leave me alone.

Miranda was looking down at my file. She kept scribbling things in her notebook. I winced.

"I don't like when you write like that," I said loudly.

Miranda stopped. She looked up. She put down the pen. "I'm sorry," she said.

"Do you have other people also coming?" I asked. "Witnesses?"

"Yes. Do you?"

"I am the only one."

"You are hesitating, Gittel."

"I know."

"Why don't you tell me what happened?"

"I will."

"We could do this anonymously. No one needs to know."

"Of course they will know."

"How?" she asked.

"I'm the only witness for this. I'm the only one who could have told."

"Gittel, are you scared they will hurt you?"

I bit my lip until it hurt.

"Do you have other cases like this?"

"Yes. We do," Miranda answered.

"How do you know?"

"There are many ways of knowing. Reports from the emergency rooms. Reports from school nurses. Psychologists working with children sometimes contact us."

"I'm scared, Miranda."

"I know."

"I don't want to be here."

"But yet, you came."

I bit my pinkie nail hard. It was a new habit, this biting of my nails, and I forced myself to stop. I looked down at my shoes. They were new shoes. My mother had bought them for me only yesterday. She said they were expensive, but a girl in *shidduchim* in only a few more months had to look good. I looked up at Miranda.

"Does it become evidence once you write it down?"

"After you sign it, yes."

"What if I change my mind after?"

"After all this?"

"I could say you made it up. I almost did that once already."

"Do you want to?"

"Don't write anything down yet."

"Gittel . . ."

I thought of how to say it, how to explain it all from the beginning. I had been so certain last night, but now . . . now, it was physically painful trying to open my mouth and talk.

"Maybe she was really only depressed," I said.

Miranda stared at me quizzically. "Do you think so, Gittel? You were there."

"Well, she was very depressed."

"Why?"

"She was always strange. Different. She knew too much."

"Like what?"

"Like . . . things. . . . She read too much. They said she was too smart for her own good. It isn't good to be so smart. It makes a person unhappy. It's better to be dumb and good."

"Did you like her?"

"She was my best friend. We had fun."

"What did you like about her?"

"I don't know. I don't even know if I did like her. She was just always there, like my twin. We were even born together in the same hospital."

I twisted the ring on my finger. There was a streak of red on my skin where I rubbed it. I bit my pinkie nail again. "She was born in the wrong place. She should have been born somewhere else. It's like the whole thing was a mistake, that she came here."

"Maybe she was strange because of all she suffered."

"Many suffer. Holocaust survivors went through worse. My teacher said it was because she could not accept her suffering."

"Nobody can accept such suffering," she said quietly.

"How do you know?"

"I know. We have other cases."

"Like that?"

"Yes."

"By us?"

Miranda nodded her head. "Of course."

"Tell me who?" I asked.

"I can't."

"Then why don't you have witnesses?"

She looked at me quietly. "They are all scared," she said. "Like you."

CHAPTER FOURTEEN

1999

Chanukah was over and Hashem had made no miracles. Devory had come over the following night, and it was as if she did not remember anything that had happened. We played hero and dragon and left the garden looking bald after we had pulled out most of the grass in a desperate effort to save the sinking ship from the evil witch. Our survival was a miracle! Then we talked about real miracles. It was our favorite discussion—the miracles Hashem could make right here in New York if only he was in the mood. All *Yiden* loved miracles. Hashem had made quite a few exciting miracles in our history, and anytime the goyim would start up again, Hashem would pull out a miracle that He kept handy just for suffering Jews. But it seemed as if those goyim had no intention of ever doing anything wicked again, and we were getting impatient.

My teacher said that Hashem made miracles every minute, though they weren't as dramatic as the biblical ones, but we weren't interested. We were looking for the real stuff, and though I had

62 EISHES CHAYIL

prayed for one, promising to sacrifice my entire sticker collection, it seemed as if nothing could penetrate the scattered gray clouds hovering over Brooklyn.

But one day Hashem did make a miracle. He made it for Kathy's *goyishe* cat, and I never quite forgave Him for it. It was on a rainy day, and I was walking home from school when I heard a screech that was louder than my mother's after I gave her wig a haircut. It was Kathy. I could see her jumping up and down in front of the gate that locked my neighbor's driveway, screeching hysterically, "Kootchie Mootchie! Kootchie Mootchie! Oh, no! Kootchie Mootchie!"

I ran over to Kathy, who was crying that she didn't know what to do because she couldn't get to her little cat. "I was walkin' down the block takin' Kootchie Mootchie on a walk when he suddenly ran away and squeezed under the gate of the neighbor's driveway. Maybe he'd seen a mouse or somethin', I don' know, but then this big bad dog came growlin' and now he's gonna kill Kootchie Mootchie. Oh, what'm I gonna do, what'm I gonna do?"

Kathy wailed loudly, and I stood near her staring at the terrified cat and the big dog. The bulldog's back was arched, his tail stood stiffly in the air, and he growled so scarily, I was glad to be on the other side of the gate. Kathy rattled the gates and yelled at the dog, "Shoo! Shoo! Get off my li'l cat!" The dog didn't even notice and just stared at the cat, never taking his mean red eyes off him.

Kootchie Mootchie was so terrified he didn't move. Kathy shook the gates again and screeched at the cat, "Run, Kootchie Mootchie! Run, Kootchie Mootchie!" but he didn't run. He just stood in front of the dog as if paralyzed, and it looked like that was the end of the furry fat cat.

Kathy ran to the door of the house and banged on it with all her might, but the driveway was empty and I knew that nobody was home. The dog growled furiously, moved forward, and lunged. Then, as if electrocuted, Kootchie Moothie sprang up and ran. There was a flash of white and a flash of black as the cat flew down the driveway and the dog ran after him.

They ran around and around the long, narrow driveway, and every time it looked like the dog would get him, Kootchie Mootchie gave an extra lunge and barely got out of the way. The cat was fast, but the dog was faster, and I didn't know how much longer Kootchie Mootchie could run around the driveway like that.

Kathy clutched on to my arm and she cried so hard, her face was red and splotchy from the rain and tears. She kept on looking up to heaven and begging, "Oh, God help us, oh, Jesus, help us. . . ."

Suddenly she turned to me and begged, "Oh, Gittel, pray to God! God loves little girls like you and He always listens. God smiles when little girls pray. . . . Oh, Gittel, pray to God and tell Him to save my little cat."

I quickly skimmed through all the prayers I had learned in school but could not remember a single one that saved fat white cats from big ugly dogs behind the gate of a neighbor's driveway.

The situation behind the gate was becoming desperate. Hoping Hashem was only smiling and not laughing, I looked up to the raining heavens and sheepishly muttered, "Hashem save the cat, Hashem save the cat." And He did.

There was a tremendous clap of thunder as the gray sky turned black and then a fiery yellow. It all happened in the space of a few seconds—a yellow flash of lightning rushed out from the heavens, like an arrow lunging downward, down through the layers of the atmosphere, through the endless streets of New York, and right down to the plain brown beech tree at the corner of the driveway of my neighbor's house.

The tree quivered once and fell, and when the sky cleared up the dog was dead. He was stuck under the fallen trunk, his stunned red eyes staring blankly ahead from between the tangle of branches that covered him. Kootchie Mootchie didn't wait. With one last surge of energy he jumped, fat, fur, and all, over the gate and down to safety.

Kathy and I stood there in the rain that poured down from the plain, gray heavens in stunned silence. Kathy moved first. In joyful ecstasy she grabbed Kootchie Mootchie from the ground, smothered him in her arms, and cried, "Oh, Kootchie Mootchie, God likes you. God likes you!"

We walked back home together, me in shocked silence and Kathy in jabbering ecstasy. Kootchie Mootchie sat in Kathy's arms, looking around contentedly as if he had just caught three mice. Kathy went on and on about the great miracle that Hashem made just for her cat, and I could hardly disagree with her. She thanked me for my prayer and said she knew that Hashem loved me and that He would listen to me and look how good Hashem was for saving Kootchie Mootchie from that big wicked dog, though she didn't know what the neighbors would say when they came home. But she didn't care; it was his fault that he had started up with the poor cat, and Hashem punished him, and he deserved to be dead. She then asked me if I would pray for her friend's cat who was sick and dying, and for the keys that she lost last week, and for the raise her husband wanted, and I said no, no, no! But she didn't even hear me.

Finally, we arrived home. Kathy climbed upstairs with her fat cat and I knocked on the door on the first floor, which led to our apartment. My mother opened the door but I barely said hello. I dropped my briefcase right there near the entrance, ran to my room, slammed the door, and plopped down on my bed.

I was furious with Hashem.

Not only didn't He make a miracle for me when I'd been praying for one forever, he made it instead for my upstairs neighbor, the gentile, and her *cat*.

When I told my father about it, he laughed and said that it wasn't a miracle. It was just a coincidence. Hashem didn't make miracles for cats. But I saw it happen, and I knew it was definitely a real miracle. I told that to my father and he said that maybe the cat was a reincarnation from a past generation *tzaddik*—learner—and that's why he earned the miracle. I said maybe, but I wasn't quite sure. If the cat was a reincarnation of a past generation *tzaddik*, then how come all he did was eat night and day and watch TV on Kathy's couch? My father laughed again and said that trees got struck by lightning all the time, and the stupid dog had been in the wrong place at the wrong time and I shouldn't let it bother me so much.

But it did. It bothered me even more after I told my sister Surela, and she laughed and said that I was stupid. Hashem didn't make such miracles today. I stuck out my tongue at her, but I knew that she was right.

A miracle had to be at least one hundred years old, when nobody was sure exactly when and how it happened, so that everyone would know that it was absolutely true. Once they knew it was true, it then became sacred and they could print it as part of the Children's Tales of *Tzaddikim* series, in which all the men were *tzaddikim* with tall, fur, round hats, and the children had black *payos*—side curls—with big black *kippas*. I loved the Children's

Tales of *Tzaddikim* books. They were small, thin, laminated blue books, with a big picture on one side of the page and big, clear words on the other. We had about twenty of them at home and I knew them all by heart. All the stories took place in a *shtetle*—an all-Jewish rural village—in Eastern Europe, and they were all about the great miracles that Hashem did to save the poor, long-bearded, *shtreimel*-wearing Jews from the wicked duke, or the vicious king, or the anti-Semitic baron who persecuted them.

My friend Shany even once told me in school that her grandmother lived a long time ago in one of the *shtetlech* mentioned in the books and she saw a miracle that Hashem made, but I said that it couldn't be. There were no women in the *shtetle*. They were only created sometime afterward. I knew that because there were never any women or girls in the Children's Tales of *Tzaddikim* books. All the stories and miracles happened only to men with long beards and fur hats. But she said it was true, and I said it wasn't, and she said that I wouldn't dare call her grandmother a liar. I said I wasn't calling her a liar, I was just saying that it wasn't true. The argument would have gone on all recess if my teacher hadn't intervened and reassured us that there were women all the time; they just weren't shown in the books because it wasn't modest, and I said, "Oh."

CHAPTER FIFTEEN

2008

Dear Devory,

    Sarah Leah was engaged last night. She is the first girl in our class to be so. It is only two weeks after graduation, but Sarah Leah had turned eighteen already two months ago, so it was time. We all went to the L'chaim in her home yesterday. Sarah Leah was glowing with happiness. She wore a beautiful navy dress, three-inch-high heels, and even a little makeup. She looked so different suddenly, out of uniform, all dressed up with lipstick and mascara. We couldn't stop gushing about her.

    Our entire class bought her flowers and balloons. Everyone chipped in to buy her a cookbook and a hand blender for her new life as a wife. It was wrapped up beautifully inside the flowers, and stapled on the rose was a small prayer for a long life filled with happiness and joy.

    They say marriage completes you. They say that as long

*as one is unmarried, one is really only halfway done. It is
funny to think of oneself like that, only half-done, but I hope
that soon when I am engaged, I will be as happy.*

It is strange to think that there is a Chassid *I don't know
who I will raise a family with. But it seems that everyone does
it, that it is the only way for things to happen.*

*It is hard for me to write this to you. How old are you
now . . . nine? Do the dead grow older? Does the spirit go on,
developing more even without the body? I don't understand.*

Gittel

CHAPTER SIXTEEN

2000

Some time passed since the great cat miracle. I was still angry at Hashem, but less so now that I was busy with other things—like the night He almost made me pregnant and I was so scared I didn't even tell Devory.

Every night before I went to sleep I said *Shema Yisroel*, begging the heavens for kindness, love, and general forgiveness—but most of all to give me a good dream. A while back I had had a terrible nightmare concerning some Nazis that followed me all the way home until finally Hashem woke up from His nap and turned them into pillars of salt. I had awakened trembling, sweating in fear, and then in anger. I threatened Hashem that if He would ever send me such a pointless horror dream again, I would . . . I would . . . I would . . . do something that He really didn't like. But I was still afraid that the dream would somehow come slinking back, which explains my nightly prayers.

That night He took me very seriously and made me pregnant.

I'd shut off my bedroom light and was just drifting off when I saw myself standing in front of my mother's large bedroom mirror. My mouth was open in fear, and I was staring at the perfectly rounded stomach that poked out of my shirt. Somehow I knew with complete horror and certainty that there was a baby inside.

The first time I had thought about the strange state of pregnancy was in third grade. My English teacher walked in one day carrying a well-rounded ball right on her belly. I had stared at her in complete shock, wondering how on Hashem's good Earth she had arrived at that sudden inexplicable shape when she had been so fine and thin the day before. When I told my mother of Mrs. Gross's new stomach, she laughed and said there was a baby growing inside. I stared at my mother and wondered how it was she could say such an absurd thing, and how it was she really believed that someone would go and stuff a baby inside Mrs. Gross's stomach. That was a full year earlier. Now here I was, baby stuck deep inside and no earthly idea of how to get it out. Hashem, in His peculiar way, had made me pregnant. It seemed He had forgotten that I wasn't married.

I woke up paralyzed with fear. What if there was really a big, round stomach hanging off my waist? I stared at the ceiling, too scared to even cry. I closed my eyes tightly and rolled off my bed onto the cold floor. I lay there on my stomach trying to sense, without touching, any strange bloating where my stomach would normally be. There was none, but I still wasn't sure. Finally I scrambled off the floor, and, pulling up my pajama shirt, I forced myself to look down.

My flat stomach had never seemed so beautiful. Greatly relieved, I lay back down in bed and simply breathed. And staring at the ceiling I decided to have an important talk with my friend

Hindy, who had seven older sisters and always knew everything. But then I heard my mother yelling from the kitchen for me to wake up, and I was really glad that I wasn't pregnant that morning. If I was going to be pregnant it had to be when my mother was in a good mood. If not, I knew I would never be able to convince her that it was Hashem's fault. She would just blame me and say that I was careless or something. But maybe I was still pregnant. Maybe the baby—however it got in there—was still really small and would soon grow bigger and pop out. I pulled on my sister's larger sweater just in case. I shouted to my mother in the kitchen that I wasn't hungry and ran outside to wait for the van. I clutched on to my briefcase and pushed it into my stomach with all my might. I looked at my sister to see if she noticed anything strange, but she just walked right past me.

Finally the van arrived. I stumbled on, holding my briefcase like a shield, and plopped down near Hindy. She demanded that I get up because Goldy had agreed to sit next to her that morning and she was coming on at the next stop. But I whispered into her ear that it was an emergency—I had something really important to tell her. Hindy looked really excited and said okay, she would tell Goldy to sit on the roof. She then sat really close to me and whispered dramatically, "What happened?"

I told her that I had been pregnant that morning. Hindy's eyes opened wide. "Wow," she said. "How did you become unpregnant again?"

I looked fearfully down at the bulky sweater. "Maybe I still am." I explained to her that it was really all a dream, and in the dream Hashem had somehow forgotten that I wasn't married and had made me pregnant.

Hindy thought for a moment, then crunched up her nose and

said, "Neh, it can't be. Number one, Hashem never forgets. Number two, you never got married in the first place."

I asked her what exactly that meant, and she sighed and said that it was a complicated process and would take her all the way to school to explain. I offered her my new eraser but she only stared ahead. So I pulled out my onion-and-garlic flavored Super-Snack and dumped it on her lap and she said all right, she would tell me. She knew all about it because she had an older sister who got married last year, and another three or four who were already married forever. The one who got married last year cried all day because she didn't have a baby yet. She had been married eleven whole months and all her friends had had babies. Hindy explained to me that eleven months was a very long time and something was wrong with her sister if she didn't have a baby yet. Hindy knew that because she had heard her mother say so, and she looked at me to see if I understood the tragedy of the situation.

I nodded my head wisely while I crunched on some pretzels and wondered if Hindy would finish my whole Super-Snack. But then Hindy said that her other sister also cried all day long. She did so because she was fat and she couldn't become skinny like she was before she had four babies in four years. She was just going to tell me about another sister who also cried all day long because of some reason or other, but I wasn't interested because we were almost at school and she still hadn't told me how people got married.

Hindy swallowed the last of my Super-Snack, sighed again, and said, "Okay, this is how you get married. First, you have to get a diamond ring. Without that you can't ever get married. Then, a long time later, you have a wedding where the *kallah*—the bride—with the diamond ring has to wear a big white gown. Hashem can't know that you are married until you put on a white big *kallah* dress for the wedding. And if it's not at least this white," she said, pointing to her dirty homework sheet sticking out of her briefcase, "Hashem will get totally mixed up.

"Then comes the *chuppah*, the canopy." Hindy pointed her chubby finger at me for emphasis. "That is when you really get married. The *chassan*—the groom—stands under the *chuppah* shaking and mumbling, and then the *kallah* walks down the aisle with her mother and the *chassan*'s mother. The *kallah*," Hindy explained, "must shake so that you can tell she is crying. The mother and the *chassan*'s mother also must cry, but not too much, because they are holding torches in their hands and can't even wipe their makeup. When they reach the *chassan* they walk around him seven times, and then everyone in the family has to be very serious and cry at least a little, or at least wipe their eyes with a tissue and hold one another's hands. Then when they finish going around and around, the sobbing *kallah* stands near the shaking *chassan* and a lot of different men say a lot of *brachos*—prayers—and after all that, the *chassan* has to smash a glass cup under his foot, and everyone screams *mazel tov*—good luck—and the *kallah* and *chassan* walk together down the aisle holding hands, and that's when Hashem knows that you are married."

Whoa, that was a long wedding.

And then I jumped.

"Holding hands?" I asked.

"Uh-huh." Hindy nodded her head hard, up and down. "Uh-huh."

Yikes. I looked straight ahead at the torn leather on the back of the seat in front of me, trying with all my might not to look too stupid. Truth be told, perhaps I could deal with holding hands, but I was really nervous about all that crying. Carefully I asked Hindy if I really had to cry and shake just so much in order to get married. Hindy said, yes, absolutely. It was the main part of the wedding, and if I wouldn't cry Hashem would never guess I was married. I asked Hindy what happened then, and she said, oh, the rest was just food and dancing and everyone was happy and forgot they ever cried.

"But what about the pregnancy part?"

"Well," she said importantly as we got off the van, "once Hashem sees you in a white dress crying and shaking just a little under the *chuppah*, with the finally-got-smashed cup, He makes you pregnant whenever He wants."

I was relieved to hear the long ordeal I would have to undergo to be married, for surely Hashem remembered that I had done none of that. I did not have a diamond ring or a *chassan* who shook and mumbled. I had never worn a fancy white dress and I had certainly never cried. Yet I had my doubts about Hashem not forgetting. I'd been asking for gold earrings forever and He always forgot. I mean, I knew, I knew, of course Hashem wouldn't forget, but still.

CHAPTER SEVENTEEN

2008

"God doesn't forget," Kathy said. "He can't forget; He's God." And she was a gentile. "Look how many miracles God made for the Jews. He made Chanukah, and He made the Passover miracle, and He did Purim for you—and all the other stuff you got done by Him. Such a God doesn't forget."

She was right. Hashem did not forget. He allowed children to suffer without forgetting. While watching and knowing everything.

"Man creates suffering," Kathy said. "Man. Why you mad at God for something He never did?"

I told her no. Man also made slavery in Egypt. But Hashem, He made miracles there to help His people. Man does everything bad. Sometimes Hashem looks and helps; sometimes He doesn't.

"Oh, Gittel," she said. "Jesus knows what suffering means. This whole world is made from that—"

"I don't care about J—"

"You don't got to. Jewish, Christian, everyone worships the same God, and you gotta talk to Him 'cause He's not like that."

"I don't want to."

"Pray to Him," she suggested.

"I don't have to."

"It'll make you feel better."

"It doesn't. The miracles, He made them only a long time ago to show off."

"You love God, Gittel." She put her hands over her chest. "When you were a little girl with that pink, flowery skirt, you always sang that song—how's it go? Hashem is here, Hashem is there, Hashem is truly everywhere." She laughed, delighted at the memory. The bunny ears on the slippers wiggled as she stretched them out on the coffee table. "You remember?"

It was funny. I did remember. We were six, maybe, or seven. It was Kathy's birthday, and Devory and I had made her a big happy birthday sign. We wrote on it, "Happi birthday to Kathy, May Hashem give you helth and welth and hapines."

We had done it in secret. Surie, my sister, said we shouldn't be talking to a neighbor like that and Kathy even went to church, which made her a real goy and Hashem didn't like such people. Devory and I had been terrified. We weren't sure why Hashem didn't like Kathy yet but decided not to start up with Him. Kathy, however, would feel bad. On my birthday just a few weeks before she had made me a pretty card and bought me a Hello Kitty balloon. So Devory and I compromised. We made a card and put it by her door, and sang loudly, "Hashem is here, Hashem is there, Hashem is truly everywhere," while looking up at heaven or the stained ceiling but never directly at Kathy. And we hoped Hashem didn't mind too much.

"I don't love Hashem," I said. "I'm only scared of Him."

Kathy sighed. She pressed her pudgy cheek into the palm of her hand. She told me that it wasn't true. Hashem was good.

I thought of that. "I'll go tell Devory," I said.

"Gittel. Oh, Gittel." Kathy stood up heavily. The floor creaked under her feet. She threw her hands up in the air. "Why'd you stop coming here for so long?"

"My mother, she didn't let me."

"Why?"

"Because . . . she . . . because."

"Is it because I'm a gentile?"

"Yeah."

"She don't like when you come up here talking with a goy?"

"No."

"But still you came up. Why'd you come up?"

"'Cause you're a gentile. . . . You won't tell anyone. Also because Devory is here. . . . She likes to come here."

Kathy looked around the room. She looked at the empty space between us. She smiled happily, as if she had finally noticed something she hadn't before. "Oh," she said. "That's good."

CHAPTER EIGHTEEN

2000

School wasn't good that day. Aside from not having my Super-Snack anymore and my fearful jabs at my stomach, Devory got kicked out of class twice: once in Hebrew class when she was caught scribbling all over the *chumash*—the books of the Torah—with a black marker and once during math when she was caught reading a book. A *goyishe* book.

I was sitting at my desk at the time, disturbed by a sudden thought that had occurred to me. Miss Goldberg was talking about the afterlife and how every Jew had an assured place in paradise. Did that mean that my principal was going to be there too? Because if it did, then there was no way I was ever going to let myself die. And if I had no choice about that, then I figured that wherever my principal was going to settle herself in heaven, I was going in the opposite direction. Then I remembered my grandmother, my teacher from last year and the year before, and Sarah Leah, who always fights with me, and Shany, who never shares, and all the other annoying people who were going to crowd in on paradise and I wasn't quite sure I wanted to go up there at all. I was thinking that this called for an urgent discussion with Devory when Miss Goldberg's loud voice cut across the classroom to the back seat where Devory sat.

"Devory Goldblatt! Not only are you not listening, not only are you eating taffy—a forbidden snack—not only is your desk a wreck and your head in the clouds, but you are reading a book in the middle of class!" Miss Goldberg grabbed the book and stared at it, horrified.

"A *goyishe* book!" She pointed an angry finger at Devory. "Where did you get this book? Get up now! Go to the principal! Immediately!"

Still munching, Devory took out a piece of cake from her desk and ran toward the classroom door.

"Your shoes!" screamed Miss Goldberg. "Where are your *shoes*?"

Everyone stared at Devory's shoeless feet. Devory looked down curiously at her stocking feet as if discovering her toes for the first time. She then giggled quietly and continued walking.

Miss Goldberg furiously grabbed Devory's shoes from the floor and dumped them into her hands along with the book.

"Go! Go right now to the principal with this book and the shoes and tell her what you did! I will speak with her at recess time!"

At recess time Devory skipped into the classroom humming happily. I asked her what happened, and she giggled again and said, "Oh, she just gave me a whole long speech."

But that wasn't the end of it. At the end of class Miss Goldberg gave us back our writing assignment. When she called up Devory, she stared at her sternly and handed her a white envelope with the assignment inside.

"Give this to your mother," she said.

I went home with Devory that day; my mother was at the dentist with Yossi. Devory hummed all the way home. She slammed open the door, dropped her coat and briefcase near the closet, and bumped right into her mother standing angrily at the staircase, and I knew that she was in big trouble.

"Gittel, please wait upstairs." She glared at Devory. "And you"—she pointed a warning finger at her—"come into the kitchen right now."

I could hear her angry voice all the way at the top of the stairs.

"I don't understand you! What is wrong with you? Every week the principal has to call me with a new story. Not only do you eat in class, day dream, have the messiest desk, and not listen to anything—anything! The teacher says you also read non-Jewish books that you got who knows where! And now this! This! What is this supposed to be? Not only did you write the assignment on pink paper with red crayon and chocolate smudges in an illegible handwriting, you also write about *Cratzmich*! Where do you think you come from? How dare you write such a thing? Who put these *shtism* into your head? How dare you embarrass your family like that? Answer me! Answer me right now!"

There was a tense silence.

"I don't understand you! I just don't understand you! Why are you behaving like this? Why are you doing this to me? What happened to you? How much trouble are you going to give me until you stop? Answer me!"

Silence.

"Take this assignment upstairs right now and write it over using *only* Chanukah! I never want to see that word—*Cratzmich*—again! You are a *Yiddishe* girl and there's no such word in your language! Did you hear me?"

"No!" Devory shrieked. "I'm not changing it to Chanukah. It doesn't fit! It will ruin my story."

"Ruin your story? Ruin your story? Ruin your mind! That's what it will ruin! Take this paper now! I want to see it in one hour on this table written with pencil, on a neat white paper, and written with the word *Chanukah*. Is that clear?"

Devory stomped upstairs crying. I followed her into her room and she sobbed angrily that they were ruining her perfectly beautiful Christmas story. Chanukah would sound ridiculous; it just didn't fit. Devory stamped her foot. "Christmas! Christmas! Christmas!"

I stared at her in awe. Christmas. I never heard the whole word *Christmas* so many times in my entire life.

Devory stomped around the room, sobbing that she would not write over a word of that story. But I told her that we would stay in the room for the rest of the day.

"Just write it over, Devory, and then we can go out and play. You know what?" I jumped up and down. "Write 'birthday'! Not Chanukah and not Chris-whatever! Just 'birthday,' Devory, just 'birthday.'"

Devory agreed somehow and, using my pointy sharpened pencil, painstakingly rewrote the story in angry, small lettering. We then ran downstairs, where she threw the paper on the kitchen table and ran out after me to the small backyard.

We played until dark. I was the pirate Groondledu and wore a red-and-white-checkered kitchen towel on my head, and she was the pirate Foondledu and wore her mother's kerchief tied tightly around her neck. We chased each other in circles and slashed at each other with fallen branches until one of us would fall down dead. We sat in cardboard boxes rowing our stolen boat through the great seas, fighting storms, flying dragons, and evil spirits. We even ate our supper outside. Mrs. Goldblatt usually had us sit inside around the kitchen table with the whole family, but this time she didn't seem to care.

I had just finished taking Foondledu into captivity when my mother arrived in her small blue car to pick me up. I was very proud of my mother's blue car. Only three other girls in my class had mothers who drove, because driving was a modern thing to do. Our teacher once explained to us that *Chassidish Rebbes* didn't allow women to drive because . . . of all sorts of reasons that I didn't remember, except for the one that said that it wasn't *tzniesdig*—modest—for a woman to drive a car. I told that to my mother and asked her if it was true. And anyway, I said, wasn't it more *tzniesdig* for a woman to be in the car than out in the street? My mother just pursed her lips and said that she had to drive because of different reasons and that plenty of women drove. She looked very annoyed, so I didn't tell her that only three other girls in my class had mothers who drove and they were all more modern. I liked being more modern, if only just a little bit. When my friends said that my mother was modern because she drove, I told them they didn't even know why she drove and it was for all different reasons that I couldn't say and it was none of their business anyway.

Now I sat in the front seat near my mother and listened to her talk with Mrs. Goldblatt about Devory.

Mrs. Goldblatt leaned over the car window and, shaking her head, spoke in a low voice. "I don't know what to do with the child anymore. I'm telling you, I don't know what to do. Did I tell you about today? Yes, I already told you on the phone before. . . . I'm telling you, the teachers don't want her in the classroom. Her teacher Mrs. Greenstein is being really helpful, but I'm at my wit's end. She used to be so different. What happened?"

My mother shook her head and stared into space for a few moments. She promised to call her later in the evening, and then drove down the block. At the red light she turned to me. "What happened in school today with Devory?"

I told her everything. How Devory had been kicked out of class in the morning, then in the afternoon for reading a book—a *goyishe* book—and how she had walked out without her shoes, munching on the cake, and Miss Goldberg was so angry she was screaming, and she never screams. I laughed, remembering how Devory had looked down at her toes as if they didn't belong to her. And then I just found the whole scenario so funny I couldn't stop laughing. My mother didn't agree. She just shook her head and muttered to herself about "that child."

My father was in the kitchen when I entered the house.

"Where is my missing little girl?" he boomed as he strode out of the kitchen with his arms opened wide.

Delighted, I dropped my briefcase and coat and ran to the dining room. My father chased after me, and around and around we went until I caught him and climbed up to his waist. He threw me up in the air, hugged me tight, and warned me that I still owed him fifty-seven kisses from yesterday's game.

"Totty!" I shrieked happily, dangling over his shoulder. "I can't give you so many kisses—it hurts my mouth!"

He plunked me down on the couch, and I tickled him so that he fell backward onto it, and I sat on his stomach and kissed him up until my mother came in laughing.

"Hashem should bless you two. You could make a comedy.

I never saw such a pair. What are you gonna do when she gets married?"

My father sighed and let his arms dangle over the couch. I groaned.

"Oh, not again. I don't want to hear it." I stretched out my neck, trying to imitate my father's deep voice.

"In just a few short years," I intoned, "you're gonna grow old, and get married, and fly far, far away from your father. . . . And of course, you won't even remember who he is anymore."

My parents laughed as I skipped out of the dining room singing.

"Get ready for bed!" my mother called after me. "It's late."

When my father came to tuck me in, he threatened me with at least twenty kisses.

"Totty!" I demanded. "It makes me wet. Why can't you give me just one kiss?"

My father looked at me sorrowfully.

"But I am giving you only one kiss. One kiss for every day of your life. One day when you grow older, you'll get married and fly away, and then I'll never be able to kiss you again."

"*Oy*, Hashem," I said, and covered my face with the blanket. Then I remembered something.

"Totty," I asked him, "do I *have* to get married and have a baby when I grow up?"

My father chuckled.

"And will I have to make supper every single day for the rest of my life?"

"Why are you suddenly worried about such things?" my father asked, laughing. "You still have plenty of time. . . ."

"Yes, but why don't boys have babies also? The mother could

have half the babies and the father the other half. All boys do is wear a hat and have a *Bar Mitzvah*, and why don't girls have *Bar Mitzvahs*?"

"Whoa, whoa, what do you mean? Of course you have a *Bas Mitzvah*."

"Oh, that's not the same!" I protested. "Boys have fancy *Bar Mitzvahs* in a fancy hall, with a big meal, and a lot of people and presents. Girls don't have anything like that."

"Well." My father pondered. "Well. Maybe it's because the boys do things afterward that girls don't, like wearing a hat, putting on *tefillin* every morning, and *davening* and learning all day."

I thought about that some. "Maybe," I said.

My father kissed me good night and left the room. I stared at the ceiling, thinking. I did want a fancy *Bar Mitzvah* like Yossi and Leiby had. But then again, after their *Bar Mitzvahs*, when Yossi and Leiby walked down the street, they had to keep their heads down. They told me that they were keeping their eyes pure and thoughts holy by not looking at women, especially *shiksas—goyishe* girls. Purity of mind strengthened one's spirituality, and the only way to do so in this temptation-filled world was to keep one's eyes clear of all evil. Yossi and Leiby also had to wear a black *Chassidish* coat and a hat, and although they were very proud of it, I most certainly did not want to wear a black *Chassidish* coat and hat every day for the rest of my life. I liked my colorful clothing. Neither did I like the idea of waking up every morning at six a.m. to go *daven* in *shul*, like Leiby did. My father would scream at him that if he didn't wake up he would be the biggest bum in the class.

Praying once a day in school was enough for me. Three times was exhausting. I also didn't like the idea of having to learn and learn and learn all day long. The boys did nothing but that. Even in the summer, after *Bar Mitzvah*, the *Chassidish* boys weren't allowed to do anything like roller-skating and sports and amusement parks. My brother told me that the only break they had in camp was swimming. Only the bums did anything else. On the other hand, the boys didn't have to study math or science. They didn't learn any English or get diplomas, while my sister Surela had to study all day for exams. But Yossi learned Torah from seven a.m. until six p.m., and my father once told him even that wasn't good enough. A true Torah scholar studied at least until ten, if not midnight.

I turned over and closed my eyes, comfortably resolved. *Bar Mitzvah* or not, it was much more fun to be a girl.

CHAPTER NINETEEN

2008

My mother was furious. "Look at your skirt; it doesn't cover your knees when you sit. How do you expect to get married?"

I didn't know how I expected to get married. I just would—like everyone else—wherever their skirt was. I didn't mean not to cover my knees when I sat. It got pulled up accidentally as I was sitting down, and I hadn't pushed it down fast enough. My mother was always upset with me these days. We just couldn't seem to get along. My father said it was because I was turning into a woman, and it was always hard for a mother to see her daughter become a woman.

The change in our relationship started when I was thirteen and my cousin Moishe, just *Bar Mitzvah*ed, ate by us on *Shabbos*. Moishe and his four younger siblings came with my aunt Yitty often to eat by us on Friday night, and sometimes we would talk. We liked to read mystery books together, especially the ones by Gadi Briskman. But two weeks after his *Bar Mitzvah*, Moishe stopped

talking to me. He had taken two steps inside my room that Friday
night, noticed me standing near the bookshelf, gave a startled jump,
and ran out. I said, "Hey, where are you going?"

He said, "I'm not allowed to be in the same room with a girl."

"But why not? I'm your cousin."

He fidgeted awkwardly. He looked down at the ground, blushing as he spoke to me. "My *Rebbe* said if you are in the same room
with any girl, a baby would come."

I took a step away from him. I imagined a baby sprouting in
the air between us if we were only in the same room long enough.
I told him his *Rebbe* didn't know what he was saying. Babies didn't
come until one was married, and then only when Hashem decided.
But he said, "No, no, that's what the *Rebbe* said, and we are forbidden to be in the same room," and he quickly walked away to the
dining room.

After they left, I asked my mother if what Moishe had said was
true. She said, "Take the glass cups to the sink. Why is your sleeve
dirty? Don't you know the laws of *Yichud* yet? Didn't they teach
them to you in school? Of course boys and girls are not allowed
to be in the same room. Yossi, go to bed now—you have to wake
up early for *shul*!"

"But what does it have to do with a baby?"

"Put the salt shaker in the closet, behind the *kiddush* cup—not
near it, right behind it. Be *careful*—my father gave that to me
when I was married; you think I have a spare one? If the *Rebbe* told
Moishe that, then that is what is true. You'll learn about it when
you grow up. Now clean the challah crumbs off the table. I can't
believe the Baums are eating over tomorrow. Never invite people
on Monday for *Shabbos*. What was I thinking?"

She picked up the edge of her turban in one hand, deftly tucking in a loose hair above her ear.

"But the baby—how would that come?"

"Here they are! The prayer books from Segal's wedding! I was looking for them all over! Come, Yossi, sweep the floor, do a *mitzvah*. That's my boy."

I cleaned the challah crumbs off the table. I thought of asking my father, but I already knew he would just tell me to ask my mother.

My father always told me to ask my mother about "women things," as he called it. But my mother did not like talking about "women things" either. When I had asked her about what a period was when I was twelve, and if it was true (Hindy, youngest of eight sisters, had warned me of it) she said it was complete nonsense. A few months later she changed her mind. It was when I was in seventh grade, after everything had happened.

She had informed me suddenly, while standing in Landau's supermarket and choosing avocados, that I was now old enough to know "things." I asked her, "What 'things'?" and she answered, "Women things," but then busied herself with the avocados. They were tricky to choose. I asked her again, but she ignored me and only looked more closely at her list. Finally, pulling a plastic package from aisle six, she gave it to me. It said "Always: Regular Maxi with Flexi-Wings."

Oh, I knew that stuff. She had told me once that it was for children who wet their beds. Old people too. It happened. But now she changed her mind. She said it was for me. For my period, when blood would come out from between my legs for a week. This "thing" had been happening to women ever since Eve ate the forbidden apple from the forbidden tree, and Hashem cursed her, saying,

"Thee shall suffer when thou shall have children." It was a good thing to get my period, she reassured me, because that meant that though cursed, I was healthy and would have many babies as soon as possible. It meant that when I grew up and became pregnant by Hashem's will, the bleeding would stop. What one had to do with the other, I hadn't the slightest idea, but I had my pads.

I clutched the pads tightly. I looked at the shelves. I saw that there were many kinds of pads lining the aisle and they offered all sorts of protection. There were the Long Super Pads with Flexi-Wings and the Long Super Pads with the Flexier-Wings and the Long Super Fresh Pads with the Flexiest-of-Wings. There were the Overnight Maxi and the All Day and Night Maxi and the Make Your Period Disappear Maxi—which wasn't there, but I kept searching for it anyway.

I grabbed all of them. But still I wasn't sure. What if I used the wrong pad? What if I bled until my heart gave out but was too embarrassed to say anything? Would I just lie there dying alone? And what if a baby just got in there somehow despite the bleeding, not knowing there was a period going on? Regardless, it was extremely important that I have those wings, all of them. I explained to my mother between the produce and the Pantene that I needed all those maxis, because one could not know what unexpected circumstances might require the Extra Heavy pad or the Flexiest-of-Wings as I lay somewhere and died a sad and lonely death.

My mother told me to quit babbling. She could not find the coupons she had certainly put in her pocketbook and I should put all fifteen maxi pads back at once; they were all the same. They were certainly not, I countered. My mother looked at me. She looked at the pads. She sighed and said, "Put them back."

I dumped them all in the cart.

"Put them back!"

She said this because the pads were choking her avocados. But I ran back to the aisle for more. My mother thought otherwise. She followed me to the shelf and plucked out package after package, placing them in my arms, and said that she would buy me one—and only one—pack for the period I did not yet have. I could choose which one.

I chose one. Then I chose the other one. Then I chose still another. My mother changed her mind. "I will choose," she said. She picked the Long Super-Fresh Maxi with Super-Fresh-Flexis and Wings.

But then we had to pay. And the cashier, the one who would pick up my Super-Fresh-Flexi Maxis with Wings and know, just know, that I had my period, was a male. A *Chassidish* male, with curly little *payos* dangling from each ear, drumming his fingers on the cash register as he listened to Avraham Freid warble into his headphones.

I pulled on my mother's arm. I held her back. I whispered that there was no way she could pay for the pads. We must sneak them out under our largest coats that we had stored away for next winter. My mother said nothing. She simply walked over to the cashier and threw everything out on the conveyer. Mortified, I watched, standing far away behind the brooms, as the cashier, with a bored gesture, rolled the pads right by the scanner as if they were nothing more than a can of condensed soup. I felt anger. Also wonder. Had he no respect for basic modesty and Hashem's glorious curse? I waited until everything was safely in shopping bags. Then I flounced to the exit, away from my mother. I had nothing to do with those bags. So I did not ever speak with my mother about "women things." And she would not tell me now about babies and how one would come into the room where Moishe and I had stood. It had been annoying back then, when I could no longer talk with my cousin the way we used to—though I had known the day would come. By seventeen, the only boys I was speaking with were my brothers, who I wished would shut up. And my father, of course. My father would often sit with me and tell me how he couldn't believe that I was already of marriage age.

"You're a big girl already," he'd sigh. "Seventeen . . . Look at you. Soon you'll get married, and get busy with your husband, and then you'll forget all about your old, *fakachtah* father at home."

"Of course I won't," I reassured him. "I'll still need your money."

My father would chuckle and stroke my head. "Yes, that's true. How could I forget?" He pointed a hand to heaven. "Thank you, Hashem, for Your money. I wouldn't have children without it."

And we'd laugh and go outside for a breath of air, because, my father said, "There's nothing like New York's polluted air to energize the system." Then he'd tell me all about his first year of marriage with my mother, and how they didn't get along all at once, but eventually they ran out of things to fight about, and look, today they were the best of friends.

He also told me about my aunt Rivky and how she had gotten married by seventeen because it was easier having babies than studying useless things, and about his parents and how they had been married back in the *shtetle*, not much different from today—but never, ever anything about how those babies happened in the first place.

CHAPTER TWENTY

2000

My mother woke me up that morning at least four times. She pounded on my bed, warned me that she would send me onto the van in pajamas, and why, oh why, couldn't I be ready like Surie always was. I jumped out of bed and pulled on my clothes so fast that the right shoe was on the left foot. I put on one blue sock and one black, along with my dirty skirt from last week, my sister's clean shirt from this week, and my little brother's blue sweater that looked like the school sweater anyway. Yet before I finished, the van was outside with its long, squeaky beeps so that the whole neighborhood heard I was late.

I ran out of my room and down the hall with my mother yelling that I was always getting up at the last second and why couldn't I be like my brother, who was waiting for the van ten minutes before it came. Here was my lunch, there was my briefcase, and who knew where my homework papers were—why didn't I put them in my briefcase last night—and, no, she didn't make me a peanut butter sandwich, the tuna would do just fine. And why was I running around like a chicken without a head, just go already! The van was *leaving!*"

After school, Devory came home with me. Hashem had stuffed another baby in her mother's stomach and she wasn't feeling well. Miriam was caring for the younger children while her mother rested. Devory, though, was too much of a handful because she never listened to anyone.

My mother wasn't home. I had forgotten she had told me that she was taking Sruli to the doctor for a small checkup. I couldn't find my key, so we went up to Kathy's, hoping to watch some good TV.

My mother didn't mind me going up to Kathy sometimes, but she didn't know that I watched her TV. In general, my mother didn't like goyim. But she said that Kathy was a nice goy who was just a little strange, so nothing would happen if I went up. Surie, though, said that she didn't know how I could visit such a weirdo, with that *ichy* white cat and all those *goyishe* pictures. But I didn't care. Fat Kootchie Mootchie never bothered me. Though he and I had never quite gotten along, we had reached a point of mutual toleration and completely ignored each other. All he did was eat and sit on the couch watching TV.

Devory and I sat comfortably on the yellow couch in front of the dark TV looking at a photo album of Kathy's family. The pictures in the album were all black-and-white, as Kathy had been a child about a hundred years ago, though she always said it was only fifty years ago. Kathy pointed out to me a pretty picture that showed her mother holding her as a baby. I asked Kathy where her mother was today, and she said that her mother was in heaven. I was completely surprised and told Kathy that I didn't know her mother was Jewish. Kathy looked even more surprised and said that her mother wasn't Jewish. She was Catholic.

"Well, then," Devory said, "she isn't in heaven. Only Jews go to heaven." But Kathy insisted her mother was in heaven. She said that all good souls went to heaven and it didn't matter what religion you were. But we knew it *did* matter, and we told Kathy that the only way you could get into heaven was if you were Jewish and, of course, wore a hat. She laughed and said, "No, no, there are no hats in heaven, only souls."

We felt terrible disappointing her, but Devory whispered to me that she must know the truth. I agreed and earnestly informed her that there was just no way her mother was in heaven and if her father didn't wear a hat of some kind he wasn't there either.

Then it suddenly struck Devory that Kathy's father did wear a hat. She pointed excitedly to the picture in the album showing Kathy's father wearing the very bend-down kind of hat like the *litvish* wore. I was relieved and told Kathy that her mother could get into heaven after all.

"Maybe," I mused gravely, "your father was a secret Jew who never told anyone but only wore the hat." But Kathy only laughed again and said, "No, no, *everyone* wore a hat then."

"But if everyone wore the hat," Devory said, puzzled, "it must have been awfully confusing to Hashem. How did He know who was Jewish and who wasn't?"

Kathy claimed that we didn't have to worry about Hashem. He knew. I asked her if she was absolutely sure all Christians wore hats then, and she said yes, absolutely sure, though today no one wears hats any longer except for the Pope. I asked her who that was, and she said that the Pope was the head of the Catholics, and he wore a great, tall, white hat. I was surprised to know Christians kept

Hashem in their hats too. But Kathy said no, Christians kept Hashem
in their church and sometimes forgot Him on the way out, but the
Pope was a holy man who kept Hashem in his heart.

Devory and I didn't have much to say to that one, and we were
forced to agree with Kathy that the Pope—with the great, tall,
white hat—and all those goyim from the 1950s might somehow
push their way into heaven. But as for the goyim today, it was hope-
less. Perhaps they could even get away with not being Jewish, but
they simply couldn't make it in if they didn't wear a hat.

Kathy, though, was terribly stubborn. She said that, even
today, her hatless Catholic uncle who had recently died had gone
straight up to heaven with her mother and all the other hatless
souls in her family, and that she and her husband, Leo, had every
intention of going to heaven too.

We argued some more, but despite everything our teacher said,
Kathy insisted that souls went up to heaven and hats stayed firmly
on Earth. We left Kathy's apartment very annoyed. She had completely undone our heaven and Earth, and I could not stop thinking of that tall, great, white hat prancing around in heaven without
anyone knowing he wasn't Jewish, and of Kathy going up there and
being stuck outside the gates of heaven, crying to be let in. We
weren't worried about other goyim. We knew that except for Kathy
and maybe her family, they were all evil and mean. But what would
happen to Kathy? How would she get into heaven if she ever died?

Devory thought about asking Miss Goldberg, our teacher, but I
told her that she shouldn't dare. Miss Goldberg would tell my parents, and my parents would never let me go back up to visit a goy
whose family dared to be in heaven.

CHAPTER TWENTY-ONE

2008

My brother Avrum, the one ahead of me, is getting engaged tonight though he does not know it yet. In the last few weeks there have been all-day phone calls, passionate meetings, and fierce Yiddish arguments, as the matchmaker persuaded my parents to take the Cohen girl, that perfect *maidel* from a rabbi-filled family, with rich grandparents and genius hands that would bake three-layered cakes to feed to the many healthy children she would produce for their genius and future rabbi son, Avrum. My parents had made their final decision yesterday, after the *Rebbe* gave his blessing for the *shidduch*, but had then decided that it was useless to interrupt the young man's Torah learning with distracting thoughts, when he would not meet his future wife anyway until later today when the *L'chaim* was ready.

Today was hectic and panicked in our home, as my mother brought in two cleaning ladies to sparkle up the house, prepared enough salads for the whole neighborhood, and put red roses and

snow white dandelions in every room. So she hardly noticed when
I left the house, mumbling something about buying tights on Thirteenth Avenue. Instead I came here, to the police precinct, and
asked to speak to Miranda.

Miranda nodded her head. "But what made you come now? It
is so many years later. Why did you come now?"

I did not know why I came here now. Actually, I did, but I
didn't want to explain, did not want to talk about Devory and me,
how we had dressed up like brides when we were nine and promised each other that we would be married on the same day, in the
same hall, wearing the same dress. It had made sense at the time.
We had just been to our very first wedding, when our fourth-grade
teacher got married. We had stared at her in wonder: at her flowing
white gown, at her face shining with happiness, at her soft, pale
hands and the jewelry that sparkled on her neck like little stars.
One day we would be brides too, we told each other, and then to
make it more fun than ever, we would do it together. We would sit
near each other in two great white chairs. I would hold a bouquet
of red flowers; Devory's would be white. We didn't think much
about the grooms. They would work it out somehow on the other
side of the hall by the men's section. We had even drawn our
dresses out in detail, meticulously copying Cinderella's ball gown
from a book on a white sheet of paper.

For a time, I had forgotten about all of this. And I would have
gotten married alone, just fine, if I hadn't seen that picture—the
smiles flashing out at me, our eyes sparkling ecstatically, our ten-
dollar bridal dresses drooping on our small bodies.

Maybe Devory could not forgive me for this, for getting married without her.

I told this to Miranda.

"You are very brave," she said. "You are courageous for coming here."

"I am not brave," I said.

"You are. You just don't know it yet." She pushed a cup of water toward me. "Drink," she said, half smiling. "I won't write anything down."

I drank. Miranda leaned back in her chair. She thought. "Is it your parents you're most afraid of?"

"Yes."

"Will they beat you?"

"No."

"Then why are you afraid?" she asked.

"Because I need to look at them afterward. I need to look into their eyes and tell them why I destroyed their family for something they did not do."

"How will it destroy your family, Gittel?"

"It will destroy our reputation, our *shidduchim*, everything. It is difficult to explain. I will be a *moser*."

"What is that?"

"A traitor. Someone who tells things to the goyim."

"Do you feel like a traitor?"

"Yes."

"Yet you came."

"I did."

"Why?"

"Because I *am* a traitor. . . ." And I did not explain Devory's white, white face by the window, her knocking, knocking in the wind, and why she would never let me sleep again. It was too hard to say that this was my fault, because I should have screamed out loud the first time she had come to me and held my hand so tightly from fear that I had almost cried from my own.

"Do you want to get married?" Miranda asked, after waiting for me to explain.

"Of course . . . ," I said, chewing on a nail. "I think. I don't know. That's what we do. Of course I'll get married."

Miranda bit the pen cap. She twisted the pen between her fingers as her eyes narrowed, and she looked at me, trying to understand without speaking.

"Do such things happen by the goyim?" I asked.

"Which things?"

"That."

"Gittel, what's *that*?"

"The thing that happened to Devory."

"But you didn't tell me what happened."

"You know what."

"I don't. I just know the end. But I don't know the why."

"But the police asked questions. It should be in the files."

Miranda sighed. "But when there are no witnesses, when we have only half a story, there is nothing we can do."

CHAPTER TWENTY-TWO

2000

A few days after our visit to Kathy, my mother informed us that she was running away to Israel. Actually, she said that she was going for only one week, but I knew that she was really abandoning us forever.

It was all my fault, really. The night before, my mother had tucked me into bed at seven thirty, my father had kissed me good night, and they had left my room looking quite relieved. I had lain in bed staring at the ceiling, waiting for sleep, imagining it to be a small fluffy cloud floating slowly into my room, hovering gently over my head so that I could drift off into a deep, deep . . . death sleep. I smiled mysteriously. Being dead was fun. I got to lie completely straight, my arms and legs in a perfect line, my head laid back romantically on the pillow, my eyes closed prettily, and my lips just slightly open . . . like that. Perfect.

Then my parents would come in and wail and my siblings would stand at the door, their scared eyes wide open, and I would lie there as pleased and as dead as could be. I hadn't quite figured out how I would see the whole scenario if I couldn't even open my eyes. At first I just ignored this, but then I realized that there was simply no way I could see through my eyelids, and what was the point of being dead if I couldn't see how sad everyone was. So I stopped playing dead and to my great annoyance found that I was still not sleeping. I tried counting sheep. I counted and counted and in the middle I switched to cows and then to monkeys, who were, on the whole, a lot more interesting. That's when I heard the mice. Actually it was the steam making all those squeaking noises, but it occurred to me that perhaps they were trapped. Horrified, I visualized the tiny gray mice stuffed into the narrow metal tunnels, scuttling desperately back and forth, scratching at the iron with their tiny paws, squeaking mournfully while I lay in bed.

Quickly, I jumped off my bed. Quietly, I tiptoed downstairs to the basement. Slowly, I pushed open the heavy metal door to the boiler room and stared at the huge round boiler and the pipes tangled all over the ceiling like metal hissing snakes. I could not hear the squealing anymore. Maybe the mice had already escaped. I turned back to go upstairs, and that's when I saw the closet near the boiler room wide open with a neat stack of chocolate bars piled on the top shelf.

My heart lurched. So that was where my mother hid those chocolates. I felt hungry. It was hard work trying to sleep. So I settled down on the floor near the closet, tore open a chocolate bar, and ate.

My mother found me just like that, munching on chocolate at ten o'clock at night. She stood there, her eyes opened wide, and

I began muttering something about mice and pipes that did not convince her at all. I began telling her another story, this time about sleep and sheep, but my mother's eyes only grew wider. So I stopped talking, stuffed the last piece of chocolate into my mouth, and watched her eyes slant angrily. She shook her finger threateningly into my face and said that she had had enough of my nonsense and she simply could not believe that I had been up all this time. She followed me all the way up the stairs, raving about what *chutzpa* I had and that I would not get chocolate for the next month.

I explained to her that it wasn't me; it was my hormones. (My sister had told me that she was learning about hormones in science, and that they were the things that made you grow and jump.) My mother said that she didn't care. I should carry myself and my hormones back into bed this split second if I knew what was good for me. I went glumly back to bed wondering what hormones really were.

But that wasn't all. The next morning I woke up late again, lost my shoe, my gloves, and my glue, had a big argument about what I would eat for breakfast, spilled the milk, dropped the egg, burned the bread, and finally, with the van beeping crazily outside, pulled on the wrong coat. At first my mother yelled, then she threatened, and finally she sighed and said that she was thinking of giving up this whole mothering business. I sat worriedly in school, wondering exactly what that meant, but between recess and a spelling game forgot the whole issue. And that very evening at the supper table she revealed her escape plan to us.

"Okay, everybody," she had said, looking very serious as she poured too much ketchup on Sruli's schnitzel. I stuck my plate out underneath the ketchup bottle and she squeezed even more onto mine.

"So, everyone," she repeated distractedly. "I have something very important to tell you."

We licked at the ketchup.

"Remember Mommy's friend Shaindy from Israel?"

I stuck out a pointy tongue and tipped it with thick red paste.

"She stayed here a few years ago, and she brought those talking dolls."

I crossed my eyes, trying to see the red tip of my tongue waving delicately in front of my face.

"Her daughter is getting married in two weeks, and it's very important to her that Mommy come to the wedding."

I snuck the ketchup out from behind the vase of flowers. I quickly squeezed out more.

"Her husband died last year, and it's important to make her happy."

My sister glared at me. I crossed my eyes again.

"So Mommy is going on Sunday to Israel for a week so I can go to the wedding."

My eyes uncrossed abruptly. Ketchup dripped off my chin. There was complete silence around the table.

My mother smiled. "Hey, I'm not going to the moon. I'm only going to Israel for one week."

Israel, for one week? And she wanted me to believe that? Once she got on that plane I would never see her again. But my mother was calmly instructing us.

"Now, Totty will be home with—"

"It's not true! It's not true!" I yelped. "You're running away from us!"

"Are you crazy?" she demanded. "You would think that I'm leaving you for a few months!"

"Oh, yes," I wailed. "Oh, yes. You even told me that you don't want to be my mother anymore, and now you're going to be someone else's mother."

My mother stared at me. "Gittel, your imagination will eat you up one day. Now, listen to me—"

But I kicked the table and sulked angrily. My mother sighed and ignored me.

"Totty will be home with Surela and Avrum. Yossi and Leiby are anyway in *yeshiva*, and Sruli will go to Aunt Sarah. Gittel will stay by Devory for the week. I was thinking of keeping her home, but"—she waved her hand dismissively—"Totty will never manage her."

Stay by Devory's for one whole week? I stared at my mother in utter disbelief. Oh, boy. I shrieked happily.

"Yay! I'm going to Devory's! So when are you going already?"

My mother looked at me, surprised, and then burst out laughing. She ran over to me and hugged me tightly. I stared at her curiously, wondering what was so funny, but I didn't really care. I was going to stay by Devory for one whole week. I would eat Cocoa Pebbles in the morning, peanut butter for lunch, and hot dogs for supper. I would play with her every day after school, never do homework, and we would even sleep in the same bed. Why, we would really be just like twins.

But when Sunday morning arrived, I stood unhappily at the doorway to Devory's house with a small suitcase, my purple jump rope, and a bar of chocolate, feeling very abandoned. My mother had kissed me good-bye just now at home and I had cried. Then she gave me a bar of chocolate and I smiled. My father drove me

to Devory's and I cried again. But then as I sat in Devory's room I
felt happy once more. It was very confusing. Finally I settled permanently into bliss. It was just so much more convenient.

Devory and I unpacked my clothing, stuffed it as neatly as we
could onto her shelves, and ran around the room playing catch.
We played until we reached the dining room, where Devory's
mother sent the ball careening out the window and us into the
kitchen to do our homework.

We had a fine time that week. We pretended to do homework,
played teacher, house, and pirates, and took turns scratching each
other's backs at night. Devory's mother wasn't strict like mine was,
and she let us stay up until almost nine o'clock every night. Only
one night did she punish us. Instead of studying for a math quiz,
we scared the twins, whooshing and whooping around them in
circles, covered with white linen as if we were ghosts.

The twins cried, we laughed, and her mother scolded us right
into bed at seven. Devory got a hundred on the math test anyway.
I got a seventy-five. We both scribbled up the test papers with red
and blue marker and then folded them into planes and flew them
straight out the window. Her mother called us "double mission
impossible" a few times, but then she just laughed and said, well,
at least it's only for a week.

We had only one argument, on Monday night when I spelled
the word *ridiculous* incorrectly on a homework assignment. I looked
it up in Devory's dictionary, but when I saw how they spelled it, I
scrunched my nose and told Devory that her dictionary spelled
"ridiculous" in the most ridiculous way and that was not the way
you spelled it. Ridiculous, I informed her, was spelled r-e-e-d-i-c-
u-l-i-s and they got it all mixed up. Devory said it couldn't be.

"The dictionary can't spell anything wrong," she countered. "That's why it's a dictionary."

I said that I didn't care what the dictionary said. I was going to spell "reediculis" the right way, and with a newly sharpened pencil I did just that.

My mother called on Tuesday evening from the hotel in Israel and told me that she would buy me earrings as a present. She wanted to know how much I missed her, and though I didn't miss her at all I did want the earrings. So I said that I couldn't wait till she came home on Monday. Then I ran upstairs to tell Devory about my new earrings. Devory's room was small and crowded, with mismatched closets lining the wall and other old furniture from her grandmother's house. There were two wooden bunk beds in the middle of the room that were so low, we would swing ourselves onto the top bunk and pretend we were climbing the rigs of a ship. There was a high-riser over by the wall, where I slept, while Devory hopped from my bed to hers. The twins and the baby slept in the next room, and in the middle of the night I would hear Devory's mother and father cooing the crying baby back to sleep, while Devory, her limbs sprawled widely over the bed, slept right through it.

Devory used to share her bedroom with Miriam, Shmuli, Leah'la, and Tzvi. But now we had the room all to ourselves, because Shmuli moved into his *yeshiva* dorm after his *Bar Mitzvah* and Miriam had recently moved into the storage room in the basement with Leah'la. They had painted the tiny room white, put up a big "Teenage Zone—DO NOT ENTER" sign on the door, and nobody dared violate the warning except their mother when she did the laundry. Tzvi had also wanted his own room, and proposed moving into the backyard shed. His mother refused, and he ended up sleeping on the couch in the dining room. At nine p.m. he would claim property rights to the dining room until the morning. He would hang a cover over the doorway, and anyone who entered without permission would be blasted with a cup of water placed strategically over the upper ledge.

One night we heard an angry shout from downstairs. Devory's father had pushed the cover aside and entered the dining room. That was the last cup of water Tzvi ever put anywhere. Devory's father was different from mine. He was taller, his eyes were a dark blue like Devory's, his beard was darker and longer, and he was hardly home, even at night. Sometimes he came home after we ate supper, but he never stayed. Devory's mother would pack the food into little plastic containers and he would take it to *shul*, where he would study Torah until ten thirty. Every evening Tzvi went with his father to *shul* for an hour, where they would study together. Sometimes they would study at home like my father did with my brothers. They would sit at the dining room table across from each other, and we would hear their voices chanting the holy words, discussing interpretations, arguing over the meaning of the Talmud in front of them. The conversation would grow heated with Tzvi arguing in the Hebrew language and his father answering in Yiddish—back and forth, back and forth, swaying, shaking, curling their long *payos*. Tzvi's lilting voice and his father's—gentle and deep—joined in a lively ancient song, a song that always ended with his father proudly proclaiming, "Now that's how a *Yiddishe kup*, a Jewish mind, works."

Devory's mother was very proud of Tzvi. She said there was nothing as sweet as the sound of Torah learning in a Jewish home. Once, when Miriam complained that Totty was never available to help her with her assignments, her mother told her that having a father who was such a *Talmud Chacham* and studied Hashem's Torah was a lot more important than anything else. Besides, she could always help Miriam with her assignments. But Miriam never asked her mother for help. They barely spoke to each other. When Miriam washed the dishes every day after supper there was a gloomy expression pasted on her face, as if she wanted to disappear.

Mornings were the worst. We would sit munching our cereal, and Miriam—her hair in a bun and her shirt untucked—would slouch into the kitchen, grab an apple, and then walk quickly toward the door, her backpack hanging over one shoulder.

"Did you think of saying good morning to your mother before you leave?" Devory's mother would demand, her hands moving swiftly over the countertop, wiping it down.

Miriam would mumble something incomprehensible and open the door. Her mother, pointing an angry finger at her, would call her back.

"Miriam, come here right now! Do you think I'm blind? How many times do I have to tell you that your uniform skirt is too short? Stop folding it up!"

"Leave me alone!" Miriam would snap.

"The skirt has to be four inches below the knee. That skirt is not longer than two inches. Aren't you embarrassed? Are you looking to get into trouble? Is this the kind of example you're setting for your sisters? You are ruining your name for *shidduchim*, don't you realize?"

Miriam would march angrily out of the house.

Devory and I stayed as far away from her as possible. We played with Leah'la and Tzvi, who were a lot more fun. Tzvi showed us how to build a house out of the couch pillows. Devory's mother tried to join us, but when she crawled through our house with us cheering her on, she got stuck, and our little house went scattering in all directions.

"*Oy*, I'm not so skinny anymore." She laughed, pulling down her house robe. "Believe it or not, I used to do this when Miriam and Shmuli were small."

On Thursday evening, Devory's father came home early.

"Okay!" We heard his booming voice from downstairs. "We are playing the Kazooooola!"

Devory, who had been sitting one foot away from me, was suddenly no longer there. With a wild shout of delight she was running down the stairs and I heard feet, big and little, stampeding from all corners of the house. I ran downstairs after them. The entire family congregated in the small dining room.

Mr. Goldblatt then closed his eyes, held up his hands, whistled, and the Kazoola began. I ran after Devory, who was grabbing canned food, chairs, anything she found, though I had absolutely no idea why. I followed the mad dash back to the living room, where we laid the stash, including cups, a small table, cardboard boxes, spoons, and forks, out on the floor. Only when the room looked like the aftermath of a burglary did Mr. Goldblatt yell, "Kazooooola!" And in a split second we all stood in a line in front of him.

"Okay," he said, winding his watch. "We're starting. Miriam first."

I stared at Miriam, bewildered, as she quickly began jumping over objects, skipping over cups, and swiftly stepping over the chair—without touching a thing. If you touched any of the scattered items you were out. Whoever finished the Kazoola the fastest won and got turned upside down while everyone tickled him. We all had our turns; I was out within seconds. With an undignified crash I landed on the floor trying to tiptoe over the small table. Devory won. She screeched happily as she ran around the table, everyone running after her, until her father caught her and the tickling ceremony began, and ended with cherry ice cream in the kitchen.

Mr. Goldblatt said that Shmuli had invented the Kazoola, and he held the fastest record so far.

"Remember what a troublemaker he was?" he said to Mrs. Goldblatt as we crowded around the table. "It's amazing how he settled down."

"Is Shmuli coming home for *Shabbos*?" Tzvi asked, jumping on the couch.

"No, not this week," Mr. Goldblatt answered. "He wants to learn extra for the Talmud competition next week."

Tzvi kicked a pillow into the air and caught it with one hand. "*Oy*, all he does is study all day."

Devory's mother pursed her lips. "You should learn like him. There is no better *nachas* that a parent can ask for, no greater pride for a mother or father. Shmuli has the best name in the *yeshiva*," she said proudly. "He is such a *Talmud Chacham*. He's only fifteen and his *rosh yeshiva*—head of the *yeshiva*—already told me that he would be the biggest match in *shidduchim*."

Mr. Goldblatt nodded proudly in agreement and fondly pinched Tzvi's cheek.

On Friday afternoon Devory and I helped Mrs. Goldblatt bake challah for *Shabbos*. We sat near the kitchen table—that is, I sat near the kitchen table; Devory sat cross-legged on the table rolling the dough. I tried braiding the challah, and though Devory said it looked like the baker's work, it struck me as rather messy looking. We were working on our third challah when Shmuli walked into the house.

"Shmuli!" Mrs.Goldblatt ran to him. "I thought you were staying in *yeshiva*! What a surprise!" She hugged him tightly. "*Oy vey*, you'll have to sleep on the couch with Tzvi, because Gittel is here too."

"I was planning to stay in *yeshiva*," Shmuli said, smiling broadly, curling his long side curls around his finger. "But a group of boys, guests from other *yeshivas*, came for *Shabbos*, and I decided that I'll never be able to learn there in all that noise, so I might as well come home."

He noticed Devory and me sitting in the kitchen and waved at us from the hall.

"Hello, Devory, and her friend Gittel."

"Hello," I said shyly.

When Devory and I were five years old, Shmuli would give us piggyback rides around the dining room table. He would play hide-and-seek with us and teach us Torah songs. But since his *Bar Mitzvah* he had suddenly become like an adult, with that deep, ugly voice, like my brother's, a blond curly beard sprouting over his chin, and the huge black *kippa* covering most of his head. I no longer saw him, except when he came to see my brother when they were home for *Shabbos*, and even then, they would usually go to *shul* together. But Shmuli was a big helper, I heard Mrs. Goldblatt tell my mother. Whenever he was home, he would help out with the younger ones. He has the patience of a real father, she would say fondly. He even used to bathe Devory and put her to sleep until he went to *yeshiva*.

And now Shmuli played with the twins outside, while Devory and I fooled around in the backyard. He then bathed them so they should be clean for *Shabbos* and helped Devory set the table for *Shabbos*.

"I bought you a new book on the way home," he told her as he handed her glass cups. "I'll read it to you with the funny voices. Remember?"

"I wanna read it myself," Devory said, placing the cups quickly near the plates.

"Hey, Gittel." Shmuli turned to me. "Do you want to hear me make funny voices?" His blue eyes winked mischievously as if he were my secret friend.

I shrugged.

"I want to read it myself," Devory repeated. She put the cup upside down near the plate and walked into the kitchen.

Shmuli took a pile of forks, spoons, and knives and spread them out on the table. "Look," he showed me. "It's the three soldiers Jim, Joe, Jan."

He placed a fork in my hand. "Meet Jim. He goes first." With a flourish of his hand, he dropped the fork on the table. "Now, where's Mr. Joe?" He took the knife out of my hand, twirled it in the air, and put it by the fork. "And now, Mr. Jan." He held up the fork, cocked his head, then threw it high up in the air and caught it with his other hand.

"See," he said, smiling dramatically. "Jim, Joe, Jan. Now if I say to you, hey, pass Mr. Jan, you'll know what to do."

I giggled. He was funny.

"I'll read you the book soon," he said as he finished folding the napkins. "Maybe we'll have time before I go to *shul*."

But an hour before *Shabbos*, the twins had turned on the

shower and soaked themselves completely and then ran around the house with wet shoes. By the time Shmuli had changed them again, he said he had to go to *shul* because he liked to learn the Torah before *Shabbos*.

Mrs. Goldblatt, mopping the floor for the third time that day, tiredly told Devory to watch over the twins until *Shabbos*, when she would put them to sleep. We took them out to the backyard, where they ran around in circles and then rolled in the dirt, giggling. I wanted to play a trick on them, but Devory, sitting dully on the steps, said she was not in the mood. We sat there until it was time to light candles.

CHAPTER TWENTY-THREE

2008

When I returned from the police station, I couldn't bear the tumult of Avrum's *L'chaim* and all the jabbering conversations. So I ran up the stairs and banged on Kathy's door. I looked down over the staircase furtively. I could hear my parents' tense conversation and Avrum's nervous voice floating up the stairs. The door to the house was opened downstairs. I saw Surie, the top of her perfectly coiffed wig, and the large cake she held carefully in her hands.

"The Schwartzes sent this," I heard her say out loud as she opened the door to our apartment. "Isn't it gorgeous? *Nu*, so when's the girl arriving?"

I knocked again, more quietly. I closed my eyes, praying Kathy would be home; I could not go downstairs like this. They could not see me this way. Finally, I heard the creaking floor and Kathy's slow, sure footsteps. She opened the door and pulled me inside.

"Gittel," she cried, "you're white as a sheet!"

I dropped my pocketbook on the floor. "I told Miranda what happened."

"You did?"

Kathy held my hand and took me inside.

"I told her the truth," I said, and again I couldn't stop crying.

She said, "Gittel, Gittel, it's good. It's good that you told what happened."

"Why did I tell her what happened?"

"It's good, Gittel," she repeated. "It's the only way it could be."

"You said I should tell her. . . ."

Kathy took me over to the couch. She pushed me down till I sat.

"You'll feel better soon," she said.

I bent over, putting my face between my knees.

"She lied," I said.

Kathy put her hand on my back.

"Why are you saying that?" she asked.

I pushed her hand off. "She lied . . . after I told her what happened. . . ."

"How did she lie?"

"I tore up the file," I said. "I'm never going back. And I can't go downstairs right now. . . ." With Avrum getting engaged tonight, I had to get back home fast and put on the new suit my mother had bought me and smile at everyone brightly so that they should see how beautiful and perfect I was and that I was next in line for marriage.

My mother was calling my name. There was that frantic note in her voice, the one that came right before she completely freaked out, wondering where I was.

Kathy stroked my cheek. She said, "Gittel, Miranda didn't lie. You didn't want to hear what she said. It just hurt too much."

CHAPTER TWENTY-FOUR

2000

Shabbos in the Goldblatt home was like *Shabbos* at home. Then again, *Shabbos* was the same in all Jewish homes. Mrs. Goldblatt lit the *Shabbos* candles, one for each child, and then prayed, covering her face with her hands and swaying with emotion. We sat on the couch and sang the Friday night prayers, and when we finished Mrs. Goldblatt took a nap until Devory's father came home with the boys from *shul*. The men sang the holy *Shabbos* songs and then Mr. Goldblatt made *kiddush* over a cup of wine. Mrs. Goldblatt then told us that every Friday night when Jewish men sing *Eishes Chayil*, the angels of heaven sing along and Hashem is happy because it is only because of Women of Valor building homes of *Torah* that the *Yiden* survived everything. We then went to wash our hands and said the blessing over the warm, fresh, homemade challah. In between eating the fish, soup, and chicken, we sang special *Shabbos* songs, called *zemiros*, and Shmuli said a *D'var Torah* sermon.

As soon as the meal was over, Devory ran upstairs. Shmuli, Leah'la, and I helped clean up the table, while Miriam and her mother were washing the dishes.

"It's amazing how Devory disappears as soon as it's time to help," her mother said.

"Oh, none of us liked to help too much when we were nine," Shmuli said with a smile.

"Oh, no, this girl is something special," Miriam said sarcastically. "Never saw anyone so messy."

"Well." Mrs. Goldblatt sighed. "She'll just have to grow up, like everyone does."

When I went up to our room I found Devory jumping on my bed.

"Let's see who could jump the other off." She smiled mischievously. "I already jumped myself off."

I bounced off at first try, but when I fell off the bed and bruised my elbow I stopped the game right there.

"All right, then," Devory gave in. "Let's play ghosts and scare the twins again."

"Yes!"

And we did. We brought the twins into the room, and then chased after them, wrapped in sheets. "*Whooooo! Whoooooooo!*"

We had fun. They didn't. Miriam heard the noise, yelled at us that we were acting like disgusting babies, and took the crying twins out of the room.

Devory still wanted to play, but I was tired already. She was not and was jiggling around the room like a jack-in-the-box. Even her freckles seemed jittery, and I told her if she wouldn't stop jumping they would bounce right off her cheeks. They didn't, even as she sang the most ridiculous songs out loud and danced around the room as if she were powered by batteries.

I lay down in my bed and closed my eyes. But when Devory saw me falling asleep she sat down right near my head and tickled me all over.

"Stop that!" I shrieked.

"I'm going to dress up like Haman on Purim," she said suddenly. "What are you going to dress up like?"

I sat up in the bed. "I don't know," I said. "I want to dress up like a *shnorrer*—a beggar—then everyone will give me money."

"I wanna dress up like Haman," she repeated. "With a rope around my neck." She twisted my purple jump rope around her neck and began spluttering, pretending she was choking. We giggled.

Haman was an evil man. Long ago, in ancient Persia, Haman was the grand vizier to the king. He convinced the king to kill all the Jews living in Persia and hang their holy *tzaddik*, Mordechai. But the king's queen, Esther, was a beautiful Jewish lady who pleaded on behalf of the Jews. And in a miraculous turn of events, Haman was hanged in the city square, on the very gallows he had built to kill Mordechai. Since then, that day is celebrated every year on Purim. But girls never dressed up like Haman. Until Devory's plan.

"Does it hurt to hang?" she asked me.

"I don't know."

"It doesn't hurt to hang," she said firmly.

"How do you know?"

" 'Cause I read about it."

"You did?"

"Uh-huh, if you twist around the rope like this"—she stood on the bed demonstrating—"and you hang it onto something high, then it just takes a second 'cause it breaks your neck over here." She bent her neck forward so I could see. "And then you're dead just like that."

I stared at her clenched fist clutching the imaginary rope.

"Ich," I said.

She sat down on my bed. I pushed away the blanket.

"But for Haman it hurt to die," I said. "'Cause he was evil."

"Maybe," she said, crossing her legs. "Maybe not."

"Are you gonna have a horse?" I asked.

"Uh-huh. A cardboard horse, like Leiby had last year." She giggled. "And I'll wear a purple turban and a long black mustache. It'll be fun."

"Yes," I said. "And let's make each other *mishloach manos* again. Like last year. But this year let's make it a surprise."

We giggled excitedly. *Mishloach manos* were holiday gifts of food that friends gave to one another on Purim, and that was the only time of the year that we could eat as much nosh as we wanted to. It was a generous day.

Devory's father knocked on the open door and clucked his tongue.

"All chickens into bed immediately! The sun rises in only eight hours. Into bed now!"

He strode toward my bed smiling. Devory jumped off and ran giggling around the room.

"End of fun," he said, scooping her up and dropping her, bouncing, right into her bed. He pointed a warning finger. "No kidding," he said seriously. "No getting out of bed."

He left the room, and there was quiet. I was drifting, in between dreams, when Devory nudged me hard.

"You know what else I am going to do on Purim?"

I muttered in response. I was tired. I wanted to sleep. Devory nudged me again.

"Come on, wake up. It's Friday night. We don't have school tomorrow."

I grunted and closed my eyes. She pulled at my blanket.

"Come into my bed!" Devory whispered into my ear. "Come into my bed."

"Leave me alone. . . ."

"But I can't fall asleep, come. . . ."

"Don't wanna. . . ."

She pushed me hard, and I opened my eyes, annoyed. "Stop it!" I protested. "I want to sleep. I'm tired!"

She stared at me, her blue eyes wide open with fear.

"Come sleep in my bed," she pleaded.

"I can't," I said. "Your mother doesn't let us. And then she'll yell at me tomorrow."

"I don't care," she said urgently. "Come into my bed."

I was angry. "Leave me alone. I'm not getting into trouble again. . . ."

Devory stared at me. She stood by me for a few moments, and finally, as I was about to push her away, walked back to her bed. But the house was dark and silent and I was scared and annoyed. I hated being awake at night, and I was angry with Devory. She was lying in her bed quietly, and I could see her staring up at the ceiling.

I thought about my father. He was alone at home without me, and I wondered how he was surviving. Surela was home, as was

Avrum, but I wasn't—and I was his favorite child. That's what he said when I spoke to him the day before on the phone, though I told him that I knew it wasn't true because Yossi and Avrum and Sruli told me that he always told them the same thing. He laughed and said that it couldn't be. Whenever he looked at me or even thought of me I was really his favorite child. The thought of it confused me, and I wondered how one person could have so many favorite children. I couldn't imagine ever loving my brothers Yossi or Avrum even if I was their mother, though I wouldn't have such a hard time loving myself. Or would I? I was giving up on the whole love thing when Shmuli walked into the room. In the dark he looked like a shadow, and for a moment I thought it was a thief. But then he moved forward and when I saw that it was him, I sighed deeply in relief.

Shmuli walked quickly across the room. When he reached Devory's bed he stood over her, staring down at her as if he could not make up his mind. Devory lay unmoving, and I wondered how she had fallen asleep so fast and what it was that Shmuli wanted to ask her in the middle of the night. He then turned around and walked back to the door, but he never left the room. He stood there for a long time and stared into the dark space. He lifted his hand as if he was still unsure and slowly pushed the door closed. He stood still; only his fingers were moving, habitually curling his *payos*, waiting—as if listening for a sound. Then quietly, he walked back to the bed.

I wanted to call out to him in a whisper, to tell him that Devory was sleeping and he should come back tomorrow, when I saw him lift up the edge of her blanket. I wanted to tell him not to wake her up now, she had finally fallen asleep, when I saw how she jumped, as if he had touched her with fire. I wanted to tell her that it was only a dream, it was her brother Shmuli, when I saw how he sat on the mattress and pushed her head down. I wanted to ask him what he was doing, why he was pulling the blanket over them, why his breathing was so loud and heavy, why he disappeared inside with her, but something froze inside of me, and fear—the kind I had never known—rushed over my body and I dared not move. I saw the blanket, how it moved back and forth and back and forth so fast I thought they were playing tug-of-war. But then the blanket moved angrily as if someone was fighting with it from inside. I saw Shmuli's dark head, how it bobbed up and down from beneath the covers, and I could hear him panting like my father did when he carried in the heavy grocery deliveries. Finally he stopped. His breathing slowed down, and he sat up on the bed.

Nothing moved in the darkness. I saw him pull off the blanket, and it struck me, suddenly, horribly, that he had remembered I was there. I closed my eyes and held my breath. My throat was clenched so tightly I could not feel myself breathe. I heard his footsteps. They came carefully toward me and my body turned to stone. I could hear him breathe, could see him in my thoughts standing over me, watching my still form. Then I heard him move away. He moved quickly, silently, until he reached the door and opened it slowly until it was the way it had been before. His footsteps moved down the hallway, a soft, shuffling sound, and then I could hear him no longer.

I could not open my eyelids. They weighed down heavily on my face, as if someone had glued them together. I was scared to open them, as if I would be in an evil dream of monsters and ghosts. I struggled to breathe. Forcing my hand onto my face, I pinched my eyes and pushed them open. I sat in my bed and watched Devory. She lay still. I watched her for a long time, but she did not move. Maybe she was dead! He had done something and it had killed her. I wanted to get up and run to her, but my legs lay like two boulders and I could not budge them.

Then she moved. Her small hand fell limply over the blanket and I could feel my hot, relieved breathing against the blanket I had stuffed against my mouth. We lay there in the darkness and we did not dare move again that night.

The twins woke me up in the morning. They pulled out my ponytail holder and yanked my hair hard. I shoved my face into theirs and growled, but they only ran away delighted. I stumbled out of bed, annoyed, and got dressed. Devory was reading a book on the couch downstairs. Her mother was yelling at her to please help set the table for the *Shabbos* meal, but Devory was completely ignoring her.

I helped set the table while Mrs. Goldblatt and Miriam prepared the salads in the kitchen. The twins were running around throwing their toys all over the place and the baby was crying in the bassinet. Devory was reading the book as if she were alone on an island. I sat near Devory, but she ignored me too. Mrs. Goldblatt stared at her grimly as if deciding whether or not to grab the book away. She shook her head, turned around, picked up the baby, and went upstairs.

Even after Mr. Goldblatt came home, Devory placed a book on her lap and read straight through the *Shabbos* meal. Shmuli was singing *zemiros* the entire time. He closed his eyes, looked up to the ceiling, and swayed so hard, as if he were praying, and Mrs. Goldblatt smiled proudly and said that he looks like such a *tzaddik*, a *mensch*—an honorable and decent man. There was a guest at that meal, a young man who had come from a different country for cancer treatment. Leah'la whispered to me that he was bald from the chemotherapy, and though I stared intently trying to see, he never took off his hat.

The young man sang along and then asked to give a *Shabbos* sermon. I did not understand most of it until he began talking about the community. He stared down at the plate as if hypnotized by it, and the words came out slowly, with difficulty.

"When I found out I had cancer I thought it was the end. . . . Besides the diagnosis itself, I come from a poor family. We didn't have money for anything, certainly not for treatment. . . ." His voice cracked. "I would not be alive if not for the *chessed* in the Jewish community. They take care of everything. . . . Everything! *Chai* lifeline, *Bikur Cholim*, *Rofeh*, I can't even remember all the organizations that helped me with money, food, doctors, advice. . . . They even pay for the car service that takes me to the hospital. . . ."

Mrs. Goldblatt nodded her head. I could see the tears in the corners of her eyes.

The guest looked up. His fingers played nervously with a fork, but he smiled and shook his head in wonder.

"There was not one *Shabbos* I was alone. Not one meal that I had to wonder where I would be. . . . They have built an empire of *chessed*—good deeds—in New York. . . . It is unbelievable. I heard of the charity that is given here . . . who hasn't? But until you witness it, until you are in a situation where you need help, you cannot believe it. Every patient is treated like a VIP, like there is no other life that is as important."

"*Baruch Hashem*," Mrs. Goldblatt murmured. "Blessed

Hashem." And we could almost touch the warm pride that spread over the room.

There were baked apples with cookie crumbs for dessert and then ice cream with cherry sauce.

After the meal we played outside with the neighbors. Devory was running around wildly, and we got into a fight because she didn't want to play school with me. She wanted to play cops and robbers, but I told her she was too much trouble to catch as a robber and had too many freckles to be a cop. She said that plenty of cops had freckles, and I said that there was no such thing. A cop who had freckles was fired on the spot. All cops had to be tall and big and have unfreckled skin. At that moment, Avigdor, a six-year-old neighbor, threw marbles at us. We took after him and played catch-the-annoying-freckled-boy for the rest of the afternoon.

When Mrs. Goldblatt said that we should come in, Devory wanted to run away around the block. I told her not to. I said that we would play poxa moxa, her favorite game, inside. Poxa moxa was a game of made-up words. We each took turns coming up with new ridiculous words and the other had to guess what it meant. We then wrote all the words down and had a long, profound conversation in poxa moxa.

"Time for bed!" Mr. Goldblatt said when he stuck his head into our room later that night.

"*Twadril mokri bo!*" we screamed at him.

"What?" He cocked his head. "Oh, not again!"

"*Waiz wallayeo xain bryomy,*" we protested.

"All right! *Hootchka pakootchka lamootchka* now! That means—get into bed if you know what's good for you, in space language."

"*Jay.*" Devory threw up her hands in laughing frustration. "*Proksiani puksadowdla iyenvee.*"

"*Tway, tway,*" I agreed. It was the only word I remembered. It meant yes.

He moaned mockingly and slammed the door. We giggled helplessly.

Devory came to me that night when everything was dark. She pushed the blanket from my face and clutched on to my arm.

"Come into my bed."

I did not move.

She put her face close to mine.

"Gittel," she whispered. "Come into my bed."

She was scared, so scared, but I could not move. I just stared at her.

She came into my bed. She climbed over me and slid under my blanket. I moved a little to the side. She wanted me to hold her hand. She put her palm over my clenched fist. I was too scared to move. I don't know why.

We lay in my bed, staring at the ceiling. She clutched my hand, lying limply under the blanket, and squeezed it tightly, so tightly, but I did not pull away.

Then she began to cry. She did not cry out loud. Her mouth opened and closed as if it did not dare make a sound, and I heard the long, silent screams of agony again and again.

I wanted to scream, to run away, but I was frozen—as if I were holding the hand of a ghost. I could not think of anything but the hand that had become part of mine, and the deep swirling fear and revulsion that consumed me.

Afterward, Devory left my bed and she said she was going to

the bathroom. I watched her walk away, her long white nightgown trailing behind, her small fists clenching the worn sleeves. I turned over and thought of the pretty gold earrings my mother was bringing me all the way from Israel. They would be heart-shaped earrings, each with a small pearl dangling from it, the kind we weren't allowed to wear. I would wear them to school, and all my friends would stare at them and touch them and be so jealous. It was a nice dream and I didn't want to leave it, so when I felt her nudging me again, my eyes stayed tightly closed. I did not open them. She would take my earrings away, my beautiful gold dangling pearl earrings, and I wouldn't let her. They were mine, and they looked so nice on my ears with my hair in a pony so everyone could see them. She was shaking me, but I ran away to Shany and Chani and Miri on the other side of the classroom to show them my new earrings. They said, Wow, you are so lucky, and we played jump rope together and I was first on line. I heard her calling my name—"Gittel, Gittel, come"—but I was jumping up and down, up and down so hard, and dashed away after Miri to catch my next turn. When I jumped up and down my earrings dangled and I could hear the pretty tinkling of the pearls. I heard her calling me, saying she didn't want to play jump rope, she wanted me to come with her. And I said, No, no, I'm first on line, and jumped and ran harder than ever. Then she walked away, and I couldn't hear her anymore, and I pushed away the jump rope but I got tangled inside. I screamed, "Devory! Devory!" and tried to pull off the long rope, but my hands moved with such painful slowness, as if they were being slowly paralyzed, and when I tried to run after Devory, still tangled, I could not see her anymore.

Then there was nothing. I sank deeply into the peaceful nothingness, where it took me down, down, down, as if I were drowning

in warm, gentle waters and did not care to breathe. I could hear the
scream from deep within the quiet, jolting through the gentle darkness like an electric current forcing me out of the silence. And next
there was the blinding sunlight through the bedroom window, and
Mrs. Goldblatt stood over me, pale, shaking, holding a piece of
white paper in her hand.

"Where is she?! Where is she? Where is Devory? Where did
she go?"

I sat up. She jammed the note into my face. I read it slowly.

"I WANT TO DIE."

I stared at her uncomprehendingly.

She spoke hysterically. "She left this note on the kitchen table.
Didn't you see her go? Didn't you hear her?"

I pulled up my blanket. "No. I didn't hear her, I was sleeping. . . ."

"She ran away. I can't understand. She ran away. . . ." And she
turned around and staggered out of the room.

Two big policemen were standing in the kitchen when I
came downstairs. Miriam was pouring coffee into foam cups, and
Mrs. Cohen, the next-door neighbor, hovered worriedly over the
sobbing Mrs. Goldblatt. Mr. Goldblatt was driving around in the car
with Mr. Cohen, searching the neighborhood.

I ran back upstairs. I was scared of the policemen. Maybe they
would think I did something and then they would take me away. I
sat on my bed and tried to say *tehillim*, which I knew by heart
from school. But then I remembered what Devory had written.
She said she wanted to die. Her words confused me. How could a
person want to die? Only Hashem could make someone die; no
one could do that on their own. And anyway, children couldn't die.
One had to be old, ill, and cranky for Hashem to finally get tired

of the complaining and make you dead. Unless you were bad. Maybe if you were bad enough Hashem made you die. In the stories, bad people always died and always after suffering so much.

Mrs. Goldblatt walked into the room right then. She sat down near me and turned my face gently until I was looking at her.

"Gittel," she said, almost in a whisper, "you must speak to me. I know Devory is unhappy, but I don't know why. Why is she acting this way? Why is she writing so many angry things? I found writings that don't make sense. She is writing strange things, so many angry things for such a small girl."

She put my hands in her own trembling ones.

"Gittel, now is not the time to keep secrets. Tell me what you know. Sometimes friends know things that mothers don't. Is there something wrong in school? What happened to her? Tell me; it's very important. Don't be scared, Gittel."

I looked at her, her dry, pale skin, her large green eyes smudged with yesterday's mascara, her snood falling back so that the short pieces of graying hair fell in every direction.

And I told her. I told her that Shmuli came into the room, how he went under her blanket in the middle of the night. I told her how Devory was so scared. I didn't say the whole thing, but most of it, though I wasn't quite sure myself what I was saying. She listened quietly while I spoke and when I finished she looked straight ahead blankly, confused. Then suddenly she jolted as if she had been electrocuted. She began shaking.

"What? What did you say? Who told this to you?"

Terrified, I was silent.

"Who told this to you? Did Devory tell this to you? Did you see it? Did you?"

And I lied. I answered, No, I did not see it. She had told it all to me.

Again Mrs. Goldblatt jolted, and then jumped up and walked quickly out of the room. I could hear the bathroom door slam. I could hear the water run. I could almost hear the terror closing in on us. She came back into the room. She grabbed my arm and held it tightly.

"Did you tell this to anyone? Does anyone know? Did you tell?"

"No," I said. "No!"

She looked at me wildly. "Devory makes up stories. You know that. She likes to make up stories. You must never tell this to anyone." And she jerked her head in the direction of the stairs, her voice rising in a half-stifled high-pitched scream. "You must not tell this to the police. Okay? This is very dangerous. Just stay in the room and don't talk to anyone. Okay? Okay? Do you understand?"

I stayed in Devory's room until eleven o'clock, when they found Devory walking on the boardwalk near the beach at the far end of Ocean Parkway, without shoes. The police brought her in, and I could hear the frenzied screaming and the neighbors' voices all talking at once. I was scared. Very scared. I began talking with Hashem because I was so afraid I did not know what else to do. I promised Hashem that I would be good. I promised Him that I would never misbehave again, never eat candies from Kathy, never watch TV when my mother didn't see, never think things I wasn't supposed to, and He would make Shmuli stop pushing Devory at night and Devory wouldn't want to die. Hashem listened to children's prayers, I knew. Our teacher told that to us many times.

The police finally left. I watched their cars from the bedroom window pulling out of the driveway and down the block. The neighbors left soon after. I could hear Devory's father reassuring them. "But really, it's all right, we just need some time alone." And the door of the house finally closed.

It was silent for a few moments, a lying kind of silence. Then her mother began to scream.

"How could you?! How could you, how could you, how could you?"

There were seconds of mad silence, and then bursts of shrieks that came closer and closer together until there was one long scream that wouldn't end, screaming with no words.

"Why, why, why, why? The *siddur*! The *siddur*! I went all over! Spent the entire day! Tired, aching body, running from store to store! For the nicest *siddur*. I went all over, yesterday! From one end of Borough Park to the other! To engrave your name in gold lettering on the prayer book! To the other end of Borough Park by foot. I wanted to give you a present, a *siddur* with your name on it! I knew you wanted it. A *siddur* like that! And this is what you do to me? How much attention? How much attention do we give you?! How could you make up such stories? What will everyone say? Do you want to kill me? Only when I die, lie dead on the floor of a heart attack, will you finally behave?! How much attention do we need to give you?! How many presents? Trips? Why, why, why?"

I could hear her father's footsteps pacing heavily downstairs, stalking up and down the dining room like a trapped animal. It stopped suddenly, and then he was in my room. He told me to pack my things and he would take me home. My mother was arriving tomorrow morning and I could sleep at home tonight. I showed him my little black suitcase, and he picked it up and told me to come after him. I followed him quickly, running down the stairs, clutching my briefcase, terrified of seeing anyone. But when I reached the bottom step, I saw Devory. She stood in the kitchen facing me, turned away from her mother, who was sitting at the table, her face in her arms like a crying child. Devory looked like my doll after my brother had smashed its head on the floor and it stared at me, its eyes blue, dark, and empty.

CHAPTER TWENTY-FIVE

2008

Miranda said it was called rape. It was called rape. I knew not to believe her. I told her that she was making a mistake because there was no such word in Yiddish and that he had only pushed her. I explained to Miranda that she didn't know what she was saying, but she just said, "Gittel, such things happen everywhere. Only in some places, they don't call it by a name. They think maybe if they don't name it, that will mean it can't happen."

I didn't like her calling it by a name like that. Hearing that word made me go crazy. I told her again that it wasn't rape, that rape was a word from the other side, and she had no business using it here. But Miranda insisted. She said, "Gittel, rape can happen anywhere, and Devory was certainly raped by her brother," and I kicked at the desk hard.

I didn't plan it. It happened so fast, the rage welling up, exploding like a volcano. I still don't understand it. I grabbed the file with my name on it. I tore it up. I ripped it fast, shredding it into little pieces before Miranda could get to me, could take it back and write things down. I screamed at her. I screamed, "I'm never talking to you again!" I kicked the desk again. "Don't tell me such things! Why are you lying—I wish I had never come here! How could you say such things! You don't even know what you're saying! You just want to say bad things about us. It's true, you do. I'm never coming back here!"

Miranda did not move from her chair. She looked at me sadly, calmly, and that made me even angrier. Words had no shame to goyim. They were said with no shred of respect for what could and could not happen.

I ran out of the room and left the police station. Because it wasn't true. Nothing like rape had happened. It was terrible what he had done, but it was something else. It had to have been.

CHAPTER TWENTY-SIX

2000

When Devory came to school the next day she sat at her desk all through recess and read. I asked her to come out and play, but she said she didn't want to and that I should leave her alone. That entire week Devory read books. I told her that if she wasn't feeling so good she should stay home, but she said that her mother wouldn't let her. She said that Devory was just making up excuses. Even our teacher noticed and came over to Devory one recess to ask her why she had stopped going out to play, but Devory just turned the page and ignored her. I sat near her during recess sometimes, but then I would get bored and run back out of the classroom.

Devory read books during class time too. She read during lunchtime. She read all the time. It was as if she wasn't there at all. Miss Goldberg at first rebuked her, but after two days of warning glances, she ignored her. Only at lunchtime would Devory get up, and, together, we would walk through the crowded hallway. One day, she told me that she was writing a book.

"Am I in it?" I asked.

"Yes," she answered thoughtfully. "You're one of the main characters."

"What is the book about?" I asked excitedly.

"It's about us two going on adventures in a faraway place to fight evil *Yiden*."

"*Yiden*?"

"Yes, but fake ones. Just dressed up like *Yiden*, and only we know they are not."

I didn't understand. "But how do we know that?"

Devory waved her hand dismissively. "I have to write the book first, and then you'll know."

When my mother heard that Devory ran away, she asked me why she had done so, and I told her I didn't know. I looked at her as she looked at me, her eyes demanding an explanation. I said, "I don't know why. She just did."

"That poor mother is going out of her mind," my mother muttered to Surela. "That girl is driving her crazy."

My mother had brought back wonderful presents when she came home from Israel. When she placed a beautiful gold necklace with a Star of David pendant around my neck, I was so excited that I quickly promised to behave myself for the rest of my life. That meant of course that I had to be like Surela for at least a month, and that was besides the promise to Hashem at Devory's house that I needed to keep and keep and keep because one could not break promises to heaven. But after an entire week of jumping out of bed on time and washing the dishes after supper, I was tired. Being good was exhausting and it drained me of all my energy. So that *Shabbos*, with great relief, I returned to my own self-reassuring heaven just for one day, to gather more strength so I could be good again on Sunday. I forgot to add hot water to the coffeepot, I fought with Sruli over chores, I broke a glass, and worst of all, I leaned against the wall and shut off the kitchen light.

My mother stared at me with that expression reserved for times she had all intentions of giving me up for adoption.

"I didn't do it on purpose!" I cried. "I'll go get Kathy."

Kathy was our *Shabbos* goy. On *Shabbos*, the day of Hashem's rest, it was forbidden to deal with electricity or do anything that resembled the daily grind of work. So anytime we forgot to turn on the air conditioner or the light, Kathy would come down to do it for us.

Kathy enjoyed coming down to help us out, but sometimes she forgot to go back up. My mother would blink nervously and snap her fingers the way she did when she was impatient, while my father listened calmly to Kathy's long speeches.

"Oh, Shimon," she began after she turned the light back on, "you wouldn't believe the miracle that Kootchie Mootchie is. He chased all the mice out of my apartment. Remember those mice I was always complainin' about? They'd run aroun' my apartment as if they owned it, and Leo got tired of puttin' those sticky traps all over. But since Kootchie Mootchie came into my life, the mice stay so far away, they forgot they were ever there at all."

She stood in front of my father and gestured animatedly. "And you know what I do to keep him fit and in shape? I got *Your Cat* magazine, and it says in there that exercise is very important for cats, or they get lazy. 'Specially if they live in the inner city. So besides taking him out ever' day for a little walk, every mornin' Kootchie Mootchie and me, we do exercises together. He's one lazy cat, and at first he would stare at me like that, and he even tried to scratch me when I pushed him off the couch, but now he just goes right along and he's really keepin' fit. It's a very important exercise. In the magazine it shows all kinds of things you could do, but I just do this."

And she began to sing and dance, her red curls bouncing, as she demonstrated the entire routine to my *shtreimel*-wearing, blushing father.

"Kootchie Mootchie, up! Kootchie Mootchie, down, now Kootch Kootch Kootch, turn around! Oh, Kootch, oh, Kootch, come on, let's go! Oh, Kootchie Mootchie, get into the flow!"

Just then the guest, my father's friend from Israel, walked into the house. My mother thanked Kathy profusely and apologized for the interruption, and I walked her back up to her apartment.

The guest was an important man. I knew that because my mother prepared the kind of dishes she made only when special guests arrived. I didn't like those fancy dishes. They were spicy and Polish-tasting, as my father proudly described it. But more than the spicy dishes, I certainly didn't like the presence of a guest because that meant I couldn't sing *zemiros* with my father. A woman's voice was forbidden in front of a stranger—it was immodest— and so whenever we had guests only my father and brothers sang. Besides being unable to sing, Surela wasn't feeling well and was in bed so I had to pitch in with two full hands, or else. I didn't do a good job, and my father tried to help. He came into the kitchen after the fish course, carrying a tall pile of dirty plates. My mother was fuming.

"What are you doing here?" she whispered angrily. "Get back to the table, sit where you belong, and don't move from there. What, are you trying to embarrass me? A man helping in the kitchen on *Shabbos*? And why aren't you singing *zemiros*? What do you think, this is a hotel?"

My father placed the pile in the sink, mumbled an apology, and did not dare move from the head of the table for the rest of the meal.

I was relieved when the meal was over and the guest, who gave a "short" Torah sermon that was longer than my teacher's and principal's combined, finally left. We then cleaned up the table and my mother gave each child a bag filled with nosh, which meant that we were to keep quiet while my parents napped for the next two hours.

I did keep quiet for the next two hours. I was waiting for Devory to arrive, but she didn't come, so I sat on the couch and read the *Bais Yaakov* Times, my favorite book series. Leiby was outside playing, Avrum and Sruli went to a neighbor's house, and my parents and Surela were sleeping, so only I was in the dining room when the doorbell rang.

I jumped off the couch. Who rang the doorbell on *Shabbos*? It was probably Sruli. He always forgot that it was forbidden to touch the doorbell on *Shabbos*. I ran to the door. There was no one there. I ran to the other door, the one rarely used at our front entrance, and angrily swung it open. And there stood . . . There stood . . . There stood . . .

A priest.

A real, live, white-collared priest.

My mouth dropped open.

"Hello," he said in a friendly voice. "I am looking for Kathy Prouks."

My mouth opened wider.

"Hi," he repeated himself loudly. "I'm Father Frank. Is Kathy Prouks in?"

I closed my mouth. "Um . . . um . . ."

He stared at me curiously.

"Um . . . um . . . one minute." And I turned around and ran—and I mean ran—upstairs to tell Kathy that there's a PRIEST STANDING AT OUR DOOR! He had come to the wrong entrance.

"Oh, good," she said, clumping down after me, breathing hard. "Kootchie Mootchie stopped breathin' last night, and I called 911 but they said they weren't coming for no cat, and I don't know when he's gonna suddenly die on me, he's old already, so I said I would call a priest to say the last rites on him. That should cover his death whenever God wills it to come."

I ran ahead of her so I could get another good look at the priest. The priest stared at me, laughed, then stuck his hand into his pants pocket and handed me a candy.

I grabbed the candy and stared at it. A candy from a priest. It could only be poison. In the stories, the evil priest always gave poison to the Jewish children who wouldn't convert. I held up the candy and peered into it suspiciously. It looked good.

"Oh, Father." Kathy smiled happily at him. "Come on upstairs, this way. This is my landlord's house."

And in complete horror I watched as the priest himself, poison candies and all, Walked. Across. Our. Dining. Room. Floor.

What would I tell my mother?

My mother would kill me. I pushed the candy into my underwear. Then I had an idea. I ran upstairs to the third floor and into the living room, where Kootchie Mootchie was relaxing while the priest talked to Kathy in the kitchen. I scanned the area. All was clear. I hurriedly removed the candy's wrapping and placed it on the couch in front of Kootchie Mootchie. With one swift flick of his pink tongue the poison candy was gone. I then sat on the couch across from him, folded my legs, and stared at the cat—waiting for him to die.

Forever passed. At least nine minutes. I simply could not believe it. The cat was as alive as ever, staring at me with the same bored expression, twitching his whiskers as if asking for another one. The candy was not poison, and now I wanted it back! I folded my arms across my chest angrily. But the candy, I knew, was long gone, deep inside the soft, overfed Kootchie Mootchie's stomach.

Life just wasn't fair. I thought of pushing the cat off the couch and out the window, but I was afraid he would scratch me. So I stuck out my tongue at him and stomped back downstairs, leaving him to the priest and his evil last rites, without saying good-bye.

CHAPTER TWENTY-SEVEN

2000

That night, after *Shabbos* was over, my father, wearing his black *Shabbos* coat and tall *shtreimel*, made *Havdalah* over a flame and a cup of wine. *Havdalah* is the prayer that separates the holy from the mundane, the *Shabbos* from the workweek. My father, his eyes closed, his strong voice pronouncing every word, swayed slowly to the rhythm.

"*Oomayn!*" we all answered when he finished.

Nearly every week, after *Havdalah*, my parents and Surela would sit on the couch discussing all sorts of interesting things, such as how Mrs. Yuskavitch could afford to buy a new house, what the *Yushive Rebbe* told my third cousin three weeks ago when he went in for a blessing, and *shidduchim*.

Shidduchim was an important subject. In fact, it was the single most important subject in the community and was a traditional and passionate part of our weekly family conference.

"You wouldn't believe what Chavie Goldberg told me before

Shabbos," my mother said as she settled down on the couch. "I'm telling you, you have no idea how angry she is with Mrs. Cohen. She told me that that lady thinks just because she is a *shadchanta* for thirty years, she could offer her the most ridiculous *shidduchim*."

Surela leaned closer to my mother. "Who did she suggest this time?"

My mother shook her head indignantly. "You know the Mandl-baums from Fifty-seventh Street—her sister *davens* in the Fifty-sixth Street *shul*? So Mrs. Cohen thinks that Mrs. Mandlbaum's daughter would be perfect for Chavie Goldberg's son! Could you imagine? Chavie was fuming and, boy, did she give it to her. She told me that she told her, 'Would you take a girl whose grand-mother was divorced? I don't care what kind of girl this is! You have no right to suggest my son for a girl whose grandmother was once divorced!'"

My mother pressed the button that released the leg rest and leaned back.

"And she is absolutely right. I mean, if there had been a problem in the family, then I'd understand. Mrs. Teitlebaum made a *shidduch* with—what's his name, *nebech*, that poor boy who doesn't have a father—oh, yes, Bloom, because her daughter stuttered. So she figured, the boy is a top one, he's smart, he's a top learner, so fine. She didn't have a choice and she took an orphan. But a presti-gious family like the Goldbergs with money and good background *yichus*—good family—why would they ever take a family like that, whose grandmother was once divorced? I just don't understand that *shadchanta*."

"Wasn't Mrs. Cohen the one who suggested that adopted boy to my sister?" my father asked.

"Yes!" my mother exclaimed. "That was her! Only she could go and think that any family would take an adopted boy for a son-in-law!"

"She doesn't talk with Mrs. Cohen to this day," my father mused. "And they used to be good friends."

"Well," said my mother. "If someone would offer you someone who's adopted, Hashem forbid, you wouldn't talk with them either."

"Hey, Surela," my father said with a teasing grin. "So are you all ready to get married?"

"Totty!" Surela turned red. "I'm only seventeen."

"And three-quarters," my mother retorted. She then laughed. "But all right. We'll leave you alone until you graduate."

"Don't worry," my father said, ruffling Surie's hair. "We'll find you the best catch in all of Borough Park, with the best *yichus*, and a little money won't hurt either. . . ."

"But I have to finish seminary even if I'm married." Surela giggled nervously. "Or I won't be able to get a teaching job."

"What about the rest of your class? What are they all doing?" asked my mother.

"Well, everyone's going to *Bais Yaakov* Teacher's Training Seminary. Some half day, some whole day." She chuckled. "I mean, if a girl wants a good *shidduch* she better go."

My father turned serious. "I heard that Toby Fried, that curly-haired girl in your class, is not going to seminary. She wants to go to Touro College. Is it true?"

"Touro College!" My mother stared at him, horrified. "I don't believe it! Her parents let her?"

"I don't know," Surela said. "You know how she is. She was

always a little weird, always asking all those questions and reading those weird books. The principal must have spoken with her ten times this year. If she weren't related to the *Yushive Rebbe*'s cousin's assistant they would have kicked her out long ago."

"*Nebech*," my mother sympathized. "Her poor parents."

"Yes," my sister agreed. "She just does what she likes. Her parents don't have a choice about it."

"College is a dangerous place," said my father. "They teach you all sorts of things that are against the Torah. Once you start opening a boy or girl's mind like that, forget it. *Nebech*, how will they ever marry her off? Her brother also made problems. At age eighteen, when he wasn't even engaged yet, he left *yeshiva* and went to work."

"That's horrible," my mother said. "Just terrible."

"So what kind of boy do you want?" my father asked Surela, his eyes filled with love.

"I want a boy who will learn Torah his entire life," Surela said seriously. "Whatever happens, my husband will never work! I'll teach and we'll make do with what there is."

"Well"—my mother cocked her head proudly—"with a girl like you we should have no problem finding that."

"Last week, Rabbi Steinman came to speak at school." Surela smiled. "He's one of the best speakers I ever heard. And you know what he said? He told us that for every minute the husband learns, his wife gets a share in *Gan Eden*. He said that only when one feels the taste of *Gan Eden* does one suddenly realize that every moment of hardship and sacrifice for Torah learning was a luxury, not a burden. And then he picked up his hands like this, and cried, 'Oh, how lucky we Jews are that we have the holy and great

Torah. Oh, how lucky the woman is whose husband's soul is filled with only Torah. And oh, how we must thank Hashem for every opportunity, for every millisecond that we have a chance to keep Torah alive for our people.'"

She sighed happily. My mother dabbed her eyes.

"Oh," she said, sniffing. "That was so beautiful. I wish my father were alive to hear his own granddaughter speaking like that."

"Yes, that was very inspiring," agreed my father. "I can't believe my own daughter is already of marriageable age. You were just this little tot waddling around the dining room."

My parents and Surela talked on and on, but Sruli and I weren't listening. We were discussing our life goals.

My dream was to be a garbage collector. I would ride in those wonderfully huge white trucks all night long and never sleep again. My brother grunted disdainfully at that idea and said he would be a skyscraper-window cleaner. It was much more fun. We would have gone on arguing, but my mother had somehow heard us, and as she rose from the couch she laughed and said, "Enough of that nonsense. You, Gittel, will be a teacher, and you, young man, will be a Torah scholar, and it is so late, I can't believe you kids are still up."

And that's when Devory walked in. It was pouring outside, and she was soaking wet, but she strolled into the dining room without a coat or hat, as if she had never noticed the rain.

My mother stared at her, shocked.

"What are you doing here at ten thirty p.m.?"

Devory glanced at her and said calmly, "There's no room in my house."

My mother folded her arms across her chest. "Does your mother know that you are here?"

Devory didn't answer. My mother strode straight to the phone and dialed.

I heard my father muttering to himself, "That girl is becoming more unpredictable by the day."

I walked over to Devory. "Why didn't you take a coat?" I asked.

Devory looked down at herself. "I'm wet," she said, surprised.

My mother hung up the phone abruptly. "Shimon," she said to my father, "please take Devory home now. Her mother is furious."

Devory looked blankly at my mother, turned around, and walked back out of the house.

My father ran after her with my raincoat, and my mother shook her head again and again.

"I don't know what to say anymore," she said. "Is that child normal?" She turned to Surela. "You know what my father always used to say. Don't ask for a child that's too pretty, too talented, or too smart. You don't want a genius for a child; you want a well-adjusted child. Too much is no good. It can only bring trouble."

I ran upstairs to my room and looked out the window. I saw my father's car drive off with Devory sitting near the window of the backseat. The house was quiet. I was scared. I knew Devory still wanted to die. Maybe it was because of the priest. Maybe it was because I had promised Hashem never to eat a *goyishe* candy again, but I had taken one on the holiest day of the week, *Shabbos*, from a priest. A priest who had walked across our dining room floor. And my mother didn't even know. I repented that night before I got into bed. I spoke to Hashem for a long time, convincing Him that I was

for real this time. I would never do anything wrong again. I would
be good forever and he would take away Shmuli forever. I looked
outside the window at the dark, quiet sky. Hashem was somewhere
in there, I knew, but I could only see the stars silently blinking down
at me. I was still scared.

CHAPTER TWENTY-EIGHT

2008

Avrum, my eighteen-year-old brother, was officially engaged.

I could hear the happy shouts from downstairs, my father's booming, *"Mazel tov, mazel tov!"* blending in with other new voices of the in-laws, relatives, and neighbors. I had not heard my name for a while, my mother being too busy with the new family and Surie probably clenching her teeth, preparing a long speech for me for when I returned while she hosted the guests. I did not care. I was still up on the third floor, crying. I could not stop trembling.

"So why did you go?" Kathy asked, holding me in her arms. "Why did you go to them? What'd you think she would tell you?"

"I don't know."

"You knew. It just hurts so bad to hear the truth out loud."

"But you never said that word when I told you."

"No, I didn't."

"Why didn't you use that word?"

"Because the fear you got in your eyes. I was afraid to touch it."

"So why did you tell me to go?"

"You had to believe her. The police ain't weird, like me. I thought you'd believe them."

"I did."

"That's why you got so mad."

"I screamed at her. I made a *Chillul Hashem*. Why did I scream at her like that?"

"Because you can't scream at Shmuli. Because you can't scream at your parents."

I breathed heavily. I could not cry anymore.

"It was was my fault," I told Kathy.

"It ain't your fault," she said.

"Don't say that. It was my fault. When she came to my window that night for real. She knocked on it in the middle of the night, and I opened it and she came into my bed and she held my hand so hard, I almost cried. She didn't want to go."

The tears came.

"I made her go back home. I was scared. I told her to go back home or my parents would see her there and know what had happened and that we had done such a terrible thing. . . . She went back out the window. It was cold outside. She ran back home in the cold. I watched her. I didn't"—I choked on my breath—"let her stay."

"Oh, Gittel," Kathy said, engulfing me in her arms. "You poor girl. You poor, poor girl." She rocked me slowly to and fro. "Talk with God," Kathy murmured. "Talk with God. People don't die, they only become part of God. When you talk with God you can talk with them too."

CHAPTER TWENTY-NINE

2000

It was Purim, three weeks after my week at Devory's house, and I was dressing up like a *shnorrer*. My mother had insisted I be Queen Esther but I said no way after I found out that Miriam, Esty, Chani, and Yehudis were all also going to dress up like Queen Esther. I changed my mind the day before Purim, and my mother said that it was too late; I had to be Queen Esther. I cried and said that every single year, since I couldn't even remember when, I had been Queen Esther and it was *boring*.

I had decided to dress up like a *shnorrer* after I had seen Crazy Head Yankel marching down Eighteenth Avenue banging his *tzeddakah* box, screaming "*Tzeddakah* for the poor! *Tzeddakah* for the poor!" and my mother, with a small pitying smile, dropped a quarter into his box. I saw lots of people giving Crazy Head Yankel money, and I concluded it was a worthy investment. I was going to be a *shnorrer* and get rich.

My mother said no way. Purim was a time for giving, not taking.

But I stomped my foot and said that I was gonna stay in my room a whole Purim if I had to dress up like Queen Esther. She sighed and frowned and said okay, but I had to give the money to *tzeddakah*, and who would I give it to?

I said nobody. The money was mine. Why would I give it away? My mother looked annoyed and reminded me that Jews gave *tzeddakah* to other Jews and didn't keep the money to themselves and I couldn't be a *shnorrer* unless I promised to give the money I got to charity.

I said, fine, okay, okay, I would give a little bit to Sarah Leah in my class. Sarah Leah was so poor she barely had a sticker in her sticker collection. In fact, she was so poor, she didn't have a sticker collection at all. She always looked at my stickers, especially the shiny Hello Kitty ones in the front page, and stroked them softly, and said that she wished she also had a collection like mine. It was a tragic thing not to have a sticker collection, and I promised my mother that I would give Sarah Leah some of my Purim money so she could buy stickers too.

My mother frowned, then smiled a little and said that it wasn't quite what she meant. Then she sighed again and left the room, and I wondered why it was that adults so often didn't quite know what they meant.

Devory dressed up like Haman on Purim with a pointy black hat, a long curly mustache, and pointy shoes. Her mother had also wanted her to dress up in the Queen Esther costume that her two older sisters and three cousins had worn, but Devory said it was Haman or Osama Bin Ladin and she tore up the Queen Esther costume when her mother wasn't looking.

Purim night we went to *shul* to hear the *megillah*—the scroll with the retelling of the Purim story. The *Yushive shul* was located in a long, narrow room on the first floor of a small brick house right near our school. It was a simple, clean space with white walls, plastic chairs, some benches, and shelves and shelves of holy books. In the middle of the *shul*, there was a *mechitzah*—three wooden partitions on wheels that could be moved to make the space needed for the men's side on *Shabbos* when few women arrived to pray. There were small slats on the top part of the *mechitzah* so that the women could see through to the men's side.

We sat on a bench near the wall together with the Goldblatt family and looked at everyone's costumes. There were babies dressed up like Queen Esther and Mordechai, runny-nosed toddlers dressed up like Queen Esther and Mordechai, and teenagers dressed up like Queen Esther and Mordechai. There were also some clowns and lions and a King Achashvairosh. Everyone was holding noisemakers called *graggers*, a *megillah*, and a baby. My mother was talking with Old Mrs. Goldman about her husband, who had Alzheimer's, when Miriam Goldblatt and two of her friends entered the *shul*. Everyone turned to stare at them. Mrs. Richter muttered something under her breath. Surela looked horrified. Mrs. Bloom nudged her daughter-in-law in front of me.

Miriam and her friends were wearing terribly nonmodest costumes: long orange wigs that reached their waists, thick dark blue eye shadow, fake eyelashes, and bright red lipstick. They wore long earrings that shook with every move, short leather skirts that covered their knees by no more than an inch, and bright pink fitted shirts. They even wore high heels and glittering jangling bracelets.

Devory's mother looked straight ahead, her eyes tense with anger and embarrassment. Miriam and her friends stood in the corner of the *shul* near the door giggling nervously and whispering to one another.

"At least they should wear masks so nobody should see who they are," I heard Mrs. Lefkowitz whisper to my mother. My mother nodded sympathetically and raised her eyes to heaven in a "what-can-one-do?" expression that quickly turned into "what-the-heck-is-going-on-here?" when Shloimela, the son of Mrs. Miller, threw his Mordechai-the-*tzaddik* hat on her while fighting with Duvidel the Lion over who was the strongest.

Mordechai hit the lion and Duvidel opened his small mouth in an angry roar, just as an impatient Mr. Lefkowitz stood on a chair on the men's side of the *mechitzah* so that the top of his face could be seen and, throwing up his hand, gestured angrily to the back of the room.

"*Nu, shoin,* what's going on here! You want to hear the *megillah* or *nisht? Zah shtill! Zah shoin shtill!*"

The *chazan*—the cantor—ignored it all and began reading the *megillah*. His powerful voice cut through the noise and Old Mrs. Goldman stopped right in the middle of a long speech about this most disrespectful generation unlike the one before the Holocaust when even babies dared not cry in *shul*, to listen to the singsong chant of the *chazan* telling the story of the evil Haman.

Reading the *megillah* was a difficult task. A man had to practice long and hard to be able to read the Purim story with the correct rhythm and beat. I loved hearing of the terrible Haman, who tried to exterminate the Jews, and of his complete defeat at the hand of simple, long-bearded Mordechai. I loved hearing of the mean queen Vashti, and the tail that sprouted right from her tush, and how they chopped her head right off her neck after she refused to come to drunken Achashvairosh's party with nothing on. And of course there was Queen Esther, who, though her mask was dreadfully boring, saved the Jewish people with her prayers and bravery. But the best part of the *megillah* reading was Haman. With each "Haman!" announced by the *chazan* the *shul* went wild, stamping their feet, whirling the *graggers*, and I, rattling my *tzeddakah* box as hard as I could.

By the time the *megillah* was over, the men began to dance. They sang *La'Yehudim*, an old Purim song, and, linking hands, kicked their feet in the air, dancing around and around as the old men thumped their fists on the tables and the boys jumped wildly up and down in the middle, their *payos* flying in every direction. The women swarmed to the *mechitzah*, peering through the slats in the partition. I stood under the slats, jumping frantically up and down, trying to see my father through the hole. I tried a lower slot, but Mrs. Lefkowitz blocked my way, her armpits directly over my nose. I squirmed out, dragged a chair through the crowd, and pushed it against the partition, but every slot was taken. I did find a small crack between the slats, though, and when I squashed my face between Mrs. Richter and Mrs. Broida and their screaming babies, I could see the top of the *shtreimels* bobbing up and down. I found another, larger crack to my left side and if I looked at the right angle I could see the side of some beards.

Then I lost my balance and fell onto the floor. I crawled out from under the crush of high heels and saw Devory climbing on top of some chairs near the wall, dangling casually over the *mechitzah*, perched on top of the thin wall happily shaking her *gragger* to the beat. I climbed after her, but Mrs. Goldblatt saw us and strode over quickly.

"Devory, get down now!" she called worriedly. "What are you doing? It's not modest and it's dangerous. Get down here now!"

Devory didn't hear and I pretended not to. Mrs. Goldblatt pushed into the crowd, trying to reach her. Then someone pushed someone else, who leaned against the *mechitzah*, which began tipping over. Devory screamed, and her mother reached up to grab her, pushing against the partition even more. A *shtreimel* flew through the air, someone's *gragger* whirled loudly, and the whole thing fell to the floor with a crash—with Devory spread out on top of it.

The dancing stopped. *Shtreimels* froze mid-dance, men on one side, women on the other, and everyone stared at the fallen *mechitzah*.

Devory giggled. She tossed the pointy hat on the floor, jumped up, and began dancing a jig, first right, then left, then all around.

Mrs. Bloom gasped. Mrs. Lefkowitz of the smelly armpits shook her finger. Old Mrs. Goldman glared. And Mrs. Goldblatt grabbed Devory's arm, pushed her through the angry crowd and into a corner where she yelled and screamed, then grabbed her coat and marched her right out the door.

The men quickly picked up the *mechitzah*, and my mother, trying to hide a smile, said it was high time we left. So out we went into the crisp cold night and crowded into the car for a ride home, where my mother, sitting in the front seat near my father, turned on Purim music.

"Did you see what Miriam was wearing!" she yelled at my father over the music. "You should've seen her and her friends, *oy vey*! Let me tell you, you can really tell a person from the way he dresses when the rules don't apply."

"*Nu*, Mommy," I said. "But it's Purim. It's just a costume."

"There's no such thing as just a costume," my mother admonished loudly. "The kind of mask you choose reflects your inner being! Purim is not an excuse to look like a goy. And those who dress up like modern Jews, well, it shows." And then the van came to a screeching halt.

A small truck lined with streamers and balloons swerved around our van, jolting to a stop. A group of *yeshiva* boys dressed like delivery boys and holding a booming stereo jumped out of the back, ran up the steps laughing loudly, and disappeared into a house.

My father fumed. He poked his head out the window and shouted, "*Meshugunah!* Are you trying to get someone killed?" But they were already gone, they hadn't even turned off their headlights, and my father moved angrily around the truck and drove on furiously muttering Yiddish expressions we weren't supposed to hear.

"You see," he said, looking into the rearview mirror. "On Purim it's a *mitzvah*, Hashem's commandment, to dress up and be happy, but you can tell what kind of person you are by how you honor the *mitzvah*." He pointed his thumb back at the receding truck. "Those boys chose to get drunk and act like hooligans. Then there are boys like Devory's brother and yours, Shmuli and Yossi. What are they doing now? They are sitting in *yeshiva* and learning an extra *blatt* of *Talmud* in honor of Purim. They are treating Purim like a *mitzvah*, not like Halloween! And what do you think they are dressing up like? Delivery boys? No! They are dressing up like *Chassidish Rebbes* and tomorrow they are going to collect money for *tzeddakah*. Now that's the kind of mask every Yid wants to see on his child."

Purim morning I got rich. After hearing the *megillah*, I helped my mother prepare *mishloach manos* and packed them into the

back of the car, where I sat with two *mishloach manos* on my lap,
three at my sides, four under my feet, and off we went from address
to address. I ran out of the car delivering the packages, rattling my
tzeddakah box hard, and received one dollar from Mrs. Lieberman,
five dollars from Mrs. Bloom, fifty cents from the Kriegers, and a
twenty from Mrs. Cohen—the mother of a wealthy family who
had a large front lawn *and* a backyard.

I danced into my house after the first delivery shift as rich as Job
before Hashem selfishly took everything back. I told Surela that I
would save my piles of money for my wedding, but she said the
money would be rotten by then and that I should give it to her. I
stuck out my tongue and ran to show my mother the riches,
when she handed me an apple strudel and asked me to give it to
Mrs. Yutzplats, the old witch at the end of the block. I stared at her
in horror. She lived in that old, pointy, corner brown house across
from Tovah, and I wasn't going anywhere near her. When I told this
to my mother, she laughed and said, "Go!" I dropped the strudel
on the table and patiently explained to her that I could not go.
Mrs. Yutzplats would turn me into a frog and I would never be able
to get married. My mother said it was high time I stopped believing
such fairy tales and that Mrs. Yutzplats was nothing but an old,
lonely woman and it was a big *mitzvah* to give her *mishloach manos*.
I told my mother that all witches were lonely and old. There was no
such thing as a young and friendly witch, but she wasn't interested.
She told me that if I didn't go give her the *mishloach manos* I could
not go to the Gottliebs, who always gave twenty-dollar bills. I
thought about that some and decided that if I wouldn't go, then
Surela would get the twenty-dollar bill and that was far worse than
turning into a frog.

I walked slowly down the block, knocked carefully on the door, and was about to drop the strudel on the steps and run for my life, when the witch appeared at the threshold. I stared at her, my mouth open in fear. Mrs. Yutzplats was old, short, and wrinkly. She wore an ugly wig like my grandmother's, a green sweater like Devory's grandmother's, and old ugly shoes like, well, all grandmothers'. She did not have a long tail; she did not have pointy shoes; she did not even wear a pointy hat. Mrs. Yutzplats smiled widely and said that she was so happy to see me. "May your mother be blessed forever for remembering an old lady who lives down the block—thank you so much, thank you so much. You are a good *maidel*," and she handed me a small chocolate wafer and a one-hundred-dollar bill!

When I showed my mother the one hundred dollars she opened her eyes so wide I was scared they would fall out. She nodded, shook her head, opened her mouth, and then closed it. Finally she said, "Wow, not bad for a witch."

I also brought *mishloach manos* to the Goldblatt family. Their house was filled with *Yushive* boys singing in the dining room, high school students laughing in the kitchen, neighbors and relatives walking in and out bringing their packages, tasting a slice of Purim cake, and wishing one another a happy Purim. Miriam was nowhere to be seen, but the twins were jumping on the table with their clown costumes, Leah'la was organizing *mishloach manos*, and Shmuli, back from collecting money for the *Yushive Yeshiva*, was dressed up like a *Chassidish Rebbe* with a short, fur *shtreimel*, a long white beard, and the mask of an old saintly man.

Mrs. Goldblatt, wearing a curly, gray wig with a funny hat on top, pushed a quarter into my hand and said I could take whatever nosh I wanted from whatever mess I found it in and that I should go upstairs. Devory was there.

Devory was sulking in her room. She had been sent upstairs when her mother punished her after she refused to take off a rope she had put around her neck so she could be like Haman hanging from a tree. She had also tried pulling the tree out of the backyard, and her mother had said it was off with that dangerous rope or her room for the rest of the morning.

I gave Devory the small *mishloach manos* I'd prepared for her, and she gave me a new pack of stickers and gum. She had a fifty-dollar bill on the table, and I asked, "Who gave *that* to you?" She shrugged her shoulders and said Shmuli did, then stuffed the bill inside her drawer. I told Devory she could come to my house for the rest of Purim—we were having a big party soon with my aunt Rivky from Lakewood and cranky grandmother. But Devory said her mother wouldn't let her. I went downstairs and told Mrs. Goldblatt that I forgot Devory's *mishloach manos* at home, then asked if she could come to my house now. Mrs. Goldblatt, stuffing one basket with cookies, another with nosh, and talking with a student, hastily looked down and said, "Okay, okay, just go, that girl is making me *meshugah*—crazy." I told Devory that she could come to my house, and, giggling, we ran all the way home. We played with my cousins, ate two whole bars of chocolate under the dining room table, and received ten dollars each from Savtah.

CHAPTER THIRTY

2008

My mother was furious with me again. I had gone and bought makeup on my own, without her permission.

"Two hours ago you graduated from high school!" she shouted angrily. "And already you're doing things as if I'm no longer your mother!"

We had graduated from high school that morning. It was one week after our last day of school—two days after Avrum had gotten engaged—and I had lied to my mother about Kathy. I told her that I had fallen asleep on the bus on the way back from shopping and had woken up at the end of the line.

"For two hours you sleep on a bus and miss your own brother's *L'chaim!*"

She was angry enough about that. I had missed a chance to be seen. I had missed the chance to be shown off just when it was most important for me. How did I ever expect to get engaged, she demanded, if I didn't show up like a normal person? If I trudge around, pouting all day, barely a smile—and now the makeup. "What is wrong with you?"

The graduation had been a long and boring ceremony. My classmates and I had sat in the front of the school auditorium, our mothers and sisters in back, holding balloons, flowers, and beaming smiles. We had listened to many speeches. The principal spoke, the teachers spoke, and *Rebbitzen* Ehrlich spoke, at which point I fell asleep on Hindy's shoulder, who shrugged me awake when I began to snore.

I told Hindy that I don't snore. She whispered, "You sure do." Chani, sitting to my right, nodded her head. I stared sleepily ahead. I do not snore. *Rebbitzen* Ehrlich was still speaking. I heard her vaguely, spouting things about modesty and motherhood and something or other. I fell asleep on Hindy again. I jumped when they called our names. The audience applauded as one by one we marched up the steps to the stage and received our diplomas.

My mother took pictures of me with Hindy in front of the stage after the graduation. She also snapped pictures of me with Sarah Leah, Ruchy, Esty, and Malky, who was two grades younger but she didn't care. And did I know that before I turned around I would be at my own daughter's graduation? And did I realize how fast life passed? Sarah Leah's and Hindy's mothers had been her classmates just twenty-five years before and here they stood, snapping pictures. How unbelievable. It was truly incredible. "I know," I said tiredly. It was fascinating.

As the chattering clusters of mothers and daughters dispersed, I told my mother I was going shopping with Hindy. She, Sarah Leah, Chani, and I were having a sleepover that night at Hindy's house to celebrate our graduation. Soon we would all be married and could never have this kind of fun again.

"Yes, it's a tradition," Hindy's mother piped up from behind my mother. "My oldest started it, and since then every one of them and their friends invade my basement on graduation night and have the time of their lives." She chuckled. "Let them take advantage while they can."

My mother laughed. She remembered her own graduation night, how they had done the same thing, and as the two chatted and giggled over the long-gone days, Hindy and I left the building. We walked to Thirteenth Avenue, a few blocks down.

"I can't believe I will never wear this skirt again," Hindy murmured. We stared down at our dark, pleated uniform skirts.

"I know," I said. "It's so weird—that's it—it's over."

Hindy gave a sudden leap into the air. "It's over!"

She ran down the block. I chased after her.

"Are you crazy?" I said, panting.

"Yes," Hindy said, imitating my principal's voice. "How are you ever going to get married if you behave this way?"

We burst out laughing. Hindy pulled a fifty-dollar bill out of her pocket.

"Guess where we're going," she said, leading me into the Rite Aid Pharmacy at the corner of Thirteenth.

"To buy congratulations cards for ourselves?"

Hindy pursed her lips importantly. "That too, that too." She then turned to me and with a curtsy and a flourish, whispered, "I'm buying makeup!"

"Makeup?"

"All my seven sisters started wearing makeup only after they were engaged," Hindy announced. "But being the spoiled youngest brat that my mother announced me to be, she agreed, after a temper tantrum or two, that I could start now."

Hindy strode down the makeup aisle, stopping by the Revlon section. "The best stuff," she said, pointing dramatically.

So we bought makeup. Not too much, not too loud, not too glittery. Or flashy, or heavy, or creamy. We bought only the natural colors: a tube of pink lipstick, mascara, and light brown eye shadow. Hindy grabbed lip gloss and an eyeliner too.

"Your mother's gonna flip," I said, pointing to the liner. We had just finished learning about makeup and its pitfalls. In the Torah it speaks of the Jewish women of the second temple who wore blue eye shadow and heavy makup and because of their immodesty brought down the Jewish nation. Eyeliner emphasized the eye, and for a girl right out of high school, it was certainly off the list.

Hindy shrugged. "I'll put it on at my sister's house."

All right, so Hindy had always been a bit of a troublemaker. More stylishly dressed, more self-absorbed, more—how does one put it—*vildeh*, wild. But me? What had happened to me?

My mother fumed when I returned home with the makeup. She held up the lipstick in her hand, dangling the Rite Aid shopping bag in front of me like a dead rat.

"What do you mean you just go and buy makeup without my permission? You think you're seventeen and you can do what you want? Are you crazy? Now's the time to be careful for *shidduchim*. Your first day out of school, and you're putting on mascara already!"

I grabbed the bag out of her hand.

"What are you talking about?" I screamed. "Ruchy and Chani and almost every girl in my class wear some makeup! Yes, I saw with my own eyes, Ruchy with mascara—yes, mascara—at her second cousin's wedding."

My mother snatched the eye shadow out from the bag. She glared at it. "Eye shadow! Eye shadow! Who wears eye shadow at your age? Didn't they teach you something in school? Who are you trying to attract? What kind of attention? Even if I do let you wear makeup, you ask first. And certainly not eye shadow! Wait till your father sees this!"

"It's natural eye shadow!" I held up the cosmetic close to her face. "See, it says light brown. It's not blue! You wear light brown eye shadow—then why can't I? Anyway, it's only for *Shabbos*. I wasn't planning to wear it every day!"

My mother pointed a warning finger at me. "Watch the way you talk to me! How dare you speak with such *chutzpa*? What happened to you, talking to your own mother like some goy off the street."

I stomped away from my mother. I ran upstairs and slammed the door of my room. I stared glumly at the makeup. I couldn't wait to be married. Then she couldn't tell me what to do. Only my husband could, and what would I do if he didn't like mascara? I tore open the package. I was putting on the mascara, and now.

I read the instructions. I looked closely in the mirror. I held the brush horizontally over my eyelashes and softly pressed against it. I pushed it up gently. My eyelashes looked nothing like the ones in the picture. I tried to smooth it, but it only smeared until it looked like ink had spilled on my face. I looked terrible. I ran to the bathroom. I scrubbed my eyes, rubbing them with water and soap. This was Satan's work, I knew, and it was all my mother's fault.

I heard my father's footsteps on the stairs. I ran to my room and locked the door. My father knocked.

"Leave me alone," I said loudly.

"Gittel, Mommy is really upset," he said through the door. "She doesn't mind the makeup so much; she was just upset that you did not ask permission. She said that you could wear a little blush and maybe some lipstick. When you are engaged, you would put on mascara and all the *shtism*—junk. I know you're mad, but you know this thing. What were you thinking?"

I said, "Okay, whatever, I'm sorry. Just leave me alone."

I packed a nightgown and clothes for the sleepover. Hindy had asked me to come before dark. She needed help dragging down the mattresses and putting on the linen. I had planned to leave later, but I decided to go right then. It was really early, barely evening yet, but I was nervous that my mother would call Ruchy's or Chani's mother to ask about the makeup business. Ruchy's and Chani's mothers certainly did not allow their daughters to wear any cosmetics. They had put it on just once, for fun.

But I didn't care. I wanted to wear makeup, mascara too. I hid the thin black tube in the back of my bookshelf. I placed it carefully between the book of Genesis and the book of Prophets, the ones I used to study for school. She would never look there.

CHAPTER THIRTY-ONE

2000

On a fine Sunday afternoon two weeks after Purim, Devory and I went to Tovah's house to play, and she let us watch a video of *Cinderella*. We were mesmerized. The last time I had watched an animated video was in the doctor's office. But then my mother had asked the nurse to shut it off because they started kissing in one scene, and she said that it would put *garbage* in my head. Now Devory and I did not budge from our positions on the floor in front of the VCR for two full hours until the screen started blinking crazily, which Tovah said meant it was the end and we could get off her floor. We weren't supposed to be in Tovah's house anyway; we were only to play with her outside in the yard, but we didn't care. Cinderella was singing with the mice, and soon she would turn into a princess, and that was a whole lot more interesting then anything else. But it was late when we finished. We were supposed to have been home twenty minutes ago, and now I would have to lie to my mother.

"Okay." I drilled Devory as we walked back down the block. "We were playing with Tovah at the end of the block and forgot the time because we were looking at the bird that fell out of the tree."

But suddenly something struck me and I spoke without thinking.

"I don't want to be a Yid any longer."

Devory stared at me in terror. "What?"

"I don't want to be a Yid any longer."

Devory stopped in her tracks and stared at me in total horror. Then her expression changed. She became doubtful, pondering. She looked furtively around.

"I don't either," she said. "Let's be goyim."

"Yes," I repeated. "Let's be. Then nobody could hate us just because we are *Yiden*."

"Yeah," Devory agreed as we strode confidently toward home. "And we're gonna be the nice goyim. We'll never be mean or horrible to anyone, especially not *Yiden*."

"And then," I said excitedly, "we could wear pants and watch TV like everyone else!"

"And we'll never let anyone say bad stuff about Jews," Devory added triumphantly. And that's when I told Devory my deepest and darkest secret that I had never told anyone, not even her.

"Sometimes," I said very quietly, "I make believe that I am really adopted and *goyishe*, and one day, soon, my *goyishe* family— who live near the beach in Australia—will come take me back."

We climbed over the gate to my house and sat behind a bush in the garden.

"My *goyishe* parents will have nice long hair and a cute little puppy, and I'll wear jeans and socks with little knitted flowers on them, and it will be so much fun."

But by the time we stood at the steps leading up to the front door, I had fully repented. Realizing the infinite gravity of my sin I swore to Devory that it was just a joke, and we fervently and solemnly promised to do *teshuvah* to repent—and ask Hashem for forgiveness the very next morning.

"Ich," I said, laughing as I pushed open the door. "Who would ever want to be a goy?"

"Yeah," Devory said. "Puppies are dirty."

My mother never noticed that we were gone. She was busy cleaning her bedroom closet for Pesach.

It was four weeks until Pesach and my mother was beginning to panic. Pesach, or as Kathy called it, Passover, was the most exciting holiday in the year. It was hard work for mothers though. What happened was that some three or four thousand years ago the Jews had been slaves in Egypt for some four hundred years. Then this big *tzaddik* and the first leader of the Jewish people called Moishe Rabbenu—or Moses, as Kathy says—rescued the *Yiden* out from Egypt after Hashem punished the evil Pharaoh and his people with the ten plagues. But Pharaoh was so traumatized from the plagues, he kicked the *Yiden* out of Egypt so fast they didn't have time to bake their bread. So out they went carrying flat dough that baked in the sun into something called matzos.

To remember that whole long story, which really included a lot more details, the *Yiden* celebrate Pesach every year by eating matzos for seven days and cleaning out the house of all *chametz*. *Chametz* means any food with leavened flour in it. The entire house must be cleaned. Devory's mother would start cleaning the house on

Chanukah. No one dared go upstairs with food, and by Purim, the rooms were sterile. My mother had a cleaning lady once a week, so she reserved her hysterics for the week after Purim. That's when she and Surela set up an airtight schedule of exactly what would be cleaned on each day so that a week before Pesach everything would be done.

That Sunday, as I trotted in after my secret *Cinderella* viewing, my mother had begun cleaning and was already talking Pesach jargon. I was *not* to go downstairs with food, I was *not* to dare go into her room with a drink, and I was *not* to go into the study at all.

Devory and I held hands and ran to my room, where we played until dark, then my father took her home.

Spring had finally come and we played dangerous games in our backyard every afternoon after school. Devory said it was healthy to do so; it would make us stronger and braver. She took my purple jump rope, climbed up on the garage, and tied it to the thick branch of the cherry tree. She then held on to the jump rope, ran across the sloping roof, and pushed herself off the garage. I screamed at her that she was breaking my favorite jump rope and I would never be her friend again, but she just laughed and swung wildly. Angrily, I climbed up after her, and she jumped nimbly onto the roof, turned the glittering rope in her hand, and said, "See, it didn't even break."

We also played "Kill the Dragons," then "Kill the Lions," then "Kill the Bad People." By the end of the week we had killed so many of everything, I told Devory Hashem would never let us into heaven. Not that I minded staying on Earth forever, considering the unpredictability of the people of paradise. Devory said it was all fake killing, so it didn't matter. But then she wanted to play jump off the roof, for real. She stood on the garage roof, her short blond hair flying in the wind, her arms stretched out, her eyes closed, and said that she would jump off the roof. I told her that she would break her hands and feet, but she only giggled happily at the thought. Finally, after she dared me to jump, I grew angry. I told her that if she wouldn't come down now, I would call my mother. She said, "Okay, then let's kill some more." But I was tired of playing mean games and said that I was going inside to read. I did, and Devory went home alone.

Two weeks before Pesach my class went to visit a nursing home. Every year each class went to visit a nursing home, where we would sing songs, give out cards, and walk around chatting with the residents. My teacher told us it was a big *mitzvah* to visit the nursing home because the people in there were lonely and they loved to have visitors to keep them company.

Devory and I said hello to some old drooling people who barely looked at us. I told Devory that I was never going to do anything as stupid as grow old. In fact, I had no intention of ever growing past *Bas Mitzvah*, when life seemed to be too annoying to be much fun. Devory said I was being dumb and took me over to a tiny old lady in a too-large light blue bathrobe, staring at us from the door of one of the rooms. I smiled dutifully and held out our card, which had a picture of two girls smiling with the words *Have a great day* printed on it.

She did not take the card. "Which school do you go to?" she asked.

I told her. "Oh, that's a *Chassidish* school," she said.

I was surprised because she said *Chassidish* with the right accent, yet she did not cover her hair.

"You know," she said, the wrinkled skin around her mouth sagging as she spoke, "I came from a *Chassidish* family when I was a young girl. Here, look." She pulled up her sleeve. We saw the familiar green numbers etched into her wrinkled skin. "But this is where I stopped. After God murdered my whole family. He is a cruel God, a very cruel God, and only I, who survived, know His ugly, merciless face."

She bent over us, her small face close between ours.

"You know what He let them do? You know? He let the Nazis take the babies, live, screaming babies, and He let them throw them alive, alive into the fire. That's what they did. I saw it; they played it like a game—grabbed them by their hand or foot and threw them into the fire."

She pointed a crooked finger at me.

"That is the God I survived. That is the God you worship."

Stunned, we stared at her.

"But . . . but He punished them," Devory said.

The old lady laughed. She laughed long and hard and it scared me.

"He punished them with what? How do you punish for millions of dead, twisted, burned bodies? Punished whom? He has a very short-term memory, that God. Look at Germany today." And she laughed again.

That's when Miss Goldberg arrived and firmly led us away.

"Thank you very much," she said sweetly, her heels clicking softly on the shining waxed floors. "Have a nice day."

I wanted to go home. I cried that I did not want to stay any longer. Miss Goldberg held my hand and said I shouldn't listen to the old lady. Sometimes they went a little crazy and it was hard to judge them, but we just must stay away from those. She pointed to an old black man sitting in a wheelchair and said, "Why don't you go talk to him?"

"Him?" I asked.

"Yes," she answered. "He looks lonely, and it would be a big *kiddush* Hashem—a good deed to sanctify G-d's name—to show him how good *Yiddishe* girls behave."

So we went and spoke with the old black man. We gave him another card and spoke to him about the bike race Devory and I had had yesterday, because he couldn't talk. He just nodded his head and smiled at everything we said.

My teacher said we did a big *mitzvah*.

CHAPTER THIRTY-TWO

2008

Sarah Leah had brought *Oprah* magazines to the sleepover.

It was almost midnight when we finally settled in Hindy's old basement after a long dinner with her older sisters. They had come over with gifts and balloons for their youngest sister, shrieking and giggling over baby pictures of her while her mother wiped tears over her youngest, grown so fast.

Sarah Leah had arrived a little later. She was the oldest of nine and first had to put the house in order and the younger ones to sleep before she marched down the stairs holding a large bag of too much food and magazines.

"What?" she asked as we stared at her sitting on the floor pulling out *cocosh* cake, homemade cookies, jelly rolls, tuna salad, and hot soup in plastic containers. "My mother said we might be hungry." She shrugged and pulled out a foil-wrapped something, staring at it curiously. "I have no idea what this is. What? What's wrong?"

"Nothing," Hindy said as she set down bowls of popcorn, pretzels, chips, and salad. "We are all famished."

But Sarah Leah was not done. Smiling secretively, she pulled a thick glossy magazine out of the bag and held it out. "Guess what I have," she said excitedly.

We looked at the magazine. It said *Oprah* on top.

I looked closely. "Who's that?"

Sarah Leah's eyes widened. She opened her mouth as if in stunned surprise. "You don't know who Oprah is?"

I looked at Chani. She looked at me. We looked at the picture again. Hindy waved nonchalantly. "Oh, of course I know. She's this big singer. Or politician. One of them."

Sarah Leah rolled her eyes. "She is not a singer."

Hindy hurled a pillow at the mattress across the room. "Not a regular singer," she explained. "An opera singer. It's her name—see? Op-r-ah."

"Then why is she publishing magazines?"

"She's a really big opera singer."

Sarah Leah flipped back her pony. "I can't believe you don't know who Oprah is. She's, like, this huge actress by the goyim. She's all over the TV. My mother buys it sometimes, and when she's finished she hides it in the storage room in the basement. I brought a bunch of them. You wanna see it?"

We sat on the bed and huddled eagerly over the magazine. Sarah Leah turned the pages. We read, curiously. We saw advertisements for brand names we did not know and luxury brands we could not pronounce. We saw pictures of models who were sort of dressed, halfway dressed, not even pretending to be dressed—Sarah Leah turned that page fast.

"Ugh," I said, carefully covering one eye. "How is she not embarrassed to show her whole front off like that?"

Chani snorted. "You're asking questions about these ladies?"

Hindy turned back the page to the model. Sarah Leah put her hands over the picture. Hindy pushed it away. I quickly turned the page again. Chani turned it back. I turned it again. Back and forth, back and forth, until we flipped the page back together. We stared. There was a loud thud on the stairs. We jumped. Chani ripped the page out of the magazine. She crumpled it up fast in her hand. We looked at the doorway, toward the stairs. There was silence. Hindy threw the unholy model in the wastebasket.

We then read an article on how to lose weight. And another article on how to maintain weight. And another article on what to do when you regain the lost weight. We read an article about love, how to know if he's Mr. Right. And another one about divorce, when after all, he's Mr. Wrong. We read about self-esteem. A nutritionist explained how to feel satisfied and happy with one's body, no matter what size, which we would have read had we not been staring at the skeletal model advertising chocolate-chip cookies on the adjacent page. Then we read more on love.

"It's amazing how they live," Chani commented. "They really think marriage is love, love, love."

"Yes," I agreed. "Which is how they all end up divorced, divorced, divorced."

We giggled. Then Hindy's mother came down the stairs. Sarah Leah threw the magazine under the high-riser. We began to sing loudly.

Hindy's mother came in holding a plateful of homemade Rice Krispies peanut chews. We sat on the floor chewing as she sank onto the old mattress and remembered her girlhood days when there was only one *Bais Yaakov* high school that every Orthodox girl attended.

We argued about it, if it was better that way or worse. After all, if every religious girl had to attend the same school, they would be susceptible to one another's ideas. And who knew what ideas could enter a girl's head from a classmate whose father wore a different hat. There were major differences separating the ultra-Orthodox sects, Sarah Leah explained. Like the accent.

"Why should my parents who pray in one accent want their kids to attend a school that teaches the prayers in a different Hebrew accent?"

Chani agreed. It made sense, she explained, because having only one accent as opposed to many would certainly confuse Hashem come prayer time. How was He supposed to know who was really *Chassidish* and who was not? This way it was clear immediately.

Hindy's mother did not agree. She took a bite out of the peanut chew, sighed, and said, "Oh, like my father used to say— today's fanatics are tomorrow's moderates. Then, we thought we were better than the goyim. Now with every group in their own school, everyone thinks they're also better than the *Yiden*."

"So why didn't you send me to a different school?" asked Hindy.

Her mother winced. "Are you crazy? How would you ever get married?"

She then went upstairs, and we read *Oprah* magazines till dawn.

CHAPTER THIRTY-THREE

2000

It was nearly Pesach. All the girls' schools were on break until after the holiday so that we could help at home. This was not a vacation. My mother was nervous and screechy and tense, and I could not move one inch without being told that I should *not go anywhere* without cleaning first. The cleaning lady who was supposed to have arrived at seven a.m. did not show up, and my mother complained furiously to my aunt on the phone.

"This *goytah*, may she burn in hell! One week before Pesach and she doesn't show up!! What am I supposed to do now?"

I stuffed my mouth with a cookie and looked up at the ceiling.

"Please, Hashem," I whispered ever so quietly. "Could you make me a goy just until Pesach?"

But a Yid I remained, and I found myself scrubbing and rubbing and cleaning out all my crumb-filled drawers until my mother left the house to do some shopping. Sighing in relief, I sneaked outside when Surela wasn't looking. Devory showed up soon after.

She told me that she had made such a mess cleaning for Pesach that her mother had kicked her out of the house and told her not to come back until late.

We made sure that no one was in sight and then climbed the tree and up onto the garage. My mother always warned us that it was a dangerous thing to sit on the sloping roof of the garage and that we might fall, but we never did. We used the rough trunk of the cherry tree standing by the garage as our ladder and after much scratching and giggling, we pulled ourselves onto the roof. We sat there, hidden by the branches of the tree, surrounded by hundreds of candylike cherries, and Devory told me that she was sleeping by me for the whole Pesach, starting tonight. Pesach was in a week and I was really excited that Devory was coming.

"From now until the end of Pesach," she explained to me. "Only to sleep, because my brother is coming home tonight."

"Yes, yes," I said happily. "We'll have so much fun. But how did you get your mother's permission?"

Devory shrugged. "I'm coming to sleep in your house for the whole Pesach," she repeated matter-of-factly.

When I told my mother about Devory sleeping by us for Pesach, she said, "Huh? What in the world is the girl talking about? Why would she come sleep by us for Pesach? She has her own home. Oy, I feel bad for those parents when it comes time to marry her off."

But sure enough, at promptly six o'clock, Devory appeared again at our house with a small bag that held her nightgown and toothbrush. She walked upstairs, settled herself down in my room on my bed with a book, and said that I shouldn't bother her. She wanted to read. I went downstairs to my mother and told her that

Devory was sitting on my bed and that she had brought her night-gown and toothbrush, so could she sleep in our house after all?

My mother looked at me strangely and went straight to the phone. She dialed the number, waited, and then rather impatiently said, "You might want to know that your daughter is upstairs in Gittel's bedroom. She brought her nightgown and informed us that she is sleeping here tonight. Is that all right with you? It doesn't seem like you know."

I could hear the exasperation clearly in the faraway voice through the phone. "What? Sometimes that girl is crazy!"

My mother listened for a few moments, said, "Yes, yes, no problem," and hung up.

She climbed the stairs determinedly, opened the door to my room, and said, "Devory?"

Devory did not even hear her.

"Devory?" My mother moved toward my bed.

She did not look up.

"Your mother said that you should go home right now. I don't mind if you sleep here, but you need your mother's permission and she is waiting for you." Devory shrugged and went back to her book.

My mother looked at her, blinked her eyes in annoyance, and repeated, "Devory, you have to go home now. Your mother is wait-ing for you. You cannot sleep in this house tonight. I am waiting."

Devory did not move.

My mother strode over to her, grabbed the book, put it in the little black bag with her nightgown, and handed it to her. "Take this bag," she said firmly, "and go home now. Your mother is waiting for you."

Devory stood up, took the bag, and walked out of the room. My mother followed her straight to the bathroom, where Devory quickly slammed the door and locked it from inside. My mother sighed.

"*Oy*, Hashem," she groaned, and she went to the phone again.

A long time passed and I stood by the bathroom door waiting for Devory to come out. I knocked on the door and told her that no one was there anymore except me. Finally she opened the door a crack and her freckled nose and twinkling eyes peeked through. "You wanna play ghosts?" she asked with a mischievous smile.

"No way," I said. "My mother would kill us."

Devory came back to my room and we sat down on my bed. "I think my mother called your mother again," I said.

"I don't care," she replied, opening up the book again. "I'm sleeping here tonight."

"Maybe you could sleep on the dining room couch in your house," I suggested.

"No," she said. "My mother doesn't let me. And anyway, I don't want to sleep at home at all."

"Why not?"

"Because."

"But your brother is only here for two weeks. Then he's going back to *yeshiva*."

"No. I'm not going home."

I did not know what to tell Devory. She was bothering me, lying like that, saying things she knew our parents would refuse. Her stillness scared me. I wanted to tell her something so badly, but I didn't know what it was. I wanted to shake her hard and then she would scream out loud and everyone would get scared and ask what had happened. But she wasn't there anymore. Her small, narrow face was burrowed in the book, her blue eyes scanning smoothly over the lines, and she was already in some other world.

I stood up to leave. I had just reached the door to my bedroom when I heard Mr. Goldblatt's voice downstairs. "Upstairs? I'm so sorry for this bother. I'll go get her right away." And his strong footsteps were on the stairs.

I turned to Devory. She jumped off my bed, threw the book on the floor, and stared at me, her face pale and drawn.

"No, I'm not sleeping at home. I'm not sleeping at home."

Her father had reached the landing when Devory rushed past me and into the bathroom. She slammed the door and locked it. Then there was silence. Her father looked at me and pointed to the closed door.

"Is she in there, Gittel?" he asked.

I nodded.

He walked to the slammed door and knocked sharply.

"Devory?" he said sternly. "It's Totty. Open the door."

Silence.

"Devory, open the door immediately. I am very angry with you. Open the door now."

It took half an hour to get the door open. At seven o'clock, her father pried the door using a knife. Devory screamed when she saw him, and he carried her out of our house kicking and crying that she didn't want to sleep at home.

My mother was very upset. I could hear her talking to my father on the phone at work about Devory, and when she saw me she demanded that I go to sleep now. I went upstairs and found Devory's book lying on the floor near my bed. I tried to read it, but I got bored and fell asleep instead.

It was a beautiful sunny day the next morning. I came down

to breakfast planning to play with my new purple jump rope outside, but my mother told me that I was cleaning my drawers for Pesach today, and that was all I could do.

Sulking, I left my rope in my bedroom and sat down at the kitchen table for breakfast. I was slurping loudly from a bowl of Cocoa Pebbles when Devory walked into our house. She didn't even knock, just opened the door and walked in. She didn't even say hello. I only glimpsed her through the kitchen door, going upstairs, still in her nightgown. My mother barely noticed, being busy on the phone.

"Hello, Devory!" I yelled.

She didn't answer, and I could see my mother's annoyance with her nonchalant stroll into our house.

I finished my bowl of Cocoa Pebbles, licking the bottom until it shone. I wanted more, but my mother said no way, she couldn't believe she was letting me have this junk altogether. She then went back to talking on the phone and motioned for me to wait. She finally finished arguing with my grandmother, and then, still annoyed about something, hurriedly told me to take the basket of laundry downstairs to the basement, put it in the washing machine, and turn it on. Then I should go upstairs and start cleaning. Maybe Devory would help me.

I ran downstairs with the laundry basket, dumped everything into the machine, pressed some buttons, the big one twice, and waited for it to start groaning. I stared at the swirling colors for a while and then ran upstairs to my bedroom, calling Devory's name. I looked in my room, but it was empty. I looked in my sister's bedroom, expecting to find her there. She liked to sit near the shelves filled with books and browse through them until she finally found a book that she hadn't read yet. But she wasn't in there either.

I walked down the hallway calling her name, but she didn't answer. I passed the bathroom and knocked on the closed door. When there was no answer, I pushed it open. I noticed the open toilet seat and I was thinking that I had better close it—my mother hated when it was left open—when I saw Devory hanging like a broken rag doll from the curtain rod.

The chipped wooden chair from my sister's room stood near her small limp body. My purple jump rope was wound tightly around her neck like a snake, and her head fell sideways over her shoulder, twisted, unmoving, the white, white skin stretched over her face like plastic. Her eyes stared straight at me, cold, ice blue, dead eyes with a straight line of dark lifeless red where her mouth used to be.

I screamed. And screamed and screamed and screamed.

Totty came first. I felt him come up from behind me, heard him shout, and collapsed onto him as he grabbed me, pushing my face hard against his chest, crushing out everything else. He ran with me, carried me to my room, where he lay me on my bed, holding my arms tightly, yelling for my mother, "*Hatzalah!* Mommy, *Hatzalah!* Call for emergency help!"

His voice sounded like thunder. I heard my mother's rushing footsteps, her terrified voice, vaguely, from so far away. She was shrieking now, shrieking, saying words, our address, her name.

My father was holding me tightly so I could not look, could not see, only screamed and screamed until suddenly I could not breathe. Everything was white, and my throat was closed shut, choking so that no air came in, and I thrashed about wildly. I felt my father's clutching hands shake me. He slapped me hard; I could hear the sound of it but could not feel anything at all. He thumped my back again and again, and then my face was deeply

in his hands and I saw him looking at me, heard him say somewhere, "Breathe deeply, breathe deeply, breathe deeply, like that,
yes, breathe deeply. . . ."

I wet my skirt. I could feel the warm water moving down my
thighs, my skirt, my legs—and then two *Hatzalah* men were lean-
ing over me and everything went black.

When I opened my eyes I was lying in a small white room on
a hospital bed. My father was sitting near me and talking to a lady
who didn't look Jewish. When my father saw that I was awake, he
jumped up and called the nurse, who came in immediately and
asked me what my name was, how old I was, and what today was,
until I whimpered that I didn't want to answer any more stupid
questions. I sat up in the bed, and the nurse brought me orange
juice and a doughnut, but I didn't want them. My father turned
on the small television hanging from the ceiling, and while I
watched a funny show, he spoke quietly with the lady. When the
show was over, and the doctor had poked me all over and said I
was just fine, my father told me that the lady wanted to talk with
me. He said that she needed to ask me a few questions, and that if
I didn't want to answer I didn't have to.

The lady standing near my father wore long navy pants and a
light blue shirt. She smiled and nodded at me while my father
spoke. Her face looked nice, so I kept quiet as she told me that she
didn't want to hurt me or make me cry but it was very important
that she know a few things. She then asked me if I was good
friends with Devory. And then I remembered and could only nod
my head.

She told me quietly that she knew Devory wanted to sleep in
my house very badly and maybe I knew why. I felt a little dizzy

and leaned on my father's chest. I didn't want to answer but I wanted her to leave, so I said, "Because she didn't want to sleep with her brother."

"Why didn't she want to sleep with her brother?"

"Because he came into her bed and she just didn't want to sleep with him."

"Is this the first time she told you that she didn't want to sleep with her brother in the same room?"

"No, she never wanted to. She also ran away the last time when her brother was sleeping in her room."

"Did she tell you that her brother came into her bed? How do you know about this?"

"I don't know, she just didn't want to sleep with her brother," I whined. There was silence for a few seconds. I buried my face in my father's chest. "Totty, tell the lady to go away." I sobbed softly.

My father stroked my hair and spoke quietly to the lady, and they decided to continue "a different time."

When I arrived home that night the house was hushed. Everyone tiptoed around my bedroom, and even Surela's usual babble on the phone couldn't be heard. I was put straight to bed, and my mother brought up a small tray with a big cup of sweet hot chocolate milk and my favorite cheesecake. My father sat near me while I nibbled and read me two chapters of the *Bais Yaakov* Times book until I fell asleep. I woke up sometime later in the dark of my room and I was scared. I plugged in the little night-light near my bed and was staring at the full yellow moon through the open window shade when I heard my mother crying from her bedroom. At first it sounded like a mumble of confused voices, but then my mother's voice rose.

"My daughter will not be involved in this!"

"*Shah*, quiet."

"My daughter will not be involved in this, you hear? Enough! Everyone will know! No one will come near us in *shidduchim*. Our lives will be ruined!"

I could hear my father's low voice trying, persuading, and then lagging. "I am obviously not going to advertise in the *New York Times*."

"Do you realize what you are saying? They've been our neighbors forever! They are an important family, *chashuva* descendants of the *Rebbe*! No one will believe it anyway. . . . Yes, I spoke with *Reb* Speigel. He said that you're just assuming things, you have no idea what really happened! The child was always a bit strange. . . . He said we should do everything to help them now. It's too late."

"Do you remember what happened to the Wiesfeld family when they reported Sruli's *rebbe* to the police?" my mother continued. "Shimon, do you remember? Look at them today! Look what happened to them! Nobody goes near them! They can't find schools for their children. Forget about it. I don't care what you say. Think about your daughter! What happened, happened. The child is gone already. There is nothing to do. I absolutely forbid you to talk to the police ever again."

More mumbling, arguing, and then soft crying. I fell asleep again.

Devory came to me that night. She came to me and everything was white. I was blind and I couldn't see anything except for her face twisting sideways over her shoulder, dead. But then she was alive. I couldn't breathe. Couldn't breathe, couldn't breathe because she was choking me. She was choking me with my jump rope. Her icy dead eyes were staring out of her face and she never smiled never smiled never smiled—her mouth like a red-painted line silent and dead dead dead. I couldn't close my eyes, couldn't breathe, had to see the blue glass eyes falling from her face all over in front of me. She was choking me choking me choking me— dead eyes cutting me into a million pieces.

I screamed a lot after that. Every night and sometimes in the day I would scream, huddled on the floor, and could not stop. My mother would cry, wring her hands, but my father would say, "Let her scream, she needs to scream," and he would stand over me until I stopped kicking and let him hold me on his lap.

My mother told me they would take me to a good psychologist who could take away those terrible dreams. She would stop the dead eyes from falling all over.

CHAPTER THIRTY-FOUR

2008

Dear Devory,

    Please read this letter. Please don't ignore it because you are dead. I know you are mad at me. I know that it is my fault, and you can never forgive me. I know I am terrible. What I did then was so horribly wrong. But I was only nine. Now I am almost eighteen. I will never ignore you again.

                    Your best friend,
                    Gittel

Dear Devory,

    Devory.
    Devory.
    D e v o r y.
    I like writing your name. It makes you feel real, like you're still here somewhere.

                     Your best friend,
                     Gittel

Dear Devory,

*My brother's getting married in six months. My parents
are getting calls every day about me from the* shadchanim.
*Devory, I don't think I am going to give evidence. Not now.
I'm sorry.*

Gittel

CHAPTER THIRTY-FIVE

2000

After Pesach, when I returned to school, everybody wanted to know about Devory. I said nothing, because just as I got off the van at school, my principal was waiting for me at the school gates. She told me to come to her office. I sat behind her desk, but she sat right near me and held my hand in hers. She said that she knew it was hard for me, and that I must be very sad after what happened. But one day I would be happy again and have new friends. Then, holding my hand tightly, she looked into my eyes.

"It is very important that you understand not to talk to anybody in the class about what happened. Nobody will understand and they will only bother you about it, and most of all it is *loshon harah*—evil talk—because everyone will talk bad about Devory's family. And you know what a big sin that is. *Loshon harah* could ruin people's lives, and there is nothing we have to be more careful about. You can talk to any adult you want, like me, or your mother or father. They will help you as much as possible. I'll tell the girls in the class that I do not allow anyone to talk about it. Devory was a very sick and sad girl and that's what made her do what she did."

"It's not true," I said. "Devory did it because she hated her brother."

My teacher cleared her throat and smiled hesitantly. "Gittel, we don't really know why Devory did it. But I just want you to try to remember what I said. It is very, very important not to tell any girl in the class anything about Devory."

She then gave me three chocolate-chip cookies and walked with me back to the classroom.

After *davening*, my teacher announced that Devory wasn't coming back because she had been very sick and Hashem had taken her away to heaven, where she would be happy.

During recess, I was eating Super-Snack at my desk when Chani came over to me and said that she heard her mother saying Devory was a little crazy and that's why Hashem took her away. Hindy heard and quickly came over and said, *nuh-uh*, her mother said that Devory was jumping when the jump rope got stuck on her neck and she choked. Rivky, who sat right behind me, told Hindy that she didn't even know what she was saying, 'cause her father said that Devory died in the bathtub by mistake. Esty said it was *loshon harah* and her sister said that nobody was allowed to talk about it. I walked away.

When my father came to pick me up from school, I asked him why everyone said that Devory was very sick, when she had been perfectly healthy. He said that Devory was sick, but a different kind of sick. She was a very sad girl and didn't know what to do with her sadness, until it made her do what she did. I said it wasn't true. Devory was only very sad because she didn't want to sleep in the bed with her brother. My father nodded and said that when I grew up I would understand, and for now we would just try to forget the whole thing as best as we could.

My father came to school because he was taking me to a psychologist. He told me that the psychologist was a very nice lady who would help me forget things.

The psychologist *was* a nice lady. Her office was pink and full of nice pictures. But she wanted me to draw, and I wasn't interested. She then explained to me that I was a big girl and she would try to help me understand what happened to Devory.

"No."

"Depression," she explained slowly, "means a terrible kind of sadness."

"Devory did it because she hated her brother."

The nice psychologist looked at me quietly for a long time. "Do you want to tell me what is in your dream?"

I said nothing.

"Do you want to tell me what Devory told you?"

I said nothing.

For a long time there was silence. Then she told me that if I didn't talk or didn't tell her how I felt and what I was scared of, I would never be able to forget.

I said nothing.

CHAPTER THIRTY-SIX

2008

Dear Devory,

Today we started seminary. Summer is over, and most of our class is attending Bais Yaakov Teacher's Training Seminar to learn how to become teachers for our schools. Today we learned that people who kill themselves don't get to heaven. Is it true? We also learned that children under eighteen can't go to hell. Where are you then? I am only asking you because I have no one else who is Jewish to ask. So I don't know.

Gittel

CHAPTER THIRTY-SEVEN

2000

The Goldblatt family was moving to Israel.

"Yes, there were difficulties," I heard my mother explain on the phone that evening while I slurped on my bowl of soggy Cocoa Pebbles. "But, *Baruch Hashem*, everything was taken care of. *Agudath Yisroel* got involved and Chaim Cohen had connections with the police. Shmuli is in Israel already. They put him on a plane two hours after the police tried questioning him. Yes, of course it's a lie! You know the police, the first thing they do is open investigations, make up stories! I'm telling you, instead of sympathizing with this poor family, the only thing they could do is give them another heart attack. You should have seen the men yelling at the police when they came. They did a good job keeping them out. *Oy*, these goyim, may Hashem erase their name.

"Yes, yes, only Miriam stayed. She'll live with Itty Green. Of course you know, the aunt on Sixteenth and Forty-ninth. Anyway, so she'll stay there till she finishes her senior year. *Nebech, nebech*.

What could one do? That's right, only Hashem knows. I don't ask any questions these days anymore. I just say, Hashem, You are the master planner, I don't understand what You're doing, but I guess You know. Yes, these days. I'm telling you. . . . There's just nothing to say. But that's it, these are the times before *Mashiach*, the Messiah, and we can only *daven* and *daven* that He should come already.

"*Baruch Hashem*, she's fine. I have nothing to complain about. . . . Yes, of course I'm going to the wedding tonight. Zisi will never forgive me if I don't show up. . . . No, no, I'm wearing the navy dress. I look much better in it. *Oy*, in the gray I look like a hippopotamus. What are you wearing? Okay, good-bye. *Be'ezras Hashem*, you too, you too."

I couldn't sleep that night. I sat on top of the staircase and listened to my parents arguing in the kitchen.

"I can't believe it, I just can't believe it."

"It's true." My father's voice was tense. "I spoke with Mrs. Weinberg herself. She told me that her son has never been the same since. And that the *Rebbe* is still teaching in the most prestigious *litvish cheder*. Who didn't she speak to? The principal, the teachers, the *Rebbe*. Even the police told her that they couldn't help her. They said gathering evidence of molestation in the Orthodox community was impossible and that she would lose the case. None of the parents dared to say anything. When she sent that last letter to the head of the *yeshiva*, she started getting threats. She just shut her mouth and that was it."

The running water made small splashing sounds as my mother washed the dishes.

"Look," she said. "You are just assuming things that we have

no right to assume. Do you know how badly they beat up *Reb*
Spitser because he agreed to talk to the police? Do you remember
that other girl, how they kicked her out of school after she called the
police for help from her father? Just forget this whole thing. I refuse
to burden my children with suffering they don't deserve. That child
was emotionally disturbed, and that is that."

There was silence for a few moments.

"Who would believe such things?" My mother sighed. "*Oy,*
one hundred years ago, such things would never have happened."

My father laughed bitterly. "And if it did happen, would we
ever know?! They certainly didn't record it."

There was no answer, only the clanking of the dishes.

When my father came up, I was still sitting on the stairs. I told
him that I was scared to go to sleep.

"I am taking you to the psychologist again next week," he said,
carrying me to bed. "You will like her better with time."

"No, I won't," I said stubbornly. "I don't want to go."

"Do you want me to go with you?" he asked.

I nodded my head.

"Okay, I will go with you into the office. It is very important,
Gittel. It will take a lot of time to understand. But you must learn
to talk about how you feel."

And that's when I told him. I don't know why.

"Totty, he came into her bed. I saw him. I saw how Shmuli
came into her bed and pushed her under the blanket."

My father turned white—white like my school paper under his
curly, black beard.

"Oh, yes," I continued angrily. "He came into her bed that
night when Mommy was in Israel and I was sleeping in Devory's

room. I saw him. He pushed her inside the blanket, and I thought she was dead, Totty. Why?"

He turned his head away as if I had just slapped him hard. His beard quivered. He stared at me as if I were a ghost. And then he put his head down on his knees and cried.

I had never seen my father cry before. I never knew he had tears the way I did, that his cheeks could get wet, that his eyes could look so sad. He held me in his arms, my father. He held me in his arms, and he cried for a long, long time. That scared me most of all.

CHAPTER THIRTY-EIGHT

2008

Dear Devory,

Kathy says that you are at peace with Hashem. She says you feel only love and tranquillity. She said the dead can't suffer, that only bodies could break but souls stay whole eternally. Then why do you come to me in my dreams? Why do you come like that knocking at my window? Are you ever going to stop?

Your best friend,
Gittel

CHAPTER THIRTY-NINE

2000

After I told my father about Shmuli, I did not feel well the next morning. When I complained to my mother, she covered my forehead with her cool hand, then brought a thermometer and placed it under my tongue. The results were not impressive, but she said I should stay home anyway. I lay in my bed listening to the rushed morning sounds filling the house: the hurried footsteps clumping down the stairs, the kitchen chairs scraping against the floor, the clanking of the frying pan, my mother nervously repeating, "You'll be late, hurry up, you'll be late, hurry up." And I felt like I was on a small island of peace in the quiet of my bed.

On my desk across the room lay a new book my father had bought me, a book about death for children. He said when I felt ready I should read it; it would help me. My father had also bought me a big art notepad and a large box of markers, crayons, and pens. He said it would help me express myself in an artistic way. He wanted to buy me a fish. Maybe I would talk to it, and it would be like a friend. Or maybe, he said, a small recorder, the kind we saw in the toy store, so I could record myself playing on it and it would be only mine to listen to. But my mother put a stop to it and told him to quit thinking up things to buy and just let the child think alone.

I padded across the carpeted floor to my desk and opened the drawer that held my school notebooks and a small photo album of me since I was a baby. It was gone. It held pictures of Devory and me as babies, as toddlers in the park, on the swings, at my brother's *Bar Mitzvah*, at the aquarium last year. The album had been lying in the drawer of my desk under my school notebook, but now nobody seemed to know where it was. When I asked my mother where my album was, she said the cleaning lady had thrown it out in the frenzy of the Pesach cleaning.

I wanted those pictures. I wanted them now. Then I remembered Kathy had once taken a picture of Devory and me with Kootchie Mootchie, sitting on her couch. I wanted to go up to her apartment and get it. Just then, my mother came into my room. Her shoulder-length wig was neatly on her head, and her summer dress fit her trim body perfectly.

"I'm going to the supermarket. Do you want to come with me?"

"No," I said, burying my head in my pillow. "I want to rest and read."

She looked at me, worried creases near her eyes that had become a permanent part of her face deepening.

"I'll be back soon."

The door closed and I could hear the clicking of her heels fade as she walked down the block. I put down my book and ran up to Kathy's apartment.

"Gittel!" Kathy said happily when she opened the door. "How was Passover? It was beautiful in Greece. I tol' you that I was going didn't I? We were visitin' Leo's family for a few weeks. I just came home two days ago and it's been too quiet round here. Come in. Come on in. Hey, you're not in school. You got enough of it already?" She giggled. "Come, you wanna see what Kootchie Mootchie did? He tore my bathroom curtain to pieces when I thought he was sleepin'. Oh, my." She wiped her forehead. "I don't know what I'm gonna do with that ol' cat."

"Kathy," I said, "do you have a picture of me and Devory with the cat on the couch?"

Kathy squinted her eyes. "Oh, sure." She smiled, remembering. "That's a sweet picture. There it is." Kathy pointed to the picture on the wall. She took it down and held it.

"Beautiful girl, Devory. How's she doin'?"

"She's dead," I said.

"What?"

"She's dead. She hanged herself in our bathroom."

Kathy raised her eyes to the man on the cross hanging on the wall, and I could see her lips moving softly, like my mother's did when she prayed. She sat down heavily on the couch, staring at me intently.

"An' I'm sittin' up here all day like an old hermit and I didn't even know." Her small eyes crinkled sadly.

"Give me the picture," I demanded, and grabbed it out of her hand. She held on to my wrist. I pushed her away. She pulled me toward her, wrapping me in her arms. "You poor girl. You poor, poor girl." She rocked me slowly to and fro and I could feel the firm thud of her heart beating steadily against my head. "Talk with

God," Kathy murmured. "Talk with God. Devory's now up in heaven with so many wonderful people an' angels, and she's a part of God."

I pulled myself out of her arms. "I have to go back downstairs. I just wanted the picture."

I hid the picture in my undershirt and ran down the steps.

"You're a beautiful girl, Gittel," Kathy called after me. "God loves you."

The picture, pressed against my stomach, rubbed against my skin. I pulled it out and hid it under the mattress in my room. But I changed my mind. I took out the picture, holding it facedown in my hand. I was afraid to look at it. Would she still be smiling, her light brown freckles decorating her face like tiny stars? Or would she stare out at me the way she did when they took her away? I turned it over. Devory smiled at me. Her eyes twinkled. Her hand waved cheerfully at the camera.

I did not know dead girls could live in a picture. I did not know they could still smile, as if pretending they were still alive. I held the picture tightly. I did not want anyone to see it. I could not bear the thought that anyone would ever touch Devory again. I hid the picture deep in the middle of my *Bais Yaakov* Times book on the second bookshelf on the top of my desk. It was a better hiding place than my bed. The cleaning lady would shake out the mattress and throw Devory and me into the garbage again.

When my mother returned from the supermarket, she asked me if I wanted to go back to school for the afternoon. I said no. It wasn't that I didn't like school. Everyone in my class had already forgotten Devory. Other than a few fights I had had with Chani over whether I was allowed to have a goy living in my house, I was friends with almost everyone. My teachers didn't bother me as they had in the beginning, when they asked me how I was doing and reminded me kindly again and again not to talk to anyone in the class about what happened. Even the principal left me alone. She used to call me out of the classroom every two days and tell me that if I *davened* every day with a lot of *kavanah*—sincerity— Hashem would help me forget about what happened. I told her that I didn't want to forget Devory. I wanted to remember her all the time. She said that wasn't healthy. I had to forget.

When my father came home that evening, he picked me up and held me tightly in his arms.

"Oh," he groaned, setting me down. "How do you expect me to swing you into the air, if you keep on growing?"

After supper he and my mother went into their room. They stayed there for a long time. I sat in the adjoining bathroom and listened.

"Maybe it's not such a bad idea," I heard my mother say. "I don't want people to go around saying we got everyone into trouble. Maybe Gittel should say something to someone from the police, a nice police lady, so she won't be scared."

My father's voice rose angrily. "You forbade her from speaking to the police to say the truth. But you want me to allow her to speak to the police in order to lie?"

"I just don't know what to do." My mother sobbed. "I don't know what to do. What will this do to our family . . . ?"

I heard her blowing her nose hard into a tissue. I pressed my ear against the wall so I could hear her more clearly.

"I spoke with Chaya Goldblatt today. She said Ashdod is a nice city and they have a new apartment. At first she sounded strong, and she was telling me what a friendly neighborhood they live in, and how the younger children were catching on to Hebrew so fast she could hardly keep up with them. But then"—I heard the tremor in my mother's voice as it grew thick with tears—"she started crying and I could barely hold myself back. She said her husband has completely withdrawn. He doesn't want to talk to anyone, not even her. He literally sits all day in *Bais Medrash*, and sometimes all night. He is a broken man. She was crying so hard, she kept repeating, 'Why me, why me, why me? What sin have I committed to receive such a punishment?' I tried to calm her down but she was crying too hard. She was almost screaming at me, 'Why was I such a bad mother? Why didn't I take her to a psychologist a year ago when I saw that she was so different from all the other children?' Shimon, I didn't know what to do. She was just sobbing and sobbing, and I couldn't even hear what she was saying anymore. . . ."

I pictured my parents sitting on their beds across from each other, my father staring at the wall, my mother fumbling with the tissue.

I heard my mother sobbing softly. "What are we going to do? Surela is almost in *shidduchim*. . . ."

My father spoke firmly. "Look, this is a hard time for our family," he said. "But there's nothing we can do about it. I won't allow Gittel to lie to the police. Sometimes we build such high walls for protection that we forget that our greatest enemy can grow from within. My daughter's soul will stay pure." There was an angry thud as he thumped his fist on the night table. "She will speak to no one."

CHAPTER FORTY

2008

Dear Devory,

I am no longer writing you letters. We are not nine anymore, and we know that letters don't reach heaven. I am writing this for myself, I guess. I know you are mad at me. I know that I should have done more, screamed louder, told other people, but they wouldn't listen. They are too scared of the truth.

I want so badly to speak with you. I want so badly to know about the dead. Is it true that without eyes you can see so much more? Without the limits of a body, you can understand everything? Is that why you come to me in my dreams? Is that why you are angry, the way you could not be when you were alive?

I finally went to the police, Devory. They said it's called rape. They said you were raped by Shmuli. They also told me *it happens everywhere. Did you know that, Devory? Did you read that in your books? That it could happen by us too? In the goyishe books did they talk about this? In our stories they never write about such things. Maybe they think that if they don't, it will never happen.*

Kathy told me I should not be mad at Hashem. She said to be angry at the people who hurt us. I am not angry at anyone anymore. I am only very tired and scared.

Please stop being mad at me, Devory. I will open the window for you, and you can come in. We will lie talking and talking forever because dreams don't need to end. I promise. I will hold your hands and never tell you to go home again. I am sorry I did that. So sorry.

When we finish talking, we'll go to a meadow. I know exactly which one. The one that looks like paradise, with rolling hills of green and lush flowering trees and perfect blue clouds. It is only just for us. There we'll run and dance and play like we used to, before anything happened. We'll make our own heaven. No one can tell us how to dream. If we are dead together, they can't catch us. They can't tell us what to do. We'll float above them, never looking down, and no matter how much they scream and shout, we won't hear them.

I know you'll never get this letter. But maybe because you're dead, you can feel it. Maybe you can know what it says from wherever you are and you'll come back. And then we could talk again.

> *Your best friend forever,*
> *Gittel*

CHAPTER FORTY-ONE

2000

School was almost over and we were already starting to pack to go up to the Catskill Mountains when Kootchie Mootchie died, just like that. His fat body curled up by the kitchen stove, his whiskers drooping over a half-eaten cheese snack. He simply gave out. He was an old cat, almost eighteen years old, though he had eaten so much over the years it was a miracle he could even breathe.

Leo knocked at our door that morning. My mother, clutching a pair of my brother's torn pants, opened the door.

"Good morning," she said impatiently. She looked at Leo's arms. He was holding what seemed to be a cat covered with a small blanket, one limp paw and the unmoving tail hanging down.

"Cat's dead," he said.

We could hear Kathy's footsteps trudging heavily downstairs. Her hair lay flat and damp; her small eyes were red and swollen with grief and tears. Her nose, a bright pink from the crying, sniffled sadly.

"Kootchie Mootchie died las' night. I stayed up all night sayin' goo'-bye. We gotta bury him. We gonna bury him near the back fence, in back of the garage, okay?"

My mother blinked. I could see the disgust pass over her face as she tried not to grimace at the dead cat.

"Sure," she said. "Okay, uh, I gotta go." And she turned away from the door.

Kathy and Leo walked slowly out of the house. Pulling on my brother's slippers, I followed quickly after them.

"How did he die?" I asked Kathy. I'd never seen a dead cat before. I stared at the tail swaying imperceptibly in the wind.

"God took 'im," Kathy said. "He was a good cat, and the time came to take 'im." She wiped her nose. "He had a good life."

Behind the garage, near the back fence, was a patch of neglected earth, a few feet away from the small garden. Leo placed the cat gently near the wall, took the shovel out of the garage, and his muscular arms heaved up and down as the dirt whipped out from the ground. Kathy, on her knees, bent over the dead cat and stroked the blanket.

"Oh, poor Kootchie Mootchie." She sobbed. "This is a special blanket. Warm and fuzzy, his favorite, so he shouldn' be cold in there even in the winter."

She grunted and pushed herself up. "He'll be fine in his next life, my little Kootchie. . . . He was a good cat. I'm gonna make him a nice headstone. It'll say Kootchie Mootchie, a good cat. May Jesus give him a good and loving family in his next life."

"What next life?" I asked.

"Cat's got nine lives," Kathy told me. "If they good in one life, they get a good next life. And I know my Kootchie Mootchie's gonna do just fine. He gonna get a nice little family with a sweet girl like you who gonna love him and care for him jus' like I did."

Nine lives. That sounded like an awfully long time to be on Earth. But I supposed cats liked it. What would they do in heaven? I didn't like Kootchie too much, but I hoped he got a good next life, maybe a family with a pizza shop or something so he could do nothing but eat all day. Kootchie would like that. Everyone got their own kind of heaven, I guessed. Even cats.

I did not tell my mother of the little funeral and certainly not about the grave with the J— sign. She was muttering when I came into the kitchen that she could not believe she let Kathy bury the cat in her backyard. She just wanted that dead cat out of her face. She sliced the tomato into two perfect halves. "And that is the last animal that woman will ever bring into this house.

"Hashem." She pulled her snood over her forehead. "The things these goyim fall in love with. . . ."

Kathy gave me a handful of candies that afternoon, after I went up to talk with her, she being so sad and lonely after Kootchie Mootchie's death. She showed me some pictures she took of the cat and said he was the best companion she had ever had—after Leo. When I came downstairs with the candies, my mother wanted to know what it was I was eating. I told her it was candies I got from Kathy. She said she couldn't believe I was eating candies from a *goyishe* house and who knows what it was that she gave me. I told her they were kosher candies that Kathy had bought from a kosher store and there was nothing wrong with them.

"What do you mean, nothing wrong?" she demanded angrily. "You don't eat food that comes from a goy, no matter what. You say 'thank you' nicely and then throw it out just in case it's not kosher enough! Where did you grow up anyway, in goyland?"

Something snapped in me, deep inside. I told her that Hashem had more to worry about than candies that were just-in-case-not kosher-enough. I told her that kosher was kosher wherever it came from because Hashem was everywhere. I didn't have to climb the tower of our house or chant along with my class during prayer in school to reach Him, because if I closed my eyes, and reached inside of me really high, I would touch the heavens from wherever I was.

My mother stared at me, her face gone white, her eyes stunned. I walked away from her, back to my room, and sat on my bed. I said a blessing to Hashem out loud, tore open the wrappers of all five candies, and stuffed them into my mouth.

And they were very good.

CHAPTER FORTY-TWO

2008

I walked up the gray concrete steps of Precinct 66. I pushed open the heavy doors. The policeman sitting at the front desk told me to wait in her office; Miranda would come in a few minutes.

I sat down in the folding chair and looked at the desk. The metal sheet covering the front of the desk was bent inward. I had kicked it hard. I looked down, embarrassed of how I'd behaved. Miranda came in immediately after. She smiled at me hesitantly. She then pulled the chair around the desk, bringing it to the front, right across from my chair. She sat down empty-handed. She waited.

"Maybe after I'm married," I said.

Miranda folded her hands on her lap. "Okay. . . . Why then?" she asked.

"Too many people will be hurt now."

She was quiet.

"Do you want to get married?" she finally asked.

That question. Always that question. "I want my parents to love

me," I said. "I don't have anywhere else to go. I don't want to leave.
I have siblings who will suffer. Schools that will kick them out, *shuls*
that will ostracize them, a community that does not forgive. Shmuli
won't be punished, only *we* will."

Miranda was silent.

"I can't do it," I said. "Maybe after I'm married."

"Do you think you can forget?"

I nodded my head. Then I shook it. I nodded again.

"Do you still have dreams?"

"No. The dreams went away. She stopped coming. I don't see
her anymore. Maybe she just wanted to know what had happened."

"Are you upset you came here?"

"No. I . . . I just needed to know. I just needed to know what
had really happened." I bit my lips. "Are you disgusted with me?"

"You are only seventeen."

"Still . . ."

"You are the one who suffers. Only when you are ready, maybe
after you are married, you'll come back."

I looked at the desk. It was empty. Just a bare surface with no
paper.

"Do you still have her file?"

"Of course. I rewrote it."

"Will it stay open?"

"Of course."

"Okay."

CHAPTER FORTY-THREE

2000

It was the first week of summer vacation. I held my father's hand as we walked down sunny, blossoming Ocean Parkway. Every week, after the heavy *Shabbos* meal, my father liked to take a long walk to settle his food before the traditional *Shabbos* nap. My mother and sister usually came along, but this week I was the only one. Everyone else was too lazy. We were strolling together, hand in hand, pointing at the tiny white-petaled flowers springing from the grass, when something happened—and this time Hashem was almost crushed.

My father was telling me some old jokes he knew from his childhood, but I wasn't in the mood to laugh. So we walked quietly down the long, shaded block, watching the birds chattering and running on their tiny, pencil-thin feet when a *shaygetz*—non-Jewish boy—passed by us, the kind I often saw from the safety of the school van window, laughing loudly in the streets. As he passed us, he grabbed my father's *shtreimel* off his head and sped down the block. My father yelled at him to drop the hat and took off after him, *kippa* in hand, *payos* flying in the air. When the goy reached the end of the block, he was forced to stop. There was a green light, and cars were speeding by him so he had nowhere to run. My father had almost reached him when the goy, realizing he wouldn't get away with it, raised the *shtreimel* and threw it into the rush of speeding cars. He then fled back down a side street and disappeared.

My father and I watched the *shtreimel* as it rolled beneath one car and then under another and another. Beneath the speeding vehicles it looked like a helpless penny rolling, turning, spinning between flashing wheels on the black asphalt street oblivious to the trembling hat that held Hashem deep inside.

Somehow the thought passed through my mind that maybe Hashem, realizing His danger, would make the green light turn red and then the speeding cars would stop and my father would save the *shtreimel*. But He didn't. Stunned, I watched as a long, sleek limousine, its metallic tire rims flashing in the sun, rolled right over the tall fur *shtreimel* as if it were a mere hat, crushing it completely. When the light finally turned red and the limousine was long gone, all that was left of Hashem's hat was a mangled piece of fur, flat as a pancake, stuck savagely onto the black asphalt pavement.

I cried all the way back home. I wanted to know what had happened to Hashem. Was He crushed in the hat beneath the heavy wheels of the passing cars? My father hadn't even bothered to pick up the hat. He left it there in the middle of the street, saying that there was nothing left of it anyway. In tears, I looked behind me until I could no longer see the mutilated hat abandoned on the road. I wanted to tell my father that it was all my fault—my fault that Devory was dead, my fault that Hashem was crushed completely beneath the wheels of a car. I had wanted to be a goy; I kept going up to see Kathy; I had eaten five entire candies from goyland and they had been really good. But I didn't tell him. He would never believe that I could do such things, that I could hold such thoughts in my head.

My father smiled at my tears. He held my hand and said that I shouldn't worry for Hashem. He had escaped and was safely up in heaven. But he cursed the goy who had killed the hat and said that he would go straight to hell for what he had done. He called him a wild *shaygetz*, and now he would have to buy a new *shtreimel*—and they were so expensive. I asked my father if Hashem would be in his new *shtreimel* too, and he laughed and said that Hashem was wherever righteous Jewish people were.

The next day my father came home with a new *shtreimel*. He showed us the new hat, so tall and majestic with its shiny new fur. When he put into its box, he turned it gently, around and around, so all the fur would lie in one direction. He then took the hat box and placed it up on the shelf near my mother's $180 Versani shoes, and once more, it stood there, tall as my father, round as a pancake, and as confusing as Hashem.

PART TWO
2008–2010

CHAPTER
FORTY-FOUR

The price of fur had gone up. It seemed as if there were no more foxes in North America, Mr. Weiss of The Hat Store on Sixteenth Avenue said, scratching his scraggly beard behind the glossy counter. *Shtreimels* were now mostly imported from Asia. It was a bit more expensive, but what can one do?

My father didn't care. He said, "For my daughter's groom? Only the best!"

His fingers ran expertly over every strand of fur, closely observing the stitching, gently stroking the silk lining inside.

Standing near the wall-length mirror balancing the *shtreimel* on my own narrow head, I laughed. The tall fur hat fell lopsided over my face, looking absurd on my thin, brown, shoulder-length hair.

My father smiled when he saw me. "It's a heavy hat, isn't it?" he said, turning back to the *shtreimel*. "He'll get used to it. . . . Come look at this one. It's perfect."

And it was. Fur so new it glowed, so black it shone, so smooth it left a velvet touch on the skin, every last lustrous strand bent in perfect circular symmetry.

I had never been in a hat store before, had never seen the rows of black *shtreimels*, *shtreimlichs*, and fedoras, bent-downs lined up like soldiers on the slanted, dark wood shelves lining the store's walls.

"At one thousand dollars a hat, a *Chassid* only buys a *shtreimel* once in twenty years," my father had said. "It's important that you help me choose the hat that will be on your husband's head until your own child's wedding."

My mother laughed when she heard that my father and I had bought the *shtreimel*. "Hashem! She was engaged only two days ago! She still has ten months till her wedding!" But she ooohed and aaaahhhd as my father pranced proudly around the dining room table parading in the hat and said it was truly a *gezinta shtreimel*—a great hat—and that we had better put it away somewhere safe.

On December 2, six months after I had graduated from high school, one month after I had turned eighteen, and two weeks after the third girl in my class had gotten married, I had finally become engaged.

The engagement was made by Yosef Yitzchak, the *shadchan's* idea. He was *Yushive's* biggest matchmaker. He said he had thought of the *shidduch* months before I had even turned eighteen. Yosef Yitzchak the *shadchan* used to live in Borough Park before he moved to Israel five years ago. He had *davened* in my father's *shul* and they had kept in touch after he left. My father always described Yosef Yitzchak as a good man with a large heart and a larger mouth. There was no detail the man did not know about every *Yushive* family going back three generations from both sides. He knew that Mrs. Blumbaum's great-grandmother's sister, back in Lodz, Poland, in the 1900s had run away from home with Yoneh Goldberg's great-great-uncle's brother, then a neighbor, to join the Zionists. He knew that Brachala Zalts's sister had cancer, back when it was a classified secret because people still thought it to be contagious. He knew that the rich Reich family was no longer rich. They had gone bankrupt a while back, but kept it secret till he'd married off the last of his children.

My mother said Yosef Yitzchak had made over seventy *shidduchim* in the last two decades by sheer persistence. He never gave up until the families agreed and the couple was engaged. He had even once finished a *shidduch* over the phone. The groom, from Belgium, was supposed to fly into New York with his parents, but the flight was canceled and the next one was in three days. Yosef Yitzchak explained to the parents that there was no reason to wait. The poor girl was so excited, why drag it out three long days, and since when did the customary twenty-minute meeting between the boy and girl before the *L'chaim* make the marriage any better?

So they spoke on the phone and then got married and were miserable, and the *Chassid* blamed the *shadchan*, who said, "Eh! Phone or not, they would have gotten engaged the same. What's a useless conversation to blame for a bad marriage?"

But that was a rare incident. Uusally, a boy and girl had to meet for at least twenty minutes but no more than forty before the *L'chaim*, set up since the night before, to see that they weren't repulsed by each other. And if they were, there were usually ways to fix it. When my sister, Surela, met her husband, Moishe, she couldn't bear his crooked teeth, ugly glasses, and bad skin. My mother said, "Crooked teeth you can straighten, ugly glasses you can change, bad skin you can clean." The main thing was the kind of husband he would be, and she would have to get married to know that. So they got married and she got used to his crooked teeth, ugly glasses, and bad skin, and five years and three children later they were perfectly happy. He took out the garbage, helped with the children, and even cleared off the *Shabbos* table whenever they came for a meal. A true *mensch.*

Yosef Yitzchak said that the boy he had in mind was just as perfect. He had thought of it when he noticed the boy walking down the Jerusalem street where he lived. He had been looking out the window of his small apartment on a sunny afternoon when he observed a fine young *bachur,* a son of the Geldbart family, two buildings down, walking along, twirling his nice, long, curled *payos*— and a boy who knows how to curl his *payos* like that—it shows something about him, especially one strolling up a hill immersed in an energetic Talmudic discussion with himself. And that's when it hit him. Of course. It was a perfect *shidduch.*

The Geldbart family was a good one. Chaim Geldbart, the great-grandfather from Lodz, had already been a *Chassid* eighty-five years ago. He had been one of the first *Yushive Rebbe's* closest *Chassidim,* and according to Yosef Yitzchak, who swore he knew from a reliable source, the man didn't dare *pish* without asking the *Rebbe.* They say that he was so faithful to his master that when the *Rebbe* died, the poor man fell ill and never quite recovered from the shock. The Geldbarts had eleven children, all of them *Chassidim,* but *nebech* they were all killed in the Holocaust except

Lazer Geldbart, who eventually moved to Israel and opened up a small bookstore on Strauss Street.

And the boy's mother? Now, she has a real *yichus*. Her great-great-grandfather from her mother's side had met her great-great-grandfather from her father's side in the *Yushive Rebbe*'s home in Poland. The *Rebbe* had commanded they make a *shidduch* between their sixteen-year-old son and daughter back home in Lublin. It took them so long to get back home, the engaged couple did not know they were engaged until the day of the wedding. And her great-aunt Leah from the grandfather's side, who used to bake special carrot *kugel* for the *Rebbe* that only she knew how to make, was the only woman in the entire *shtetle*. Every Friday that carrot *kugel* was delivered promptly to the *Rebbe* himself, and that was the only *kugel* the holy man would eat. And her great-aunt, murdered by the Germans, may their names be erased from Earth, was the closest friend of the *Yushive Rebbe*'s second son's wife herself. A family with solid foundations, indeed.

The first time my father heard of the *shidduch*, a few weeks back, he refused to listen. Yosef Yitzchak had called him up from Jerusalem excitedly.

"*Mazel tov, mazel tov!*" he practically shouted. "Your daughter is engaged!"

"Is she?" asked my father.

"Well, she will be," he answered. "I have the perfect boy for your daughter, believe me. The *Rebbe* himself would take him for a son-in-law."

My father protested. "My daughter's not yet eighteen!" he said. "The day she turns eighteen in two weeks you can call me back. Until then, leave me alone."

So he left us alone for two weeks, until he arrived in America on some fund-raising mission for a *yeshiva*, and with a grunt and an "ahhhh, it's nice to be back," he sat down in our dining room. I listened excitedly from the kitchen to his enthusiastic banging on the table as he extolled the virtues of his next-door neighbors.

My parents were impressed.

"Chaim Geldbart, named after Lazer's father, had a small grocery with which he supported his wife and eleven children, but with his wife Golda's agreement, he stopped working so that he could spend more time with the *Rebbe*, and Golda, a Woman of Valor, a *tzaddekes* herself, took over the business." He jabbed a finger at my father's nose. "And remember the carrot *kugel* I told you about? I tell you, it was the only cake in the entire *shtetle* the *Rebbe* would eat—and if he trusted Chaim's wife's great-aunt Leah from the grandfather's side, then so could you."

My parents were very impressed.

"Everyone in Jerusalem knows the Geldbarts! You could ask who you want! Chaim is a good man with long *payos*, a longer beard, and a mind of a *rosh yeshiva*. Until today, his son learns every night with him in the main *shul*. He never misses a night."

My parents were so impressed, I could almost hear the excitement swirling through their minds.

"I'm telling you," the *shadchan* continued, clapping his palms together, "he is a *sheineh bachur*, the best! I would've taken him for my own daughter, except I don't have one, so I'm offering him to you, unless of course you don't want him, and I could call up the head of the *Yushive Yeshiva* in Israel. He would *love* to have him."

And so on, until the last cookie crumb was finished, and the bottle of soda was emptied, and my parents, holding their hands over their hearts, promised they would seriously consider the *shidduch*.

My father walked Yosef Yitzchak to the door. My mother came into the kitchen. She put the plate in the sink and chewed her lower lip the way she did when she was thinking intently about something. "Well," she finally said. "It sounds worth investigating."

"It does," I said elatedly. "But what's the boy's name?"

My mother looked at me. "The boy's name?" She blinked, then ran to the door.

"Yosef Yitzchak! Yosef Yitzchak!" she shouted. "What's the boy's name?"

"The boy?" He sounded startled. "Ah. Yes. The boy. His name . . . Eh, well, he is eighteen years old and the *Yushive Rebbe*, *Reb* Yaakov Meir, died around that time, so probably his name is Yaakov Meir, or Meir Yaakov, or something similar. The entire generation of boys born then was named after the *Rebbe*, so what else could it be?"

He chuckled. "Look," he said reassuringly. "What could his name be? It's either Yaakov or Yosef or Moishe or Srulcha! One of them for sure! Don't worry, the boy has a name, I promise. I'll find out and get right back to you."

My mother returned to the kitchen. "He said he'll find out his name."

"But what about English? He lives in Israel. Does he speak English?"

My mother ran back. "English, English! Does he speak English?"

I could hear the door open. "English you also want?" he said. "Actually, he happens to speak English. His mother grew up in Los Angeles so they speak English at home."

And the investigations began. My mother called my brothers; my father called my uncles; my cousins called their friends, and information poured in.

The boy didn't wear glasses. He was thin. There were eight children in the family and he was the fifth or sixth or seventh. My brother Yossi had once seen him when he learned in Israel in the same *yeshiva* some years back, and if he recalled correctly, he remembered that someone had pointed Geldbart out to him in the study hall and said that he was one of the best learners in the grade. He was almost sure.

My brother-in-law had actually learned with the second to the oldest Geldbart brother and said that he had a brilliant mind and could not be beaten in Talmudic debates. Yet he was also a likable man, one who thought simply of himself. The mother was thin. She volunteered twice a week at the hospital. She baked the best *lokshon kugel*—noodle strudel—in the neighborhood.

My cousin had a friend whose friend learned in the grade under the boy's grade and he promised that he was a *bachur* with many other friends and a kind heart. Did he know him personally? No. But he had seen him learning vigorously in the study hall and someone who learned vigorously in the study hall evidently had many friends and a kind heart. And he wasn't bald. He was eighteen and four months. His friends loved him. His brothers adored him. He did not have dandruff. And his name was Yankel. Yankel Geldbart.

My parents and I were satisfied: a grandfather from Lodz, a great-aunt with a chosen carrot cake, and a boy with a name. What more could a girl want?

We met on a cold, sunny December afternoon. My brother had gone to the airport to pick up the parents and the groom; my mother had chased my younger brother out of the house. She nervously spread the guests-only embroidered tablecloth in the kitchen, where we would meet, and the gold-trimmed glass cups with schnapps in the dining room. I wore a new black suit with white trimming, and my father, pacing anxiously around the table until my mother yelled that he should stand still already, smiled briefly at me and said that I already looked like a bride.

I brushed my hair again. I touched up my lipstick. My sister, Surela, had applied the makeup earlier and my mother and I had sat in front of the mirror staring intently into my reflection, trying this lipstick then that, smudging on beige eye shadow then brown, until we agreed that it was just so—not too much so I looked modern and not too little so I looked too young. I put on the Versani shoes, my first $180 high-heeled shoes, and my parents had proudly watched as I clicked precariously around the room. Now was the time to spend, they said.

My mother warned me not to wear any jewelry for the fateful meeting. "The less your in-laws see you have, the more they'll buy you," she advised me, so I removed the necklace, watch, three rings, and large pearl earrings my father had bought me, and left only the simple gold earrings my grandmother had given me for my *Bas Mitzvah*.

The house was tensely silent as we waited. My father swayed over a Talmud, my mother rearranging the crystal salad bowls for the fourth time. When the bell rang my parents jumped. They stared at each other in terror, and I burst out laughing. My mother reached the door first. My father, tossing the Talmud on the shelf, ran after her. My mother turned the lock. My father fumbled with the doorknob. Together they opened the door.

I stood near the dining room table as my parents politely welcomed in the Geldbart family. Mrs. Geldbart looked as she did in the pictures we received: a short, slender woman wearing an elegant shoulder-length wig framing a soft, pretty face. She wore a classy beige suit with intricate gold buttons and matching flat shoes. I liked her immediately.

"Hello." She smiled widely, embracing me gently. "You look as pretty as you do in the pictures."

I blushed. My parents, each pulling out a chair by the table, asked them how the flight was, how many hours they waited at the airport, was it too cold for them, they must be used to a warmer climate after all. . . . And of course, hiding behind his father, was Yankel, the *bachur*, the *tzaddik*, the *mensch*—a tall, thin *Chassid*, nervously twirling his *payos* and pulling at his small, dark blond beard as if trying to make it grow longer.

In the picture Yosef Yitzchak had brought us, Yankel had light green eyes. Now, as he stood close behind his father, concentrating intently on the strawberry shortcake at the corner of the table, I couldn't see his eyes at all. He looked down, jutting his head up occasionally as our parents smiled, nodded, and chatted—and finally, smiling sweetly, motioned for us to meet alone.

Yankel followed me to the kitchen. My mother, with a small, apprehensive smile, closed the door behind us. We sat down at the table. He stared at the tablecloth with fascinated interest, his fingers nervously outlining the embroidered flowers, as I stared at his pale face, deeply relieved that I didn't have to talk at all.

Yankel spoke quickly. He looked down, blinked his eyes, and

mumbled something about the *Rebbe* and how he was told by him to speak to me about the sacredness of marriage. In the *Talmud* it speaks about a Torah scholar who, though he was one of the greatest of his generation, never married. After he died and went up to heaven, he was told that he could not enter Hashem's presence because he had not completed his soul's work. He must go back down to Earth and marry. Only then could he enter the gates of heaven.

I observed Yankel's nose. It certainly wasn't bad. It was narrow at the sides but rounded out nicely in the front. He had the looks of his mother with the same smooth skin and large eyes, and the beard of his father, short and scraggly, stubbornly refusing to grow a respectable length, though my brother-in-law's was much worse. Having a nice beard was really all a matter of luck. *Chassidim* did not trim or touch facial hair in any way. In the Torah it said, "You shall not round off the corners of your heads, and you shall not destroy the corners of your beard," and this has been the law for generations.

At the end of the short speech, while I was observing his ears, Yankel said that he and his father had gone to the *Rebbe* before leaving Israel and he had blessed the *shidduch*. He then sat at the table in silence, his eyes darting from one embroidered flower to the other as I thought of something appropriate to say. Perhaps I would ask him about the story of his great-aunt toiling at the carrot *kugel*. But I could not say a word. I had never met a strange boy before in my life and knew nothing about the Talmud, so what was there to discuss? And after five minutes of awkward silence, Yankel's finger patterns growing more frenzied, I pitied the tablecloth my mother had so meticulously ironed, and stood up. He stood up quickly after me. We both breathed a sigh of relief and the meeting was over.

L'chaim!

- - -

The flowers arrived from all over that night. Our dining room looked like a blooming garden had sprouted from the granite floors as the bell rang incessantly and bouquets of every size and shape and color came through the door.

I spoke with my new sisters-in-law, cousins, and aunts on the phone to Israel, stumbling over the Hebrew and English until we just settled for *Mazel tov, Mazel tov! Mazel tov!!* MAZEL TOV! I ran to the door when my friends arrived, struggling through the doorway with a mass of balloons, and we screeched and screamed unintelligibly over the occasion. They wanted to know exactly how many minutes I'd met with him and how he looked and what had I heard about him. Was he brilliant, compassionate, pious, smart, and was his beard shorter or longer than Rivky's groom's, whose beard was so long he tucked it under his chin and stuck in bobby pins? Did my mother-in-law give me jewelry, did they have money, who was going to buy the *shaitel*, the wig, and oh, what was his name? Panting, I said that I have absolutely no idea, I can't remember, I would have to ask my mother-in-law.

That night I smiled, shook hands, hugged, screamed, giggled, was kissed with lipsticks of every brand and color, switched to shaking with my left hand, and grinned so brightly, I thought my hands and my jaw would fall off.

Half the Geldbart family lived in New York, so I met Bubba Yuskovitz from the mother's side, Zaida Geldbart from the father's side, Aunt Zisel from one of the sides, and Bubba Geldbart, who had come along from Israel especially for the occasion. Various relatives I did not know existed wandered in and out wearing elegant clothing and pretty smiles. My mother rattled off first names, last names, and long convoluted family connections to me as I nodded my head blankly and listened to every person I knew or didn't who had heard from his uncle, brother-in-law, cousin, or whatever, what a genius, *tzaddik*, and *mensch* Yaakov Mier/Mier Yaakov Geldbart was.

My mother-in-law, squeezing through the boisterous crowd, excitedly called my name. She held up a small blue velvet box and my mother squeezed my shoulder hard and said, "It better be big."

And big it was. Aunt Sarah grabbed my hand, held it up closely to her eye, and declared it was at least one and a half karats. Zaida Geldbart, who hobbled over from the men's side, nudging everyone out of the way, said it was more. My friends oohhed and aahhhd and said it was the most stunning ring they'd seen, and my mother, satisfied with the respectable size, said who cares, the marriage is what is important, not the diamond.

The crowd spread back out to the cakes and ice cream tables and Bubba Yuskovitz, giggling like a little girl, hobbled eagerly over to me, stretching out two trembling hands. She hugged me tightly, straightened my collar, and waggled a finger in my face. She stepped back, shook her short, curly wig, and observed me, her eyes widening and narrowing as she moved from the bottom of my shoes up to the top of my hair. "You are too skinny. How are you going to have all those babies?" She wiped her eyes and sniffed dramatically. "Oh, but you are beautiful. Perfect. Perfect for Yankel. He will be the best husband. I know, I know—let me tell you I took care of him when he was a tiny baby before they moved to Israel, and even when you are a baby you can tell a lot about you. Yankel, he was just a little *pisher*, but oh what a *pisher*. His little *pipikel* the size of a jelly bean it was. But I'm telling you—he used to *pish* so hard, it spritzed straight up and hit the ceiling like that. I still have a stain on my ceiling. Not one of my grandsons could do it like that." And she put her hands on her cheeks, sighing. "*Oy*, my little *pisher*, all grown up and engaged. . . . I just can't believe it, I can't believe it. In my days girls weren't so skinny." And she hobbled away toward my mother, who was holding a tray of ice cream.

More flowers arrived; more people came and left. My father snuck in from the men's side to see my ring. There was no room for the plants inside, so my mother began lining them up on the porch. It was well past midnight when the house finally emptied and Yankel and I posed for pictures, I, on one side of the room, he on the other, as it wasn't appropriate for an unmarried couple to stand closely together. But my mother complained that she couldn't get us both into the lenses, would we move in a little more; my mother-in-law hastily placed three large flower arrangements on the floor between us so we were only eight feet apart. Two limp smiles, a flash, and now I had pictures to show off to my friends. Pictures were an important part of one's engagement and my friend and I, using a ruler, measured precisely how many feet stood between each couple in their engagement pictures. The really *Chassidish* ones stood so far apart you could see only half of each person; the normal *Chassidish*, like me, only several feet; the modern *Chassidish* left barely a few inches between them. But none of this was really important of course. Flowers, pictures, jewelry. . . . The crucial thing was that I had my groom tucked safely away in *yeshiva* for the next ten months, as my father tenderly said, "Ah, marriage. . . . Only Hashem could come up with that idea. . . . You have ten months to pray, Gittel, ten months to pray. . . ."

CHAPTER FORTY-FIVE

And pray I did. I prayed I would have a happy marriage, I prayed that I would recognize him in ten months, three hundred and ten days, seven thousand, four hundred and forty or so hours when I would see him for the second time under the canopy. I also prayed that we would have something to talk about. What *would* we talk about now that I was thinking about it? But when I asked my mother she said it would all come, and she spread twenty-one pictures of me on the table as we worked on the *kallah* album, the customary gift to the mother-in-law, showing pictures of the new daughter-in-law from babyhood to bridehood.

I sifted through the pictures, laying them out in order of age. There was only one picture of me as a toddler. The rest were of me as an adolescent.

"Mommy, where are all my baby pictures?" I asked.

"Oh, here." My mother thrust a picture of one-year-old me, smiling, my right arm cut right down the middle where it reached out to someone else.

"Wasn't that Dev—"

"We could blow it up, make it bigger, you can't tell," my mother said brightly, scribbling some ideas on a paper.

I held up the strange-looking picture. "Don't I have any pictures of myself, I mean—"

"We should go shopping in Amazing Savings," my mother interrupted. "They have some adorable scrap paper and pretty knickknacks you could play around with. This is your first gift to your mother-in-law, so it has to be impressive."

"But it looks weird," I said. "I need baby pictures. I can't start from fifth—"

"Oh, I know!" my mother exclaimed. "Rivkah has pictures of you! Remember when you were in second grade our two families went on a trip to the safari park together?"

Rivkah was my father's *litvish* sister from Lakewood, New Jersey. We used to go on outings with her that I did not remember, when she still lived nearby in Borough Park with my then-small cousins.

My mother snapped her fingers. "That's it! Call her up and ask her to send over the pictures. She had the camera then and kept promising to send over the photos. Of course, I never saw a single picture and then totally forgot about it. There should be some really nice ones."

So I called up Aunt Rivkah, and she said, sure, of course, she would send over the pictures right away. She also said it was ridiculous, *Chassidish* boys getting married so young. Before twenty-one, she declared, she would never let her son as much as think of dating.

"What's an eighteen-year-old boy?" she proclaimed. "He's just a little *shnuck* who doesn't know his right from his left!"

But my mother, sitting on the chair near mine, overheard the

statement and grabbed the phone. She told her that boys sitting
and learning all day in their cloistered *yeshivos* didn't know their
right from their left any more than when they were twenty-five
than when they were eighteen, and the only way for one to learn
one's right from one's left was to get married. That was when real
life started, and would she just mail over the pictures, we needed
to send the album.

My *litvish* aunt from Lakewood and my mother had never gotten along quite that well. My mother said that she was a narrow-
minded *litvish* who thought only the *litvish* were holy. She called
my mother a small-headed *Chassidustah* who knew only about
Chassidim, but my father said it was really all about a fight they
had that nobody remembered anymore twenty years before when
my aunt had called my mother a fatso after my mother had called
her a *ganuv* and a thief because she had taken the larger share of
silver after my great-uncle had died.

"There is really barely a difference between *Chassidim* and the
litvish today," my father said. After all, he chuckled wryly, "Every
Jew today learns Torah, wears a hat, and believes he is the chosen
within the chosen."

My aunt wasn't just *litvish*. She was *Yeshivish*, a group whose
name derived from the word *yeshiva*, study hall. Back in Lithuania
in the late 1800s, *Reb* Shapiro Lubling, one of the greatest Torah
scholars of the century, opened the doors of the first *yeshiva*—a
place where young men would come, leaving their families and
homes behind, and dedicate themselves completely to a life of
Torah learning. The idea spread fast among the *litvish* and then
the *Chassidish*. In a deteriorating world where morality was sinking fast into the dark abyss, they realized that it was Torah, only

Torah, that could save the Jews from the darkness. It was Torah, only the sweet sounds of Torah learning, the swaying of a thousand bearded Jews, that would stand as the spiritual pillar and support for a joyless world of goyim and materialism.

But what had started out as a small exclusive group back in Lithuania quickly grew over the decades to a phenomenon unseen in the history of the Jews, a mass production of Torah scholars, an ideal that turned into the law, especially among the *litvish*. And it was in Lakewood, a small city in New Jersey, where cheaper housing could be found, that the core group of *Yeshivish* families settled, quickly growing into a city of ten thousand scholars. A place so holy, they said, that the beautiful sounds of Torah learning rose up to the heavens creating a halo over the polluted skies of New Jersey.

My aunt from Lakewood was a true Woman of Valor, an *Eishes Chayil*, she said so herself. Years before, when she had had her fifth child, she had spoken with the famous *Reb* Aharon Kotler, Grand Rabbi of Lakewood, and had asked him whether her husband should go out to work now that they had no money for food.

"No," he had ruled. "There is no greater reward in heaven than for a woman who encourages her husband to bury himself in the wisdom of Torah." And bury himself he did while my aunt supported her growing family by teaching in the local high school in the morning, tutoring at night, sewing after midnight, and giving birth to a blessed child every January.

"I have eleven children," she once boasted to anybody who bothered listening, "and all seven sons and three-sons-in-law are learning only because of the Torah they saw at home, because we listened to the *tzaddik*, the angel in the body of man, *Reb* Aharon Kotler."

But my aunt had a terrible secret. Avigdor, son number three, father of six children, named after Avigdor Miller, the greatest scholar of this generation and last, had left *yeshiva* to go to work not long before. My aunt had cried as hard as my mother would have had my brother removed his *shtreimel*. She sobbed brokenly to my father on the phone that the way to heaven was lost, if she, *she*, had a son who had stopped learning Torah for something as trivial as bringing food home to his family.

In fact, Aunt Bluma's daughter, Chevi, just a few months older than I was, had recently gotten engaged to Chaim Kamenetsky, a budding scholar. Well, they almost broke off the engagement when my aunt and uncle found out that the budding scholar was attending the gym twice a week to exercise. Exercise? My aunt was aghast. "I don't know," she fretted. "It *past nisht*, it sounds wrong. What *yeshiva bachur* who takes Torah seriously does *exercise*?" Only Chevi herself, insistent on getting married, promised she would persuade him to stop the offending action after the wedding. Exercising for a boy was really a strange idea. It was a waste of Torah time and showed that his head was elsewhere, and I knew that if Yankel exercised, the *shidduch* would never have come through.

Chevi and I had become close friends as teenagers. Though we had grown up in different cities, we often visited each other for *Shabbosim* and attended the largest seminary in New York, *Bais Yaakov* Teacher's Training Seminary, together. Shortly after my engagement, we went strolling down Thirteenth Avenue after seminary browsing through stores and discussing our upcoming weddings, when we passed by Boutique Lingerie. A bright orange sign on the window declared a half price sale on all items inside. We ran inside looking through the rows of bathrobes, nightgowns, and

lingerie, when Chevi—with a small gasp of excitement—tore a
hanger off the rod.

"Look!" she said.

I looked.

The nightgown was sleeveless, it was short, it had a slit at the
side. It was gold satin, cut low in the chest, with barely two strings
to hold the whole thing up.

"What is that?" I asked in shock.

"It's a nightgown for my wedding night!" Chevi answered giddily, holding up the nightgown like a prize. "The bedroom is a
place where you're supposed to attract your husband."

"What?" I envisioned Yankel's pale face upon seeing the nightgown.

"Yes!" she said, carefully folding the garment. "You're supposed
to attract your husband so you can have a good relationship."

Yankel, I believe, just fainted somewhere.

"If a man doesn't feel fulfilled with his wife," Chevi explained,
"then he can't concentrate on learning Torah."

I considered fainting myself.

"If a man is fulfilled with learning Torah," I retorted, "then he
doesn't need all this *shtism*! And what does a nightgown from goyland have to do with a good relationship?"

Chevi grimaced. "Of course it has to do. It says in the Talmud
that a woman is supposed to attract her own husband."

"It says in the Talmud that a man is supposed to watch his
eyes . . . even in his own home."

Chevi continued to clutch the devious nightgown.

"The most important thing is Torah, that a man's mind should
be only on Torah and not on anything else. If a man is satisfied in

the bedroom, then he is not distracted and can think only holy thoughts."

I didn't know what she was talking about and told her that with a nightgown like that a man would be distracted out of his brain. How can one's lips repeat the holy words with visions of satin cloth held up by two strings waving in one's mind!

Chevi turned to me furiously. She said that I had no idea what I was saying, the *litvish* who put a greater emphasis on Torah learning were much holier, the *Chassidish* just knew how to dance around their *Rebbe* and curl their long *payos*.

I said that I had never heard such nonsense. The *litvish* thought that as long as you sway over the Torah, you are the holiest. One has to apply what is *in* the Torah to life, and wearing *goyishe* clothes is not part of it.

She said that of course the *litvish* apply Torah learning to life. She would never let her husband as much as wipe one dish because then three seconds of Torah learning are lost. A husband is not expected to lift a finger, so he can concentrate on Torah every second of the day.

"It says in the Torah that behaving like a *mensch* comes before learning Torah," I retorted. "If a man can't help his own wife and family, his Torah learning is not worth the dish she is washing and a relationship is dependent on respect to each other, not on a nightgown," and on and on until we were out of breath and decided to stop the useless argument and go have pizza at Mendel's.

When I told my mother of Chevi's nightgown and the dish her husband would never wipe, she said that they had their own way of doing things and we had ours. And anyway, we should not be having these discussions. What each couple did behind closed doors was absolutely no one else's business. She then took out a pile of fashion catalogs and we began leafing through them.

Though there were still some months until my wedding night, my mother decided we would do our shopping right then. There were holidays, other weddings, work, and who knows what else in between now and the big night and relying on time was never a good idea.

We had already begun shopping for clothing. We combed through Macy's, cleared out Lord & Taylor, and began exploring Bloomingdale's. We made long lists of items needed, stores to check out, and hints to convey to the in-laws. There was the Wedding Night Itself, The Day After, and Life in General, which required an exhaustive investigative committee of experienced wedding people that included my aunt—who married off five; my second cousin—seven; and my mother's former classmate Mrs. Frish and her eleven daughters. Shoes, clothes, lingerie, head coverings, house appliances, linen—all this needed expert advice on what to buy where, and for how much, and most important of all, how long it would last. Elegant's linen lasted at least until the third child's bed-wetting. We weren't to bother with cheaper brands; they could barely absorb one child's vomit. Ralph's shoes with three-inch heels were good until the sixth month of the first pregnancy; Versani, though, was a better choice. Mrs. Frish had stumbled in them until at least the seventh month of the seventh child, when the heel broke clean off the shoe right in the middle of Thirteenth Avenue and she had to hobble to the nearest car service with the twins in the carriage. Wilhelm's porcelain plates were by far the best—my cousin knew. Her sons had used them for trampolines and most of the set remained intact. And as for the fridge, and most appliances, we were to go directly, without turning our heads in any direction, to Yoily's Electronic. They were the cheapest, installed them for free, and even had a package deal where you could get a washer and dryer at a discount.

We ran from store to store, comparing prices, bargaining with the salesmen, making lists for the lists. By the end of the week, my mother had purchased the dishes, towels, and cutlery, my grandmother had pledged a dryer, my aunt a mixer, my friends the cookbooks, and my sister-in-law two sets of fine linen, but she had promised to buy me a bracelet for my *Bas Mitzvah* five years earlier—and hadn't—so I decided not to wait.

As for clothing, it never ended. There was the Before, when a bride had to look like a bride, the After, when a just-married bride had to look like a just-married bride, and the General After After, which my mother insisted was not an excuse to look like a *shluch*. There was the elegant wear for *Shabbos* and special events, the elegant-but-simpler-wear for work and every day, and the very-simple-but-still-elegant wear for staying home.

Dressing a bride, she said, was a mission unto its own, and she had five sons but only two daughters on which to spend her life savings. She strode purposefully through the wide aisles of every store in New York City, chewing her lips, narrowing her eyes, clicking her heels as she picked out clothing of every design and texture and tried to predict which one Pessy, the only daughter of her best friend, Goldy, would never buy. A month before, my mother had bought me an expensive suit for Sarah Leah's upcoming wedding. After long deliberations, we had purchased the suit at Estee's Exclusive on Coney Island for a price she never told my father about, only to see Pessy wearing the very same dress at the very same wedding after Estee had explicitly promised that she would sell it to no other *Yushive* girl.

This time my mother took no chances. Every dress was scrutinized, redesigned on paper, and sewn up in a slightly different version by the good Asian seamstress Dia, whom Goldy did not use. The dresses were stylish and elegant but modest, the way a Jewish girl should look.

Then there were the shoes. The saleslady at the new Shoe Center store recognized my mother from seminary some thirty years before, and they laughed as they reminisced about this teacher and that, and how one absolutely needed two shades of black because patent leather reflected differently on silk black than on velvet black.

And the lingerie. A girl had to stock up on practical items, and my mother bought two wired bras, three wireless bras, and two and three of the same in a bigger size for when I got pregnant. A dozen liners to wear beneath every outfit, lest the strap of the bra or such immodest sight could be seen, a dozen slips, flimsy silk skirts to wear beneath the first skirt for the same reason. We also bought a few long simple nightgowns, with wrist-length sleeves and ankle-length hems that buttoned up to my collarbone.

"Romance, shmomance," my mother scoffed at the modern Orthodox saleslady when she suggested something more "you-know" for the young bride. "You want your husband to respect you in the kitchen, between the dirty dishes, and not only under the starlit sky with makeup. . . ."

And the wig—the hair-covering that symbolized the higher level attained upon entering womanhood. The two-thousand-dollar, 100 percent human hair wig that announced to the world—at least the one that noticed that it wasn't my hair—that I was married! A wig to cover my hair, the way every *Eishes Chayil* had done since the rabbis had legislated so some ten centuries back, and even Hashem dared not disagree.

But choosing a wig in itself was a complicated matter. Pregnant Shany said I should buy only Shevy's. It was two thousand dollars but worth every penny. Chani, snorting loudly, said, No way, Shevy was nothing more than a brand name and I should go with Glida's, which was cheaper, had a two-year guarantee, and lasted just as long. Surela said not to listen to any of them and to purchase a Frieda that had hair as soft as silk and a cap as comfortable as a slipper. There were endless brands sold throughout Brooklyn, and I sat for many an hour in wig salons trying on wigs of every shape and color until we finally settled on a Chevi's that was almost like the Shevy's, with a guarantee as long as Glida's and a cap as comfortable as Frieda's slipper.

I discussed all this and more with my friends for long hours on the phone, until my mother told me that none of this stuff was important. The main part of marriage preparation was not the shoes, clothing, and other *shtism* we had just spent ten thousand dollars and three months shopping on, but the bridal classes—the premise and foundation of a Jewish marriage.

It was in the bridal class that Mrs. Kryman taught Jewish women about the beauty and sanctity of the Jewish marriage. It was there a woman studied the laws of family purity and the premises of the Jewish nation. It was there she realized her sacred role as an *Eishes Chayil*, a wife, homemaker, and mother.

And it was there I learned that beneath the fine white linen, the one my sister-in-law was supposed to buy and the saleslady

promised would last until my third child, I was supposed to do
the strangest thing. Only three weeks before the wedding, after the
last bridal class, Mrs. Kryman had a private lesson with each bride.
And it was there, in her small, moldy basement, with the door
closed and window shades pulled down and a bottle of water
standing vigilantly by, that she told me that, No, we did not do *it*
with needles, and no, Hashem did not do *it* Himself. With a prayer
on my lips and a fear of Hashem in my heart, I must open my legs
and receive my husband.

I blinked.

Whyever would I do that?

Mrs. Kryman stared at me intently. When I had looked back
at her blankly for long enough, she continued.

"Every soul is divided in half when sent down to Earth. It is
marriage that unites them and once more the soul is complete. But
there are three partners in a marriage, as I taught you—the woman,
the man, and Hashem. Whatever you do in marriage, especially
in the intimacy of the bedroom, you must always remember the
holy presence is there, right with you, and you must treat the relationship with Hashem with the sacred respect it deserves. You have
to always think: what kind of space are you creating for Hashem in
your own home—will it be one of *shmutz*, dirt, and materialism or
purity and holiness? And with that thought always in your mind,
that is how you take every step of your life. But in order to fulfill
the most important *mitzvah* where Hashem commanded to be fruit-
ful and multiply, man and woman must come together and do *it*. *It*
is the most important *mitzvah* in the Torah. *It* is what enables us to
do our sacred duty and obligation, which is the essence and purpose of marriage. *It* is what gives us the privilege to give birth to

precious Jewish souls and raise them in the way of Hashem. *It* is
what allows us to be true *Chassidim* by obeying the way we do *it*
from the way the *Rebbe* from three generations ago and down told
us. *It* is what—well, okay, this is how you do *it*."

She drummed her pen on the table and closed her eyes. She
mumbled a short prayer, and in a flat, monotonous voice proceeded:
when we came home from the wedding, I was to pull up my nightgown to the waist—no more—lie in bed with the light off, spread
my legs, and with a prayer on my lips and fear in my heart, my husband would come onto me and do *it*.

She poured me a cup of water. I moved my seat a few inches
away from her.

"*It* will only take a few minutes," she reassured me. "You have
to remember that *it* is a *mitzvah* from the Torah and the obligation
of every man and wife. But the most imporatant part of *it* is that
during *it* one must pray with all one's power that one's children
should be blessed by Hashem and the *Rebbe* and the angels." She
banged her pen on a notepad for emphasis. "For it is at that crucial moment, that most crucial moment, when a Jewish soul is
sent down from heaven, that every word of prayer will influence
the kind of person that child will be."

She was silent.

"Do you have any questions?" she asked.

I had none.

She then spoke of the *Rebbe*, and how it was important for a
Chassid to keep close to him to maintain the level of holiness he
had had undisturbed in *yeshiva*. How I was to encourage Yankel to
go to the *Rebbe*, to learn, to keep his eyes clean and heart pure,
and some other things I was to do or not that I heard not a word

of. My head felt heavy, my feet felt light, and I walked unsteadily out the door as she called after me that *it* was all *L'Shem Shamayim*—in the name of heaven.

I came home and sat in my room for a long time. My world had just fallen apart. I needed desperately to discuss it with someone, anyone, who wasn't my mother. The betrayal that she had had me in such an unfathomably un-*Chassidish* manner was too much. I had known there was something mysterious that had to be done. Hindy had once spoken to me of the matter. She had said that goyim did things you wouldn't believe in order to have a baby, things like Mrs. Kryman had explained to me. But Hindy had said with certainty, we did it with needles or a squirter. The man put something into the squirter (or needle) and the women squirted it inside. From there, Hashem took care of things. People who did things the goyim did were terrible. It was un-Jewish, forbidden— and like rape. Miranda had explained it to me then. She had clearly said when a male forces his thing into a girl's thing, it is called rape. I had never known that there were two different kinds: one like *that* and one to have babies.

I called up my sister.

"Um, Surela," I began, almost crying, and though my mother was still at work, I kept peering out into the hallway. "Um . . . um . . . I just came back from Mrs. Kryman's last class. . . . She says that . . . she said that . . . that . . ."

My sister listened to me fumble for a few minutes and then burst out laughing.

"*Oy*, Gittel," she said breezily. "Don't worry. Everyone goes through the same thing. You sound pretty good though. I didn't talk to Mommy for a week after I had that lesson. I know, I know, right now you think it's the end of the world, but in a year you'll laugh at yourself because that's how Hashem created the world and that's how it goes. It's just something that has to be done, and it gets better with time—usually—and if you think you have it bad, the men have it worse. They're told the day of the wedding, when *Reb* Ehrlich talks to them a few hours before and tells them what they have to do. It makes sense that way, because if they told them a few weeks before they'd be walking around like ghosts and not learning one word of anything. So this way they get over it fast. You remember the day I got married—when my husband fainted before the *chuppah*? In fact, he had fainted three times that day. . . . *Oy*, don't ask. But don't worry," she said casually. "Everything works out in the end. . . . Oh boy, am I happy it's five years later. You know what Mommy told me after that week I didn't talk to her? She came into my room and said one sentence: 'If the *Rebbe* can do it, so can we'—*oy gevald*. It's so late, I have to run take Leah'la from the babysitter. Okay, I'll talk to you later. Come by and I'll help you choose the colors for the invitations. Bye!"

I tried not to think about *it* as I ran to the store to buy more shoes, more linen, another tablecloth for *Shabbos* in case the first one got dirty.

It was ten days before the wedding. I was organizing long lists of invitees. My mother was in the other room generating lists of lists of the lists we hadn't yet listed when my father entered and said something, and their tones suddenly, conspicuously lowered to a whisper. My ears instantly pricked up.

". . . But she might be so insulted if I don't send her an invitation. As if she is no longer in existence. . . . I don't know what to do. . . ."

My father's deep voice: "No, no, don't send anything. Can you imagine how painful it will be for her, our daughter walking down the aisle, while Devory is buried somewhere? It will be too painful. Besides, you haven't spoken to her in years. . . ."

"I know. . . . I couldn't. . . . Every time she would hear Gittel's voice from our side of the line it was as if she was accusing me for having a daughter that was alive. Those two were like sisters. . . . It just cut our relationship afterward. She couldn't take it and I couldn't either. It was better for both of us this way and certainly for Gittel. . . ."

". . . But what if she finds out? I mean, *of course* she'll find out that Gittel's getting married, someone or other will tell them, and they'll be so hurt. . . . I don't know what to tell you. . . ."

"You know what I'll do? I think I'll call up Miriam, their oldest. She lives in Monsey now. . . . I'll ask her what to do."

I walked into the room with a question about some names. The conversation stopped. My mother picked up a box of crackers on the desk and put one in her mouth.

"Come, Gittel," she said, walking back into the dining room. "Let's finish those invitations already. They are haunting my dreams."

As I sat down across from her she said distractedly, "Your mother-in-law just called before. She finally sent the watch with Bubba Yuskovitz, who just came back from visiting them in Israel. Go tomorrow to her house, she lives on Twelfth and Forty-fifth Street, pick it up and be nice to her. She's all excited to see her new *kallah*, don't ask. Your mother-in-law told me she is preparing a whole meal over there. . . ."

She took the phone book from me and began swiftly checking

off names, the edge of the cracker between her front teeth. The pen hovered over column G, Goldblatt, the third name from the top, but only for a second. Then in short blunt strokes, she crossed it off.

"That watch better be big," she muttered to herself. "It better be big."

CHAPTER FORTY-SIX

And then it was my wedding day, the holiest day of a person's life, the day a Jew is reborn. The day the bride and groom are reunited with the lost half of their soul the day Hashem forgives them for all past transgressions, the day they recite the Yom Kippur confession in their prayers, the entire Book of Psalms. The day they are finally complete. It is a day of rebirth, of forgiveness, of fasting. A day devoted to blessings and prayer from sunrise until the makeup lady arrived at 12:30 (though she was supposed to arrive at 12:00 sharp). The day that the hair stylist decided to come down with the flu and my sister-in-law lost the pearl-decorated hairpins. The day my sister did not answer the phone the entire morning. When did she think the wedding was anyway? And the belt on my mother's gown ripped at the back—she would never use that seamstress again. The day my father paced around, smiling sadly, and urging us to hurry, *nu*, hurry. We had to be in the hall at three p.m.—the photographer was *waiiitinnng!*

The makeup, wig, tiara, gown. Pictures in the hall with my mother posing at my side, her hands on my shoulders, in my hands, on my back, hugging me while facing the camera, the wall, the door. My nieces lined up in front of me, looking up at me, sitting in a circle around me.

And then it was my *chuppah*. My family and friends stood tearfully around me. My father, Yankel, and a small crowd of men walked toward me. My eyes clenched tight in prayer as Yankel, holding a white veil, threw it hastily over my head and then my father, his hands placed gently on my head, whispered words of prayers as he blessed me. And blessed me and blessed me, until my mother, sobbing into a handkerchief, whispered angrily into his ear, "Are you *meshugah*? Bless her after! The music is almost finished," and then, my crying mother on one side, my sniffling mother-in-law on the other, we walked slowly up to the *chuppah* room and down the aisle to Yankel, shaking like a *lulav*—a palm tree frond—under the canopy, and my father, standing stoically, staring at the floor, as we circled the groom to the cantor's wailing.

Though I could not see through my veil or my tears, I could hear the sobs of my sister, and relatives praying for me, and the cantor as he called up my uncles, grandfather, and *Reb* Ehrlich to recite the blessings of the ceremony. And then from underneath my veil, I saw a trembling hand holding a gold band and I quickly pushed my finger through. More prayers, more blessings, more tears, and finally after three attempts, a smashing of a glass cup, and *Mazel tov!* Yankel—who *pished* so high it hit the ceiling—and I were married.

My mother threw off my veil. She hugged me tightly, and crying so hard her makeup would certainly have to be redone, kissed me and screamed something over the booming music that I could not hear. My mother-in-law, wiping her tears carefully with a silk handkerchief, hugged me gently, held my hand in hers, and said something else I couldn't hear but nodded my head to. Then Yankel and I, timidly holding hands, hurried down the aisle, up the elevator, and into the *Yichud* room, a room where, according to the law, a bride and groom must sit together for a half hour or so.

First we ate. Starving after our day's fast, we washed our hands, ate challah, and gulped down the hot soup placed on the table. Then we drank. And waited for the next course. And stared at the table. And at the pictures on the wall. Yankel smiled awkwardly. His nose hadn't changed. His beard had grown maybe an inch. He looked mostly the same, except taller—and of course he was wearing the *shtreimel* my father and I had bought him.

"The . . . the challah is good," he said.

"Yes," I said.

He flushed. "Which . . . which bakery do you buy challah in?"

"Um. We make challah at home. . . ."

"Oh."

We ate the chicken.

"My friend . . . he lives here, Eckstein, you know Eckstein?

"Um. Yes. I mean, there are four Ecksteins—yes, I know the family."

"He said Weiss's Bakery is . . . is the best."

"Oh."

The waiter brought in the dessert. We looked at it intently.

Yankel told me something, but I was nervously thinking about what to answer back and I did not hear. Yankel gave me a folded paper and said that he had written down a special prayer his mother had given him and said that it was a good omen, a *segulah*, for the new couple to say it at the beginning of their marriage. Quietly we prayed. I prayed that my mother would come fast. I prayed that she would get us out of there. That didn't happen. They left us in the room for a long time. After two Torah sermons by Yankel, a long pause, and an awkward silence, I finally opened the door, called a passing waiter, and asked him to go call Mrs. Klein, the one in the long blue gown.

Finally a clicking of heels over the marble floor announced my mother's arrival. She breathlessly explained that she had completely forgotten about us, there were so many people coming, you wouldn't believe it. Even the *Rebbe*'s first cousin who came from Israel yesterday showed up, and a bunch of others she hadn't seen since she was in high school, and they all had to be greeted, seated, and fed. And anyway it was time for dancing—come on, let's go. Relieved, we left the room, and Yankel went to the men's side, I, to the women's.

The music began. The crowd gathered in a close circle around me. I danced that night. Boy, did I dance. I danced with my ecstatic mother, my sniffling mother-in-law, and every *bubba* and great-aunt who could hobble across the dance floor clutching on to my arms for dear life. I danced with my aunts from my mother's side, cousins from my father's side, my relations from my in-laws' sides, and every person who knew my family from before the war. I danced with my teachers from high school, my principal from elementary, and Bubba Yuskovitz, who kept tottering over with a cup of water, pushing everyone away so the poor bride could drink, *nu*, drink, drink more. I danced with my friends who were married, my friends who were almost married, my friends who were dying to get married, and those who should have been married because they were a full year older than I was.

Then Kathy entered the circle. I had invited Kathy a few weeks earlier, over my mother's objections. My mother had not wanted that woman near her daughter's holiest night. We had argued about it all day. Finally, I had told my mother that it was my holiest night, not hers, and I was inviting Kathy whether she agreed or not. My father agreed. He said that Kathy had been our neighbor for years and had been my friend since I was a small child and it was only right to invite her.

I had spotted Kathy through my veil under the *chuppah*, her wild red hair and elegant, white silk pants sticking out in a hall filled with dark suits and wigs. Right after the *chuppah*, on the way to the elevator, I had noticed her babbling to my aunt from Lakewood, who was nodding impatiently at the side. Now Kathy happily strode into the circle and danced with me around and around, exclaiming how this was her first Jewish wedding and it was so beautiful. She wanted badly to congratulate the groom, she said, and would do so as soon as we finished dancing. I explained very loudly over the music that the groom was safely on the men's side and perhaps some other day she could congratulate him.

She said, "Oh—that wouldn't be polite! I gotta tell him what a beautiful bride he got right now! I'll go to the men's part for just one minute!"

I shook my head emphatically. "Oh, no! You don't want to do that. *Not* a good idea! *Don't!* After the wedding, okay?" I envisioned Kathy striding happily into the section of bewildered *Chassidim* and right up to the stunned groom, who had never spoken to a goy before.

So Kathy stood nearby instead, cheering and applauding everyone who danced with me. She also told anyone who would listen
that she was my neighbor, and I was a pretty, pretty baby whose
eyes changed color from green to dark when I was just this small
and the songs I used to sing—and so on. During dessert, between
dances, she sat next to me at the head table, right in my mother's
seat (she was hosting the guests) and regaled me with tales of her
own wedding and her grandmother, who fainted right in the middle of it after drinking one cup too much, never to wake up again.

Three hours and a worn pair of white shoes later, the dancing
was over. Kathy asked if I wanted her to stay, but I hugged her
tightly and explained that the rest was just for family and relatives. Kathy kissed me softly. She said she had never seen me quite
so stunning, and she just knew I would have a long and happy life.

Long lines of people saying *mazel tov* still trickled in and out
of the hall. Eventually, only close family and friends were left,
awaiting the holiest part of the wedding, the *Mitzvah Tantz*.

The *Mitzvah Tantz* is an ancient *Chassidic* custom with a basis
in the Talmud. It is when the father, uncles, and groom dance in
front of the bride after the wedding feast. It is the time of the wedding where the spirits and souls of the ancestors come down from
heaven to bless and dance with the young couple on the holiest
night of their lives.

The partitions separating the genders were pushed away and
the chairs were set up so that men and women face one another
across the hall. A *badchan*—a comedian—stood on a chair in the
middle of the crowd singing songs praising the families' ancestors
and moving down to the current generation. In a lively *Chassidic*
tune, the *badchan* began with the stories and the legends about

the people—oh, what saints they all were back then when the world was a so much purer place.

The *badchan* went on for an hour, two, and then three. I had fallen asleep in my chair, mumbling an apology to the legion of ancestors who had come the long way from heaven to dance at this unearthly hour, when my mother pinched me on my arm.

"Get up! It's time! It's time!"

And time it was. Yankel, my mumbling, jumbling husband, stumbled to the middle. His eyes clenched shut, his head bent over, his *shtreimel* precariously balanced at the edge, he held my hands at the tips of my fingers. Back and forth he swayed, back and forth he shook, because it said in the Torah that to dance in front of the bride and bring her joy was a *mitzvah*. Next he dropped my hands and turned in a near frenzy, around and around, until the song was over. Then he rushed back to his chair.

I clutched my mother's hands as she cried, and my father winked at me, and I could see the tears in his eyes that insisted that I was just born.

More dancing, more singing, and my mother remembered that Yankel and I had not taken a single picture together yet.

"Everybody out of the way! Quickly, only the couple together! No, not *so* together. Okay, like that together. Look at them. They look so sweet, like they are married a month already. *Oops*, the groom just fainted. It's nothing, he's fine—just one more picture."

Finally, the wedding was over.

We arrived at our newly rented basement apartment at 3:30 a.m. My mother and sister came in with me to help me out of my dress. After three fruitless attempts, gripping the dresser, the bed, the closet door, first one leg out, then the other, I was finally free.

A teary kiss, a close hug, and they were gone. Yankel and I were left alone. Very much so.

At 3:57 a.m. we went into our bedroom. At 4:06 a.m. I walked out hoping Hashem's holy presence was still hovering and hadn't stumbled down from shock after what we had done in that room.

CHAPTER FORTY-SEVEN

On my first night of married sleep I had the strangest dream. I watched Shmuli push her. He pushed her hard, inside the dark, thrashing blanket. He pushed her. And she was choking. Choking, choking, and I couldn't feel a thing. Just watching. It hurt. It hurt. It hurt so much. *Devory? Can you hear me? Devory?*

I was only watching. Watching him push her inside the blanket. I wanted to call out to him in a whisper, to tell him that she was sleeping and that he should come back tomorrow, but he wouldn't listen and lifted the edge of the blanket.

Don't come back to my room. You are dead and I am alive.
Devory?

Then there was nothing. I sank deeply into the peaceful nothingness that took me down, down, down, and I did not care to breathe.

I woke up. First I saw the ceiling, the smooth, newly whitewashed ceiling. Then the embroidered monogram on the linen. Then Yankel, already awake, staring worriedly at the wall.

The pictures, the *chuppah*, the dancing, the *Mitzvah Tantz* . . . I was married. Married!

I had better be pregnant.

"Good morning," Yankel said when he saw I was awake. "How . . . how . . . how was your sleep?"

"Fine," I said and, arranging my nightgown, stepped carefully out of bed, walked courteously out of the room, and then ran, and I mean *ran* to the bathroom to check if I was pregnant. I took off my nightgown and stared at my waistline in the mirror. I looked closer. A bit closer. My friend Shany, who had become pregnant the first night they did *it*, told me she could see the next morning, something, a difference, and she just knew it had happened. I searched for a bulge. A something, a difference, just a tiny little bump that meant I could run to the phone and call my mother, who would swear not to tell anyone except my aunt, who would promise to keep it a secret from every relative except my cousin Chevi, who had gotten married just before me, so it wasn't really fair not to tell her. She would whisper the news to my other cousin because what if she heard it on the street, and she would tell my neighbor, who would reveal the news to my friends, who would titter to their husbands, who would swear on the Talmud they would not say a word in *shul* to Yankel—whom I would have completely forgotten to tell. I shook my head, annoyed. I shouldn't have ever told my mother. Why did everything have to get around like that? I stared at the mirror. Wait. I wasn't even pregnant. I touched my stomach. I poked gently at my belly. There was nothing. Disappointed, I left the bathroom.

At 9:03 a.m. there was a knock on the door. It was a delivery from Breakfast Bagel with a bouquet of flowers and a tray of ready-to-eat, fresh-from-the-oven bagels, lox, eggs, and two salads.

To the young Geldbart family: From your loving parents.

I spread out my new floral tablecloth that was meant for *Shab-bos*, but Surela said I should use it for the week of *sheva brachos* to impress my new husband. *Sheva brachos*, meaning "seven bless-ings," are the blessings that are recited over a cup of wine as part of a festive evening meal that continues every night for a week after the wedding.

I set the table with the floral cutlery, and then said the morn-ing prayers, sending up an extra word for a happy marriage, a long life, health, and wealth—but first a baby—and waited for Yankel, who had left for prayers as soon as he got out of bed, looking fur-tively around as if guilty of a secret crime.

I wore my simple-but-elegant-for-home house robe, applied not-too-much makeup, and waited. Yankel had gone to *shul* with my brother Yossi, who would be his guardian for the week. For seven days after marriage, every bride and groom needed a guardian, any available relative, who accompanied them anytime they left the house. It was a tradition, or a law, begun in ancient times to protect them from evil spirits.

I heard quiet footsteps coming down the carpeted stairs. I grabbed my wig, pulling it over my head, and I looked in the mir-ror. It was crooked, definitely crooked. The bangs were hanging over my ears, the side was in the front, and my real hair stuck out everywhere. I pulled the wig frantically to the right. Too fast. The bangs were now hanging over my other ear. I shoved it hard to the left. Still crooked. Forget it. I would wear a kerchief.

But the wig would not come off. I pulled at the tip and yanked it hard. A clump of hair came out, my scalp tingled, but still it hung on. A bobby pin in my hair had gotten tangled in the net and I stared in the mirror, unable to keep the thing on or take it off.

Yankel was walking into the kitchen. I rushed to the door of the

bedroom and shut it. In tears I stared at the phone. Should I call
my mother to come help me? *However* did they get their wigs on? I
tried once more. This time I pulled it off gently from the back.
Then, reaching in for the bobby pin that had ruined my grand and
regal entrance, I yanked it out. Holding the cursed wig in my hand,
I shoved it back onto the foam head that held it. Then I put on a
kerchief.

When I walked into the kitchen, Yankel was sitting at the small
table, smiling shyly. Flustered, I sat down. We stared at the food
spread out in front of us. We each picked up a fork. Yankel began
with the lox, trying to cut it with the knife, but it kept slipping
everywhere.

"It's good," he finally said.

I cut up the bagel into small pieces. I daintily placed a square in
my mouth. Pieces of lox slid out from between the bagel. I pushed
them back with a fork.

"Y-y-yes, it is."

"Where did your parents buy it?"

There was a hair in the lox. A brown, curly hair. I considered
vomiting the lox onto the table. I reconsidered it and forced myself
to swallow.

"Bagel Breakfast. I mean Breakfast Bagel. Your parents also
bought it."

I pushed the hair and hid it in a napkin.

"Oh? . . . That's nice."

"Yes. It is."

Somehow, we finished breakfast. I jumped up to clear off the
table. Yankel wiped off some crumbs from the table, folded them
in a napkin, and looked around.

"Where is the garbage?"

Garbage? Garbage. Where was the garbage?

I opened the closet door under the sink.

"Here it is," I said, relieved.

He laughed awkwardly. "The most important place in the house—the garbage."

I giggled.

"Wait," I said, pointing near the door. "There is your suitcase. Your mother dropped it off here before the wedding."

"Oh, yes," Yankel said as if surprised to see it. He pulled the small suitcase to the bedroom, opened it up, and began unpacking. There were two neat piles of white shirts and undergarments. The rest was black. A black *bekeshe*, a black plastic raincoat, a black spring coat, a black heavy coat, a black cotton home robe, black slippers, black *kippa*s, black socks, black pants—cut specially loosely on top so as not to mistakenly show any bulge—and a black watch. There were also off-white woolen *tziztis*, which *Chassidish* men wore over their white shirts, and a bottle of white antidandruff shampoo. I picked it up and put it in the bathroom.

Yankel tried to make conversation. He said that he still had an entire box of antidandruff shampoo bottles in the hotel where his parents were staying, and he hoped we would have room to store it.

I said oh. I asked him if he had ever had dandruff and he said, um, uh, he, uh, used to have a little but then his mother began sending antidandruff shampoos to *yeshiva* with instructions to finish them all completely, so no, he no longer had any. I said okay.

We then went back into the kitchen. It was only 10:03. Yankel stared at me; I stared at him. "I . . . I think I'll go prepare lunch,"

I said, and ran to the closet and pulled out the other new table-cloth for when my in-laws came. Yankel sat and watched.

"Do . . . do you need help?"

"No," I answered promptly.

Fourteen minutes later, lunch was ready. It was now 10:17 a.m. I took out a book to read; Yankel sat in the chair and swayed over the Talmud. At 10:42 a.m. I called my mother. She picked up after half a ring.

"*Oy*, finally! Good morning, I was waiting for you to call! I was wondering if I should call you or not, but Surela said I shouldn't dare. Would I want my mother to call me on the first day after marriage? Well, come to think of it, she did, and I remember how relieved I was. Your father and I had *nothing* to talk about. *Nu*, so *how* was the breakfast? Did Yankel like it? Did you ask him if he likes avocado? Sruli says that is all they eat in the *yeshivas* in Israel, and I wasn't sure whether to include it or not. In the end they did not have fresh avocado anyway—only from yesterday—and I said no way. I am not sending a new couple avocados from the day before. Tomatoes I wasn't so sure if they were from yesterday or today, but, look, you can't have a salad without tomatoes and Israelis *love* salad. Bubba Yuskovitz called me and told me—don't you dare send breakfast without salad, Yankel simply will not eat, so I told the man, okay, include the tomatoes."

At 11:03 a.m. we called up Yankel's mother. She asked me how my *shaitel* was. It was difficult in the beginning, and how when she got married thirty years back they only had synthetic wigs. *Oy*, how it itched! It was one hundred degrees, summer in Jerusalem, don't ask, and there she was trying to get used to horsehair that felt like straw in the simmering heat. I just didn't know how lucky I had it, human hair wigs were nothing to adapt to, though I really had to know which wig stylist to use, so many of them had no idea how to take care of a good wig and after twelve months, there you are, two thousand dollars in the garbage. . . .

At 12:03 p.m. we ate lunch. Yankel kept eyeing the lox and finally asked me if I minded him eating lox with his fingers. His brother-in-law told him that in America the girls ate only with a fork, and I said, *neh*, who cares, and grabbed the last piece of lox, tore it apart, and after throwing aside the forks, we finished lunch.

At 1:03 p.m. my brother came to take Yankel to *mincha* prayers. When he returned, I asked him if it was true that before they were married grooms made lists of what to talk about during the first few days. Moishe, Surela's husband, had told her that *Reb* Ehrlich, the *Yushive rav*, gave them subjects to speak about—but she had promised not to tell me. And I had promised not to tell Yankel, so that it shouldn't get back to Moishe, who would be mad at Surela for telling me. Yankel turned as red as the fresh tomato I was cutting and said, "No way. Well, yes, um, *neh*, um, maybe, it depended, I'm not sure. . . ."

At 2:03 p.m. I began preparing for *sheva brachos*. I ironed my suit, chose a matching pair of beige tights, and stared admiringly at Yankel's perfectly starched white shirts folded, layered, and piled like a stack of freshly cut white paper.

At 3:03 p.m. I took a nap. When I awoke I found Yankel, his head on his arms, sleeping on the kitchen table. When I walked past him he jumped up. I told him to go to bed, but he hastily said no, no, no, no, it was just fine, just fine, but when he saw that I had finished napping, he closed the door to the bedroom and went to sleep himself.

At 6:00 p.m. I called my father and said I was dressed and ready to go to *sheva brachos* right then, and he should come pick me up. I was bored, had nothing to do, and we'd been married for eleven whole hours, which was a long time to talk about nothing.

"Are you crazy?" he asked. "It's called for seven and nobody shows up till nine. . . . Go read a book. What do you think? A relationship happens in one minute? You know what your mother and I spoke about the first month? The weather. So how's the weather? The weather is fine. Is it bad weather? Could be worse weather. It looks like nice weather. Yes, it looks like nice weather. What is the weather today? I am in the bed across from yours. I do not know what the weather is today. What we would have done without the weather, only Hashem knows. But after a month, I left my filthy socks on the floor, and *oy*, did she have some other things to tell me."

Eventually, the clock struck eight and we arrived in the newly renovated basement hall of the Satmar *yeshiva*. It was a beautiful evening. Everyone said I looked absolutely stunning, more beautiful in the wig than without it, and wow, you could never tell it wasn't a Shevy. And oh, so *how* does it feel to be married? *How* does it feel the day *after*? A relief, wasn't it? And don't worry; it gets easier; simpler, smoother, better.

"I also didn't have a thing to say for the first month," Chaya, a relative of one kind or the other, told me. "Until the first time he walked over my newly mopped floor, and we haven't stopped arguing since, ha-ha." She patted my back and glanced at my waist. "Just checking for extra movement. Don't worry, don't worry, it'll come faster than you think. . . ."

It happened on Wednesday, on the fourth day of *sheva*

brachos, at 3:00 p.m. I had just placed a full bag of garbage by the front door after washing a small pile of two dishes, three spoons, and one cup. I meticulously dried them, admired the towel with the cute little embroidered apples on it, and hung it up on the hook before walking to the closet, putting on my coat to take out the garbage, and going to the door. That's when I noticed. The garbage was gone!

It had happened . . . only four days after marriage! I dropped my pocketbook on the floor, ran across the room, grabbed the phone, and called my mother.

"Yankel took out the garbage," I announced breathlessly. "He took out the garbage!"

My mother gasped. She threw the phone on the floor and called my father from her cell phone. "You hear me? He took out the garbage. Even earlier than Surela's husband did—remember it took him two weeks to think of it. I thought I would *plotz*—but it's only four days and already Yankel took it out. I knew he would be a good husband. I just knew it!" Then I could hear her dialing someone else on her cell phone, "I'm telling you I can't believe it . . ."

Within two minutes my cell phone rang. It was Bubba Yuskovitz.

"I knew it! I knew it!" she screeched. "Did I tell you my grandson was special? Did I tell you? He is a *mensch*! A *mensch*! My grandson, may he live till one hundred and twenty, as soon as I saw him in the nursery when he was born, I *knew* he was something special. . . ."

"*Nuuuuuu*, so what do you *say*?" Aunt Sarah asked when she called, as if it had been a little secret between us. "Your parents picked the right boy after all, didn't they? See, trusting one's parents is the best idea . . . *pah*! Those *modernishe* who think that they'll fall in love and all the other *shtism*. Taking out the garbage! That's what counts. . . ."

And Surela, who called just as Yankel walked back in from afternoon prayers, said, "See, marriage is not so bad. Before you know it they start learning that hey—life is not *yeshiva*, and they even learn to help."

But my aunt from Lakewood advised me otherwise. It was the last day of *sheva brachos* and she sat near me as we munched on the cranola dessert she had brought special from Lakewood. She shook her head disapprovingly.

"A husband shouldn't take out the garbage. He's a Torah scholar; you must treat him with the appropriate respect. Imagine wasting a minute of Torah learning on taking out garbage! You want a garbageman for a husband, let him take out the garbage. You want a king, treat him like a king. . . ."

My mother, admiring Goldy's new dress nearby, overheard somehow and in less than a second was standing at our table.

"If he is a king, then she is a queen," she said sweetly, "and as this is a kingdom without servants, it would do well to treat each other royally." Then she pulled me away to meet a friend she hadn't seen since seminary.

On Thursday, a day after the last *sheva brachos*, Yankel's parents returned to Israel. On the way to the airport, they stopped in for a last visit. His mother described her harrowing trip to Manhattan in the morning, where she had not been for so many years, and how she had forgotten what it means to live among goyim.

"Once you live among only Jews, you could no longer imagine living this way. America is a good country, good to the Jews, for sure, but goyim are goyim, and as we saw in Germany, they are capable of anything. . . ."

I agreed, but told her that Israel wasn't exactly safe either. The Arabs would be perfectly happy to take over for the Germans, and we then argued about which one was more dangerous, who was inherently crueler than who, and how long it would all last before there would be another Holocaust and so on and so forth until we reassured ourselves once more that regardless of where and when, we were Jews, and we were chosen, and everybody hated us.

Then my mother-in-law hugged me, kissed me, and wiped a tear from her eye. "Oh, why am I crying. . . . ?" She patted my cheeks gently and shook a finger in mock warning at Yankel. "You can always call me if he gives you problems; I'm still good at screaming."

That night Yankel and I had our first argument: one week, seven avocado salads, and three garbage bags after the *chuppah*, Yankel insisted that *Chassidish* women did not have breasts.

I had hung up my bra on the bathroom rod to dry that afternoon, after I had washed it. Yankel had used the bathroom, but when he exited, he seemed upset. He had seen that "thing," what was it called? It doesn't matter. He had never seen a "thing" up close before. Wasn't it the stuff *goyishe* women wore to make men look at them? Wasn't it the stuff he had seen as a child in Tel Aviv, where he went once for a doctor's appointment, and his mother pushed him fast close to her and told him to look down, so he shouldn't see *shiksa* things—?

I disagreed with him. I told him that *Chassidish* women also had "that," they just didn't show it off—which was why he had never seen it before. But Yankel just stared at me suspiciously. He was worried, disturbed, and frustrated.

"It can't be," he said. "They" were *goyishe* and Jewish women were not allowed to have them.

We argued for a long time. He said that there was no way his mother or sisters had "that," so I should stop talking nonsense. And I said "that" was something that Hashem gave for children to drink milk from. Yankel stared at me as if I were insane and said that there were cows for a reason, and a *Chassidish* woman would never let her child view such "things" and maybe just in America they had "that." Things were a bit more modern here, and that in Israel, forget about it, if a woman had "that" she would never be able to make a *shidduch*. I argued that he would see in the wedding pictures, his mother's fitted gown showed "that" clearly, and that he had no idea what he was talking about.

I hid my bra in my drawer immediately, but at supper—though my mother had sent over my favorite meal—we ate in dead silence.

After Yankel left for prayers, I stood in front of the mirror, staring intently at my chest. The sweater lifted a bit, two small points on a flat surface. In seventh grade I had cried when they had first grown, because I was only the third girl in my class to have them. My mother had dragged me to the store and said that Hashem gave everything for a reason. One day my babies would be nourished by this special gift, and I should just thank Hashem I didn't have big ones like Shany. She had already grown to a B cup, and her mother ran around desperately trying to find the tightest underwire bra to make her chest look smaller. Surela had always been jealous of me because I had such small ones. Hers stuck out in every outfit she bought, so embarrassing. I thought of calling her immediately to ask her where one bought a bra that made them disappear all together.

But that night, after prayers, Yankel returned smiling sheepishly. He said that he had gone to *Reb* Ehrlich and asked him if it was all right for his wife to have "that" and the *rav* had confirmed that indeed it was okay. *Chassidish* women were allowed to have "that" too. I sighed in relief.

On Monday morning my father drove me to the *Yushive* elementary school for a job interview. After he dropped Yankel off at the *kollel* where he learned, he peered into the rearview mirror hesitantly and asked me how, well, you know, it was all going. Of course he didn't mean to butt in, but he was still my father, and as he had said before my wedding, marriage could be difficult at times. And though of course it was a private thing, there were common difficulties and if I needed, I could talk to him. He could always give some useless advice.

I said, sure, yeah, it was fine, I guess. I mean, it could be worse, ha-ha. I suppose it was all too new, weird, and strange. We still needed time for a few *gezinta* arguments to warm up to married life. My father hastily changed the subject. He said that perhaps I would consider doing a degree now that I was married. He heard that there were girls doing a BA in special education in Sarah Sheneirer, the ultra-Orthodox, completely kosher, *Bais Yaakov* girls-only school. As my father pulled up in front of the school building, I said I would discuss it with my friend Pessy, a teacher in the school, who was getting married in two weeks and had studied in the program.

The interview with Mrs. Katz, the principal, went smoothly. I promised I could control a fourth-grade class anytime. She said she knew my mother since high school when they went to camp together. I said a salary of thirteen thousand dollars a year for a full-time job would be fine. She said she remembered my aunt from when they were still young and skinny, and that I would start teaching as soon as the regular teacher had a baby. After the meeting, I went to the teacher's room, where I met my friends, who gave me a hearty *mazel tov* and said I looked so cute in the *shaitel*, and now suddenly that they were looking at me from *that* angle I looked just like my mother and my sister. Was I planning to finish seminary? It was a waste of time and you could get a job without it. It's not as if you got paid one penny more with or without the seminary diploma—experience was all that mattered.

I discussed it that evening with my father, who said I should do it because an advance degree never hurt anyone. Surie said I should ask my mother because how would I make supper, be pregnant, teach, and study at the same time? And my mother said, what is your father talking about? Who needs a degree? It costs a fortune. You could make supper, be pregnant, teach, and take care of babies without it.

CHAPTER
FORTY-EIGHT

Two weeks after my wedding night I discovered I wasn't pregnant. Then there were five days of blood, seven clean ones, and some ten nervous rechecks to see that I had followed the laws of family purity down to the last detail. Now I sat on a leather chair in the *mikvah* waiting room. I was ready, sort of, to immerse myself in the water of the *mikvah*—the ritual bath—to cleanse myself from all impurities, for only then could a Jewish woman receive her husband again.

The six-block walk from my apartment to the *mikvah* had been one of knee-jittering fear. I hurriedly ran the whole way, my face buried in a shawl. Every person I passed, knew, just knew, exactly where I was heading. My heart thumped and jumped as I prayed to Hashem that I wouldn't meet my teachers, my cousins, or my mother in the *mikvah*, or I would drop dead of embarrassment right there on the granite floor and never have children to raise in the sacred way of Borough Park and its *Chassidim*. I entered the unmarked building, received a number, and sat huddled in the corner of the couch reading my Psalms near another fresh-faced bride.

It was finally my turn. The bathroom was pretty. There were pink tiles, a long mirror covering half the wall, and lush, white towels folded neatly on a shelf. There was a bell to ring for help; a container filled with scissors, clips, and Q-tips; and a package of disposable slippers.

I prepared myself. I filled the bath with hot water, scrubbed and rubbed every piece of skin until it shone red, and kept a relentless stream of prayers heading in the direction of heaven that He send me children, but before Chevi had them or I would have a heart attack.

After the obligated hour, I rang the bell. The *mikvah* lady arrived to check me. She checked my toes, rubbed my fingers, looked over my back to see if there was any *chatzitsa*, a scratch, a nail, or a hair that would block the space between the holy *mikvah* water and my skin.

I followed the *mikvah* lady down a long, narrow hallway past the other closed bathrooms into a small room. In the room was a narrow, deep pool with steps going down into the water. It was there I would immerse myself.

I removed my bathrobe. She held it high up so that it covered her eyes. I walked tentatively down the steps into the water and stood on my tiptoes in the deepest part. She then looked down over the railing and watched me submerge, in and out, in and out, in and out, six times—saying a prayer between the third and fourth submersion—*Blessed are you, Lord, our G-d, King of the Universe, who has sanctified us with His commandments and commanded us concerning immersion,* coming up each time to her voice echoing through the small room, "Kosher! Kosher! Kosher!" and I focused reverently on the cleansing of all sin, but most of all on getting my hair all the way under the water—for if as much as one blasphemous hair surfaced, if as much as one tip of one strand reached the surface, if only one split end detached itself from my scalp floating unsuspectingly up above the water unnoticed by the *mikvah* lady, then I would give birth to miserable children with spiritual defects, physical maladies, and mental disabilities, and it would be all my fault. What would I ever tell Yankel?

"Kooosher!"

I coughed up the water in my mouth. Too much chlorine. I looked up at the *mikvah* lady. She motioned to me. One more submersion, just one more—deep, deep into the water—every inch of disobedient hair, deep inside the holiest of holies.

I rubbed my eyes. I stumbled up the *mikvah* steps dripping wet, looking back frantically for wandering hairs. The *mikvah* lady helped me with my robe, shaking my hands, and smiling kindly. "*Tizsku Li'mitzvos*, may you merit more *mitzvos*, may you merit more *mitzvos*."

Yankel was in the kitchen when I arrived home. A weak smile, an uncomfortable nod, and a blush as he turned back to the Talmud.

At 10:14 p.m. we entered the bedroom. I lay in the darkness, my nightgown up to my waist, and advised Hashem's presence to leave the room. He could hover right outside in the kitchen, just not in here, around all this—it was outrageously immodest; there were things even Hashem shouldn't see.

At 10:28 p.m. Yankel fell off my bed. He stood up quickly, mumbled something, and hurried to the bathroom. I heard the shower running and, relieved that it was over, fell into a deep sleep. I dreamed of Devory, could see her clearly staring at me in the shadows, when I suddenly felt him touch me. I did not know if I was awake or still dreaming, only that I was frozen and did not move as he came near me.

It was still in the darkness. I could see Yankel through my half-opened eyes as he lifted my blanket, gently, hesitant. He touched it again, lifting it slightly. I closed my eyes and held my breath. My throat was clenched so tightly I could not breathe. My body turned to stone. I could hear him breathe, could see him standing over me, watching my still form. Then I heard him move away quickly, silently, sitting on his bed, then pulling up his blanket until I could hear him no longer.

I wanted to get up, to run. I wanted to pound on his bed, to scream at him that a *Chassid* did not love, a *Chassid* did not touch in the depraved ways of goyim. How dare he lift my blanket that way? What would the *Rebbe* say, a scholar, standing over his wife like that, and in the presence of Hashem? But I could not open my eyelids. They weighed down heavily on my face, as if someone had glued them shut. Perhaps I was dead; he had done something and it had killed me.

Then I sank down deep into sleep, and misty shadows quickly turned dark. Black. *Come into my bed, Gittel, come into my bed.* Why was it so dark? I hated when it was dark and I was awake, the only one in the house. *Why are you crying, Devory? Don't cry.* Her mouth opened and closed, but she didn't dare make a sound. Her long screams of agony echoed loudly in my head. I covered my ears, shuddering, but I could still see her mouth opened in horror. *Devory, don't scream like that; Devory, don't scream.*

Then it was morning. Yankel was gone when I awoke, to *shul*, to prayers, to his guilt. I did not see him until after work, when we met by my parents' home for dinner. The table was set with the guest tablecloth, guest dishes, and guest cutlery. There were three main courses and six sides, all recipes from my mother-in-law of Yankel's favorite food: moussaka with inlaid pepper, tahini with extra spices, and chicken soup with *kneidlech* as soft as cream. "A little of this, a little of that," my mother preened, gently pulling at the white tablecloth to even out a wrinkle. "When Surela first got married, she and her husband ate here for almost a year before she began cooking at home, remember, Gittel?" I nodded.

"It takes time to learn how to cook," she said, sprinkling a dash of red pepper on the tahini. "How long did I eat by my mother?" She tucked a wayward hair into her snood. "I don't remember, but the first time I cooked at home, she cried. Was she ever over-protective."

No one moved during those first weeks of sparkling dinners. My youngest brother stared in awe at Yankel, my father cracked jokes he had prepared beforehand, and my mother fussed politely, "*Oy*, leave the poor new *chassan* alone. You want more moussaka? More soup? More salad? Just a little more potato? It's not that different than in Israel, is it? Where there are Jews, there are Jews. . . ."

We ate dinner by my mother the next day, the day after, and the next. At home I made sandwiches for lunch as Yankel concocted salads I'd never heard of and took out the garbage whenever it was full. Friday, I made a *letcho*, some conglomeration of fried vegetables my mother said that his mother had said that he liked, and Yankel, sitting at the table, said it was delicious. Really. No, of course he couldn't tell I had never made *letcho* before, even Bubba

Yuskovitz would enjoy it. With a satisfied sigh I sat down across from him, spooning a generous forkful into my mouth. And spat it out all over the table. My mother screamed at me when she heard.

"You put in what?! How can you read two tablespoons of pepper where it says a teaspoon?" My father laughed at my tears. "It is the husband's duty to suffer through the first year of marriage food," he informed me. "Your mother still has no idea how much food poisoning she gave me that first terrible year."

That evening I found Yankel hunched over the two high school albums I had brought from my mother's house. He wanted to know what a tennis racket was. And a basketball. "I didn't know girls are allowed to play ball," he said, sitting on our small couch looking curiously at pictures of camp and school trips. "The last time I played ball was when I was in seventh grade. Only the bums played ball past *Bar Mitzvah*, and in *yeshiva* there were no balls allowed."

He was fascinated by the games we played and the places we went. "At *yeshiva* we go once a year on a hike to different nature places where there are no women or inappropriate people. The rest of the time we spent at the *yeshiva*, except of course when we go to the *Grand Rebbe*."

When I asked him for pictures of his friends, he laughed at my question.

"There are no cameras allowed in *yeshiva*."

And he was shocked at the mixed seating on buses right in the center of Borough Park. He had wanted to take the bus home from *kollel*, but a woman sat right near him as if he weren't there, and he had quickly run off.

"It was mixed," he said. "How could they allow that? In Israel, on all the religious buses, the women sit only in the back, the men in the front."

But Yankel knew how to open a book, my father proudly said. That boy had a real head. It was a pleasure learning with him on *Shabbos*. . . . The *Rosh kollel*—the head of the *yeshiva* for married men—announced to my father when he met him at a wedding that indeed Yankel was truly what they said he was—a *masmid*, a *tzaddik*, a *fineh bachur*. Eh, would he donate a few hundred dollars more to the *yeshiva*? It was especially tight this year. Ah, one could indeed tell the man was the proud descendant of a *geshmake* carrot *kugel*.

But life was not all good. I had just gotten my period. Again. I was not pregnant yet. When I first felt the familiar monthly cramps, I cried. I told my mother that Hashem was punishing me. Sarah Pessy and Rochel Leah, who had gotten married two weeks after me, were already pregnant.

My mother told me not to worry. Surela had waited seven months until she had finally become expectant. Now that was something to cry about. But two months? Give it some time. . . . But I did worry. I worried as we walked to my parents' house in the snow to light the Chanukah candles. I worried as we ate the *latkes*—potato pancakes—and *suvganiyot*—sugar jelly doughnuts—my mother-in-law sent fresh from Jerusalem. I worried as my aunt peered down at my waist and said, "*Nu, shoin*, anything doing? Don't worry, it'll come, Hashem willing, Hashem willing, they'll come so fast you won't know what to do." I worried as I went to the *mikvah* again, came home, did *it*, fell asleep praying, and worried, really worried, when my husband tried to kiss me. Like Leo and Kathy. In the middle of the night.

Again, he stood over me. Again, he lifted my blanket. My eyes were closed; I pretended to sleep. But then he bent over. I felt his warm breath on my cheek and his lips, flushed and hot, brushed mine. I jumped as if touched by fire. Yankel straightened up and stared at me in shame and horror. He fled to his bed. I went to the bathroom and washed my face. I sat on the toilet seat for over an hour.

When I entered the kitchen at dawn, unable to sleep, Yankel already stood near the table. He was pale and trembling. He had tears in his eyes.

"I'm sorry. It was a *goyishe* thing to do. I don't know why I did it. It's my *taavah*—my evil desires. I wasn't allowed to do that. I'm sorry. . . ."

I advised him to speak with *Reb* Ehrlich. This was a serious matter. He turned crimson. "No, no, no. Never. He will not believe I did such a thing. I can't do that. He'll think I am a *shaygetz*, he just won't believe it, I can't do that."

We did not talk much that day. I went to work. He learned. We ate in silence. That night he came near me again. I watched him through my slitted eyelids, pacing up and down the room, coming closer, moving back, coming closer, and finally returning to his bed. The next morning after he had gone to learn, I called *Reb* Ehrlich. I told him who I was.

"Of course, of course," he said kindly, his low voice in heavily accented English. "So what's on your mind? Tell me, something is bothering you?"

I blushed but, determined to put an end to this horrifying business, I told him everything—the kiss, the walks, the pacing, the lifting of the blanket. What was wrong with my husband?

"I hear . . . I hear . . . ," he said, his voice rising, slowing in a singsong chant. "It's not the worst thing, don't worry. I know it is bothering you, but there is men and there is men, *vus ken min tun*—what can we do? Hashem gave some men more hormones than others. . . . I know you are a good girl, you don't want this, but sometimes it is too hard for men. . . . We try, we try, of course we try, and this way is the ideal way, but there are those who can't do this, so we do something else, a little more, just a little more. No, it's not the worst thing, it's the last resort, of course, but one more time a week, and I tell you, he'll calm down, he'll calm down. . . . You want me to talk with him? I'll talk to him, I'll talk to him, don't worry, I talk with every new *chassan*. . . . Of course, we have to make sure it doesn't go too far, always keep the lights out, the covers on—this is the holiest time, Hashem is there, right there with you. We must always do this the right way, but Yankel is a *fineh yingeman*, a fine young man. He's just a little mixed up now. . . . Call me back in a few days and tell me if things get better, okay? Don't let it sit on your mind, you can always call me."

— — —

Distracted, I arrived at the teacher's room at the *Yushive* school in the early afternoon. As if twice a month wasn't enough. . . . Shany, pregnant already with her second child, ambled over to me, a tuna sandwich in hand. She told me that Chani, a classmate of ours, was separated from her husband. I stared at her, stunned.

"I'm telling you," she said. "Everyone is talking about it. I'm not sure why, but I heard that there were, you know, problems in the bedroom. . . . He wanted to do all sorts of things. Shany told me that he acted like a goy. I knew they were never a match. I have no idea how that *shidduch* happened—I could have told them right away that it would never go." I took out a pile of tests and began marking them. Shany munched on her sandwich. "But you know, I have really good friends from other *Chassidish* schools, I mean not everyone obviously, but a lot of them, these people do *everything* . . . could you imagine?" She lowered her tone until it was merely a whisper. "They don't even wear a nightgown or *anything*."

It was 12:41 p.m. I had to go into class in ten minutes. Annoyed, I turned to my papers, but Shany continued.

"I asked my friend, the Satmar one, if—I mean I didn't ask her, of course not, but she told me, you know, hinted to me that they just did *it whenever* they wanted. He gives her *massages*. Hashem, could you imagine? It's weird . . . I mean, it's not allowed, is it? She told me that she really admires us. We must be going straight to *Gan Eden*." She sighed tiredly and stroked her swollen stomach. "I have no idea how I am going to manage with this baby. My one-year-old is so wild. I don't know what I am going to do. I mean I'm not complaining, however many Hashem gives . . ." She sighed, slowly got up, and walked away.

I had little patience for her nonsense. There was something more profound bothering me. Why wasn't *I* pregnant? Besides Shany, who was already with her second child, and Sarah Pessy, in her third week of pregnancy and wearing maternity clothing, I had just found out that my cousin Chevi, who got married three months before me, was pregnant. I had been married more than two entire months now. What could be wrong with me?

After class, I called up my mother from the teacher's room

depressed and wanting to talk. My mother, breathless and agitated, told me that she had been trying to contact me all morning.

"Listen, eat dinner at home today, I have too many errands to do. I prepared food for you—it's on the counter. I have to go talk with Totty. He is so upset, I don't know what to do. You know Mr. Weinstein, who works with Totty? His brother *Reb* Duvidel Weinstein teaches in the *Me'or Ha'Talmud cheder* and was arrested today. Someone accused him of, you know, doing inappropriate things with his students. It's probably nothing, but of course it's all over the *Daily Post*, and Mr. Weinstein's mother *nebech* has cancer, remember her? She used to be in our bungalow colony. I must go help her, poor woman. She must be devastated. She helped me so many times when I wanted the bungalow facing the lake, and when I was giving birth to you, she took the rest of the kids for two weeks. . . . Anyway, I just wanted to tell you that I won't be home in the evening, so I prepared delicious food for you in plastic containers. And, Gittel, get rid of your stuff piled up all over the house! There are boxes of pictures just sitting there, notebooks, arts and crafts, and every prize you ever got since first grade! You haven't looked at these things in years. You have your own apartment now and I don't have room!" And she hung up.

It was empty and silent in the house when I arrived, and I sat in my old room and sorted through the pictures. My entire life was there in photos, from fifth grade until my engagement. Chani and me as Queen Esther on Purim, hugging Surela in camp, laughing with my friends in a pizza shop, smiling gleefully holding my Chanukah present, laughing on my father's shoulder, waving with Devory at the aquarium.

Devory! What was that picture doing here? She had completely disappeared from my drawer years ago. Devory. I stared at her twinkling blue eyes, the wide mischievous smile, and her hand waving cheerfully at the camera. Devory. I grabbed the photo and looked furtively around before quickly hiding it inside my pocketbook. I laughed at myself. Why did I feel like a thief, as if I had just found something forbidden and someone might take it away?

I left the piles on the bed, packed the plastic containers with the warm food in a bag, and left the house. I met Kathy coming up the steps outside.

"Gittel!" she exclaimed. "I can't believe you're here. God must've wanted me to meet you." She smiled at me secretively. "Guess what I got in this bag." She waved an elegant, gray bag in the air. "Guess what I got inside here? I was going to give it to your mother 'cause I ain't seen you lately now that you're all married and beautiful. But I got it here! It's your gift. Look!"

She grabbed a silver frame out of the bag. "Look, ain't it nice? It's a picture frame. You could put a picture of you and your brand-new husband in it so you could remember your wedding every day. Look, it's got engraving on it—flowers. I love flowers. This is a dandelion. And this is a rose. This is a—"

I took the picture frame from Kathy. I turned it over, pushing down the metal holders to open the frame. Then I lay the picture of Devory and me in it and turned it back over.

The picture fit perfectly. Kathy gently caressed Devory's face. She stroked her hair. Then she took the frame, put it in the bag, and gave it to me.

I hugged Kathy. "Thanks," I told her. "You bought it just in time."

Kathy put her hands on her hips. "But you don't come visit me anymore," she said, pouting.

"Visit?" I explained it to her. "Kathy, I have a husband to attend to and thirteen new sisters-in-law, two grandmothers, and who knows how many cousins to go visit every week. I work too, and soon of course, I'm gonna have triplets. . . ."

We laughed.

"Oh, *Gittel*," Kathy said, patting my stomach. "They gonna be beautiful, just like you were. Did I tell you how your eyes changed colors just like that?"

When I arrived home, there was a voice mail from my mother. She sounded very distracted, talking again about *Reb* Weinstein. It was the Berger family who was accusing him, and some friends were working to release him. It was probably nothing, just nothing. Then, abruptly, she hung up. I was setting the table for dinner when Yankel walked in holding a small bouquet of limp yellow carnations. He stood nervously near the door. He faltered, then came closer inside and placed the flowers gently on the table.

"Um . . . I . . . bought you flowers," he said, flustered. "I—I bought them in the store. Your mother told me a good store. . . . I asked the man to help me, but he was busy so I chose these myself." He smiled shyly. "I don't know which flowers you like, but . . . these looked nice. . . . My mother likes yellow. . . . The tablecloth is also yellow. . . . Um . . . d-do you need help?"

I looked at the flowers, the stems cut unevenly, the petals drooping sadly. I smiled brightly. "Wow, thank you. They're beautiful. Yeah. . . . They do match the tablecloth. Thank you so much. I . . . I really love flowers. . . . Um . . ." And we both ran to the small glass closet to take out the vase, a wedding gift from one of our many relatives. Yankel filled the vase with water and placed it carefully in the center of the table. We sat down and looked at each other through the bouquet.

Supper took longer that night. Yankel told me stories, or *gesheften* as he called it, of all the things they did within the four walls of the *yeshiva*. I laughed hard.

Yankel came to me that night. He said that *Reb* Ehrlich told him he could do it once more every week, but only if I wanted to. I said okay, but that he should do it fast. I was tired.

He pulled the cover over us. I lay unmoving. He did it slowly, then faster, struggling to fit where he did not belong. He asked me if it hurt, I should tell him if it hurt, he would stop. I said no. Nothing hurt where I could not feel. I heard his breath—panting, gasping—and watched the blanket. It moved angrily—shifting back and forth, back and forth. As if someone was fighting from within.

Come into my bed, Gittel, come into my bed. Devory? A Yushive Chassid does not kiss. Are you still dead? Stop coming here into my room. You must stop. I promise you, you are dead and I am alive.

I threw Yankel off. I was suffocating. Hot breath, no space, couldn't breathe. I pushed him off: off my body, off my bed, off my blanket. He fell onto the carpeted floor. He sat still for a moment, then stood up slowly, annoyed.

"Hashem, what's wrong with you? Just tell me, I'll go. I told you that *Reb* Ehrlich said it was fine. Why'd you push me like that?"

Don't touch my blanket. Don't touch it. I watched him look at me, hurt, angry. When I did not answer he sat on his bed, gathering his *payos* in a knot under his cotton night *kippa*. I pulled up my cover and turned to the wall. I could hear his short, shallow breaths, the shuffling of his movement as he lay down. I wanted to push him off again, tell him to keep his hot breath on himself. Why'd he push me like that? Why'd he push me like that? Don't touch my blanket.

Devory?

CHAPTER
FORTY-NINE

I don't want to be crazy any longer. I couldn't breathe, couldn't breathe, she was choking me. Icy, dead eyes never smiling. I couldn't close my eyes, couldn't breathe. Don't be angry, Devory, don't be angry. You must be happy up in heaven so far away. I promise you, Devory, you are dead. You are dead and I am alive—*why why why why why?*

I woke up. It was dark, the sky filled with blinking stars. I switched on the fluorescent light in the kitchen and stumbled to the fridge. I gulped down a cup of orange juice. Then I grabbed a book I had borrowed from Surela and read. It was a nice story, all about Dinah, who after many years of choosing a secular life, repented, married a scholar, and is now living in Jerusalem with six children. I did not go back to bed that night, could not sleep. At 6:00 a.m. Yankel found me, head on my arms, slumped on the kitchen table. We looked at each other, bleary eyed.

"You remind me of *yeshiva*, when my friends and I would fall asleep over our books trying to impress the *Mashgiach* that we could learn for twelve hours straight."

He was already dressed. "I'm going early," he said, and with a strained good morning, left the apartment.

I slept until nine, then got dressed and ran to the dentist's office, late for my appointment. But April, the receptionist, had already let in another patient. I sat in the waiting room, staring at the pictures of leaves and trees, and listened to April talk. And talk and talk.

She congratulated me on my marriage and ring but warned me that gray times lay ahead.

"Marriage is a pain in the neck," she stated, chomping loudly on gum. "I'm telling you, I know. Love is what's important, not marriage. You'll see. . . . So how many times did you meet him? You met him what? How many times? Just once? You're kidding me, right? Tell me you're kidding me. No, of course not, my God! Don't tell me you people are still doing the arranged marriage thing? Aren't you a third-generation American? I can't believe it, you people are totally mad! How can they do something so brutal, marrying off an eighteen-year-old girl to some total stranger? You poor girl, you must be miserable! If I were you I would run away. I mean, there is no way in the world you could know a man if you didn't live with him for at least a year. Oh, well," she said, and popped a large bubble of gum. "The doctor is waiting for you, Gittel, go right in."

- - -

After dinner at my mother's that evening and listening to my father's worn-out jokes, Yankel and I pretended there had never been a last night. I told Yankel what April had told me.

He laughed long and hard. "You know, my mother told me before the wedding something that should help us through the next decade. She said, only ten years after marriage does a real relationship develop. The first decade you invest, the rest of your life, you enjoy the payoff. . . ."

But Yankel missed Israel, the *yeshiva*, the friends he had lived with, and the familiar life around the *Yushive Rebbe* our sect's spiritual leader. He missed the weekends in Jerusalem, thousands of *Chassidim* in one huge room, united in prayer—the singing so powerful, his mother would hum along in her apartment in the next block. And the *tish*—the crowded roundtable every week with the *Rebbe* sitting at the head of a long table filled with fruits, chocolates, and nuts, and the crowd straining, pulsing, each *Chassid* pushing forward just a little more to catch a glimpse of the holy *Rebbe*, eating.

Yankel's eyes widened excitedly at the memory. "I always stood behind my friend; they called him the *Shtiper*. He was the best shover by far. Whoever saw him quickly moved out of his way, so that we always had a front place where we could even see the *Rebbe* unwrapping a bar of chocolate down to the last movement. . . . And you know what I have? Two years ago, by a *tish*, I was standing in the front when the *Rebbe's* assistant, the *mishamish*, gave out the *Rebbe sherayim*, leftovers, from the very chocolate bar that the *Rebbe* himself had. I still have that piece of chocolate. You want to see it?"

I stared at it in wonder; a small piece of dark chocolate turning white with age, wrapped in two napkins, a silk handkerchief, and placed carefully in a small cardboard box. I had never before seen anything that had been directly touched by the holy *Rebbe's* hands, never come so close to something so tangibly transcendent. I watched Yankel lovingly wrap up the small block and tuck it into the safety of his coat pocket. "Some of my friends offered one hundred *shekolim* for this small piece," he said. "But I wouldn't sell. You don't get this every day."

The last time I had received *sherayim* from the *Rebbe* was after our engagement, when my father-in-law sent us nuts from the very table the *Rebbe* had sat by at the *tish*. And those were nuts that were only touched by the *Rebbe*.

"My father got those nuts when he told the *Rebbe* that we had finished the *shidduch*," Yankel recalled. "It was amazing. My father stood on line to tell the *Rebbe Gut Shabbos*. The *Rebbe* touched the hands of every *Chassid* as they passed by, one after the next, and when it was my father's turn and he told him the news, the *Rebbe*—without even looking up—said *mazel tov* for your son and his bride Gittel Chava! Even *we* didn't know your name was Gittel Chava. We heard your name was Gittel—but the *Rebbe* with his prophetic knowledge knew all. . . ."

It really was almost a miracle, I agreed. Almost, because my father had warned Yosef Yitzchak—the *shadchan*—back when he sent him to the *Rebbe* to ask him to bless the *shidduch*, to say my full name, Gittel Chava Klein, so that the blessing should not fall mistakenly on any random Gittel.

"Oh," said Yankel. But we hastily agreed that it was a miracle nonetheless because even if Yosef Yitzchak would not have told the *Rebbe* my name, he certainly would have known it.

Yankel picked up his hat lying on the dresser and put it on the shelf in the closet. He fingered Kathy's picture frame, which I had placed near the mirror, and looked at it curiously. "That's you when you were small," he said. "Wow, you look the same in miniature.

And who is this?" he asked, pointing to Devory—still waving her hand, smiling mischievously up at him. "Is she one of your friends in the high school pictures I saw?"

"No," I said.

"Who is she?"

"Just a girl. Used to be a neighbor."

"*Yushive* family?

"Yes."

"Who is she married to?"

"She's not married."

"What kind of boy is she looking for?"

"I don't know," I said, and took the picture and tucked it under the shirts in my drawer. "I don't really know."

I went to the kitchen and took out two glass cups. Yankel took out the orange juice and we sat by the table. I opened my lesson-planning notebook and began reviewing the next morning's lesson. Yankel sipped at his orange juice.

"Hey," he said casually. "You heard about this Weinstein story? It's all over the place today. My learning partner even had a reporter try to ask him questions in the street near the Talmud Torah, where he lives."

"Yeah, I heard."

"Crazy story. And I heard this Berger family is the one that is accusing them. I don't know how they are not terrified. You know them? "

"No, they're not *Yushive.* . . ."

"This Weinstein is supposed to be one of the best fifth-grade teachers. He's been there for almost twenty years, and yesterday morning the police suddenly showed up at the *cheder* and arrested him. Supposedly the Berger boy, today already twenty, suddenly woke up to complain that he had done inappropriate things some ten years ago in fifth grade." He grimaced. "Of course the secular media is having a heyday with it. . . . Could you imagine his family's embarrassment? Taking away a respectable *Rebbe* in handcuffs?"

He rolled his eyes.

"I remember in *yeshiva* there was a boy who also called the police on one of our *mashgichim*. This real bum, a depressed boy, was always looking for attention, making problems, and never learning. After the head of the *yeshiva* threatened to throw him out, he suddenly filed charges. Not that he could prove anything . . . crazy boy. The head of the *yeshiva* always told us a person's mind who is not in Torah can only be in *shtism*." He gulped down the rest of his orange juice. "I guess there will always be these people who don't know what to do with their lives. . . ."

Something snapped in me, deep inside. I stood up. I could not speak, could not feel, only watched my hand grab the glass cup near me, felt my arm swing back hard, and saw the cup as it flew over the table, over my husband's head, and smashed against the whitewashed wall near the small mirror by the entrance. And a million little pieces of glass shattered on the floor.

I sat back down at the table, picked up the red pen by the notebook, and continued writing my lesson plans. There was silence; a deep, long silence. I never looked up, never saw his stunned face, his bewildered expression. I just focused on finishing my lesson.

"Wh-wha . . . What happened?" I could hear the fear in his voice.

I said nothing.

"I . . . did . . . did I say something wrong?"

I said nothing.

"Gittel, why . . . why did you do that?"

My hand began to tremble. I said nothing. Nothing. Could not say a word that night at all. Yankel spoke to me, said things, asked questions. I did not hear, only clenched my hands trying to stop the shaking, the swaying of my body over the notebook. *Don't cry, Devory, don't cry.* I was so afraid. *It is good up there near Hashem, isn't it?* I couldn't breathe. *Don't be angry that you are dead. I can't be crazy anymore.*

"Gittel, look at me. . . ."

Devory?

"Gittel, what happened?"

Can you hear me?

"Go to bed. You look . . . terrible."

Devory, don't cry. . . .

CHAPTER FIFTY

So many broken dreams, a million little pieces shattered. But who had time for the fear, for little girls who would not die, when the *Rebbe* of *Yushive* was coming to America? It was Yankel who told me the news. He arrived home the next morning, after prayers, and when he saw me joking with my mother on the phone he smiled with relief, and then excitedly told me the news. The three greatest rabbis of today's generation were arriving on the shores of New York: the *Yushive Rebbe*, *Rav* Schapiro of the *litvish*, and the *Kotlaneh* Gaon, a famed scholar.

My father, sipping the small glass of whiskey my mother allowed him before she hid the bottle, joyfully confirmed the news that evening.

"Yosef Yitzchak had told me about it last week, but you know him, so I decided not to say anything until I was sure. They will be here for exactly twenty-four hours. They're also going to L.A. and London to strengthen the Jewish nation during these difficult times. Not that times for Jews were ever very easy. . . ."

The *Yushive Rebbe* would stay in the Golds' house, a simple family, and one whom the *Rebbe*'s father had already once stayed by when he came to visit New York two decades before. The *Rebbe* had refused the offer of the Cohen family, the richest *Yushive* family, who had used no small amount of influence for the unforgettable honor that would be remembered for three generations of *shidduchim*. What was good enough for the *Rebbe*'s father, the *Rebbe* said, was good enough for him, and the Gold family moved out of their house to make room for the *Rebbe* and his entourage.

On Sixteenth Avenue, near Simcha Hall where the rabbis would speak as one, hundreds of young men prepared the street, repainting the traffic poles, washing store windows, stringing yards of little white lights along the lampposts, and hanging signs on every block welcoming the rabbis to their humble abode in Brooklyn. Police set up barricades along the entire avenue blocking traffic and mounted a huge screen with an audio system right outside Simcha Hall so the women could also see the rabbis and be inspired by their words of wisdom.

Every *Chassidic* and *litvish* school in Borough Park and Flatbush closed on that fateful day one week later. I walked with Bubba Yuskovitz down Sixteenth Avenue in the early afternoon, holding her arm in mine, and watched the thousands of Jews, *payos* flying or tucked behind their ears, in their long black coats, shorter dark jackets, long beards, short beards, growing beards.

Bubba Yuskovitz cried. She stood on the corner within the barricades reserved for women and cried tears of joy. "Hitler lost his war," she said, smiling through her tears. "The ghetto is still alive, the Jewish nation is still strong, the true people of Israel still live. . . . This is how it looked in the ghetto in Poland. I was such a little girl, but I remember. This is how it looked when the *Rebbe* came, the *Yushive Rebbe*'s father. We would stand and watch how he walked by, so frail yet so powerful, so old, yet afraid of nothing—an angel of fire, a prophet of truth. This is victory; let the Germans see this! For every Yid they killed, there are now two. Look at how we've grown, look!"

Hundreds of women gathered outside the building, where we watched the rabbis speak, first *Rav* Schapiro, then the *Rebbe* of *Yushive*, then the *Kotlaneh* Gaon. They spoke of holiness, of purity, of the evils of the world and how we must keep ourselves above and away from it all. They spoke about the Nazis and how we had triumphed over them but how sometimes the biggest source of destruction could come from within; the malignant effects of college, of magazines, of movies, of immodest dress, and most of all, the insidious evil of the Internet—the new darkness that must be destroyed at all costs. The Jews must not change, they commanded. They must set themselves apart from the world in every way. The Torah was what had kept the Jews a holy nation since the beginning of time, and it was the Torah that must be preserved, studied, lived by every day, every moment of our lives.

My mother held a small tape recorder in her hand. "It's not every day that one sees and hears the *Rebbes* themselves speaking . . . ," she said. "This is something I'll share with the grandchildren."

After the speeches, the men danced—a sea of black swaying, swelling, swirling, dancing around and around, back and forth, tens of circles, ripples as each man held the arm of the other, and we women quietly hummed and tapped our feet along.

When Yankel came home late that night, after waiting in line for a blessing, he was ecstatic. "The *Rebbe* gave me a *bracha*," he said. "He blessed us that we will have a child. He said, 'It will come, it will come.'"

Yankel had waited for over two hours for a blessing from the *Rebbe*. He had only managed to get in because Laibel the helper, who stood by the door where the *Rebbe* sat, letting people by, knew Yankel through his oldest brother, who had once tutored his younger cousin before his *Bar Mitzvah* for free.

Yankel was happy for a week. He laughed more, cut the salads into even pieces, and waited in anticipation for the good news. But instead I got my period. I called my mother in panic. My mother rebuked me sharply for my hysterics but promised that if I was not expecting in one month she would make an appointment at an excellent fertility doctor, one that her friend Chaya had used after she had given birth to five children and then suffered secondary infertility.

Yankel was devastated. He said it must be his fault. There must be a *stiyah*—an obstruction in heaven—that was preventing us from having children. He told me it said in the Talmud that if a person ever as much as hurt another Jew, the Jew's pain could affect Hashem's decisions concerning that person. And then he remembered how, when he was fourteen, he had once made fun of a boy after he had lost a game of ball, and when he was eight, how he had refused to play with a neighbor, and when he was twelve and thirteen, how he had spoken back to his mother, and when he was fifteen, he had refused to study with a weaker boy in his class. . . .

"I remember how he cried when I told him no. I felt bad, but I never apologized. I must go ask him for forgiveness."

I agreed wholeheartedly. Together we made a list of potential

victims obstructing heavenly benevolence and vowed to beg forgiveness one by one if I was not pregnant within the month.

With our lists folded and hidden in the closet, Yankel was reassured. I was not. I felt depressed and anxious and did not go to my
mother for dinner that night. When Yankel returned alone from
my parents' house, he wanted to know why I was so unhappy. "It's
hard, but you can't mope like that. You didn't go to work today, you
didn't even call to tell them. . . . Don't worry! If the *Rebbe* said it
will come, it will! We must have faith. If not this month, then the
next. . . ."

But the next evening, when my husband came home from
learning, I was back in bed. I felt tired and jittery. Yankel sat across
from me near a bag of unfolded laundry, and when I ignored his
entreaties he went to the kitchen, where he washed the dishes. He
then returned to the room and pulled the undergarments out of
the laundry bag. "I'll fold them," he said, and laid my underwear
out on the bed, fumbling with it this way and that, first rolling
it, then folding it. Then he found my sports bra. Pulling it out of
the pile, he let it dangle by the strap from his finger, gawking at it
wide-eyed, observing it as one does a strange new species, his
mouth hanging slightly open in a most un-*Chassidish* manner.
Angrily, I jumped out of bed. I grabbed a towel nearest to me and
chased Yankel out of the room and around the kitchen table as I
ran after him in circles threatening to call *Reb* Erlich on the spot.
From across the table, he quickly threw the bra at me, offering his
boxers in exchange. "You could fold my boxers! You could fold
my boxers, see if I care!" I told him I had little interest in his big
boxers; he could fold them by himself. And holding my bra close to
my heart, I went back to bed.

At 7:30 p.m., Yankel went to evening prayer, and I sullenly packed shampoo, tights, and a towel and went off to the *mikvah* once more. I met Dinah there, in the waiting room. We blushed, smiled at each other, and exchanged small talk. Dinah was my former classmate in *Yushive* high school, the only one who went to college, wore skirts that barely covered her knees, and married some bum she had fallen in love with who knows where. My mother told me, "Love, shmove, such marriages end in nowhere." I observed Dinah closely, her sparkling eyes, her excited giggle, her annoying smile as if she had a secret she was not going to share, and tried my hardest to glimpse the nowhere that was nowhere in sight. Finally, I decided to ignore her, and said my Psalms while waiting for my turn. Later, sitting in the bath trying to pray, I thought a lot about Dinah, who dared look so happy but was probably secretly miserable inside, and I fell asleep right there in the warm water between one prayer and another.

When I finally arrived home, sniffling from the cold, Yankel was sitting in the kitchen reading *Chassidish Tzietin,* the community newspaper. He told me that my father had come before to bring some wedding gifts he had received from family friends for us, and as he put them on the table, he had noticed the frame with the picture of my friend and me that I had taken from the drawer and put there.

"It was strange," he said. "Your father looked so agitated. He turned really pale. He picked up the picture and kept looking at it as if he couldn't believe what he was seeing. He asked me how long the picture had been here. He asked me if I knew who the girl was, and what you had told me about her. I told him you said that she was your friend and wasn't yet married. He acted weird. Then he

said that she used to be your neighbor or something, and then just
left, in the middle of a sentence—just turned around and walked
away."

I dropped my pocketbook on the couch and walked toward the
fridge. He continued.

"Why did he act like that, so strangely?"

"Very strange."

"She used to be your neighbor?"

"Yes, they lived near us. Our families were close. She was my
best friend."

"Oh. Where are they now?"

"They live in Israel."

"Are you still friends with her?"

"Yes. I am still best friends with her."

"So what happened? Why isn't she married?"

"Because she is dead. Because she hanged herself in our bathroom a week before Pesach with my purple jump rope. I never saw
the jump rope again. Where is it? What'd they do with my purple
jump rope?"

"Wh— she what?"

"Strange."

"What are you *talking* about?"

"Shmuli. Her brother Shmuli. They lived near us, just three
blocks away. He pushed his sister under the blanket. He *raped* her.
Why did he rape her like that, why?"

Yankel stared at me blankly. "What does 'rape' mean?" he asked.

I felt my heart constrict, my breath stop, and suddenly I could not
stand. I sat down on the floor—just collapsed right there and started
talking. I don't remember what I said, only that I was overcome by

the deep swirling fear and revulsion that consumed me, the waves of anger, sadness, and fear—so much fear. Yankel's face was so white, so pale, his eyes were a pool of horror as I told him that I killed Devory. It was my fault. I had killed her. Only nine and dead. I had watched her suffer, scream for help, run without shoes for miles down Ocean Parkway, and I didn't do anything. I had killed her. I watched Shmuli when he came under the blanket in the room where I slept with her. We were born on the same day; she shouldn't have died so long before me. I saw him pushing her under the blanket that night. Why did he do that, Yankel—push her like that in the dark in the room where we slept, under the blanket? I watched her lie like the dead, watched her scream, and nobody could hear her—only me. Why didn't I get into her bed? Why didn't I get into her bed when she begged me? I didn't hold her hand. I didn't hide her under my bed when her father came to our house, didn't tell him that she wasn't there. I killed her, murdered my best friend, *Devory, Devory, Devory.*

I lay sobbing on the floor in the kitchen. I called to her but her sorrow was choking me, choking me. I tried to scream but I could not make a sound. I wanted to cry, to run away, but I couldn't see anything. Only her face, her dead eyes cutting me into a million pieces. *Why why why why why why?*

Yankel was pacing around the small space near the table. I saw the agitated movements of his shiny black shoes, the frantic strides as he circled the armchair, sat on the couch, stood up, walked to the door, back, and again, pacing as if he had forgotten the beat of a march. I pulled myself off the floor and shuffled to my room. I heard the door of the apartment close and Yankel was gone.

I don't remember falling asleep. I don't remember the night

passing, the sun rising, the broken dreams. I do remember my lenses, how dry they were when I first opened my eyes at eleven the next morning. How I pulled them, yanking them out and down the drain, rinsing my face with cold water, and mashing tuna for lunch. I did not see Yankel until late that night. He had given a message to my father that he was eating supper with his learning partner. When I did see him, we did not talk much. He said he had to wake up early the next day; he had an exam in Talmud study. He was facing the wall near his bed thirty minutes after walking in.

When he did not come for dinner a second night, my mother asked me what was wrong. A tight smile on her face, she mentioned it nonchalantly. "So what happened, he doesn't like my food anymore?" I told her, no, he loved it. Yankel had exams now, pressure and all that. No need to worry. It was nothing.

It *was* nothing. A distant, empty nothing in his eyes, the nervous tremor that told me I should have said nothing to him. He walked more quietly, he did not move his hands when he spoke, as if he was afraid of breaking a silence, of disturbing what should never have been touched in the first place. But even though he came home late that night and the next, I could not, would not, move the picture of Devory off the kitchen table. I let it stay right in the center.

Yankel stopped sitting at the table. He had put the picture in my drawer, and angrily, I had returned it to its place. He drank his coffee standing against the counter. He read the paper sitting on his bed. He learned the Talmud on the couch. Never at the table. We spoke, words here, a sentence there: You're coming home late? Yes. How was school? Fine. I have to go. Okay. I'll be home at eleven tonight. Don't wait up, I'll be home late.

He had another learning partner at night now. He was helping a young boy with learning difficulties. He needed to go visit Bubba Yuskovitz, Zaida Geldbart, some other aunts and uncles. Two weeks of nothing, of the questioning, silent glances of my parents, and then one night Yankel sat on a chair waiting for me. He asked that we eat dinner at home. I said okay.

We ate in silence. We sat across from each other, me staring at the table, he at the picture, in silence.

Then he spoke.

"I went to *Reb* Ehrlich this morning. I knocked at his door and I spoke to him for two hours. . . ."

He stared at the picture, at the waving hand, the mischievous smile, the freckles scattered over her thin face.

"He didn't say much. Just kept sighing and shaking his head and said there was no answer. . . . He deals with this all the time. In Bobov, in Satmar, everywhere—it's a problem. Once, he tried to kick a teacher out when he got complaints from parents, and he did not receive his salary from the *yeshiva* for five months. They told him he could not destroy the income of a teacher, a father of six children, based on assumptions. . . . He said the only thing he could do was persuade the teacher to leave for another *yeshiva*. He teaches today in another *yeshiva* in Flatbush. He said there was a big lawsuit now against Talmud Torah, also in Flatbush, against a teacher who did inappropriate things for over twenty years. . . . He said the police came to him at least five times over the years asking about this, about that . . . but there were never any witnesses, everybody was so fearful. He said there were no answers, he did not have an answer."

He spoke rapidly as if afraid I would respond. "I don't think you

should keep remembering this. You shouldn't let it hurt you like
that. I mean, it's over. It's gone. There's no one to blame anymore.
It will just ruin everyone's lives. You have to forget about it. Just
forget about it. The Torah says one has to forgive and forget or it
consumes the person. Now is what matters. . . . You just have to
forget. I mean, people went through *gehenim* and they forgot. All the
Holocaust survivors . . . They . . . they . . . lost everything. But they
just moved on. They didn't sit there crying all day long, or we
wouldn't have a state of Israel or the Jewish nation today. They . . .
moved on, they forgot the past and built up a whole world again.
And that is the worst thing any person could go through."

We cleared off the table. A space had settled into my mind.
An empty space, and I could not think, could not care. I washed the
dishes. Yankel wiped them. He told a joke. I don't remember it. He
asked me a question. I answered. He told me that his younger sister, Chayala, was getting engaged any day now. His mother just
told him that morning, and though the wedding was a long way
off, we would be going to Israel to attend it. Wasn't that exciting? I
said wow, it was. Who was she getting engaged to? He told me a
name, a family, a cousin in America, when I turned around and
saw that the picture was not on the table. My eyes moved abruptly
around the kitchen: the counters, the couch, the floor, a glance at
the open garbage bag—where I saw it, between the lumps of ground
meat and uneaten macaroni.

I grabbed the picture—just thrust my hand inside the bag,
held it tightly between my finger and thumb, and pulled it out. She
had gotten dirty. There was a small red stain where her eyes used
to be. I screamed.

"What did you do with my picture? Why did you throw it

out?" I pushed the photo close to his face, jabbed my finger into his chest. "Don't you dare touch my picture! How dare you! It's my picture. Do you want me to throw out your pictures? How about the *sherayim* from the *Rebbe*! Don't touch my stuff, don't touch my stuff, don't you touch my stuff!"

Yankel backed away. He told me that he didn't mean to, he didn't realize, it was a mistake; he just thought that . . . he wasn't sure . . . okay, okay, he was sorry. He would never touch the picture again.

I didn't care. Putting the picture on the counter, I pushed Yankel hard against the wall. I poked his chest with my finger. "Don't. Touch. My. Picture!" His eyes changed from scared to angry to bewildered.

"You are crazy!" he said. "You are totally nuts!" He pushed my hand away. "I'm getting out of here!"

I dropped my hand. Did I just do that? I was so tired. So tired.

Yankel ran to the closet. He pulled on his coat and hat. "If I wouldn't be embarrassed," he said, "I would tell *Reb* Ehrlich!" and he slammed the door behind him.

Devory? Can you hear me?

CHAPTER
FIFTY-ONE

We did not speak of Devory again. When he returned hours later, I was already sleeping. And by morning, it was as if nothing had happened. I could not talk about it and he didn't want to.

There was so much else to talk about. There was my sister-in-law's engagement to someone from somewhere, tests to mark, and the twins that Blimi, daughter of Goldy, gave birth to after almost ten months of marriage. There was Surela's high-risk pregnancy, her children, whom I needed to help care for every afternoon, and Bubba Yuskovitz's annual surprise birthday party for herself. There was also Yankel's annoying habit of smelling his socks at night—how could he tell if they were clean or not? I told him to concentrate on the Talmud.

And the Monday he came home at midnight instead of at ten and I did not speak with him until Thursday, when he proudly brought home a bouquet of withering yellow roses because there were no more dying carnations. I told him that I hated, hated,

HATED yellow; live, fresh, red roses would do, thank you. Could
he not tell the difference between dead and alive?

He stared, bewildered, at the roses, and said, what's the difference? Flowers were flowers, and I looked like Bubba Yuskovitz
with a bad case of food poisoning lately. So what if he came home
two hours after he said he would; get over it!

And I said, Two hours later? Two hours later? Who was talking
about the two hours later! What about the lunch he just *left* on
the table, not bothering to clean up—there were bugs eating it
by the time I walked through the door at four thirty. And his dirty
underwear—would he *stop* leaving them on the floor? Did he
think this was *yeshiva*? And the socks, Hashem help me, if I saw
him sniffing at those two-day-old socks *one more time* I would call
up *Reb* Ehrlich and ask him if it was a normal thing for men holding up the pillars of holiness and purity in the joyless world of
materialism and darkness to sniff at sweaty, made-by-goyim *socks*!

But Yankel said that I was totally *meshugah*, there was no contradiction between the two, the *Rebbe himself* used to smell his
socks. Laibel, assistant to the *Rebbe* as a boy, saw him doing it, I
mean, *gevald*, most boys wore their socks for at least a week, he
was by far the cleanest. I just didn't know how to appreciate him.
Did I realize how much laundry I would have if he changed his
socks every day?

I said, yes, I did, and he could wash his socks every day himself. What made him think I was his maid, did they have maids in
the *yeshiva*, huh? huh? huh? and huffed right out of the house and
marched straight to Surela, who told me to just calm down. Those
men, they were all the same.

There was a bouquet of fresh red roses waiting for me on the table when I came home seven minutes past midnight. Yankel was sleeping, his socks dangling on the rim of the hamper where he had aimed them from his bed. I pushed them in, flicking them with my pinkie nail, and went to sleep. The next morning I found a note near the flowers that said, "These things cost ten bucks, which I took from your wallet. Water them. I'll be home at midnight. (Okay, at 11:34.)" I also took a pregnancy test—I had missed my period by two hours. And sixteen weeks after my wedding night, four months of tense waiting, and four *mikvah* visits later, there were finally two pink lines staring back at me from the little white window.

Rushing out of the house, raincoat over my nightgown, I ran to Surela's house. She called up her husband, who drove eighty miles per hour through the streets of Borough Park to the *kollel* where Yankel was learning the Talmud with a friend in the *shul* across the street. It took an hour to find that *Chassid*. I was giddily jumping up and down on the couch; Surela was shrieking that I should stop—I would destroy the one-hour-old cell that would become a baby. Then my husband—he should live until a hundred and twenty—finally walked in. I jumped off the couch, threw the pregnancy test high in the air, and Yankel did not catch it. But he picked it up, examined it closely, and, gasping with excitement, got down on one knee, holding the test triumphantly in his hand and swearing that he would never smell a sock again. My parents— who heard my happy shrieks when they finally answered the phone— drove over immediately and said that we were all completely *meshugah*, dancing around the dining room table like clowns. Gittel, *what* are you doing in your nightgown? The neighbors would hear, the evil eye would see, the angel of death would feel, *tu, tu, tu,* we must keep this a total and absolute secret until the first delicate trimester is over.

And somehow it happened. Yankel told his mother, who did not tell Bubba Yuskovitz the news. After all, is calling up an aunt so close and dear and just repeating, "*Baruch Hashem*, thank Hashem, thank Hashem, isn't it amazing? Married already four months, she must be lighting that candelabra," considered saying anything at all? And what's wrong with Bubba Yuskovitz calling up her new favorite bride and offering to go shopping for a crib, or perhaps a mobile, but *tu tu tu tu, bli ayin harah*, may the evil eye not see, one should not discuss those things prematurely."

I complained to Yankel, but he waved his hand and said, *nu*, some things would never change, and we should just thank Hashem the wait was over. After all, most of his friends had at least one baby already. He was almost twenty, which was late to be a first-time father. Then he chuckled giddily and said that it was really way too early to talk about all this. We would no longer discuss the pregnancy until at least the third month.

We did not discuss the pregnancy until the next morning. It was Friday, almost Purim, and Yankel told me that he did not mean to scare me, but he had heard from his friend that in the first month one should get out of bed right leg first. It was a good omen. Getting out with the left leg first disrupted the newly planted soul's session of learning with the Angel of Torah and could have dangerous consequences. I stared at my legs. Did getting out of bed in the middle of the night also count? And if the left foot did not yet touch the floor, and you then switched quickly to the right, did the Angel of Torah take a deep breath and continue? My mother burst out laughing when she heard this and said that it was all complete nonsense. The only thing that mattered was that I dare not step on any fingernails. Nails were a bad omen and often brought on miscarriage. Surela told me not to worry so much, when I called her up trembling in fright. She said people were overprotective of a first-time pregnancy, scaring the heck out of the young mother for no reason, and if I just stayed away from any falling leaves everything would be fine. Falling leaves symbolized spiritual degeneration, and the child would be permanently scarred and religiously damaged.

Yankel said, "Eh, it's nothing!" and that I must rest and take life easy now. He would ask his mother not to say anything out of hand when she spoke with me, especially not about the name she had decided the child would be called—Duvid'l, after her great-grandfather if it was a boy, and Leah, after the carrot *kugel* maker if it was a girl.

"Not exactly," said I. "The *minhag*—tradition—is that the first child's name is decided by the mother's side and no one else."

Yankel smiled impishly. "Okay. My mother will just have to survive this one." He sat back comfortably in his chair eating chicken. "So who will you name the baby after? Wait, don't you also have a great-aunt Leah?"

"Yes, but not Leah," I said. "Devory."

Yankel creased his forehead, trying to recall. "Devory? Which grandmother is called Devory?"

"None. My friend. Devory Goldblatt."

He dangled the fork in the air. "Who?"

"Devory. My best friend, who died when she was nine."

There was a sharp bang as the fork hit the table. "Are you crazy? It is forbidden to name a child after someone so young, and certainly someone who died like *that*! This is . . . this is . . . it's a terrible omen. You know that. You can't call her Devory. You are not making sense! Besides, enough of that topic. I can't believe you are bringing her up again!"

"I'm calling her Devory."

"Gittel! Forget about it! A child is named after someone she can aspire to be . . . an ancestor, a grandparent, a rabbi, not a child who . . . who—"

"Devory, Devorah, the prophetess and judge of the Jewish nation."

"Gittel, stop it! And let's just hear exactly what you are going to tell everybody? My parents, yours, our relatives, my friends."

"She used to sit under the palm tree of Deborah . . . the Jews would come to her for judgment."

"So what are you, a new feminist now? My child will *not* be called Devory!"

"I'll say that I am calling my child Devory for my friend who hanged herself when she was nine years old. That is what I'll say."

"You will do nothing like that."

"I will call her Devory."

"I will go to *Reb* Ehrlich! Nobody names their child after a dead child!"

"She didn't just die. She was murdered."

"I don't care! No normal kid does such a thing! She was probably crazy to begin with!"

"Devory. Devory Goldblatt."

"Forget about it. You're acting completely emotional!"

"We will call her Devory."

"Gittel! Stop it now!" And I watched him march out of the house.

I went into my bedroom and sat on my bed. I held my pillow close to my chest and slowly rocked myself back and forth, rocking, rocking, hunched over the exquisite embroidered monogram in the center of the bed. The phone rang. It was Chevi, my cousin.

"Gittel! I have not talked to you *forever*! How are you? What's up? I heard the news! I am sooo excited, I can't believe it, isn't it amazing? I am so happy for you! Oh my gosh, we're gonna have our babies only three months apart! I can't believe it! I can't believe it! When are you coming to visit? We could go shopping together for maternity clothes! Isn't it a weird feeling to be pregnant? There's an actual human being growing inside of you!"

"I have to go," I said, and hung up.

I stared out the window. I washed dishes. I did things around the house. I tried mopping the floor but instead sat at the table for an hour waiting. *Why, Gittel, why?* I cleared off the untouched food and put it in plastic containers. I placed it in the fridge.

Yankel came in an hour before *Shabbos*. He walked in, opened the closet, pulled on his silk black *bekeshe*, and placed the *shtreimel* on his head. He then turned around and closed the door behind him. I watched him from the window, walking down the street to *shul*, his *shtreimel* bobbing up and down until I could see it no longer.

I walked slowly to my mother's house. My mother smiled secretly when she saw me and said I should take advantage of the new dress I was wearing. It would not be long before it did not fit me. Surela, lounging on the couch, stroking her own swollen belly, warned me that I should take advantage of, well, everything. She pointed to my three nieces and nephew turning over a bookshelf in the corner. "Sleep, eat, read, do everything now, Gittel. You aren't gonna have too much freedom once that comes out!" She then smiled lovingly and said that it was all worth it—every pound of fat; every ounce of energy. There was nothing as beautiful as children.

I fell asleep on the armchair and woke up to the sounds of *"Gut Shabbos, Gut Shabbos!"* as my father, brother-in-law, Moishe, and Yankel returned from *shul*. My nephew, happily tearing pages out of my old schoolbooks, screeched so loudly when my mother stopped him that no one noticed Yankel's tense silence, the rigid strain on his neck as he made *kiddush* without waiting for me, did not sing *Shalom Aleichem* and *Eishes Chayil* with the rest of the men. I heard *kiddush* from my father and helped serve the fish, humming along with the *Shabbos zemiros*. I made small challah-balls for my nephew, reassured my mother that the smell of soup did not nauseate me, and spent most of the fish course separating my three-year-old nephew from my four-year-old niece, who had taken his napkin because he had eaten from her challah after she had used his fork. I held crying Leah'la on my lap.

My mother wiped my niece's face while recounting her conversation with *Reb* Weinstein's mother that morning, after he had been released on bail from prison. She said, "Poor woman. I mean, even if the story had some truth, why did the Bergers have to do it in such a horrible public way? They are destroying the whole Weinstein family. They are all innocent, and did you see what it said in the *Daily Post* today?" She hadn't read it herself but she had heard from Mrs. Rosner that some reporter, one of those typical anti-Semites, accused the community of denial. What denial? she continued. They should just look at their own papers; they're filled every day with these horror stories and sick crimes. Hashem, you can't read that stuff without getting depressed, and they're

talking about us? They should look at the Catholics, the priests
there, such hypocrites. Remember that scandal? How could any
parent trust their child with those *people* for even one second? It
is amazing there are still so many Catholics in this world. I mean,
if they can't trust their own clergymen, then what are they *thinking*? And my father, looking agitated, said that this was not a discussion for the *Shabbos* table. Did the children really have to hear
this?

"You're right," my mother said, shaking her head. "It just made
me so mad, I couldn't help it," and then she moved on to Goldy,
mother of Blimi, and Blimi's twins—totally unexpected, nobody
had ever had twins on either side of the family, and how hard it
was. "I always said, take them one at a time. It's hard enough with
one. . . ."

"Hey," my father said, winking at me. "You never know."

I rolled my eyes.

"Okay, okay," Surela announced. "Remember? We are not supposed to be discussing this. . . ."

"Right," my mother agreed. "My mother always said, don't talk
before the fact. . . . She learned the hard way. She always told me
how she and my father fought constantly over the name of their
first baby in the first month already . . . *nebech*, they had so many
people who perished in the war to name after, but the baby never
made it past the third month. When I was pregnant with Surela,
she didn't let me as much as complain about morning nausea out
loud. She warned me that Satan will hear and take the baby away.
Be happy that you have morning nausea."

Moishe, wiping off the ketchup Chaim had splattered on his
face, laughed. "My mother still doesn't forgive my father for my

name. They had agreed on Avigdor, after her grandfather whom she was close with, but my father mistakenly said Moishe after *his* grandfather in *shul* during the naming ceremony, and here I am— Moishe. My mother didn't talk to him till I was a year old, I think. . . . My father always joked that if only my name had been Avigdor I would have done better in *yeshive*."

"What nonsense," my father said. "People treat a name as if it's the only thing that will decide what the child will be. The most important thing is the way you raise a child, not his name."

"Of course names are extremely imporant," Moishe said. "In my family we have a *minhag* that before you name the child, the parents go pray at the grave of that person to ask for permission and for a blessing on the baby's soul."

Go to the grave for a blessing on the soul. Go to the grave for a blessing . . . *Devory?* I remember standing up. I remember my voice; it came out of my mouth clearly, unafraid, as if asking about a second slice of fish, "Mommy, where is Devory's grave?"

My mother wiped her mouth with a napkin and smiled at my niece, who was finally finishing her last piece of fish. "Grave? Who?"

She poured some juice into a small glass cup.

"Devory. Where is she buried?"

My mother stared at me blankly. "Devory? Which Devory?"

"My friend. Devory Goldblatt. She hanged herself in our bath-room upstairs. Remember?"

The juice bottle came down with a bang. My mother turned swiftly, her eyes narrowing in fear. "What? What are you talking about?"

"I want to know where she is buried. I want to go visit her grave. I want to name our child, if it is a girl, after her. Where is Devory's grave? Why doesn't—"

My mother looked, her eyes widening, then narrowing, as Surela's fork stopped midair, my father's mouth opened then closed, and Yankel dropped the spoonful of fish he was holding.

She screamed, "Are you crazy? Have you gone out of your mind? What are you talking about? I have absolutely no idea! No one knows! Hashem help me, you are finally pregnant, and this is what you are now busy with? It's over, it's gone, and it went away!" She stood abruptly. "You have an appointment on Sunday with Dr. Weber for a first checkup and then you must go shopping! They have this amazing sale in Generations—gorgeous stuff. You wouldn't believe the prices! But don't forget to bring your insurance card and don't forget the co-pay. I think it's fifteen dollars. And if you meet Goldy in the street, don't you *dare* tell her you are expecting; she did not tell me a thing about her daughter and I had to find out only after the whole street knew, and I—"

Another cup. I threw it hard against the wall; another shattering crash, over her head, over the candlesticks, and against the beige and gold floral wallpaper. A million little pieces of glass scattered everywhere on the floor.

Dead silence.

"Where. Is. Her. Grave?"

My mother stared at me, her face gone white, her eyes stunned. My father looked at me, his eyes pools of pain and sorrow. He could not hold me anymore, could not cuddle me till I fell asleep in his arms. And forgot.

I watched the silence erupt into sparks of noise, rapid chatter, a desperate clamor that rose over the broken chasm, desperately pushing it all back together again. I could not hear them; I only saw their frowning mouths, disapproving eyes, downturned lips, and angry gestures. "What happened? What happened? Why now? What are you talking about?"

Yankel pushed back his chair sharply, his *shtreimel* knocking onto the floor. Grabbing the hat, he walked past me, his eyes a distant nothingness. He walked out, out, out of the house. So much silence, so much screaming silence.

"Look what you're doing! Your husband walked out! What is the purpose! What's wrong with you, ruining your marriage? Over what? *Because such a little girl died?* Surela, take the kids to the back room; they don't have to hear this. Why now? What happened? It's ten years later! What happened suddenly now? It's already ten years *of nothing, an empty space in time.* You told Yankel what happened! Are you crazy? How could you do such a thing? What did you ever do that for? Why? *Why? Why?*"

I walked out. Past my mother, past my father, past the rapid, anxious gestures. I walked away—away from the tower that had never reached heaven.

My father came after me. I heard his hurried footsteps running down the block. I heard his voice, "Gittel, Gittel, wait. Don't run, Gittel, wait!"

I ran, leaving his footsteps and his pleading voice behind me, ran back home to the little table in my small kitchen with the picture. But my father came after me. I heard his weary footsteps, his knocking on the door, his opening it without waiting.

"Gittel."

I stood up.

"Gittel."

I walked into my bedroom.

"Gittel, listen to me."

I locked my door and sat on my bed, rocking, rocking, rocking the silence away.

"Gittel, open the door."

I could see the shadow of his feet under the door. He stood there for a long time. "Gittel, open the door. I am sorry. So sorry. Open the door." I needed to listen to the screams, needed to see the shattered face, the dead blue eyes. "Gittel, Gittel, I will find you her grave. I will tell you where it is. Nobody dared ask then. . . ." *Devory, don't go.* "You were such a little girl, such a little girl. . . ."

He left, saying something about finding Yankel. Then there was light where his shadow had stood.

CHAPTER
FIFTY-TWO

Yankel came home at dawn. He lay slumped on the couch, where I found him after a fitful sleep. I drank a cup of coffee and watched him, his head on his open arm, his long *payos* dangling over the arm of the couch, moving imperceptibly with his soft breathing.

I wondered how long he had slept that way. His *shtreimel* lay carelessly tossed on the floor, his *bekeshe* thrown over the other end of the couch. I dropped my coffee cup into the sink. There was a dull bang as it rolled in the metallic basin and Yankel sat up, startled. He looked at me, his eyes bloodshot, stumbled to the bathroom, and shut the door behind him. I heard water splashing. When he came out, he sat at the table and stared at his knees. He looked up at the wall and down at his shoes. He nervously curled his *payos* and pulled at his beard, and finally he put his face in his hands and remained staring at the floor for over half an hour.

I ignored him as I sat on the couch, flipping through a Jewish women's magazine. There were pretty pictures, so many pretty pictures of flowers and babies and fresh, new recipes for the holidays directly from Roisy's Kitchen. There was also an article on how to raise agreeable children and ways to ensure your child does not befriend those who have the Internet in their homes.

I heard a small sigh as Yankel stood up. He walked to the closet near the door and took out his spare prayer shawl. He began to pray. Standing near the door, the large white cloth wrapped closely over his head and body, he swayed. The twined fringes swinging in the air, his trembling hands gripping the prayer book, his eyes clenched shut, he prayed. I shut the magazine. I put the pretty pictures away and mashed tuna.

We did not leave the apartment that *Shabbos*. Did not eat by my mother, did not answer the worried knocks of my sister, or speak of the picture lying right-side up on the table.

We slept a lot. Huddled under our blankets, we fell into sporadic states of unconsciousness, and at some point in between Yankel told me that my father had spoken to him last night in *shul*. He told me that he had listened for hours, never uttering a sound, as my father, in tears, told him everything.

We ate more mashed tuna in the afternoon and some leftover salad at night. And Yankel looked at me across the small table, fear still embedded in the darkness of his pupils, but the distance was gone from his eyes.

He nibbled on a piece of challah. "I don't know why," he said, "but I remember when I was a little boy, we had an Arab cleaning lady. She came sobbing one day to my mother about her niece, a twelve-year-old girl in Jordan, who was stoned to death after she cried to her father that her uncle . . . you know . . . did things with her. I didn't understand what they were saying, but I remember my mother talking to my father about it. She whispered about those barbaric Arabs, what animals they were, stoning their own daughters until they die. . . ."

I looked out the window. "And here we bury them, slowly, alive."

"Don't say that. Don't say that. We are not like the Arabs."

"No. We can't see the blood running."

"Gittel, why are you talking like that? Do you think we are like them?"

"No, we can't hear the screams. We talk too loud."

Yankel shook his head. He sighed. We looked out the window at the bobbing hats passing by on the way to *shul*.

My father left a message on my voice mail after *Shabbos*. In a hoarse, low voice he read the address of the cemetery where Devory was buried, repeating it slowly, twice. He had received the information from an aunt, he said, the one who had taken care of things when it happened. He asked me to call home. My mother was worried. Everyone was. Please, Gittel, call home, now. I pulled the wire out of the wall.

– – –

We paid the car service one hundred dollars to drive us up to the cemetery and back. *Devory?* I told him to stay home, but Yankel had come with me. *Don't go.* It was Sunday, he had *kollel*, but he refused to stay home. *Don't cry, Devory. . . .* He said he wouldn't let me go alone. We needed to talk. *Devory. . . .* There was so much he did not know, so much he wanted to hear. I was silent on the two-hour drive to the cemetery.

Devory?

Why was I so silent; why didn't I tell him? He looked at me, the nothingness gone from his eyes. I told him he would see by the grave. First we must find the grave, we must find the grave.

We passed hills, mountains, dark forests of bare trees, and cold, hard winter ground around frozen lakes. *Gittel, come with me.* The wrought-iron gate was open when we arrived, and the wind whistled mournfully—*Come with me.* It was somewhere in the back, my father had said. He said the headstone was simple and gray and there was a cherry tree right there, a big tree. I ran through the cemetery.

Gittel?

I rushed frantically through rows of headstones, from grave to grave.

Gittel?

A simple gray headstone, a cherry tree nearby.

Come with me. . . .

Yankel rushed behind me, afraid I would trip. "Be careful," he said gently. "You'll find it, it's here. . . ."

A grave with a name. *Devory?*

Come to me, Gittel.

"Stop running! It is not good for you. Calm down, please calm down. . . ."

Come with me, Gittel, come. . . .

And it was there. A simple gravestone in the back of the cemetery near a tall cherry tree, its bare branches hovering emptily above. A small corner gravestone with a name. *Devory Goldblatt.* No flower. No rock. No pebble. Just a name.

Devory?

I wept. And wept and wept and wept.

Yankel ran to me, his long *payos* flying in the air, his hands reaching out. I pushed him away but Yankel held me tight. I could not look, could not see, only cried until suddenly I could not breathe. Everything went white as my throat closed shut, choking me so that no air came in. I felt his hands holding me, his voice weeping for me, "Gittel, don't cry like that, don't cry," and he grabbed my shoulders, shaking me. I buried my face deeply in his chest. Finally, I looked up, and his eyes were so close to mine. "Breathe deeply, like that. Yes, breathe deeply. . . ."

I let him hold me. Then I bent over the gravestone, stroking it, caressing it. It was cold, and Yankel and I rocked, swaying with the wind, the mournful howling wind. "Why are you holding me, outside, where people can see? Why?"

His arms wrapped around me, his *payos* on my cheek, brushing against it softly, he answered, "Because you are in pain. You are in so much pain."

Why why why why did we kill her, why? Devory, don't cry anymore. I don't want you to be sad any longer. . . . I can't bear it.

Yankel and I cried together. We wept near the grave with no flower. No rocks left by visitors. Engraved with only a name.

Devory Goldblatt, only nine years old; condemned by family and community to death by hanging

CHAPTER
FIFTY-THREE

Yankel slept in my bed that night. He snuggled close to me under the blanket and softly stroked my hair. We talked late into the night. I told him about Devory and the things we had done together as children. I told him about the books she had read, the funny things she had said, and about the time we sneaked outside after midnight when we were seven because Devory wanted to talk to the stars.

Yankel told me about *Reb* Ehrlich. He told me that he had gone to him early yesterday morning for advice, before we had gone to the cemetery.

"I didn't tell you right away. I was too shocked—but he wept, Gittel," he said. "He sobbed like a small child. He said that he knew Devory's story and so many other stories like it, about both girls and boys. He told me of three boys who had been abused years ago by a *Rebbe* in the *cheder* where *Reb* Ehrlich himself then taught. One parent complained, but who believed her? When the mother said she'd call the police, they threatened her with a call to Social Services. The school warned her that they would call the police themselves and say that she was neglecting her kids—and she'd never see her children again."

Yankel sighed. He kissed me gently on the head. He said that *Reb* Ehrlich had told him he had known then that the mother was right. He had known because the teacher had confessed to him about what he had done to the boys and *Reb* Ehrlich had promised the mother he would help. But he had kept quiet in the end. The fear and the pressure were too much.

All three boys left *yeshiva* by sixteen. They went to the streets, to drugs. Only a few weeks before, when Yankel had first gone to *Reb* Ehrlich, the mother had called him and said that maybe now that he was an important *rav*, he could go out and find her son and his friends on the streets somewhere—hating Hashem, rabbis, and most of all, themselves. I won't let you forget them, she said. You who knew, you who didn't care enough to help—I want you to live with this for the rest of your life.

Yankel was quiet. Then he said, "When *Reb* Ehrlich cried like that to me, I knew that your pain was real, that this was all true. And I should start listening."

We fell asleep in my bed together.

But Devory came to me that night. She came knocking on my window, knocking, knocking.

"Devory!" I screamed, and I ran to her. But no matter how fast I ran, no matter how far I reached out, I could not get to the window. Devory cried. I could see her eyes opened wide with fear, her lips mouthing my name, begging me to open the window. I reached out to her, but she did not see me. It was windy outside, her hair flew wildly in her face, and she pressed hard against the pane, screaming.

And then suddenly a strong rush of wind came, and like an angry demon, it pulled her away. She fought the wind, her hands flailing hard, grasping at the air, calling me—*Gittel, Gittel*.

I opened my mouth to scream. I opened my mouth to answer her, but nothing came out. I was horrified because I realized that I could not say a word. I was suffocating. My mouth was tightly gagged and nothing came out.

Then I woke up. It was light outside. The sunlight streamed through the shades. I sat up in my bed, holding my pillow in my arms, resting my head on the soft, clean linen.

Yankel walked in from the morning prayers. He said that he had prepared breakfast on the table, so why hadn't I eaten? How would I get through this pregnancy if I didn't take better care of myself? Things were difficult enough.

I told him I was going to Mr. Glicksman. He said, "You are? Who's that? Come eat something. The baby is starving."

Mr. Glicksman was Devory's uncle. He owned the largest newspaper in the ultra-Orthodox world. Devory's father used to write a weekly Torah column there before they moved away. I told Yankel I was going to see him today. He said, "Why today?"

I said, "They need to write about this in the paper. They need to write about child molestation."

Yankel said, "Um . . . Oh . . . Are you sure? Okay, why don't you first eat breakfast?"

So I ate breakfast. Then I went to Mr. Glicksman. My father had called before I left. My mother was devastated at what was happening, he said. Maybe I could come over and we would talk about it. I told him that I could not talk. I needed to take care of things now.

The office of the community newspaper was located on Sixteenth Avenue. It was a busy place. There were desks and computers, and a harried secretary who wanted to know if I had an appointment. I said, "No. I am Gittel Klein—I mean, Geldbart—his niece Devory's best friend. Tell him that, and that I need to speak to him now."

The secretary looked at me strangely. She did not know who I was. She went into Mr. Glicksman's office at the end of the hall. She came out a moment later. She said, "Mr. Glicksman is really busy right now. Would you like to make an appointment and come back next week?"

"No," I said. I then stood up, walked down the hall, and opened the door to his office.

Mr. Glicksman was on the phone. He looked at me, surprised that I opened the door like that. He hung up the phone and said, "Excuse me?"

"You are excused," I said. "I am Gittel Geldbart. I was *Devory's* best friend. Remember—your niece—your sister's daughter? She was the one who hanged herself on a rope in the bathroom of my house."

Mr. Glicksman was silent.

"You know who I am," I continued. "You pray in my father's *shul* every morning."

He swallowed. "Of course I know who you are. This is just unexpected."

"I apologize," I said. "The unexpected can be really annoying, like when one's nine-year-old friend hangs herself from a shower rod after being raped by her brother."

Mr. Glicksman did not answer. He did not have to. He listened silently as I explained to him about Devory, about what I had seen, about almost a decade of denial. His eyebrows rose worriedly as I told him of his obligation as publisher of this newspaper to write about sexual abuse, to put in an article bringing awareness so that it should not be so unexpected.

The phone rang. He ignored it. The secretary came in. He told her to leave. Then when I finished talking, when I could not talk any longer, he turned to me. He said, "You are right. You are right. . . ." And no, he hadn't forgotten Devory; how was it possible to forget?

"I know there is a situation. We all know stories. I hear it all the time. But you being right won't make things happen"—he snapped his fingers—"like that. The *rabbonim* will close down this paper in one week if we put in something on abuse. They will put a *cherem*—a ban—on it, and nobody will dare buy it. There are rules and regulations I must follow. Maybe I own the paper, but the *rabbonim* are the only real bosses of the Orthodox community. We must get permission before we publish anything." He looked down at his desk. "And it will be difficult to get permission for this."

I told him I would go talk with the *rabbonim* myself.

"No," he said emphatically. "You are very naive. I know the system; I know who to talk with and who has the right connections to the *rabbonim*. It is not so simple. You are just a young woman—still a girl. They won't listen to you. It is you who must listen to them."

But he promised he would try, really try. He asked that I call him back in a few days. I told him I was going to visit Devory's grave in a few days. I wanted to know what to tell her.

When Mr. Glicksman did not answer my calls after three days, I returned to his office. He was speaking with an editor, and a line of writers stood outside waiting. His secretary told me that Mr. Glicksman had an appointment soon with an important educator about their next main issue, the evils of the Internet, and that I should return later. I did not want to return later.

I marched down the hallway. I opened the door. I asked a worker sitting there to please leave, thank you very much, and sat down in the chair.

"What happened?" I asked.

Mr. Glicksman leaned forward, his mouth open. His eyes blinked nervously. He sighed.

"It is not so simple," he said. "In fact, it is almost impossible. I went to *Reb* Shlomo, the biggest *rav* of Lakewood. He just kept saying, some subjects must be dealt with in silence. Some subjects are better left in silence. I went to the *Yushive Rebbe*; he said he would think about it. We had to be careful. It was a difficult subject and could bring a lot of *loshon harah*. I went to two others. Gittel, this could take months. Even if they do agree, they have to approve the article and it has to be written very delicately, very carefully, making sure not to—"

I stood up. I pointed at him. "There is something else Hashem gave us. It is called common sense. Hashem knows why, given how utterly rare it is." I threw down a folded paper, a letter I had written, on his desk. I had wanted to read it to him, for him to understand what I meant, but now . . .

I stepped away. I could feel my swollen belly harden and my heart constrict, beating in my chest like painful jabs. "You . . . you are a murderer . . . like all of them."

I left his office. I left the building. I walked the streets of Borough Park. I passed my old elementary schools, a boy's *cheder*, the sounds of their high-pitched voices repeating the prayers wafting out the windows. I watched a classroom of preschool children playing in a crowded school yard. They chased one another around. They jumped rope and threw ball, their tightly curled *payos* flying in the wind. I went back home.

Yankel said I must stop. I must stop trying to change what I couldn't. "We will go to a therapist. We will go every week until you feel better. But you can't change the fibers of this community. Even men can't, and you . . . you are just a young woman. It is you who must listen to them."

I spoke with my baby. I sat on my bed, stroking my swollen belly, singing Devory's and my favorite songs. I told the baby that her name would be Devory, and she would be beautiful, smart, and curious.

I did not sleep that night. Yankel, standing in his pajamas near our room, wanted to know why I was not in bed.

"It's after midnight. Come already. How are you going to wake up tomorrow?"

I explained to him that I dared not go to sleep. Devory would knock on our window and haunt my dreams. She would never let me go again.

Yankel shook his head tiredly. He began to say something but changed his mind. Instead he took a book from the shelf. He sat down across from me and studied the book. It was the *Sefat Emet*, a widely studied commentary on the Torah. He swayed as he learned. His long *payos* moved rhythmically as he rocked back and forth over the pages, whispering the ancient words to himself. His finger grasped at his side-curl. He curled it as he studied. His eyes moved slowly, intensively, like he was having a secret conversation. He turned the pages softly. He touched the lines gently. I made him tea, but he did not notice me anymore.

I watched him learn. At 2:30 a.m. I drank the last of his cold tea. Yankel was slumped over the good book. At 4:00 a.m., I dragged him to bed. At 4:15, I fell asleep myself. It was a dreamless sleep till dawn. Then I woke up again. And fell asleep again. And was jolted awake at 9:00.

It was then that Yankel rushed into the bedroom. He pulled at my blanket.

"Gittel—you must see this. Wake up!"

I groaned. "Is *Mashiach* here? Go *away.*"

But Yankel was frantic. He said, "Gittel—here it is! In the newspaper."

I sat up and took the paper from him. I scanned the page, and there it was, my letter. My letter was in it. It was in the last pages of the paper, in Reader's Forum, a popular column published weekly.

Dear Devory,

　　Last week I went to visit your grave. I am the first to visit your grave since you were buried there almost ten years ago. You died when you were nine, Devory. Only nine. You hanged yourself from the shower rod in the bathroom of my house. You used my jump rope to put an end to your life, the purple one that shone and glittered when it turned.

We all killed you, Devory. We did not let you scream. And when you did, trying to say that your brother was abusing you, that your brother was coming to you at night, into your bed, hurting you horribly, killing you slowly, everyone ignored you. They told you to keep quiet, that you were crazy, that something was wrong with you. And I, your best friend, stayed silent.

I share responsibility for your death. I am guilty because I knew and was afraid to scream. And the terror of watching, the horror of knowing, it never goes away, and always I feel like a murderer. For that I can never forgive them.

I am so sorry, Devory. I am apologizing for all of them, for those who should have known but didn't, for those who knew but ignored, and for those who put their reputations above their children's lives.

I am sorry I am the only one visiting your grave. I am sorry you suffered so horribly. I am sorry because I love you and you are my friend, Devory Goldblatt. You didn't have to die. But for our ignorance, for our deliberate blindness, for our unforgivable stupidity, you did. I hope this letter will stop others from sharing your fate.

Your best friend,
Gittel Geldbart

I read the letter again and again. He had changed some words, left out some—like sexually abused and raped—but still, my letter was there, inside, in the pages of the community paper. I could not understand what had happened. Why had he put it in?

I called up Mr. Glicksman. "How?" I asked. "How did they agree so fast?"

"They didn't," he said. "I put it in anyway."

"Why?"

He answered tiredly. His voice sounded strained and hoarse. "We've made too many mistakes already."

The letters came by the tens, then by the hundreds. They did not print them in the paper—the rabbis were furious enough—but Mr. Glicksman sent them to me from his office. Letters from brothers, from sisters, from friends, mostly anonymous; letters from a woman whose husband killed himself two years before, and only after did she find out why. . . . From a sister who watched her brother drinking bleach so he could go to the hospital and not to school, to be at his teacher's mercy. . . . From a young woman who visits her good friend in the psychiatric ward every week. She has been in and out of there since she was sixteen and raped repeatedly by a cousin. . . . And from an anonymous woman, no longer religious, who wanted to know when the *rabbonim*, those rabbis, would ever apologize.

"When will they publicly apologize themselves for the crimes they helped commit? Will they ever ask forgiveness from the dead, from the walking wounded, from each and every child whose *Rebbe* allowed them to stay in the classroom, whose parents were kept ignorant and scared, for whom reputation was more important than anything else?"

I took these letters around with me. I showed them to everyone. I made copies and put them on my high school principal's desk, on other principals' desks. I would not stop talking of Devory.

My sister, Surie, wanted me to keep quiet. Her in-laws were furious with her. They said that their daughter now had questions, she had lost her innocence.

"How dare you go against the *rabbonim*?" Surie screamed at me. "Mommy aged ten years since you started with this! How can you do this to them? You have to learn to forgive. That is not the way an *Eishes Chayil* acts. A Woman of Valor does things quietly—at least anonymously. And how *dare* you talk about the *rabbonim* like that? How will your children ever get married? And don't even try to go near my children with that garbage mouth of yours—" And she slammed down the phone.

Yankel listened on the other phone. He had picked up the cordless at the same time I did when the phone rang and Surie began to yell. I cried after she hung up. I wept by the wall, too tired to answer, to even sit down.

Yankel comforted me. "*You* are the *Eishes Chayil*," he said. "*You* are the real one. You are the only one protecting the children, and that is what a real mother does."

He held me tightly.

Those were long months. Months of fierce arguments with my mother, tear-filled ones with my father, who said that *progress* was a terrifying term in our world; it meant something had been wrong with the past, the place we chose to remain. I must be careful.

I wasn't careful at all. I met with others who had been hurt, who watched others get hurt, who saw their children falling apart and did not know how or why or what to do. I met with social workers and therapists, and I handed out books on abuse to anyone who would take them and especially those who wouldn't. It was the first painful attempts at coping with abuse within our own small world.

In September, my baby was born. We named her Devory. Devory was her name: fuzzy scalp, pint-sized fists, aimless dark eyes, swaddled in warm, cashmere pink.

Yankel announced it at the *shul* after the prayers on *Shabbos*. There were rainbow cakes and Venetian cookies proudly laid out on long tables pushed against the wall. There were small glass *L'chaim* cups, bottles of clear wine, men crowded closely to the podium when Yankel announced our little girl as Devory Geldbart. Devory, after the girl who died.

There was a shuffling of polished shoes, a shifting of prayer shawls, and whispering sounds like bewildered things floating through the air, settling on one surprised face, then another. Devory? Which Devory? The Devory who hanged?

They called me, bubbies, uncles, friends, the neighbor who happened to drop by just to ask, just to hear again what they said in the street, in homes, at the *Shabbos* table. My mother shook her head, half smiling, half crying, at the shock of knowing that her daughter had never been well behaved. They looked at me strangely, at Yankel sympathetically.

Tiny Devory, with her fuzzy scalp and innocent dark eyes— one small hand clenched around Yankel's finger and one around mine—cried in her crib, and we soothed her to sleep humming an old Yiddish lullaby. On her dresser sat the silver frame with the picture of my friend Devory. And every time I looked at it, her laughter made me smile because now she would be here forever. We would visit her grave, put a pebble there, and give her a name . . .

a memory,

a tear.

Devory, Devory, Devory Goldblatt. *Mazel tov.* This is our daughter's name.

Dear Devory,

You came to me last night. And when I opened the window you climbed into my room. You climbed into my bed and put out your hand. I took it. I held it forever.

We lay in my bed in the dark. We lay in the dark and giggled. It was a safe kind of dark, where no one could see us or get inside, because you said we were now in heaven, and the living were forbidden. This was a secret place.

We whispered and talked and giggled. We were only nine and everything was funny. We looked up at the ceiling of my room, and we could see straight up to the stars. You said we could talk for hours, for as long as we wanted, because there was no time in heaven, only one long forever.

Then we held hands and ran. We ran through the door of my room and into a sunny meadow. We played there, dancing and skipping over rolling green hills, across soft green grass, and falling into bushes that cushioned us like pillows. They can't catch us, you said, because no one can tell us how to dream. This is our heaven.

Before dawn, we returned to my room. We lay in my bed. We stared up at the orange red sky and whispered and laughed. Then we drifted off to sleep together. When I woke up, you were gone.

It doesn't matter. Now I know where you are. Now I know where your secret place is, and that you are there, still laughing.

Your best friend forever,
Gittel

AUTHOR'S NOTE

When I was twenty-three years old, I began writing *Hush*. It wasn't a book back then; it was only a story. *My* story. It became my story when I first learned what the words *sexual abuse* meant. I had known of the words, had heard of them, but wasn't quiet sure how to define them—except that they defined something that happened by the gentiles. By us, the ultra-Orthodox, the *Chassidic*, the chosen Jewish nation living in Brooklyn, New York, it wasn't a term we needed to know.

Oh, there had been stories. As children and as teenagers, we heard them all the time—whispered rumors, murmured gossip, secret scandals—all made up by some desperate people who spread lies. People who, because of mental instability, hatred for our community, or perhaps the influence of Satan, were spreading blood libels—like the gentiles do—saying things that wouldn't have dared happen by us.

But it could happen. I was a young girl when I watched my

friend being molested, though I could not understand what I was seeing. I was a young girl when an eleven-year-old boy from the community hanged himself. They said he did it because he didn't have any friends. Others killed themselves, ran away, fell apart, but we were young and ignorant and just ran outside with our friends, where we played and laughed and stared at passing gentiles, wondering at the evil they hid inside, wondering at the empty lives they led. Of this we were certain because that is what our teachers told us again and again—and that meant it was true, even if we couldn't understand why.

Okay, we weren't *completely* certain. After all, we did not have TV, did not listen to radio, watch movies, or read secular magazines; the *goyishe* media would contaminate our purity and stain our innocence. It would destroy the world they built for us, the insular, bubblelike existence that had been carefully cultivated over the generations to last until *Mashiach*, the Messiah, arrived. And we liked it that way. It was all we knew. It was all our parents knew, and their parents too—a way of life going back generations from the *shtetles* in Europe to the ones we built here, our holy enclaves tucked right in the middle of New York.

We didn't need the outside world. We had our own. We published our own newspapers, wrote our own literature, and put on our own plays—separate for men and women, of course. We attended Orthodox *Chassidic* schools, spoke Yiddish first and English second, covered ourselves with modest clothing, and never ever talked or played with anyone but our own kind. We built walls, and built them high. The walls would keep the gentiles and their terrifying world far away. The walls would protect us and shelter us—and as we built them higher, thicker, wider, we forgot to look inside. We forgot that the greatest enemies always grow from within.

This story is important to me because of what I have learned since I was twenty-three. It is dear to me because of the tens and hundreds of children—now adults—I have met, some like walking dead, others still terrified, all wounded, carrying an anger that never goes away. Ever. Watching them learn to mouth the words, to say them out loud: *sexual abuse, sexual abuse, sexual abuse, I was sexually abused*; to scream it to the high heaven and wonder if G-d, any g-d, was listening. It is a story I wrote about life in the ultra-Orthodox *Chassidic* world—about our joy, about our warmth, and about our deep, deep denial of anything that did not follow tradition, law, or our deeply ingrained delusions. It is a story told through the eyes of children, those who need to learn to understand how and why it happened to them, and those who need to find a way to survive it. This is for all the children—past and present—who still suffer.

I have used a fictitious name, Yushive, for the main sect in *Hush*. I did this because I refuse to point a finger at one group, when the crime was endemic to all.

Eishes Chayil

GLOSSARY

Yiddish is an ancient language that uses a blend of Hebrew, German, Aramaic, and Slavic. It is written with the traditional Hebrew alphabet, but in this book the words have been spelled phonetically in our alphabet to make it more accessible to readers. Please keep in mind that certain sounds in Yiddish are unusual for native English speakers.

WARNING: Do not pronounce CH as in *chimney* or *chase* in this book. Since there is no English equivalent for this sound, think about the sound you make when you're clearing your congested throat—"yucccchhh"! That end sound in *yuch* is the sound you're trying to make. Other similar words are the Scottish pronunciation of *loch* and the braided Jewish bread known as *challah*.

And TZ isn't a misspelling. Make a sound like a hiss, but put a soft "t" before the hiss.

Because Yiddish was spoken by Jews in many different countries, each sect has developed its own pronunciations for words and phrases. This pronunciation guide is meant to represent the language of the author's specific sect of *Chassidim*.

Also note that Orthodox Jews consider the name of their deity to be too sacred to be written out fully, so they have adopted the practice of spelling the name as G-d as a sign of respect.

We have used the following letters to represent vowel sounds within the words:

AH as in mod or rod	IH as in tip or flip
AY as in place or tray	OE as in sew or toe
EE as in me or flee	OO as in book or look
EH as in trek or check	OW as in how or towel
EW as in flew or chew	OY as in boy or coy
EYE as in try or fly	UH as in luck or up

Agudath Yisroel (ah-guh-DAS YIS-ruh-el): largest and most influential ultra-Orthodox communal organization, representing political and social interests of *Chassidim* to the outside world.

Ba'al Shem Tov (bah-AL SHAME TOVE): legendary founder of *Chassidic* Judaism (1698–1760).

bachur (BOO-chir): young, unmarried man.

badchan (bahd-CHIN): comedian and wedding entertainer.

Bais Medrash (BAYS MEHD-rish): Grand Synagogue.

Bais Yaakov Times (BASE yah-COVE TIMES): book series about a group of girls who attend the same Orthodox school.

Bar Mitzvah (BAR mits-VEH): celebration of a boy's reaching manhood upon his thirteenth birthday. After the ceremony, he takes his place as a full adult in the religion's rituals and responsibilities.

Baruch Hashem (BUH-ruch hah-SHEM): "Blessed is G-d"; commonly used in conversation.

Bas Mitzvah (BUHT mits-VEH): female coming-of-age celebration; see *Bar Mitzvah*.

Be'ezras Hashem (bih-ez-RAS hah-SHEM): "With G-d's Help."

bekeshe (BEHK-ish-ih): black overcoat worn by *Chassidim* on the Sabbath and special occasions.

Bikur Cholim (bih-KUHR CHO-lim): respected organization that helps the sick financially and emotionally.

blatt (BLOT): section of the Talmud.

bli ayin harah (BLEE EYE-in HUH-ruh): "without the evil eye"; religious expression believed to prevent the evil eye from cursing a person. Example: "The baby is beautiful, *bli ayin harah.*"

bracha (BRUH-chuh), *singular*; **brachos** (BRUH-choys), *plural*: blessing(s).

bubba (BUH-bih): grandma.

Chai (CHEYE): the number 18, which symbolizes life.

chametz (CHOO-mitz): bread, grains, and leavened products forbidden on Passover.

chassan (CHEW-sin): groom.

Chassid (CHOO-sid): follower of a strict form of Orthodox Judaism.

Chassidish Tzietin (chah-SEE-dish TZEYE-tin): *Chassidic Times*—a weekly newspaper.

Chassidus (CHAH-sid-oos): Orthodox Jewish sect founded in the Ukraine around 1750, characterized by religious zeal, avoidance of modern dress and customs, and a spirit of prayer, joy, and charity.

Chassidustah (chah-SEE-dis-TUH): female *Chassid*.

chatzitsa (chah-TZEE-tzuh): anything that might prevent contact between a woman's skin and water during the ritual cleansing; example: nail polish.

chazan (CHAH-zin): cantor, or the person who leads the congregation in song.

cheder (CHAY-der): boys' elementary *yeshiva*, or school.

cherem (CHAY-rim): ban; a person who violates the *rebbe*'s orders will often be put under a *cherem* and be expelled from the community.

chessed (CHES-ed): good deeds, charity.

Chillul Hashem (CHIL-il hah-SHEM): desecration of G-d's name.

chumash (CHOO-mish): the five books of the Old Testament.

chuppah (CHU-pah): canopy under which marriage is performed.

chutzpa (CHOOTZ-puh): audacity, guts.

cocosh (CUH-cush): cocoa flavored, as in *cocosh* cake.

D'var Torah (d-VAHR TOY-ruh): sermon, or a thought, from the Torah.

daven (DAH-vin): to pray by making a repeated bowing motion.

Eishes Chayil (AY-shis CHEYE-el): "Woman of Valor."

ervah (ER-vuh): forbidden; often referring to women's hair or to sexuality.

fakachtah (fah-KAHCH-tih): old and broken-down.

fineh bachur (FEYE-neh BOO-chir): fine, or good, boy.

fineh yingeman (FEYE-neh YEENG-ih-mahn): fine, or good, young man.

Gan Eden (GAHN AY-den): Paradise.

ganuv (GAH-niv): thief.

gehenim (gi-HEN-im): hell.

gesheften (gih-SHEF-tin): lies, rumors, or tricks; a deception.

geshmake (gih-SHMAHK-ih): positive expression of emphasis. Example: "That's a *geshmakeh* cake!"

gevald (gih-VALD): expression of wonder, surprise, or frustration.

gezinta (gih-ZIN-tih): expression of emphasis; see *geshmake*.

goy (GOY), *singular*; **goyim** (GOY-im), *plural*: gentile(s) or non-Jew(s).

goyishe (GOY-ih-shuh): in a gentile or non-Jewish way.

goytah (GOY-tih): female gentile or non-Jew.

graggers (GRAH-gers): noisemakers used on Purim.

Grand Rebbe (GRAND REH-bee): leader, or head, rabbi of a sect.

Gut Shabbos (GIT SHAH-bis): "Good Sabbath"; said on Friday evenings or Saturdays.

Haman (HUH-mun): historic figure in the Torah who was an evil adviser to the king of Persia and tried to exterminate the Jews.

Hashem (hah-SHEM): G-d.

Hatzalah (hah-TZUH-luh): Orthodox ambulance crew run by volunteers.

Havdalah (hav-DUH-luh): short blessing over wine and candlelight that marks the symbolic end of Sabbath.

kallah (KAH-luh): bride.

kavanah (kah-VUH-nuh): sincere focus in prayer, learning, or blessing. Example: "Do not say it out of habit; say it with *kavanah*."

Kibud Av Va'Em (kih-BOOD UV voo-AIM): the fifth commandment, "honor one's father and mother."

kiddush (KIH-dish): blessing recited over wine or grape juice to sanctify the Sabbath.

kippa (KEE-pah): skull cap worn by men at all times, as it says in the Talmud: "Cover your head in order that the fear of heaven may be upon you."

kneidlech (ka-NEYED-lich): matzo-meal balls cooked in soup.

kollel (KOY-lel): higher institution for Torah learning for married men.

kugel (KOO-gul): strudel.

L'chaim (li-CHEYE-im): "To life"; blessing used at any celebration over a small cup of wine.

L'Shem Shamayim (li-SHAME shuh-MEYE-im): "In the name of heaven."

La'Yehudim (LAH yi-HEW-dim): "For the Jews."

latkes (LAHT-kis): fried potato pancakes traditionally eaten on Chanukah.

litvish (LIT-vish): non-*Chassidic* ultra-Orthodox group originating from Lithuania before the Holocaust; just as fanatic as—and in some ways more than—*Chassidim.*

lokshon kugel (LUHK-shin KOO-gul): noodle strudel.

loshon harah (LUH-shin HUH-ruh): speaking evil of other Jews.

lulav (LOO-luv): ripe, green, closed frond from a date palm tree used as a symbol on the high holidays.

Maccabim (MAH-kah-bim): heroic warriors who defeated the Greeks and rescued the Temple in ancient Israel; their story is celebrated on Chanukah.

maggid shiur (MAH-gid SHEE-ur): Torah scholar who is a teacher of the Talmud in boys' high schools.

maidel (MEYE-del); *also,* **maideleh** (MEYE-de-luh): girl.

Mashgiach (mahsh-GEE-ach): person who supervises and ensures that kosher establishments are following all necessary practices.

mashgichim (mahsh-GEE-chim): boy's moral supervisor in *yeshiva.*

Mashiach (muh-SHEE-ach): the Messiah.

masmid (MAHS-mid): one who has the ability to focus intently and for many hours on learning.

matzo (MAH-tzuh): large crackerlike unleavened bread eaten on Passover.

mazel tov (MAH-zul TUHV): congratulations.

Me'or Ha'Talmud Cheder (mih-UHR hah-TAL-mud CHAY-der): name of an Orthodox elementary school.

mechitzah (mih-CHEE-tzah): wooden or plastic temporary partitions used to separate men and women at celebrations or events.

megillah (mih-GIL-ah): scroll containing the biblical story of Purim; read in temple on Purim night and morning.

menorah (min-OY-ruh): candelabra used on Chanukah to light eight candles in memory of the miracle of the Maccabim.

mensch (MENSH): good, decent person.

meshugah (mih-SHIH-gih): crazy.

meshugunah (mih-SHIH-gih-nah): crazy person.

mikvah (MIK-vih): ritual bath used by a married Jewish woman to purify her body after menstruation and before she can resume sexual relations with her husband.

mincha (MIN-chih): evening prayers.

minhag (MIN-hig): tradition.

mishamish (mih-SHAHM-ish): personal assistant to the *rebbe*.

mishloach manos (mish-LOY-och MOO-noys): Purim presents given to family and friends on the holiday.

mitzvah (MITS-vuh), *singular*; **mitzvos** (MITS-voys), *plural*: commandment(s) or good deed(s).

Mitzvah Tantz (MITS-vuh TAHNTZ): mystical ceremony concluding *Chassidic* weddings; the bride "dances" with the groom and ancestors are believed to come down to bless the couple.

modernishe (mud-ER-nish-ih): modern; pertains to anyone or anything not exactly in accordance with tradition or what is currently acceptable.

moser (MOY-sir): traitor, snitch.

nachas (NAH-chis): pride. Example: "She has such *nachas* in her children."

nebech (NEH-bich): expression of pity. Example: "*Nebech*, he is ill."

nisht (NIHSHT): not.

nosh (NAHSH): junk food.

oy gevald (OY gih-VALD); *also*, **oy vey** (OY VAY): "oh boy."

past nisht (PAHST NIHSHT): inappropriate. Example: "It's *past nisht* that a girl should go out in such a short skirt."

payos (PEYE-is): side curls worn by boys and men.

pipikel (PIH-pih-kul): penis.

pish (PIHSH): to urinate.

plotz (PLOTS): to go crazy with frustration.

rabbonim (rah-BAH-nim): grand rabbis of the community.

rashanta (rih-SHAHN-tuh): evil woman.

rav (RUHV): certified rabbi, knowledgeable in all legal matters of Torah.

Reb (REHB): mister.

Rebbe (REHB-ih): teacher of boys in elementary school.

Rebbitzen (REHB-ih-tzin): wife of the *rebbe*.

rofeh (ROY-feh): to heal.

Rosh kollel (ROYSH KOY-lel): head of the *kollel*.

rosh yeshiva (ROYSH yih-SHEE-vuh): head of the *yeshiva*.

schnitzel (SHNIH-tzul): fried chicken breasts.

Sefat Emet (SFAHS EH-mes): *Language of the Truth*, a widely studied commentary on the Torah, written by the Grand *Rebbe* of Gur.

segulah (sih-GOO-luh): omen.

Shabbos (SHAH-bis): Sabbath, the day of rest; begins Friday at sundown and ends Saturday at sundown.

shadchan (SHAHD-chin), *singular*; **shadchanim** (SHAHD-chah-nihm), *plural*: matchmaker(s).

shah (SHAH): be quiet!

shaitel (SHEYE-til): wig.

shaygetz (SHEYE-gitz): bad goy.

sheineh bachur (SHEYE-nih BOO-chir): good boy.

Shema Yisroel (shih-MAH yis-RUH-el): "Hear O Israel"; the beginning of the most important prayer in Judaism, said during the morning and evening prayers; the words religious Jews hold as their rallying call; a call of identity, martyrdom, faith, and belief.

sherayim (SHREYE-im): chocolates or nuts handed out by the Grand *Rebbe*, often at the *tish*.

sheva brachos (SHEV-ah BRUH-choys): seven blessings recited for seven consecutive nights for the week following a wedding.

shidduch (SHID-ihch): match between a boy and a girl; an engagement.

shiksa (SHIK-sih): female gentile or non-Jew.

shluch (SHLUHCH): unorganized person.

shmutz (SHMOOTZ): dirt.

shnorrer (SHNUH-rer): beggar.

shnuck (SHNOOK): stupid person.

shtetle (SHTEH-tul), *singular*; **shtetlech** (SHTEHT-lech), *plural*: small village(s) where most Eastern European Jews lived before the Holocaust.

shtiper (SHTIH-pir): to push; a pusher.

shtism (SHTIH-sim): nonsense.

shtreimel (SHTREYE-muhl): fur hat worn by *Chassidim*.

shul (SHEWL): synagogue.

siddur (SID-der): prayer book.

stiyah (STEE-yuh): contradiction.

sugvaniyot (SOOG-van-NEE-yuht): doughnuts.

taavah (TAH-ah-VIH): a desire that needs to be suppressed.

Talmud (TAHL-mid): the Book of Laws, a written record of rabbinic discussions pertaining to Jewish law, ethics, philosophy, customs, and history.

Talmud Chacham (TAHL-mid CHAH-chahm): Torah scholar.

tefillin (ti-FIL-in): phylacteries; two small, black, cubic leather boxes with leather straps. The boxes contain scrolls of parchment inscribed with verses from the Torah; attached to the head and on the arm, they are worn by observant Jewish men during weekday morning prayers.

tehillim (tih-HILL-ihm): psalms.

teshuvah (tih-SHEW-vuh): repentance.

358

tish (TIHSH): joyous celebration in which *Chassidim* stand around the Grand *Rebbe*'s table and watch as he celebrates with a small entourage.

Tizsku Li'mitzvos (TIZ-kew lih-MITS-voys): "May you be worthy to perform additional positive commandments."

totty (TAH-tee): father.

tzaddekes (tzah-DAY-kihs): saintly female.

tzaddik (TZAH-dihk): saintly male.

tzaddikim (tzah-DEE-kihm): saintly people.

tzeddakah (tzih-DAH-kuh): charity.

tziztis (TZIH-tzihs): four-cornered tassled garment worn by religious men in accordance with the law of the Torah, Numbers 15:38: "Speak unto the children of Israel, and bid them that they make them throughout their generations fringes in the corners of their garments, and that they put with the fringe of each corner a thread of blue."

tzniesdig (tznee-ihs-DIHG): modest.

vildeh (VIHL-dih): wild, in reference to wild behavior.

Vus ken min tun (VOOS KEN MIHN TEEN): "What can one do?"

yeshiva (yih-SHEE-vah), *singular*; **yeshivos** (yih-SHEE-vihs), *plural*: high school(s) for boys.

Yichud (yee-CHOOD): laws about the need to separate males and females in every potential situation.

yichus (YEE-choos): prestigious family background, wherein the family is descended from ancestors who played a crucial role in the *Chassidic* world. Example: "*Yichus* enables one to make a good match."

Yiddishe (YIHD-ihsh-eh): Jewish.

Yiden (YEE-din): Jews.

Zah shoin shtill (ZAH SHOYN SHTIHL): "Be quiet already!"

zaida (ZAY-dah): grandfather.

zemiros (ZMEE-rihs): songs sung on the Sabbath.

ACKNOWLEDGMENTS

These are the people who gave me a voice: Nadia Cornier, my agent and only reader for too long; Emily Easton, editor and publisher at Walker, who held the book close to her heart and never let go; Regina Castillo, Melissa Kavonic, Alexei Esikoff, and Stacy Cantor, who read the book again and again, who knew the details more than I, and whose silent hand I remain indebted to. Your time, your thoughts, your skills grace the pages of this story.

And to those whose names I cannot mention, whose haunted voices echo in my heart, your loving support and silent suffering are etched in the words I write.

EISHES CHAYIL is a pseudonym meaning *woman of valor*, chosen by JUDY BROWN when *Hush* was first published because of feared backlash from her community. Since publication, Judy's identity has been revealed. She has left the *Chassidic* community and been profiled in *The New York Times Magazine*. Judy was raised in a world of *Chassidic* schools, synagogues, and summer camps and is a direct descendant of the major founders of and leaders in the *Chassidic* world. She holds a master's degree in creative writing and has worked as a journalist for several international Orthodox newspapers. She lives in New York City.

HUSH BOOK CLUB DISCUSSION GUIDE

1. Though Gittel knows it is wrong to have a "gentile" friend, she and Kathy have a very close relationship. Why do you think this is? Also, why is Kathy the first person Gittel confides in about the incident with her best friend, Devory?

2. What was your reaction when you read about what happened to Devory? Were you surprised? How did you feel about Gittel's reaction to what she'd just witnessed?

3. Gittel's family pressures her not to tell anyone what she's seen, since it would make her a less desirable wife in the future and could put their family's reputation in jeopardy. Have you ever stood up to your family for something you felt strongly about?

4. Once Gittel finally tells Mrs. Goldblatt what happened to Devory, Mrs. Goldblatt accuses Devory of making up stories and asks Gittel not to tell anyone, including the police. Why do you think Mrs. Goldblatt has this reaction? Is it to protect her son? Her daughter? Her community? Or is it something else?

5. When Gittel is first married, she is upset because she does not get pregnant right away and worries that God is punishing her. What do you think of her reaction? What do you think it would be like to be married and have a baby at age eighteen?

6. Why does the birth of her own daughter compel Gittel to finally speak out about Devory's abuse? Why did it take her so many years to come forward? How do you think you would have acted if you were in a similar situation?

7. When Gittel tells her husband that Devory was raped, Yankel does not know what the word "rape" means. Why do you think he is ignorant of the word and its meaning?

8. If the story was told from another character's perspective, how do you think it would be different? What if Gittel's parents told the story? Or Devory? Or Devory's brother?

9. The author includes many specific details about daily life within the *Chassidic* community, such as the tradition of the *shtreimel* or Jewish wedding rituals. Did these give you a clearer picture of Gittel's life? Were there any details that you found shocking, or ones you found similar to your own life?

10. What do you think of the author's note at the end of the book? Do you view the story differently, now that you know it was semi-autobiographical?